U0107913

The Four Seasons of T'ang Poetry

英汉对照

唐诗四季

吴经熊 著　徐诚斌 译

外语教学与研究出版社
FOREIGN LANGUAGE TEACHING AND RESEARCH PRESS
北京 BEIJING

京权图字：01-2020-5435

© The Doctor John C. H. Wu Institute, LLC, 1972
Original Chinese translation copyright © Bishop Xu Chengbin, 1980. All rights reserved.

图书在版编目 (CIP) 数据

唐诗四季：英汉对照 / 吴经熊著；徐诚斌译. —— 北京：外语教学与研究出版社，2023.8
书名原文：The Four Seasons of T'ang Poetry
ISBN 978-7-5213-4725-8

I. ①唐… II. ①吴… ②徐… III. ①唐诗－诗集－英、汉 IV. ①I222.742

中国国家版本馆 CIP 数据核字 (2023) 第 146707 号

出版人　王　芳
系列策划　吴　浩
责任编辑　仲志兰
责任校对　易　璐
封面设计　潘振宇
出版发行　外语教学与研究出版社
社　　址　北京市西三环北路 19 号（100089）
网　　址　https://www.fltrp.com
印　　刷　三河市北燕印装有限公司
开　　本　650×980　1/16
印　　张　22
版　　次　2023 年 8 月第 1 版 2023 年 8 月第 1 次印刷
书　　号　ISBN 978-7-5213-4725-8
定　　价　68.00 元

如有图书采购需求，图书内容或印刷装订等问题，侵权、盗版书籍等线索，请拨打以下电话或关注官方服务号：
客服电话：400 898 7008
官方服务号：微信搜索并关注公众号"外研社官方服务号"
外研社购书网址：https://fltrp.tmall.com

物料号：347250001

"博雅双语名家名作"出版说明

1840 年鸦片战争以降，在深重的民族危机面前，中华民族精英"放眼看世界"，向世界寻求古老中国走向现代、走向世界的灵丹妙药，涌现出一大批中国主题的经典著述。我们今天阅读这些中文著述的时候，仍然深为字里行间所蕴藏的缜密的考据、深刻的学理、世界的视野和济世的情怀所感动，但往往会忽略：这些著述最初是用英文写就，我们耳熟能详的中文文本是原初英文文本的译本，这些英文作品在海外学术界和文化界同样享有崇高的声誉。

比如，林语堂的 *My Country and My People*（《吾国与吾民》）以幽默风趣的笔调和睿智流畅的语言，将中国人的道德精神、生活情趣和中国社会文化的方方面面娓娓道来，在美国引起巨大反响——林语堂也以其中国主题系列作品赢得世界文坛的尊重，并获得诺贝尔文学奖的提名。再比如，梁思成在抗战的烽火中写就的英文版《图像中国建筑史》文稿（*A Pictorial History of Chinese Architecture*），经其挚友费慰梅女士（Wilma C. Fairbank）等人多年的奔走和努力，于 1984 年由麻省理工学院出版社（MIT Press）出版，并获得美国出版联合会颁发的"专业暨学术书籍金奖"。又比如，1939 年，费孝通在伦敦政治经济学院的博士论文以 *Peasant Life in China—A Field Study of Country Life in the Yangtze Valley* 为名在英国劳特利奇书局（Routledge）出版，后以《江村经济》作为中译本书名——《江村经济》使得靠桑蚕为生的"开弦弓村"获得了世界性的声誉，成为国际社会学界研究中国农村的首选之地。

此外，一些中国主题的经典人文社科作品经海外汉学家和中国学者的如椽译笔，在英语世界也深受读者喜爱。比如，艾恺（Guy S. Alitto）将他 1980 年用中文访问梁漱溟的《这个世界会好吗——梁漱溟晚年口述》一书译成英文（*Has Man a Future?—Dialogues with the Last Confucian*），备受海内外读者关注；

此类作品还有徐中约英译的梁启超著作《清代学术概论》（*Intellectual Trends in the Ch'ing Period*）、狄百瑞（W. T. de Bary）英译的黄宗羲著作《明夷待访录》（*Waiting for the Dawn: A Plan for the Prince*），等等。

有鉴于此，外语教学与研究出版社推出"博雅双语名家名作"系列。

博雅，乃是该系列的出版立意。博雅教育（Liberal Education）早在古希腊时代就得以提倡，旨在培养具有广博知识和优雅气质的人，提高人文素质，培养健康人格，中国儒家六艺"礼、乐、射、御、书、数"亦有此功用。

双语，乃是该系列的出版形式。英汉双语对照的形式，既同时满足了英语学习者和汉语学习者通过阅读中国主题博雅读物提高英语和汉语能力的需求，又以中英双语思维、构架和写作的形式予后世学人以启迪——维特根斯坦有云"语言的边界，乃是世界的边界"，诚哉斯言。

名家，乃是该系列的作者群体。涵盖文学、史学、哲学、政治学、经济学、考古学、人类学、建筑学等领域，皆海内外名家一时之选。

名作，乃是该系列的入选标准。系列中的各部作品都是经过时间的积淀、市场的检验和读者的鉴别而呈现的经典，正如卡尔维诺对"经典"的定义：经典并非你正在读的书，而是你正在重读的书。

胡适在《新思潮的意义》（1919 年 12 月 1 日，《新青年》第 7 卷第 1 号）一文中提出了"研究问题、输入学理、整理国故、再造文明"的范式。秉着"记载人类文明、沟通世界文化"的出版理念，我们推出"博雅双语名家名作"系列，既希望能够在中国人创作的和以中国为主题的博雅英文文献领域"整理国故"，亦希望在和平发展、改革开放的新时代为"再造文明"、为"向世界说明中国"略尽绵薄之力。

外语教学与研究出版社

编者说明

《唐诗四季》作者吴经熊（1899—1986）是享誉国际的法学专家，广涉法学、政治学、宗教、文学等众多领域，著述颇丰，多以英文写就。一生致力于沟通中西法学思想，希冀通过中西思想文化的互证和互释，促进平等交流和理解融合，成为东西方文化交流的桥梁。他倡导中西文化交流的理念，于1935年创办英文杂志 *T'ien Hsia Monthly*（《天下月刊》），着力将中国文化译介传播到国外，在现代中西文化交流史上发挥了重要作用。他在"译文"专栏发表了大量中国古代及现代经典文学作品的英文译文，开创了中国文学向外传播的先河。

《唐诗四季》用英文撰写，1938年4月至1939年8月分期刊登在《天下月刊》上，后由徐诚斌译成中文，1940年3月起在《宇宙风》上连载。作者用比较文学的方式，以春夏秋冬四个季节来概括唐诗演进的历程，以通俗化的比喻来介绍唐诗不同阶段的特点，"给不同文化背景下的西方读者一个似乎不受意识形态和地方诗学束缚的唐诗全景描述"。

《天下月刊》当时的阅读对象多是懂英语的异国人士。吴经熊是虔诚的天主教徒，他写作《唐诗四季》的"初心"，是用西方读者更易于接受的话语方式和概念，通过对比、互释和印证等手段，帮助其理解唐诗，理解中华文化，以达到文化交流的目的。为呈现原著的时代特点、尊重历史原貌，除少量年份及引文订正外，未改动英文原文。

1980年，台湾洪范书店结集出版《唐诗四季》繁体中文版。1997年，辽宁教育出版社出版简体中文版《唐诗四季 唐诗概论》。本英汉对照版的中译文以前两者为底本，对生卒年、朝代起止年份、异体字、标点符号、外国专名译名等，根据现行规范进行统一。英文原文无对应译文之处、中文典籍和诗词相关内容等直接进行补充，其他整句补译用【】标示，以方便读者参阅。谨此说明，敬期明辨。

2023年6月

作者自序[*]

一、关于原著

　　这部译本是已故徐诚斌博士青年时代的作品。可是我在介绍译者之前，先须将本书的英文原稿出版的原委及其内容说明一下。此书英文名称是 *Four Seasons of T'ang Poetry*。它是为英文《天下月刊》写的，分六批刊登。第一批是民国廿七年（1938 年）四月出版的，第六批则在廿八年（1939 年）八月才始登出。

　　当时我们正在抗战，战事越来越显得白热化，《天下月刊》早已由上海搬到香港。我是月刊的主干，当然也不得不迁居于港。《天下月刊》的宗旨，是在沟通中西文化。这种文化工作，在平时比较容易，征稿也比较方便。到了战事方殷的时候，征稿就难上加难了。因此我们的编辑同人，时常促我写稿。我于是常常用化名翻译我国诗词，先后共译出二百余首，陆续投稿。由于译诗的工作，我不知不觉地对唐诗发生浓厚的兴趣，尤其对于唐诗演进的历程，我渐渐发现有四个很自然的阶段，可以用春夏秋冬四季来象征。春有蓬勃的生气、活泼的生机和海阔天空的逍遥自在。例如：

> 欲穷千里目，更上一层楼。（王之涣）
> 海日生残夜，江春入旧年。（王湾）
> 海内存知己，天涯若比邻。（王勃）
> 山光悦鸟性，潭影空人心。（常建）
> 云霞出海曙，梅柳渡江春。（杜审言）
> 行到水穷处，坐看云起时。（王维）

这些名句都具有陶渊明所说的"木欣欣以向荣，泉涓涓而始流"的意境。十足表现了天地一新的气象。

　　夏，充满了天地正气与英雄圣贤大无畏的精神，其间也不无清风解愠、时雨滋润的调剂。我在本书中以杜甫为夏季的代表，对于他的诗已加以比较充分的发挥。我觉得李白与杜甫各有千秋，犹春夏之不能互相替代。杜诗不能有"清水出芙蓉，天然去雕琢"的天真，可是李诗也达不到"读书破万卷，下笔如有神"的境界！又如杜甫的"好雨知时节，当春乃发生。随风潜入夜，润物细无声"，这些诗句，无意中反映出杜甫心中所蕴的天地万物一体之仁，不是李白集中所能寻得的。

秋，有两个方面，一是无限的感伤，一是成熟的智慧。在感伤方面，宋玉说得最好："悲哉秋之为气也，萧瑟兮草木摇落而变衰。憭栗兮若在远行，登山临水兮送将归！"（九辩）又如李贺的"不见年年辽海上，文章何处哭秋风"也深得秋意。我以白居易为秋季的主要代表，因为他的两篇杰作《长恨歌》与《琵琶行》，都是秋之心声。"上穷碧落下黄泉，两处茫茫皆不见。""天长地久有时尽，此恨绵绵无绝期！""同是天涯沦落人，相逢何必曾相识。""别有幽愁暗恨生，此时无声胜有声。""座中泣下谁最多，江州司马青衫湿。"这些句子，又有春季的自然了，令人觉有"佳句本天成，妙手自得之"的味儿。白居易是天造地设的秋天诗人。他的朋友元稹，亦复如是。元稹的三首《遣悲怀》诗，也是千古绝唱。"惟将终夜常开眼，报答平生未展眉。"文章就在这里"哭秋风"呵！

有人将元白称为"社会诗人"或"现实派诗人"，视为与杜甫同派，而称李白、王维等人为"浪漫派诗人"。我觉得这是用西洋文学史上的术语套在中国诗人头上，未免有张冠李戴之嫌。与其如此，不如以本国惯用的名词来形容各时代不同的气质与风格。

至于时人之所以把元白等人视为与杜甫同调，其理由是：元白也曾极端推重杜甫。白居易曾作"讽喻诗"百余篇，以揭发社会上不平之事。这是效法杜甫的。元稹甚至说："自有诗人以来，未有如子美者"。他也作了"新乐府"和"乐府古题"三十余首，都是有心追踵杜甫的作品。他们的动机是可嘉的。但是元白和杜子美之间，有个极重要的分别，这是研究文学史的人所不可忽视的。杜甫的社会诗，是触景生情，直接从腑肺里流涌出来的。"朱门酒肉臭，路有冻死骨。""杀人红尘里，报答在斯须。"这些话都是从灵心深处发出来的，所以其感人之深，也是无底的。总之，杜甫的不平鸣，是至诚的，无隔的；而元白的讽喻诗是理智的，有隔的。我们读杜甫社会诗，心里便会觉得非常痛快舒适，确实可以一透胸中之闷气。反之，读元白的社会诗，往往会觉得越读越闷！这是因为他们根本不是属于夏季的人，他们的灵焰，根本没有杜甫的猛烈。所以他们的讽喻诗，总不免有些勉强造作之意。我并不说他们的讽喻诗是毫无价值的。不，至少它们有宣传的作用；可是它们决不是他们的杰作或代表作。他们的代表作品，除上述诸篇以外，还有智慧诗，因为秋季根本是属于理知与哲学的。我在这里只须引征白香山的一首诗：

> 自从为骏童，直至作衰翁。所好随年异，为忙终日同。弄沙成佛塔，锵玉谒王官。彼此皆儿戏，须臾即色空。有营非了义，无著是真宗。兼恐勤修道，犹应在妄中。（感悟妄缘，题如上人壁）

无论你同不同意他的人生哲学，他这首诗是诚意的，从心底里直接流露出来的，这是不可否认的。

论到秋季，我要特别声明一点，那就是：我觉得，我在本书中，对于韩愈的评语，不够详细，而且也有失公平。我现在认为韩愈的作风，不是完全属于秋天的，其实他的心灵颇有夏气。他的文章，像《原道》《谏迎佛骨表》等篇，姑无论你同意他的主张与否，总不失其为充满正气的文章。韩文与杜诗可算唐朝文学的两大高峰。总之，依我现在的看法，韩愈似系夏末秋初的人物。

最后，我想多数读者会同意：晚唐诗在精神上是属于冬季的，而晚唐诗人之中，最能代表冬季的神态的，当推李商隐了。如云："我意殊春意，先春已断肠。""春心莫共花争发，一寸相思一寸灰。""蜡烛啼红怨天曙。""嫦娥应悔偷灵药，碧海青天夜夜心。"若不是冬季的人，决不可能产生这样想象而写出这样的诗句。

我想我是一个属于春夏的人，可是对于秋冬的诗，只要是至诚无邪的，都不会觉得不美的。

至于把李后主的词归入《唐诗四季》的书里，而且把他奉为冬季的最高峰，似乎有些奇特。我在这里不可不向读者说明缘由。当我写完了晚唐诗的研究的时候，我正在另外一篇稿件中翻译李后主的词。我越来越觉得李后主的词，具有晚唐诗的优点，而其境界则较晚唐诗人高超得多！至于词与诗在狭义上虽然不同，在广义上则一切所谓诗词歌赋，莫非是诗。其实，所谓"词"，本来也叫作"诗余"和"长短句"。难道由于句子之长短，就失其为诗的本质了吗？况且南唐究竟是唐朝的后代。因此，把南唐中主与后主的词当作唐诗一部分看待，还不能说太离谱吧！但是，这事究非文学家的惯例，所以关于这点，我要求读者多多包涵！

我新近重读了李后主的词，觉得他对文学的贡献确实是非常地伟大！我同意王国维先生的看法：

> "词至李后主而眼界始大，感慨遂深，遂变伶工之词而为士大夫之词。"（人间词话）
> "尼采谓一切文学余爱以血书者，后主之词，真所谓以血书者也。"（同上）

我认为李后主的特点是在：他的身世是属于冬季的，可是他的气魄和其词的风格，都是富于春夏气象。他是不配做君主的，因为他太文弱了。可是他是始终拒抗强权的"违命侯"！他最后的一首词的最后二句是：

> 问君能有几多愁？恰似一江春水向东流！

词的内容，虽含有无边的忧愁，但词的格调却不脱活泼泼的春意和涵盖乾坤的气象，与李白的"君不见黄河之水天上来，奔流到海不复回"同一个格局，而成为后来词人的鼻祖！就文艺而言，李后主是一个承先启后的文学巨子。

二、关于译者

我第一次看见诚斌，是在民国廿七年。当时我在香港，而他尚在上海圣约翰大学读书，还是一个十七八岁的青年。可是他对英美文学，已有相当的根基，而且兴趣极浓。他对我所发表的英文论文，似有偏爱，遽然在那年暑假时，独自乘轮到香港来探访我。那时，我才知道他是徐可陞先生的公子。可陞先生曾与我同属于上海监理会教会。我是新教友，而可陞先生乃是牧师的助理，对于教务甚是热心，我对他有深刻的印象。我初次会见诚斌时，虽然已改奉了天主教，但是因为可陞先生的关系，我对诚斌更觉有亲切之感。况且，从这个青年的谈话中，我觉得他对英国文学颇有深刻的见解。虽然我比他长了二十一年之多，友谊本来是超时间的，我们二人遂订了忘年之交。

至于翻译《唐诗四季》之事，并不是我自己托他，也不是他自告奋勇的。当我的英文原稿登完了以后，第二年初春，我接到《宇宙风》主笔周君黎庵的来信，里面有一段说：

尊著唐诗之四季，为《天下》创刊来最伟大之贡献，令人爱不忍释，久拟迻译成中文，俾可人人拜读，惜不得译者其人。去冬得交徐诚斌君，知其亲炙左右甚久，遂举以相委，蒙其首肯，遂定于三月起陆续刊载，又得吾师慨然允于翻译，并赐臂助，尤为感激。【廿九年（1940年）二月十日】

我很惭愧，由于我忙着为《天下》写稿，没有充分的时间去修正译文，只有大部分的原诗是我抄给译者的。有时，我为训练他起见，故意不给他原诗，让他自己在《全唐诗》中去找！等到他真正找不到时，我才供他原件。因为，我当时已认他为有天才的青年，天才必须以苦工培养，才始能成大器。

我和他相交，历时三十五年。对我，这个友谊是个极大的安慰，是天主赐给我大恩典之一。我亲眼看见他不但在地位上，也在内心修养上不断地继长增高。他非但没有令我失望，并且时时予我以惊喜！他地位越高，对我越显得亲热，关顾之情，与年俱深。在他逝世前二年，他遽然找到了《宇宙风》刊登着他的译稿的旧杂志，遂把它们一一复印下来，寄来给我。我本想马上给它出版，以成独立的一本书。后来因为我也忙于其他著作，而且译稿必须仔细校对一番，才可付印。哪里料得到他会这样早就逝世！他逝世后，我甚感伤，遂把出版之事搁置起来了。

去年，很意外地，我接到素不相识的秦贤次先生的电话，说他为《唐诗四季》出版之事，要来看我，我当然表示欢迎。后秦先生偕同叶步荣先生过寓来访，也携有《唐诗四季》的复印本，并且曾加以一度相当仔细的校对。我感于他们两位的诚恳，而且富于学术兴趣，因欣然同意他们的建议。我相信，这也是徐主教的心愿！

吴经熊作于阳明山

一九八〇年五月六日

* 此为《唐诗四季》繁体中文版（台湾洪范书店1980年版）作者自序，有节略。

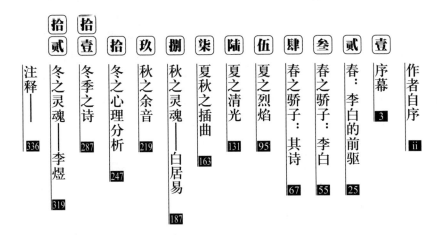

I. INTRODUCTION

It has been customary to divide the poetry of T'ang into four periods: Early T'ang, Golden T'ang, Middle T'ang, and Late T'ang. The first period was just a kind of overture; the second included Wang Wei, Li Po, and Tu Fu; the third included Po Chü-i, Yuan Chen, Han Yu and his circle; the fourth included Li Shang-yin, Tu Mu, and Wen T'ing-yuen. This classification was made avowedly without reference to social and political changes, but solely with reference to the art of poetry itself. For instance, a great part of the Golden Period of poetry was anything but golden from the standpoint of political stability and social welfare.

Some of our contemporary historians of Chinese literature have divided the poetry of T'ang into just two periods: the period of Li Po, and the period of Tu Fu. Li Po is said to sum up all the previous poets of T'ang, and Tu Fu is said to open up a new era for all its later poets. This classification has the charm of simplicity. And also it has the merit of not entirely ignoring the environmental changes. There can be no doubt that Li and Tu, who were born within twelve years of each other,[1] do belong to different periods in point of poetry as well as in point of life. I think it is within limits to say that Li Po had written his best poems before the rebellion of An Lu-shan, while the masterpieces of Tu Fu were mostly produced after that event. It has always seemed to me that Li Po sang best when he was happy, while Tu Fu sang best when he was angry. Li Po was a lark singing at heaven's gate; Tu Fu was a nightingale, singing with his throat against a thorn. The glorious early reign of Ming Huang furnished the proper environment for the blithe Li Po; just as the tragic end of the same great Emperor provided the stage for the passionate singing of Tu Fu. It is true that they both belong to the reign of Ming Huang, but then we must remember that Ming Huang himself was torn between two different periods.

I therefore think that the new classification shows a more profound historical insight than the older one. But then it suffers from oversimplification. It ignores real differences between, let us say, the poetry of Po Chü-I and that of Tu Fu, and between the poetry of Li Shang-yin and that of Han Yu, to mention but few instances. Recently, browsing over a considerable portion of the poems of the whole T'ang period, I have arrived at a classification which seems to me more natural and true to fact than either of the two I have mentioned. I feel that the poetry of T'ang falls naturally into four seasons: Spring, Summer, Autumn and Winter.

壹 序幕

　　通常我们分唐诗为四个时期：初唐、盛唐、中唐和晚唐。第一期是序幕，第二期包括王维、李白和杜甫，第三期包括白居易、元稹、韩愈等，末期包括李商隐、杜牧和温庭筠。这分法是根据诗的技艺而言，与政治社会变迁无关，其实大部分的盛唐是处于"国"不"泰"、"民"不"安"的状态下，无"盛"可言。

　　今日文学史家分唐诗为两半者不乏其人，首半是李白的时代，次半是杜甫的时代。李白总括前唐诸诗人，杜甫是后者的先驱。这分法具有简洁的优点，也不忽视时势的变迁。毫无疑问的，李杜是属于不同的时代，不论是指诗艺或指环境，虽然他们出生先后只差十二年[1]。我们可以说，李白的精华在安禄山叛乱前已出世，杜甫的杰作是事变后的作品。我以为李白精神焕发、兴高采烈时诗兴勃发，杜甫的不朽是愁眉不展时种的根苗。李白是一只在天堂前歌咏的百灵，杜甫是一种骨鲠于喉泣血的夜莺。明皇初期的辉煌，使李白适逢其时；他黯淡的结局加深了杜甫热情的诗意。这两位大诗人都是明皇的臣民，可是明皇个人的历史也可以分为两半。

　　所以我以为这简洁的分法较第一法具有更深的历史意识，美中不足的就是它过分的单调：它忽视了白居易和杜甫的区别，李商隐和韩愈也是触目的例子。近读唐诗多首，得一较前二则更自然和符合事实的分法：我以为唐诗可分为四个时期——春、夏、秋、冬。

The Period of Spring includes the earliest T'ang bards and Wang Wei and Li Po. The Period of Summer includes Tu Fu and some poets on war. The Period of Autumn includes Po Chü-i and his circle, and Han Yu and his circle. The Period of Winter includes Li Shang-yin, Tu Mu, Wen T'ing-yuen, Hsü Hun, Lo Yin, Han Wu, and many other minor poets.

Seasons are, of course, interpenetrated, one with the other, but on the whole they are distinct enough. I shall not try to define them, but I hope the reader will gradually see and feel what I have in mind as we proceed patiently together in our journey throughout the whole year.

But in order not to keep my readers too much on the guess, I will pick up a springy poet to describe Spring, a summery poet to describe Summer, an autumnal poet to describe Autumn, and a wintry poet to describe Winter.

Here is what Li Po says of Spring (see 愁阳春赋):

> The heart of Spring is heaving like waves.
> The sorrows of Spring are flying about in confusion like snowflakes.
> All emotions are roused, forming a mingled yarn of joy and grief.
> O, what pathos I feel within me in this sweetest of the seasons!

Next let us hear how Tu Fu sighs on a Summer night (夏夜叹):

> What a long day it has been! It looked as though the sun would never set!
> The boiling heat has almost smoked and steamed me to death.
> Ah for a wind of ten thousand *li* in length
> To come wandering from the sky and blow upon my garments like a large fan!
> Now the bright moon has arisen on the cloudless sky;
> The leafy trees are sifting its beams like a sieve.
> In the heart of Summer, the night is all too short.
> Let me open the pavilion doors to invite the cool air.
> In the transparent moonlight, every little thing is visible.
> I can see the winged insects flying and having a good time.

One touch of nature makes all creatures kin:

Big or small, they all love freedom and comfort.

I am only thinking of the soldiers, who, heavy laden with arms,

Stand guard at the frontiers for years on end.

They have no way of bathing themselves in fresh waters;

In the grip of heat, they look despairingly at one another.

Throughout the night, the long-handled pans keep the noisy watches;

Throughout an endless stretch of land, no soothing silence is to be
found.

春季包括初唐诗人、王维和李白，夏季包括杜甫和战时诗人，秋季有白居易、韩愈等，冬季有李商隐、杜牧、温庭筠、许浑、罗隐、韩偓及其他次要诸家。

季候是互相贯通的，可是大体看来仍是很黑白分明。我不预备为春夏秋冬划下界线，希望读者在这一年的日程内能渐渐了解我的观点。现在我举一个春季的诗人描绘春季，一个夏季的诗人描绘夏季，二个秋冬季诗人描绘秋冬，以免读者摸不着头脑。

这是李白的《愁阳春赋》：

> 春心荡兮如波，春愁乱兮如雪。
> 兼万情之悲欢，兹一感于芳节。

这是杜甫的《夏夜叹》：

> 永日不可暮，炎蒸毒我肠。
> 安得万里风，飘飘吹我裳。
> 昊天出华月，茂林延疏光。
> 仲夏苦夜短，开轩纳微凉。
> 虚明见纤毫，羽虫亦飞扬。
> 物情无巨细，自适固其常。
> 念彼荷戈士，穷年守边疆。
> 何由一洗濯，执热互相望。
> 竟夕击刁斗，喧声连万方。

Even if they wear honors thick on their heads,

The happiness is nothing like an early return home.

Hark! the melancholy notes of flageolets are coming from the northern
city.

Above my head, the cranes are wheeling about and calling.

My gizzard is fretted once more.

When, O when will peace and prosperity come back again?

Now we shall calm down a bit and lend our ears to Po Chü-i philosophizing about Autumn:

THOUGHTS IN AUTUMN (秋怀)

The moon has arisen and shines upon the northern hall;

The steps and the courtyard are drenched in its clear light.

A cool breeze is blowing from the west;

The grass and trees are withering day and night.

The *wut'ung* and the willows have begun to shed their green leaves.

The lovely colors of the orchids are fading.

Affected by these things, I meditate privately,

And find my heart in a similar condition.

Who can always retain his childhood and youth?

There is a time for blooming, and a time for decaying.

Human life is like a spark from the stone.

We often start too late to enjoy ourselves.

The following lines are taken from Li Shang-yin's poems on Winter (冬):

The sun rose in the east,

The sun has set in the west.

The lady Phoenix flies alone,

The female Dragon has become a widow.

...

Frozen walls and hoary-headed frosts

Join in weaving gloom and sending doom

To the flowers, whose tender roots are snapped asunder,

And whose fragrant souls have breathed their last!

...

The wax candles weep tears of blood,
Lamenting the coming of the dawn.

Of course, I don't mean that in the Spring period of T'ang poetry poets were singing only of Spring; in the Summer period, only of Summer; and in Autumn and Winter, only of Autumn and Winter. In fact, the same season or the same scene may evoke quite different feelings in poets of different types. For instance, read this:

青紫虽被体，不如早还乡。
北城悲笳发，鹳鹤号且翔。
况复烦促倦，激烈思时康。

现在让我们平心静气地听白居易的《秋怀》：

月出照北堂，光华满阶墀。
凉风从西至，草木日夜衰。
桐柳减绿阴，蕙兰销碧滋。
感物私自念，我心亦如之。
安得长少壮，盛衰迫天时。
人生如石火，为乐常苦迟。

以下摘录李商隐的《燕台四首·冬》：

天东日出天西下，雌凤孤飞女龙寡。
……
冻壁霜华交隐起，芳根中断香心死。
……　　　　蜡烛啼红怨天曙。

当然，我绝不以为春季的诗人只歌颂春季，夏季的诗人只关心夏季等等；同一的季候，同一的景色，能唤起绝对不同的感情，像这句：

> Night's candles are burnt out, and jocund day
>
> Stands tip-toe on the misty mountain tops.

Do you not feel that it is a springy voice that you are hearing? But compare these lines of the great Spring bird Shakespeare with Li Shang-yin's:

> The wax candles weep tears of blood,
>
> Lamenting the coming of the dawn.

Both may be equally beautiful; but the former represents the beauty of hope, and the latter—the beauty of despair.

Read these lines by Li Po:

> Natural and unadorned, the lotus flowers
>
> Are swinging freely on translucent water.

This is what I would call Spring in Summer. But read this from Li Shang-yin:

> The banana tree refuses to unfold its leaves;
>
> The clove remains a closed bud for ever.
>
> Each nurses a private sorrow in its bosom,
>
> Though all breathe the same Spring air.

This is what I call Winter in Spring.

To take an instance which may be more familiar to my English readers, Wordsworth has always appeared to me to be the Po Chü-i of England. He represents Autumn at its best. He is so ripe and mellow and *pensively* calm. Even the leaping of his heart when he sees a rainbow has not much of the Spring in it, because his heart leaps within the bounds of "natural piety." In fact, no one knows himself so well as Wordsworth does. The other day, I came across one of his poems which confirms my hunch about him so breathtakingly that I really cannot resist the temptation of quoting it even at the risk of appearing irrelevant to my present theme:

> THE NIGHTINGALE AND THE STOCK-DOVE
>
> O Nightingale! thou surely art
>
> A creature of a "fiery heart":—

These notes of thine—they pierce and pierce;

Tumultuous harmony and fierce!

Thou sing'st as if the God of wine

Had helped thee to a Valentine;

> 晚烛燃短，快乐的日子
> 在雾中的山峰上站在足尖上。

你可感觉到一种春的活跃的欢声？将这伟大的春鸟——莎士比亚——的两行比较李商隐的：

> 蜡烛啼红怨天曙。

两者都是不可多得的美诗，可是前两句代表希望的美，后两句代表绝望的美。

听李白的这两行：

> 清水出芙蓉，天然去雕饰。

这我叫作夏季的春。李商隐的这两句是春季的冬：

> 芭蕉不展丁香结，同向春风各自愁。

为了让英语读者更好理解，我打个比方：在西洋诗中，华兹华斯我认为是英国的白居易：成熟、萧条、恬静，表现秋季的精神可谓天衣无缝。在望见五彩十色的虹的时候，他的心腑跳跃也没有丝毫春的欢乐，因为他心腑活动的地带只限于"自然的虔诚"的界线内。实在没有人较他更透彻地了解白居易。日前偶读华诗，极惊喜地找到一首诗证实这两位诗人的连贯，姑录如下，虽然看上来它同我的题旨毫不相干：

夜莺与小鸽

> 夜莺！
> 你具有火热的心：
> 你尖锐的歌声
> 创造着喧嚣而强烈的谐音。
> 你高唱，
> 似乎酒神已赠你一个情人，

A song In mockery and despite

Of shades, and dews, and silent night;

And steady bliss, and all the loves

Now sleeping in these peaceful groves.

I heard a Stock-dove sing or say

His homely tale, this very day;

His voice was buried among trees,

Yet to be come at by the breeze:

He did not cease; but cooed—and cooed;

And somewhat pensively he wooed:

He sang of love with quiet blending,

Slow to begin and never ending;

Of serious faith and inward glee;

That was the song—the song for me!

This quotation is not so irrelevant to my purpose as it may appear. For if the reader will keep it in mind that the Nightingale, a creature of a "fiery heart," is none other than Tu Fu, and the Stock-dove, who sings or says his homely tale, is none other than Po Chü-i, he has already done more than half in understanding T'ang poetry. And if, in addition, he will take to heart these lines of Wordsworth, this time addressed to a Skylark, he will have acquired a valuable clue to the songs of the early T'ang poets, especially Li Po:

There's madness about thee, and joy divine

In that song of thine.

...

Joyous as morning

Thou art laughing and scorning.

...

Alas! my journey, rugged and uneven,

Through prickly moors or dusty ways must wind;

But hearing thee, or others of thy kind,

你的歌曲溢着讥嘲，
你轻蔑阴影、露珠和沉静的夜，
你鄙视永恒的欢乐与
潜藏在寂寥的丛林中的爱情。
这天我也听见
小鸽歌话它朴素的故事。
它的呼声沉埋在树林中，
轻风飘送它到你的耳中。
不息地，
它呢喃着，
忧郁地，
它恳求着。
一曲和谐的恋歌
迟缓地开始，永无完尽，
赞美着严重的信仰和深沉的喜悦。
这是我的歌，为我的！

（M. K. 译）

这首诗其实并不与我的题旨风马牛。倘使读者能会意这"夜莺"——热心的动物——象征杜甫，这歌唱它朴素的歌的小鸽象征白居易，他已懂得唐诗的大半了。倘使他能欣赏华兹华斯赠云雀的诗，他可以更进一步领会初唐诗人的精神，尤其是李白：

你有些癫狂，
你的歌
是神圣的欢乐；
……
像早晨一样的欣喜，
你笑，你揶揄。
……
嗟呼，我的路程，崎岖不平，
迂回多刺的荒野，多尘的大道。
不过听见你，或你的同伴！

As full of gladness and as free of heaven,

I, with my fate contented, will plod on,

And hope for higher raptures, when life's day is done.

With the springy poets, there is something blithe and sprightly about their joys and sorrows, and their wishes and dreams. One feels that even their tears sparkle and shine. How do you like this little poem by a contemporary of Li Po on a girl's dream (金昌绪 春怨):

O drive away the orioles!

Don't let them sing on the branches!

Their noisy songs have interrupted my dream

Before I could reach the land of my heart's desire!

How flighty are the fancies and dreams of Li Po:

The south wind blows my heart homeward.

See how it flies and lights just before the old wine-shop!

What a different world you are in when you read Li Shang-yin's:

O my heart, blow not with the Spring flowers!

My love-thoughts are turned to ashes as soon as they sprout.

Naturally, Spring is not without its sorrows, even to a springy poet. Li Po, for instance, wrote:

I hear the sweet notes of the water-nut song,

Making me tumble under the load of Spring.

But it is one thing to "tumble under the load of Spring." It is quite another thing to feel, as Li Shang-yin does:

My heart is broken even before Spring comes.

The wishes and even dreams of a summery poet are like thunder; when, for instance, Tu Fu felt pent up on a hot autumnal day, he thundered (see 早秋苦热堆案相仍):

With a heavy girdle around my waist, I am maddened by the heat,
I feel like uttering a loud cry!
And my subordinates are still pestering me with piles upon piles of
　　documents!
On the southern side I see such green pines hanging over a little pool.
Ah for layers upon layers of ice on which to walk barefooted!

充满了快乐和天堂的自由；
我，我的知足的命运，就前进，
同时祈望着更大的欢乐，在生活的末日。

春季诗人的欢乐、哀愁、希望和幻梦都是轻松活泼的，我们觉得他们的泪珠也是光芒闪烁的。你可欢喜李白同时代人金昌绪的《春怨》？

打起黄莺儿，莫教枝上啼。
啼时惊妾梦，不得到辽西。

李白的幻梦是多么地奔逸：

南风吹归心，飞堕酒楼前。

读李商隐的这两句时，我们又感到不同的经验：

春心莫共花争发，一寸相思一寸灰。

当然，春并不是没有忧郁的，活跃的李白也不免叹息：

菱歌清唱不胜春！

不过这时的"不胜春"是一回事，像李商隐般痛泣

我意殊春意，先春已断肠！

又是一回事，两者迥然不同。

夏季诗人的希望和幻梦是像雷鸣，杜甫觉得被酷热窒息时就大发雷霆（《早秋苦热堆案相仍》）：

束带发狂欲大叫，簿书何急来相仍。
南望青松架短壑，安得赤脚踏层冰。

How differently an autumnal poet would feel in hot Summer. Po Chü-i's poem on "How to keep cool in Summer" (销暑) contains these philosophic lines:

> How to clear off the vexing heat?
> By sitting quietly in your house.
>
> ...
>
> A calm heart can scatter the heat;
> An empty room induces coolness to come.

I don't know exactly how Li Po feels when the weather is very hot, but I am pretty sure that his soul would fly up to the snow-capped mountains until he forgets his poor body which he has left behind him in a seething cauldron.

Of course, even a wintry poet is not impervious to heat. But I should think his soul would not fly up to the snow-capped mountains, nor would he possess enough spiritual vigor to drive away the heat, or enough physical energy to utter a loud shriek. At most he would emit a whimpering wish that some of these days cooler weather may come, or that some mythical goblin, in which he half believes, would work a miracle *for him.* This is exactly the sentiment I find in a beautiful poem by one of Li Shang-yin's younger contemporaries, Wang Ku (王毅):

> A BALLAD OF BOILING HEAT (苦热行)
> The god of fire hails from the south,
> Whipping the fiery dragon on which he rides.
> Flags of fire are fluttering all over the air,
> Until the skies are burned red hot.
> The wheel of the sun hangs over our heads,
> Motionless, as if nailed to the skies.
> All the nations of the world boil
> As in a seething cauldron!
> The lovely green of the Five Mountains is scorched,
> And the beautiful colors of the clouds vanish.

Even the Ocean has become a frying pan;

Its waves of sorrow are dried up.

I wish only that one of these evenings

A silvery breeze will rise,

To sweep away for me

The heat of the whole world!

By this time, you may be wondering how a wintry poet would feel in Winter. Well, I have just found a poem by Liu Chia (刘驾), another late T'ang poet, called "A Song of Bitter Cold" (苦寒吟):

秋季诗人大暑时的感觉又是多么地不同！白居易的《销暑》有这般哲学化的四句：

何以销烦暑，端居一院中。

……

热散由心静，凉生为室空。

我不知道李白在大伏天气时感觉怎样，推测起来，大概他的心灵要竭力地飞冲埋入云霄积雪的山峰，直到他忘却他遗留在这沸腾的洪釜中的躯壳。

一个冬季诗人当然不能处酷热若无事，不过他不会冲入积雪的山峰，也不会聚精会神地驱散炎热，更不会暴躁嘶喊，至多不过嗡嗡地呜咽，祈望较清凉日子的到达，或者他半信半疑的神话上的鬼怪能替他行些方便。这是较李商隐年轻的同辈诗人王毂悦人的《苦热行》蕴含的情绪：

祝融南来鞭火龙，火旗焰焰烧天红。

日轮当午凝不去，万国如在洪炉中。

五岳翠干云彩灭，阳侯海底愁波竭。

何当一夕金风发，为我扫却天下热。

倘使你想知道冬季诗人要怎样应付严寒的话，这里是晚唐诗人刘驾的《苦寒吟》：

All streams are frozen, swallowing their sobs.

My songs are more and more steeped in sadness.

In the midnight I still stand leaning against a pine tree,

Until my clothes are full of snow.

The sugar-cane has its sweet end and its bitter end:

I only like to cleave to the bitter end!

Some birds sing songs of joy, others songs of grief:

I only love that bird which sings with blood flowing from his beak!

This is what I would call wintry dourness, despair turned into desperation. What a contrast it offers to the feeling of that summery bird Tu Fu in a similar weather (茅屋为秋风所破歌):

Ah for a big mansion of a thousand, or ten thousand rooms

To give shelter and cheer to all the poor scholars of the world!

Safe from the ravages of wind and rain, they will feel as calm as the
mountain.

Ah me! The day on which I shall see such a mansion rise before my
eyes,

I shall be happy to continue to live in this broken hut and frozen to
death all alone.

Indeed, Tu Fu is the most Christ-like poet that I know!

The Spring of T'ang poetry is Dionysian; the Summer is Promethean; the Autumn is Epimethean;[2] and the Winter—O, what shall I call it? I have no name for it. But whenever I read the wintry poets, I am reminded of that indescribably fascinating poem of Christina Rossetti's "Passing Away" and I often catch myself humming this stanza from the "Bride Song" in her other poem, "The Prince's Progress."

Ten years ago, five years ago,

One year ago,—

Even then you had arrived in time,

Though somewhat slow;

Then you had known her living face,

Which now you cannot know;
The frozen fountain would have leaped,
The buds gone on to blow,
The warm south wind would have awaked
To melt the snow.

　　　　百泉冻皆咽，我吟寒更切。
　　　　半夜倚乔松，不觉满衣雪。
　　　　竹竿有甘苦，我爱抱苦节。
　　　　鸟声有悲欢，我爱口流血。

这是冬天的冷酷——绝望转到心死后的固执。这同杜甫在严寒时的
精神是多么地不同（《茅屋为秋风所破歌》）：

　　　　安得广厦千万间，
　　　　大庇天下寒士俱欢颜，
　　　　风雨不动安如山。
　　　　呜呼！何时眼前突兀见此屋，
　　　　吾庐独破受冻死亦足。

诚然，杜甫是我所知悉最具有博爱精神的诗人！
　　唐诗的春是 Dionysian，夏是 Promethean，秋是 Epimethean；²
冬，我应当怎样称呼它呢？我不能替它题名，不过每逢我诵冬诗
时，总想到克里斯蒂娜·罗塞蒂美得难以形容的《过逝》，不知不觉
地我又低吟她的《王子前进》中的《新娘歌》：

　　　　十年前，五年前，
　　　　　　一年前，——
　　　　倘使你那时准时赶到，
　　　　　　虽然已经稍迟，
　　　　来看她的脸儿，
　　　　　　（你现在看不到的；）
　　　　冻凝的泉源或许会跳跃，
　　　　　　萌芽或许会蓓蕾，
　　　　温暖的南风或许会醒来，
　　　　　　融解冬雪。

Just now, after re-reading this stanza, I find myself reciting a poem by Tu Mu, another wintry poet:

SIGHING OVER A FLOWER (叹花)

O! How I hate myself for coming so late
　　In search of the flower!
Years ago, I saw her before she had blown—
　　Just a budlet was she!
Now I find the wind has made a havoc of her—
　　Her petals strew the ground!
I only see a tree thick with leaves—
　　And branches full of fruits!

And what wintry despair one finds in this poem by Hsü Hun (许浑), another contemporary of Li Shang-yin:

THE DYING WORDS OF A FRIEND (王可封临终)

From a family of scholars I have come;
　　I have only a few children.
In my life, my friends have been kind to me,
　　But I have not repaid their kindness.
This morning, I shall be buried far from home—
　　At the foot of a chilly hill!
Tell, O tell my tender-hearted old mother
　　Not to wait any more at the doorsill!

How these poems remind me of T. S. Eliot's lines:

This is the way the world ends
This is the way the world ends
This is the way the world ends
Not with a bang but a whimper.

I don't regard Eliot as a wintry poet, but certainly he describes the wintry spirit very well. I don't know about the world, but I certainly know this is the way the poetry of T'ang ends, *"not with a bang but a whimper."* A whimper, yes. But what a whimper!

The poetry of the last of the T'angs is like a tubercular girl of surpassing beauty. You may admire her secretly, and at a distance. But to fall in love with her would be fatal. And yet, at times, you are so entranced by her beauty that you feel the question of life and death becomes quite a paltry matter.

现在，我发现自己背诵冬季诗人杜牧的《叹花》：

自恨寻芳到已迟，往年曾见未开时。
如今风摆花狼藉，绿叶成阴子满枝。

李商隐的同时代人许浑的《王可封临终》，又是渗流着冬季冷酷的绝望：

十世为儒少子孙，一生长负信陵恩。
今朝埋骨寒山下，为报慈亲休倚门。

这几首诗使我想到艾略特的：

世界就这样了结，
世界就这样了结，
世界就这样了结，
一个啜泣，没有响声。

艾略特我并不认为是冬季诗人，不过他描摹冬季精神极为中肯：宇宙的落局我不知道，唐诗的落局却是"一个啜泣，没有响声"。一个啜泣，这样的一个啜泣！

唐末的诗十分酷似一个患着结核症的绝世美女，虽在相当距离之外你可以私密地爱慕她，但和她发生恋爱是有关性命的。可是，有时候我们为了她的风韵媚态而颠倒，觉得生死是无足轻重的事。

Ever since the close of T'ang, China has been whimpering for more than ten centuries. Not until now does she feel some stirrings in her soul which look very much like the beginning of a new Spring! When Winter has tarried with us so long, "can Spring be far behind?"

But if there is another Golden Age in store for my country, as I am honestly sure that there is, then let it be even more glorious than T'ang! For the flowering of Chinese culture in T'ang reminds me all too much of a stanza in Richard Le Gallienne's "A Ballad of London":

> Upon thy petals butterflies,
>
> But at thy root, some say, there lies
>
> A world of weeping trodden things,
>
> Poor worms that have not eyes nor wings.

In the coming age, let Life become Poetry, or else it wouldn't be worthwhile to sing! But lest I should be carried away by my enthusiasm for the future and forget what I am writing about, I'll draw rein and return to my present theme.

On the whole, we may say that in the Spring of T'ang poetry, there were tears without griefs; in its Summer, the poets were so angry at the phenomena of social injustice and the uncalled for miseries of their fellow-beings that they had very little time to weep for themselves; in its Autumn, griefs were assuaged by copious tears; and in its Winter, there were griefs without tears. And the great wonder of T'ang poetry as a whole is that it was such a complete year in itself, a year in which the seasons seem to come in succession so naturally and inevitably. Like the Roman Law and Greek Philosophy, it carried within its bosom all the stages of a vital movement. Rarely do we find such a phenomenon in the history of human culture.

The more you read of the forty-nine thousand poems of the whole T'ang Dynasty (618–907), by more than twenty-two hundred poets, that have been preserved for us in Emperor K'ang Hsi's edition of 1707 (one can imagine how many poems had already been lost), the more you come to wonder how it is that the poetry of the Earth could be so prolific in this part of the world precisely at a time when Europe was in the very depths of a long hibernation. In fact, for nearly thirteen centuries after Christ, poetry in Europe, with the insignificant exception of Juvenal, kept a death-like silence. It hibernated so long that when it woke up again in the person of Dante, the last poetic voice it could remember was that of

唐朝衰亡后，千年以来中国在啜泣下生存着，直到现在她方才觉得灵魂深处的鼓舞，好像新春的蓬勃！严冬延搁已久，"春天还会远吗"？

倘使祖国的将来还有一个黄金时代的话（我深信不疑），愿它的光比唐朝更灿烂，更辉煌！唐代文化的蓓蕾使我想起了理查德·勒·加利耶纳的《伦敦歌》：

> 你的花瓣上是蝴蝶，
> 你的根蒂下，有人说，蛰伏着
> 哭泣、被践踏的东西，
> 没有眼睛、没有翅翼的蠕虫的世界。

在将来的黄金时代下，生活就是诗，否则它是不值得欢唱的！想到那时候的盛况，情不自禁地神往。不过还须勒住我的思潮，继续写我的文章。

大致说来，唐诗的春有泪而无愁；在夏季，诗人被社会之不平和生活之痛苦所激怒，无暇为自己流泪；秋季汪汪的眼泪减轻了哀愁的悲痛；冬季只有愁而无泪。唐诗之奇就在这整整的一年，一季一季极自然地接踵而至。像罗马法和希腊哲学一样，它的胸怀中生存着一段有生命的天演进化。这种现象在人类文化中可说是绝无仅有。

愈读康熙年间（1707年）选订的全唐（618—907）"凡二千二百余人"所作的四万九千首诗（可想而知多少首已经散佚），我们愈惊疑：怎么在那时世界的一角是那样地丰饶，而欧洲会在荒芜的冬眠时期下。基督死后欧洲的诗，除了无足轻重的尤维纳利斯，整整地死睡了十三个世纪。这冬眠在但丁身上醒来，那时在

Virgil who had laid down his harp just before Christ was born. It seems as though our Mother Earth purposely rocked Europe to sleep for some time that she might teach Asia to sing. And what difference did it make to God whether his children were singing in Asia or in Europe, so long as He could hear some sweet music in the course of every twenty-four hours?

我们脑中余音袅袅的诗声是基督前的维吉尔。大自然好像故意催促欧洲入眠，以期专心传授亚洲歌吟之道。在老天看来，只要他每二十四小时有悦耳的音乐听，他的孩子在东方或者西方歌唱有什么分别？

II. THE SPRING

John Stuart Mill once looked around him and sighed that there were so few eccentrics. It is probably because he lived in the Victorian Age, which has always appeared to me as the mellow season of Autumn, when the sense of wonder was a bit worn out and everything tended to crystallize down into definite forms. It's only in Spring-time, when the very air is full of promise, when people are young in spirit and fresh in curiosity, when they are stirred by the growing pangs of adolescence, that the earth will be found teeming with eccentrics.

Such a period I find in the early part of the T'ang Dynasty, that is, from its founding in A.D. 618 up to somewhere around 735, when the star of Yang Kuei-fei was beginning to rise and the star of T'ang was beginning to sink.

Right at the opening of the Dynasty we come across a most eccentric Buddhist monk by the name of Wang Fan-chih (王梵志). His rugged language and shocking fancies present a marked contrast to the squeamish and refined banalities of the preceding age. Take this for instance:

> Fan-chih wears his socks slipshod,
> And everybody says it's very odd.
> I would rather have your eyes cut out
> Than have my feet covered up!

This is certainly slipshod writing, but at least here is a man who dares to be himself. What brutal frankness is revealed in this:

> When I saw that chap die,
> My stomach was hot like fire.
> Did you think that I cared for that chap?
> No, I only feared the same would happen to me!

贰 春：李白的前驱

从前英儒米尔氏遍览当代人才，不禁喟然叹道："目今狂放的人实在太少了，这就是现时代的危机！"可是我们要知道，米尔氏生在维多利亚时代，那个时代在英国文化史上可说是秋天。秋天是收获的时节，不是创造的时节，一切已上了轨道，当然狂放的人物不易复得。要是在春天，那就不同了。因为在春天，人们就觉得朝气蓬勃，创造欲摇荡着人们的心魂。同时，青春期的烦恼鞭策人们盲目前进，欲罢不能。那时节大地才会产生多数的狂放的人才。¹

孔子说："吾党之小子狂简，斐然成章，不知所以裁之。"个人固然有青春和老成的分别，其实在文化史上也有青年时代和老成时代的分别。要是时代是青年的，连老成人也会有物我皆春的气象。要是时代是老成的，连青年也会有老气横秋的态度。春天是放的时候，秋天是收的时候。在春天，即使生性拘谨的人也会晓得放浪不羁；在秋天，即使生性狂放的也会觉得畏首畏尾。俗谚道：从今学得乌龟法，得缩头时且缩头。这可代表秋天的心理。还有说，海阔纵鱼跃，天空任鸟飞。这可代表春天的心理。有海阔天空的气概，才能尽量发挥个性和天才，结果便是狂放。太白诗云：一拳打碎岳阳楼，一脚踢翻鹦鹉洲。这类的话，惟有春季的人才会说的。

我少时读少陵《酒中八仙》，我就觉诧异，为什么那时有那么多的怪物。后来才始恍然大悟，因为酒中八仙生在唐代的春季，在空气中吸入了激人心灵的晨曦，使他们不得不奔放，不觉手之舞之足之蹈之起来了。少陵本人就比他们老成些了，他不是个怪物；所以他看看这些怪物觉得他们又可爱，又可怜，又可笑。犹之中年人看小孩子在草地上打滚的样子。因为少陵不是春天的人，乃是夏天的人，年纪虽比他们轻，可是货色却比他们老。

唐诗的春季是很长的，姑定从西历618年唐高祖武德开国那一年起到735年（明皇开元二十三年），那时杨贵妃的星渐渐上升，唐朝的星也就此开始西沉了。

在这时期的开始，我们就看见一个极怪僻的和尚——王梵志。他的粗俗的文字和惊人的幻想，与齐梁间没有生气的绮罗文学绝对相反，例如下面四行就是：

> 梵志翻着袜，人皆道是错。
> 乍可刺你眼，不可隐我脚。

这可以称作"不着袜"的笔调，赤裸裸得毫不整饰，不过他至少是一个有胆量表现自己的人。从下面几句就可以看见他的坦白爽直的态度：

> 我见那汉死，肚里热如火。
> 不是惜那汉，恐畏还到我。

And then what ghostly fancies this monk has:

> None in the world live up to a hundred,
>
> But everybody seems to tune himself up for a thousand years.
>
> When you beat iron into doorsills,
>
> The ghosts clap their hands and laugh at you!

There is another poem which describes his self-sufficiency and has some Whitmanic tang about it:

> I have opened up a field of ten *mow*
>
> On the slope of the southern hill.
>
> I have planted a couple of pine trees
>
> And a few rows of green beans.
>
> When it's hot, I take a bath in the lake.
>
> When it's cool, I sing on the shore.
>
> A free lance, I am sufficient as I am.
>
> Who can do anything to me?

When you hear people sing like this, you feel that the world is beginning once more. The significance of this monk lies in his freedom from the shackles of convention in life as well as in letters. He shattered the mincing art of his immediate predecessors to pieces. There is a strange beauty in his wild notes, just as when your eyes, accustomed to see the bound feet of old-fashion Chinese ladies, suddenly see a country girl with a pair of natural feet about as big as your own.

The next eccentric to attract our attention is the grandfather of Tu Fu, Tu Shen-yen (杜审言), who was born around 646 and died in his sixties. He seems to have suffered from what modern psychologists would call a *delusion de grandeur.* He once said, "In the art of letters, Ch'ü Yuan and Sung Yu should serve as my gatekeepers; in the art of calligraphy, Wang Hsi-chih ought to *kowtow* to me."

I have no means of judging his calligraphy, as he has not left any traces of this particular art. As to his art of letters, I have searched with a microscope all his forty-three poems that have come down to us, but have only found four lines of real poetry:

The Dawn has come out of the ocean attired in robes of rosy gauze.

The Spring has waded over the River and arrived among the plums and willows.

The life-giving breath of the season has gilded the feathers of birds with gold.

The clear daylight has dyed the duckweeds in lovely green.

这和尚是多么地异想天开呵：

世无百年人，强作千年调。
打铁作门限，鬼见拍手笑。

还有一首诗叙述他的自给自足的境界，颇有些惠特曼的气概：

吾有十亩田，种在南山坡。
青松四五树，绿豆两三窠。
热即池中浴，凉便岸上歌。
遨游自取足，谁能奈我何！

听见这种诗歌时，你就觉得这世界又回复到混沌初开、乾坤肇始的时候了。这位和尚的重要性也就在他的打破生活上和文学上的俗套的桎梏。他将前人的委靡烦琐的作风击成粉碎，在他无拘无碍的音韵中却含有醒人眼目的异美。我们对他的印象，正像惯见千金小姐的三寸金莲的人突然看见一位乡下姑娘的天足！

第二个值得注意的奇人是杜甫的祖父杜审言（他生于西历646年，卒于六十余年后）。他好像患有现代心理学家所说的"夸大狂"似的，有一次他说："吾文章当得屈宋作衙官，吾笔当得王羲之北面。"

我不能评衡他的书法，因为他没有作品遗留下来。至于他的诗，我曾在显微镜下细察过，在他所遗下来的四十三首诗里只发现四行真正的上品：

云霞出海曙，梅柳渡江春。
淑气催黄鸟，晴光转绿苹。

Certainly there is Spring in these lines, and while they hardly justify his self-estimate, they will continue to be recited as long as Chinese poetry will continue to be studied. This reminds me of another poet of the same period, Wang Po (王勃), who will live for ever in these two lines:

> The existence of a single bosom friend on earth
> Turns the wide, wide world into a cordial neighborhood.

We find another interesting character in the person of Ch'en Tzŭ-ang, who was born in 659 and died in his early forties. A native of Szechuen, and a rich man's son, he started late in his studies. Only in his late twenties did he go to the Capital to take his first degree. As he was still an obscure scholar, he tried to draw public attention to himself by staging a rather spectacular scene. It happened somebody was selling a Tartar-guitar and asked for it the exorbitant price of a million cash! Tzŭ-ang bought it at the price asked for, which naturally shocked spectators. Upon being asked why he did such a foolish thing, he said, "I am an expert player of this kind of guitar." "May we have the pleasure of hearing you play it?" they urged. "O yes," he answered, "I'll give a performance tomorrow in the Hsuan Yang Terrace." The next day, Tzŭ-ang prepared a grand feast for all. As was to be expected, many people came flocking in to hear his music. But instead of playing the guitar, he took it up and made an oration! "Gentlemen," he said, "I am a native of Szechuen, and Ch'en Tzŭ-ang is my name. I have brought with me a hundred scrolls of my essays and poems, which deserve to be better known. As to this guitar, there is nothing precious about it!" Thereupon he dashed the guitar into pieces, and handed round copies of his writings. In one day, he became the talk of the town! Among the poems distributed were the famous thirty-eight "Lyrics" (感遇诗). They were written in the old style, but the language was very simple and the thought full of genuine Taoistic insights and cosmic yearnings. Let one specimen suffice:

BUSINESS MEN

Business men boast of their skill and cunning

But in philosophy they are like little children.

Bragging to each other of successful depredations

They neglect to consider the ultimate fate of the body.

What should they know of the Master of Dark Truth

Who saw the wide world in a jade cup.

无疑的，这几行里荡漾着春气。他的伟大虽然不及他自己所估计的那样，可是这四行自有其永久的价值。这使我想起这时的另外一位诗人——王勃，他亦因了两句好诗而永垂不朽：

> 海内存知己，天涯若比邻。

陈子昂也是一位饶于风趣的怪物，原籍四川，生于659年，卒年四十余。他生于富有之家，但治学颇迟，入京举进士时已是将近三十岁的人了。因为那时他还没成名，所以他用尽心思，以冀引起社会注意。《唐诗纪事》里就有如下的记载：

> 子昂初入京，不为人知。有卖胡琴者，价百万……子昂突出，谓左右曰："辇千缗市之。"众惊问，答曰"余善此乐。"皆曰："可得闻乎？"曰："明日可集宣扬里。"如期偕往，则酒肴毕具，置胡琴于前。食毕，捧琴语曰："蜀人陈子昂，有文百轴，驰走京毂，碌碌尘土，不为人知。此乐贱工之役，岂宜留心！"举而碎之，以其文轴遍赠会者。一日之内，声华溢郡。

在他所分送的作品内，最驰名的就是《感遇诗三十八首》，虽然它们是用古体写的，文字却极为清简，富有纯真的道家见识和宇宙的感怀。下面已足以为例：

> 市人矜巧智，于道若童蒙。
> 倾夺相夸侈，不知身所终。
> 曷见玄真子，观世玉壶中。

By illumined conception got clear of Heaven and Earth:

On the Chariot of Mutation entered the Gate of Immutability?

(Waley's version)

Another poem, which many critics have rightly regarded as his masterpiece, shows still better the nameless pathos of this newcomer in early Spring:

GAZING INTO DISTANCE (登幽州台歌)

I look before, and don't see the ancient sages:

I look after, and don't see the coming ages.

Only the heaven-and-earth will last through the endless years:

Overcome by pathos, my eyes are filled with silent tears.

(Teresa Li's version)

The simplicity of his language was a deliberate revolt against rhetoric. In a letter to a friend, Tzǔ-ang said:

The art of letters has been decaying for five hundred years... In my leisure hours, I have looked into the poems of the Ch'i and Liang Dynasties, and I could not help sighing when I found all genuine feeling and insight were smothered by meaningless figures of speech and squeamish refinement of words. So much rhetoric and so little sentiment! When will the grand tradition of *Shih Ching* revive?

This desire to break with the immediate past and to return to a remoter antiquity is characteristic of all the literary reforms of old China. And this is true of the reforms in other fields as well.

While it may be that Tzǔ-ang himself has not given us any really first-rate poems, his contribution as a pioneer in the revolt against rhetoric cannot be over-estimated, for he set the pace to the later poets. As Han Yu so justly said:

The art of letters has prospered in our Dynasty:

Tzǔ-ang it was who first departed from the beaten track.

In the meantime, Spring is warming up, and more and more birds come to sing. The seventh century was not to close without having produced a formidable host of poets. To begin with, there was the famous Ho Chih-chang (贺知章) who was born in 659 and lived up to 744, and who called himself "a Mad Guest from the Mountain of Sze-ming" (in the neighborhood of Ningpo). Exactly how "mad" he was we don't know, but certainly he had a great liking for wine. Tu Fu wrote a little caricature of him:

窅然遗天地，乘化入无穷。 （英译：韦利）

另外又有一首，许多批评家都认为是他的杰作，简直将新春时不可名状的感慨和盘托出了（《登幽州台歌》）：

前不见古人，后不见来者。
念天地之悠悠，独怆然而涕下！

（英译：李德兰【吴经熊化名】）

这种朴素的文字，对那时传统修辞简直是当头一棒。在他给友人的一封信里，他说：

文章道弊，五百年矣……仆尝暇时观齐梁间诗，彩丽竞繁，而兴寄都绝，每以永叹。思古人常恐逶迤颓靡，风雅不作，以耿耿也。

这种用复古的方式和口号打倒近代的传统思想，是中国历来文艺革新的通例。【其他领域的革新亦如此。】

子昂没有留下真正第一流的作品，可是他的反抗绮罗文学确是个不容忽视的贡献，因为他替后来诗人开了一条康庄大道。韩愈说得好：

国朝盛文章，子昂始高蹈。

同时，春季在渐渐地转暖，天上的鸣禽也越来越多。这第七世纪在终了前还产生了一大群诗人。那位自纪"四明狂客"（四明位于宁波近郊）的贺知章生于659年而卒于744年。我们不知道他狂到什么地步，不过他爱好杯勺是不容怀疑的。杜甫曾替他绘了一幅画：

Chih-chang on horse-back swayed back and forth

As though he were sitting in a boat.

Dizzy with wine, he fell into the water,

And was found sleeping on the bottom of a well!

He didn't write many poems, but one poem of his, I think, has been recited more times throughout all these generations than any other poem in the Chinese language:

ON RETURNING HOME (回乡偶书)

As a young man I left home,

As an old man I have come back.

My native accent I still retain,

But hairs on my head I lack!

When my boys saw me,

They didn't know their pa had come home.

Gingerly they smiled and asked:

"From where O honorable guest, have you come?"

Among the younger contemporaries of Chih-chang were Liu Shen-hsu (刘慎虚), Chang Chiu-ling (张九龄), Chang Jo-hsu (张若虚), Wang Ch'ang-ling (王昌龄), and Wang Chih-huan (王之涣), to mention but a few of the whole bunch. Space does not allow me to tell about their lives, some of them very interesting. But each of them was the author of quite a few songs which still continue to live on the lips of many of our contemporaries. I shall only reproduce here a representative piece from each of them.

(1) A QUIET STUDY ON A HILL (阙题)

By Liu Shen-hsu

The pathways penetrate far into the white clouds.

The Spring is as long as the green streamlets.

From time to time, fallen flowers are wafted on the flowing waters.

Sending puffs of fresh perfume from afar.

An Idle door, facing a mountain path, remains ajar.

A quiet study is hidden in the midst of thickset willows.

The whole place is drenched in empyrean light.

Even my clothes acquire a new luster from the clear rays of the sun.

(2) SINCE MY LORD LEFT (赋得自君之出矣)

By Chang Chiu-ling

Since my lord left,

I have had no heart to spin and weave.

Thinking of thee has made me thinner and thinner,

Just as the full moon has waned from night to night.

知章骑马似乘船，眼花落井水底眠。

他的作品并不丰富，可是他的《回乡偶书》那首七绝可说是古今最脍炙人口的了：

少小离家老大回，乡音无改鬓毛衰。
儿童相见不相识，笑问客从何处来。

和知章同时的有刘慎虚、张九龄、张若虚、王昌龄和王之涣等。因为篇幅的关系我不能叙述他们的生平，有几个是很有趣的；他们都是几首万人争诵的名诗的作者。这里可说是每人的代表作：

(一)《阙题》——刘慎虚
道由白云尽，春与青溪长。
时有落花至，远随流水香。
闲门向山路，深柳读书堂；
幽映每白日，清辉照衣裳。

(二)《赋得自君之出矣》——张九龄
自君之出矣，不复理残机。
思君如满月，夜夜减清辉。

(3) A WIFE'S SIGH IN SPRING (闺怨)

By Wang Ch'ang-ling

A young woman, newly married, she is a stranger to sorrow.

In Spring, dressed in gay array, she climbs up a lovely tower.

Suddenly, the green color of the willows meets her eyes.

"Ah," she sighs to herself, "why did I let him go to seek glory?"

(4) CLIMBING A TOWER (登鹳雀楼)

By Wang Chih-huan

The white sun has sunk behind the hills.

The Yellow River is pouring into the sea.

To see still farther into the horizon,

Let us go up one more storey!

(5) THE RIVER BY NIGHT IN SPRING (春江花月夜)

By Chang Jo-hsu

In Spring the flooded river meets the tide

    Which from the ocean surges to the land;

The moon across the rolling water shines

    From wave to wave to reach the distant strand.

And when the heaving sea and river meet,

    The latter turns and floods the fragrant field;

While in the moon's pale light as shimmering sleet

    Alike seem sandy shores and wooded wealds.

For sky and river in one color blend,

    Without a spot of dust to mar the scene;

While in the heavens above the full-orbed moon

    In white and lustrous beauty hangs serene.

And men and women, as the fleeting years,

    Are born into this world and pass away;

And still the river flows, the moon shines fair,

    And will their courses surely run for aye.

But who was he who first stood here and gazed

    Upon the river and the heavenly light?

And when did moon and river first behold

    The solitary watcher in the night?

The maples sigh upon the river's bank,

    A white cloud drifts across the azure dome;

In yonder boat some traveler sails to-night

    Beneath the moon which links his thoughts with home.

Above the home it seems to hover long,

    And peep through chinks within her chamber blind;

（三）《闺怨》——王昌龄

闺中少妇不知愁，春日凝妆上翠楼。

忽见陌头杨柳色，悔教夫婿觅封侯。

（四）《登鹳雀楼》——王之涣

白日依山尽，黄河入海流。

欲穷千里目，更上一层楼。

（五）《春江花月夜》——张若虚

春江潮水连海平，海上明月共潮生。

滟滟随波千万里，何处春江无月明。

江流宛转绕芳甸，月照花林皆似霰。

空里流霜不觉飞，汀上白沙看不见。

江天一色无纤尘，皎皎空中孤月轮。

江畔何人初见月？江月何年初照人？

人生代代无穷已，江月年年只相似。

不知江月待何人，但见长江送流水。

白云一片去悠悠，青枫浦上不胜愁。

谁家今夜扁舟子？何处相思明月楼？

可怜楼上月徘徊，应照离人妆镜台。

The moon-borne message she cannot escape,
    Alas, the husband tarries far behind!

She looks across the gulf but hears no voice,
    Until her heart with longing leaps apace,
And fain would she the silvery moonbeams follow
    Until they shine upon her loved one's face.

"Last night," she murmured sadly to herself,
    "I dreamt of falling flowers by shady ponds;
My Spring, ah me! half through its course has sped,
    But you return not to your wedded bonds."

For ever onward flows the mighty stream;
    The Spring, half gone, is gliding to its rest;
While on the river and the silent pools
    The moonbeams fall obliquely from the west.

And now the moon descending to the verge
    Has disappeared beneath the sea-borne dew;
While stretch the waters of the "Siao and Siang,"
    And rocks and cliffs, in never-ending view.

How many wanderers by to-night's pale moon
    Have met with those from whom so long apart:—
As on the shore midst flowerless trees I stand
    Thoughts old and new surge through my throbbing heart!

                (Translated by Charles Budd)

Now we come to Meng Hao-jan (孟浩然: 689–740). By nature a hermit, he once had an interview with Ming Huang. Asked by His Majesty to recite some of his poems, he picked up, for some reason or other, a particular poem which contains these lines:

Don't present any memorials to the Imperial Court!
Let me return to my old home among the hills!

Untalented, I am overlooked by the enlightened Monarch;

Often ill, I have lost contact with my old friends.

Ming Huang, naturally, was not much pleased by these lines. "Look here," he said, "you are not being fair to me. I have not overlooked you, but you never wanted any office from me. I wish you had recited that poem on Tung T'ing Lake which contains two lines I like so much:

Its exhalation warms up the marshy villages;

Its waves rock the city as in a cradle."

Ming Huang was probably in a sulky mood (it was before he had known Yang Kuei-fei), but he was subtle too. For the same poem also has this line in it:

Living like a hermit, I feel unworthy of the sage Emperor.

玉户帘中卷不去，捣衣砧上拂还来。
此时相望不相闻，愿逐月华流照君。
鸿雁长飞光不度，鱼龙潜跃水成文。
昨夜闲潭梦落花，可怜春半不还家。
江水流春去欲尽，江潭落月复西斜。
斜月沉沉藏海雾，碣石潇湘无限路。
不知乘月几人归，落月摇情满江树。　　　　（英译：布茂林）

孟浩然（689—740）天性爱好隐居。《唐诗纪事》载其轶事一则：

明皇以张说之荐召浩然，令诵所作。乃诵："北阙休上书，南山归蔽庐。不才明主弃，多病故人疏……"帝曰："卿不求朕，岂朕弃卿？何不云：'气蒸云梦泽，波撼岳阳城'？"

大概明皇那时的心境不见得十分舒畅（他尚未遇见杨贵妃），可是也相当地幽默，因为"气蒸云梦泽，波撼岳阳城"下有这么的一句：

端居耻圣明。

Be it as it may, the two gentlemen never saw each other again.

Li Po had the highest admiration for Hao-jan. He wrote:

> I love my master Meng!
>
> Who doesn't know this charming person?
>
> As a young man he threw away worldly glories;
>
> As an old man he remains a friend of the pines and clouds.
>
> His capacity for wine is admirable.
>
> He would rather look at the flowers and the moon than serve the monarch!
>
> What a high mountain he appears to me!
>
> I lift up my head and smell its fragrance from afar.

I have never seen Li Po praise a man so highly as he does Meng. Perhaps, Meng was even greater as a man than as a poet. But what charming poems on Nature he has left behind him! From his poems one seems to see a man who kept the noiseless tenor of his way "along the cool sequestered vale of life." Let me give some specimens here:

AN INVITATION TO A FRIEND (秋登兰山寄张五)

> I am enjoying myself here
>
> Among the cloud-capped hills.
>
> Thinking of you, I have climbed up to the top and gaze afar.
>
> My soul flies with the birds until they vanish from my ken.
>
> I feel a little sad because it's so near evening;
>
> But my spirit is stirring within me in the presence of such a fine sight!
>
> From here I can see some people returning to their villages:
>
> They walk on the sandy beaches, and tarry around the ferry.
>
> The trees that skirt the horizon look like mushrooms;
>
> The boats on the river look no bigger than the moon.
>
> Why don't you come, bringing some wine along!
>
> We shall have a good time together on the Double Nine.

These lines were written in Autumn, but there is nothing autumnal about them. He is intoxicated with Nature, and naturally he wishes to share his joy with his friends. How he misses his friends is shown in another beautiful poem, of which I beg to use Professor Giles' version:

IN DREAMLAND (夏日南亭怀辛大)

The sun has set behind the western slope,

The eastern moon lies mirrored in the pool;

With streaming hair my balcony I ope,

And stretch my limbs to enjoy the cool.

如此轻轻一拨，将隐居的责任完全推到浩然身上；明皇的是可儿！

李白对浩然极表钦慕之意。看这首诗：

吾爱孟夫子，风流天下闻。

红颜弃轩冕，白首卧松云。

醉月频中圣，迷花不事君。

高山安可仰，徒此揖清芬。

我从来未见太白如此推重别人。浩然的人品也许比他的作品更为伟大，可是他遗留下来的描写大自然的诗也已够风韵了，从那里我们看见一个幽静的灵魂过着甘于寂寥、遁世无闷的生活。让我举一个例（《秋登兰山寄张五》）：

北山白云里，隐者自怡悦。

相望始登高，心随雁飞灭。

愁因薄暮起，兴是清秋发。

时见归村人，沙行渡头歇。

天边树若荠，江畔洲如月。

何当载酒来，共醉重阳节。

写这首诗的时候正是秋天，可是诗里却无半点秋意。他是沉醉在大自然中，所以他希望他的朋友也来分享他的快乐。他怎样怀友可以在《夏日南亭怀辛大》（翟理思英译）中看到：

山光忽西落，池月渐东上。

散发乘夕凉，开轩卧闲敞。

Loaded with lotus-scent the breeze sweeps by,

    Clear dripping drops from tall bamboos I hear.

I gaze upon my idle lute and sigh:

    Alas no sympathetic ear is near!

And so I doze, the while before mine eyes

    Dear friends of other days in dream-clad forms arise.

The most popularly known of all his poems is a little quatrain on "Morning in Spring" (春晓):

In Spring how sweet is sleep! I don't know the day has dawned!

But what a riotous chorus of birds I hear all around!

Last night the sound of wind and rain stole into my ears—

I wonder how many flowers have fallen on the ground.

Perhaps the greatest Nature-poet of T'ang was Wang Wei (王维: 699–761). With him the Spring of T'ang poetry is at its sweetest. His naturalism is of the purest brand, unalloyed with any sense of personal disappointment, as is sometimes the case even with Meng Hao-jan; and undiluted with pale meditation and sophisticated ratiocination, as is so often the case with Po Chü-i. Wang Wei is just between the uncomfortable and awkward stirrings of early Spring and the yeasty madness of late Spring. His voice is warm and soothing like the fairest days in Spring. With fancy clean and soul clean, he "takes in all beauty with an easy span."

His personality is not easy to describe. He is not an eccentric, nor a fanatic, nor an embittered soul, and yet he is not what my friend Mr. Wen Yuan-ning would call "a moral smug." He is neither a libertine nor a prig, neither a wild ass nor a mule either. He does not belong to that class of dreary souls, who, in the words of Dante, "lived without blame, and without praise," and "who were neither rebellious nor faithful to God."

Wang Wei's soul is of the sky-blue tint, and his affinities, to borrow some words from William James in his description of healthy-mindedness, "are rather with flowers and birds and all the enchanting innocencies than with the dark human passions." This man has always impressed me as a man who possesses religious gladness from the very outset, and needs no deliverance from any antecedent burden. His religion is one of union with the divine, and he sees God not as a severe Father, but as a tender Mother.

> 荷风送香气，竹露滴清响。
> 欲取鸣琴弹，恨无知音赏。
> 感此怀故人，中宵劳梦想。

他最著名的要算是这四行绝句：

> 春眠不觉晓，处处闻啼鸟。
> 夜来风雨声，花落知多少。

唐朝最伟大的自然诗人当推王维（699—761）。在他的笔下，唐诗的春达到了中边皆甜的境界。他的自然主义是最纯粹的，不像孟浩然的自然主义还受个人生活失意的沾染，更不同白居易的自然主义掺了多量理知主义的淡水。他是处于蠢蠢欲动的初春和飞扬跋扈的晚春的中间，他的声音是像春天最快乐的日子那么地温柔抚慰，真有所谓"猗猗季月，穆穆和春"的气象。清明的幻想和纯洁的灵魂使他很轻易地吸收大自然的美。

王维的人格是难于描摹的：他既不怪僻，又不狂热；既不是一个浸淫在烦扰悲痛中的灵魂，也不是像温源宁先生所说的"麻木不仁的道学先生"；既非放荡不羁，又非墨守成规；既非野马，又非驯骡，更非但丁所说的无声无臭、模棱两可的黯淡灵魂。

王维的灵魂是天蓝色的，他好像同一切自然之美结不解之缘。【借用威廉·詹姆斯关于健康心智的描述，"他更亲近于花朵、鸟儿和其他所有迷人的天真之物，而非黑暗的人类激情"。】他给我的印象是一个素有宗教涵养的人物，【不需要从任何以往的羁绊中挣脱，他的宗教与神合一，】他的上苍不是严父，而是慈母。

His life was uneventful, and need not be told here at length. Officially, he was pretty high up. But the wonder of it was that official life did not vulgarize him in the least. He was a devoted Buddhist. But the wonder of it was that he seldom talked of Buddhism in his poems, as Po Chü-i so often did successively of his Confucianism, of his Taoism, and of his Buddhism. It is only when your faith is feeble that you feel the need to buttress it with arguments; but the irony of it is that the more arguments you use, the more is your faith sicklied over with the pale cast of thought. You cry your religion at the top of your voice, as a peddler cries his wares, but underneath your subterranean misgivings ooze and threaten to wash away your foundations. But with Wang Wei, it is different. He simply takes his religion for granted, and goes on to practice it. He was a vegetarian, he constantly resorted to the practice of *Zen* or *Ch'an* (坐禅), which means sitting silently and holding communion with the divine. As he says in one of his poems:

> In the eventide, by the side of a crystal pool,
> I practice *ch'an* to control the poisonous dragon in me.

About thirty, he lost his wife, and he remained a widower for the rest of his days. But he kept two sweet mistresses, who were not only not jealous of each other, but mutually helpful—I mean Poetry and Painting! Besides being a great poet, he was also a famous painter. Su Tung-po used to say about him that "in his paintings there is poetry, and in his poems there is painting."

For instance, what a beautiful picture he paints here:

FARM HOUSES ON THE WEI STREAM (渭川田家)[2]
The slanting sun shines on the cluster of small houses on the heights.
Oxen and sheep are coming home along the distant lane.
An old countryman is thinking of the herd-boy,
He leans on his staff by the thorn-branch gate, watching.
Pheasants are calling, the wheat is coming into ear,
Silkworms sleep, the mulberry-leaves are thin.

Laborers, with their hoes over their shoulders, arrive;
They speak pleasantly together, loath to part.

　　他的生平没有多大风波，毋庸详述。虽然身居要职，却没有官僚习气。他是一个虔诚的佛教徒，但是奇怪的是，在诗里他绝少宣传佛教，不像白居易那样俨然以广大教化主自居，将文学当作载道之器。事情是这样的：只有你的信仰薄弱的时候，你才觉得有用理论来辅助它的必要。但是好笑的是，你愈借重理论，你的信仰也愈被思想的暗影蒙罩住了。你用了尖锐的嗓子高喊你的宗教，像一个小贩高喊他的货物一样，可是你的内心中潜涌着地层下的疑虑，势必冲毁你信仰的基础。王维不是这样的，他很自然地实行他的宗教，他食甘蔬菲，时常静坐思禅。在一首诗里他说：

　　　　薄暮空潭曲，安禅制毒龙。

他的精神的专一，可在《苦热》那首诗里窥见一斑：

　　　　赤日满天地，火云成山岳。
　　　　草木尽焦卷，川泽皆竭涸。
　　　　轻纨觉衣重，密树苦阴薄。
　　　　莞簟不可近，缔绤再三濯。
　　　　思出宇宙外，旷然在寥廓。
　　　　长风万里来，江海荡烦浊。
　　　　却顾身为患，始知心未觉。
　　　　忽入甘露门，宛然清凉乐。

能将苦热化作甘露，那才真得了宗教的三昧。[3]

　　他三十岁的时候便丧了偶，终身就此过鳏夫生活。可是他养了两位极堪眷恋的情人，她们非但不彼此嫉妒，并且互相辅助，使他完成他的工作。这两位情人就是"诗"和"画"！他不但是位大诗人，还是个古今驰名的山水画师。苏东坡曾说他"诗中有画，画中有诗"。

　　你看这幅画是多么地爽目（《渭川田家》）：

　　　　斜光照墟落，穷巷牛羊归。
　　　　野老念牧童，倚杖候荆扉。
　　　　雉雊麦苗秀，蚕眠桑叶稀。
　　　　田夫荷锄至，相见语依依。

It is for this I long—unambitious peace!

With a heart full of yearnings, I hum the song of "Why Not Return?"

O dear Wang Wei! How you fill *my* heart with similar yearnings! When can I hear again "the soft gurgling music which I heard welling up from the sappy roots of the earth"? When can I see once more the "soft landscape of mild earth"?[4]

> Where all was harmony, and calm, and quiet,
>
> Luxuriant, budding; cheerful without mirth,
>
> Which, if not happiness, is much more nigh it
>
> Than are your mighty passions…

And what soothing images are evoked by this poem on "The Blue-green Stream" (青溪):

> Every time I have started for the Yellow Flower River,
>
> I have gone down the Blue-green Stream,
>
> Following the hills, making ten thousand turnings.
>
> We go rapidly, but advance scarcely a hundred *li*.
>
> We are in the midst of a noise of water,
>
> Of the confused and mingled sounds of water broken by stones,
>
> And in the deep darkness of pine-trees.
>
> Rocked, rocked,
>
> Moving on and on,
>
> We float past water-chestnuts
>
> Into a still clearness reflecting reeds and rushes.
>
> My heart is clean and white as silk; it has already achieved Peace;
>
> It is smooth as the placid river.
>
> I long to stay here, curled up on the rocks,
>
> Dropping my fish-line forever.

> (Translated by Ayscough and Lowell)

Not that he longs to escape from the world, but that he longs to live in the bosom of Mother Nature. How much at home he feels when he is alone with nature is revealed in his poem on "The Bamboo Grove" (竹里馆).

> Beneath the bamboo grove, alone,
>
>   I seize my lute and sit and croon;
>
> No ear to hear me, save my own,
>
>   No eyes to see me, save the moon.

(Translated by Giles)

> 即此羡闲逸，怅然吟式微。

【噢，王维！你道出了我的心声！何时我才能再听到"从泥土多汁的根部涌出的轻柔汩汩的音乐"？何时我才能再看到那"宜人而和煦的风景"？[4]

> 这儿一切是安谧、和谐与平静，
> 明媚似含蕾初放，却乐而不淫，
> 即使还不算至乐，但已最接近，
> 远胜过……
> 那种激烈的热情！】

还有《青溪》一诗也同样地可爱：

> 言入黄花川，每逐青溪水。
> 随山将万转，趣途无百里。
> 声喧乱石中，色静深松里。
> 漾漾泛菱荇，澄澄映葭苇。
> 我心素已闲，清川澹如此。
> 请留盘石上，垂钓将已矣。　　（英译：艾思柯、洛威尔）

他并不想脱逃这世界，他的希望是寄托在"大自然母亲"的怀抱中。他的《竹里馆》显出，同大自然孤独在一起的时候，他是多么地舒适自在：

> 独坐幽篁里，弹琴复长啸。
> 深林人不知，明月来相照。　　（英译：翟理思）

To be seen by the moon is enough of a happiness to him He is even more infatuated with Nature than Meng Hao-jan. When he is alone, he just plays the lute and enjoys himself, like a child on the lap of its mother. The mother says, "Look, look, my little baby! The moon is peeking at you!" and the baby is pleased. He does not feel, as Hao-jan does:

> I gaze upon my idle lute and sigh:
>> Alas no sympathetic ear is near!

Nor is he like Rousseau on the Island of Saint-Pierre, who cried out in ecstasy, "O nature! O my mother! Behold me under thy protection alone! Here there is no knave to thrust himself between thee and me." He would rather say to Nature, "My little ma, I am so happy here! My ma, you must never leave me alone. But, my ma, when will you have another baby to play with me and share these candies with me?"

And Wang Wei does share his candies with his friends. In a beautiful letter, rendered into beautiful English by Arthur Waley, he invites P'ei Ti (裴迪) to enjoy solitude together with him. I want to reproduce the letter here in Waley's translation, with a few alterations in italics:

> Of late during the sacrificial month the weather has been *mild* and clear, and I might easily have crossed the mountain. But I knew that you were conning the classics and did not dare disturb you. So I roamed about the mountain-side, rested at the Kan-p'ei Temple, dined with the mountain priests, and, after dinner, *sauntered forth again.* Going northwards, I crossed Yüan-pa, over whose waters the unclouded moon shone with dazzling rim. When night was far advanced, I mounted Hua-Tzǔ's Hill and saw the moonlight tossed up and thrown down by the jostling waves of Wang River. On the wintry mountain distant lights twinkled and vanished; in some deep lane beyond the forest a dog barked at the cold, with a cry as fierce as a wolf's. The sound of villagers grinding their corn at night filled the gaps between the slow chiming of a distant bell.
>
> Now I am sitting alone. I listen, but cannot hear my grooms and servants move or speak. I think much of old days: how hand in hand,

composing poems as we went, we walked down twisting paths to the banks of clear streams.

We must wait for Spring to come: till the grasses sprout and the trees bloom. Then wandering together in the spring hills we shall see the trout leap lightly from the stream, the white gulls stretch their wings, the dew fall on the green moss. And in the morning we shall hear the cry of curlews in the barley-fields.

It is not long to wait. Shall you be with me then? Did I not know the natural subtlety of your intelligence, I would not dare address to you an invitation *of so little worldly importance. But I am sure you will find the trip deeply interesting.*

明月能窥见他，他已是心满意足了。他较孟浩然更依恋大自然，单独的时候他就弹琴自娱，像一个婴孩在母亲的膝上嬉戏那般自得。这母亲说："看，看，我的孩子，月亮在觑着你！"这孩子也就欢喜。他不像孟浩然般地感觉"欲取鸣琴弹，恨无知音赏"，也不像在圣彼得岛上狂叫的卢梭，"大自然，我的母亲，看我孤独地在你的庇护之下！这里没有蛮汉闯入你我之间"。他或许会对大自然说："我的妈，在这里我是多么快乐！妈，你不可离开我。可是，你几时会再生一个孩子作我的伴侣，分享我的果食？"

王维确曾同他的朋友分享果食。在一封信里，他邀请裴迪同他共同享受清寂的味儿（韦利将这封信译成了优美的英文，英文斜体部分是我做的改动）：

> 近腊月下，景气和畅，故山殊可过。足下方温经，猥不敢相烦，辄便往山中，憩感配寺，与山僧饭讫而去。北涉玄灞，清月映郭。夜登华子冈，辋水沦涟，与月上下。寒山远火，明灭林外。深巷寒犬，吠声如豹。村墟夜舂，复与疏钟相间。此时独坐，僮仆静默，多思曩昔，携手赋诗，步仄径，临清流也。当待春中，草木蔓发，春山可望，轻鲦出水，白鸥矫翼，露湿青皋，麦陇朝雊，斯之不远，倘能从我游乎？非子天机清妙者，岂能以此不急之务相邀。然是中有深趣矣！

Although conning the classics is important, enjoying Nature is even more so. The friend did accept the invitation, and came over to enjoy solitude together. He also wrote a charming poem on the bamboo grove:

> In the bamboo grove of my friend,
> We grow daily more intimate with Nature.
> Far from the madding crowd,
> Only the mountain birds hobnob with us.

Indeed, only a very noble person can enjoy Nature in the right mood. How this letter of Wang Wei's recalls to my mind a lovely letter my great friend Holmes wrote to me over twelve years ago from Beverly Farms:

> Also for two hours I drive and motor about this beautiful and interesting region, which I am sorry you did not see. One may gaze over lonely cliffs upon the seas or pass along smooth boulevards by crowded beaches, or skirt windswept downs and fine inland farms, or evoke the past by visiting houses built two centuries ago. That is not long for China, but it is long enough for romance. I say that all society is founded on the death of men. Certainly the romance of the past is. So much so that the memorial tablets of a great war have the effect of two centuries added. I could run on for a great while, but I must stop.

Mr. T. K. Ch'uan once mentioned to me how natural and spontaneous Holmes' style of writing seemed to him. I think it is because he was such a great lover of Nature. And the style of Holmes is like that of Wang Wei, because the touch of Nature makes them kin.

Another poem of Wang Wei, written in his fifties, I like very much:

MY HOUSE ON CHUNG-NAN MOUNTAIN (终南别业)

> Since my middle age, I have taken to the cult of Tao,
> But only lately have I been able to make my home by the hillside.
> Whenever the spirit moves in me, I saunter forth all alone,
> To feast my eyes and nurse my soul with the thrilling beauties of nature.
> I walk along a water-course and follow it to its source;
> I sit down and watch the clouds as they are just beginning to rise.

Sometimes when I chance upon an old fellow in the woods,

We would chat and smile and forget to return home.

So he was not only a Buddhist, but also a Taoist. Probably, he was not even aware of the difference between the two. Nor, indeed, am I. I suspect that all genuine Chinese are fundamentally Taoistic in mental outlook,

读书固然要紧，欣赏自然之美却更要紧。裴迪接受了他的邀请，和他同居了多时，也写了一段颇具神韵的颂竹诗：

来过竹里馆，日与道相亲。

出入惟山鸟，幽深无世人。

诚然，只有优越性灵的人才能真正地欣赏自然。王维的这封信使我想起故友霍姆斯十二年前写给我的一封可爱的信：

两小时来，我的汽车在这段悦人心胸的地带上驰奔着，很可惜你没有看见。我们能看见在孤独的悬崖下的大海，我们在坦平的大道上经过拥挤的海滩，有时在高地和清风披拂的农田旁边驶过，有时停车瞻仰二世纪以前的建筑，随着唤起古意逸兴。这在中国或许不足为古，可是已经足以引起今昔之感了。我曾对你说，社会的基础是树立在人的死亡上的，过往的历史就是如此。所以纪念战争的碑碣在我看来竟无端地添上二百年的流风余韵。【我可以一直写下去，但是我必须停笔了。】

全增嘏先生有一次对我说，霍姆斯的笔姿是多么地活泼自然，我想这是因为他热爱自然的缘故。霍姆斯的笔姿和王维的笔酷似，因为爱好自然的性情使他们契合。

《终南别业》是王维五十多岁时写的，我极其欢喜：

中岁颇好道，晚家南山陲。

兴来每独往，胜事空自知。

行到水穷处，坐看云起时。

偶然值林叟，谈笑无还期。

可见他不但相信佛教，并且还深受道家思想的熏陶的。【也许他并未意识到二者的区别，我亦如此。】我想，真正中国人的心境是近

whatever the religion they may adopt. If a Chinese is a Buddhist, he is Taoistically Buddhist and if he is a Christian, he is Taoistically Christian. Taoism is no religion, but it is the way religions are received. In fact, as I have pointed out elsewhere, the greatest statesmen in the history of China have been men who acted like a Confucian, but felt like a Taoist. Incidentally, I am glad to mention that my friend Dr. Sun Fo seems to be no exception to the general rule. For, positive as he is, he used to read Taoistic books with great gusto! Recently, re-reading Holmes' letters to me, I was thrilled to find that he too was at once a Confucian and a Taoist! Who else could have written like this: "We must be serious in order to get work done, but when the usual Saturday half holiday comes I see no reason why we should not smile at the trick by which Nature keeps us at our job. It makes me enormously happy when I am encouraged to believe that I have done something of what I should have liked to do, but in the subterranean misgivings I think, I believe that I think sincerely, that it does not matter much." Now I discover why I loved Holmes so much!

But to return to Wang Wei, what is the essence of the cult of Tao that he spoke of? Listen to the words of Lao Tzǔ:

> But wherein I most am different from men
> Is that I prize no sustenance that comes not from the Mother's breast.
>
> (Waley's version)

It is natural for man to love Nature:

> AN ENCOUNTER (杂诗)
> Sir, from my dear old home you come,
>   And all its glories you can name;
> Oh tell me, has the winter-plum
>   Yet blossomed o'er the window-frame?
>
> (Giles' version)

But is it less natural to love our friends? No, not for Wang Wei:

OH TAKE ONE MORE CUP! (渭城曲)

A morning shower has cleansed the dust from the city of Wei.

The inn looks newly painted, and the willows are freshly green.

Oh, take another cup of wine before you go away!

Beyond this Pass of Yang no more old friends are to be seen!

I cannot take leave of Wang Wei without referring to a beautiful

于道家的，不论他皈依什么宗教。倘若他信仰佛教，他是一个道家化的佛教徒；倘若他信仰基督教，他是个道家化的基督徒。道家思想不是宗教，乃是接受宗教的态度。我在别处说过，中国历史上的大政治家的行动是儒家化的，而感情是道家化的。【顺便一提，友人孙哲生博士也不例外，他行事积极，读道家的书却也津津有味。最近重读霍姆斯的来信，我意外发现他也是儒道兼综！除了他，谁还会这样写："我们必须认真去完成工作，但是每周六的半个休假日来临时，我不禁对大自然莞尔一笑，这是为让我们工作所设的诡计。想到自己做了本应该喜欢做的事情，就很快乐；但是下意识里又真心觉得，做不做都无关紧要。"现在我知道为什么我喜欢霍姆斯了！】

再回到王维。他说"中岁颇好道"，到底什么叫作道呢？且听老子这几句话吧：

> 我独异于人，而贵食母。　　　　　　　　　　（英译：韦利）

这里所说的"母"，也就是王维的大自然。爱大自然是人类的天性（《杂诗》）：

> 君自故乡来，应知故乡事。
> 来日绮窗前，寒梅着花未？　　　　　　　　　（英译：翟理思）

爱朋友也是人类的天性（《渭城曲》）：

> 渭城朝雨浥轻尘，客舍青青柳色新。
> 劝君更尽一杯酒，西出阳关无故人。

未离王维之前，还须援引他的悦人的《山居秋暝》。看上来

poem called "Among Hills on an Autumnal Evening" (山居秋暝), which looks like some casual notes for a picture to be painted, but which contains two concluding lines whose meaning has grown upon me:

> Windswept hills—after a fresh shower.
> The weather—Autumn in eventide.
> Bright moon shining through the pine trees.
> A clear stream flowing on pebbles.
> Bamboos noisy—washing maids returning.
> A stir among water-lilies—fishing boats starting.
> *The Genius of Spring will stay with you for aye,*
> *If you don't mind too much its going away!*

To a springy poet, every season is Spring!

它像一幅画图的几段景色，其实结尾的二行包含着无限的意义：

> 空山新雨后，
> 天气晚来秋。
> 明月松间照，
> 清泉石上流。
> 竹喧归浣女，
> 莲动下渔舟。
> 随意春芳歇，
> 王孙自可留。

在一个春季诗人看来，四时都是春天！

III.   THE PRINCE OF SPRING: HIS LIFE

Spring is not always as dulcet and calm as the poetry of Wang Wei. Speaking of Spring in New England, Mark Twain once said that he had counted one hundred and sixty-six different kinds of weather inside of twenty-four hours. I humbly submit that this is an exaggeration; but even according to a Chinese proverb there are no less than eighteen changes in the course of a Spring day. In this sense, no one embodies the spirit of Spring more thoroughly than Li Po (李白: 701–762). A supreme romantic genius, a poet of the greatest variety of moods, he is a veritable "mingled yarn of joy and grief." But in order to appreciate his poetry to the fullest extent, we must know something of his life.

Like the wind that bloweth where it listeth, we don't know exactly when and where Li Po was born. The question of the time of his birth is easier to settle. For we know he died in 762, and we also know from a reliable source (李华 太白墓志) that he died in his sixty-second year (Chinese counting), so that we can infer that he must have been born in 701. As to his birthplace, it has been a veritable bone of contention for more than a millennium. Shantung, Kansu, Szechuen, and even Nanking have each claimed him for its own. Recently, it has been asserted with a great deal of plausibility that he first saw the light in the western part of Chinese Turkestan[1], that is, west of what is now known as Kansu. After carefully looking into the evidence, I feel pretty sure that this was the case. The fact seems to be this: by the end of the Sui Dynasty, that is, in the 610's, Li Po's ancestors, apparently for some crime, escaped *incognito* from their original home in Kansu westwards into the western part of Chinese Turkestan. It was not until 705 that Li K'eh (李客), Li Po's father, moved his family secretly into Szechuen and settled in Chengtu. But at that time Li Po was already four years old.

Whatever the place of his birth, there is no question that he spent his childhood in Szechuen, famous for its gigantic mountains and wonderful natural sceneries. We even know where he used to study his books, as may be gathered from a poem Tu Fu wrote in 761 when he was in Chengtu:

I have not seen Li Po for a long time—
What a pitiable man with his feigned madness!
All the world wants to kill him:
I alone dote on his genius.

叁 春之骄子：李白

　　春天并不是永远像王维的诗那么温柔恬静。从前，美国幽默大家马克·吐温说，春天在美国每二十四小时内统计有一百六十六种不同的气候。这当然是过分的夸张，可是中国古谚也有"春天十八变"的话。总之，春天的变化无常，是不可否认的。这样讲来，以李白（701—762）代表春天，那是可谓天造地设的了。他是一个至高的浪漫天才，一个心境不定的诗人。"春心荡兮如波，春愁乱兮如雪。兼万情之悲欢，兹一感于芳节"，这是太白描写春天的话，其实也就是一副惟妙惟肖的自绘。[2]【要充分欣赏他的诗，须先了解他的生平。

　　风任意地吹，我们能听见它的声音，却不知它来自何方。李白就像风一样，我们无法切知道他何时何地出生。出生时间相对容易解决，他逝于西历 762 年。据《太白墓志》记载，他逝于 62 岁（虚岁），由此推断他生于 701 年。至于出生地，一千多年来一直争论不休。山东、甘肃、四川、南京都声称李白是当地人。最近，有证据表明李白出生于西域，即现在的甘肃西部。经过仔细研究，我确信这个论断。事实似乎是这样的：隋朝末年，即西历 7 世纪初，李白的先祖畏罪隐姓埋名，从甘肃老家一路向西，逃至西域。直到 705 年，李白的父亲李客举家潜归于四川，定居成都。彼时李白已四岁光景。

　　不论出生在哪里，可以确定他的童年是在四川度过的，那里崇山峻岭，景色逶迤。我们甚至知道他在哪里读书，杜甫于 761 年在成都写了一首诗：

　　　　不见李生久，佯狂真可哀！
　　　　世人皆欲杀，吾意独怜才。

Quick-witted, he has hit off a thousand poems;

A waif in the world, his only home is in a cup of wine.

O my friend! 'Tis time to return to K'uang Shan,

Where you used to read books with such gusto.

(Teresa Li's version)

Where is K'uang Shan? It is a mountain lying near the city of Chengtu.

But what did he read? Confucian Classics, such as *The Book of Songs* and *The Book of History*, were, of course, among the things he took to heart. But, somehow, he liked even more to look into astrological and metaphysical books such as *Liu Chia* (六甲) and *Tai-hsüan Ching* (太玄经). His interests were moreover not confined to mere book learning. A boy of infinite curiosity, he even learned the art of taming wild birds. Like Dr. Faustus, he tried his hand at one thing after another in rapid succession. "When I was fifteen," he said in an autobiographical letter, "I was fond of sword-play, and with that art I challenged quite a few great men." By the time he was twenty, he had killed with his own hands several persons, apparently for chivalrous causes. He had led a wild life, it is true; but he was by nature generous, and open-handed with his money. He had something of the knight-errant in him.

He did not leave Szechuen until he was in his middle twenties, when he sailed down the Yangtze, passing through the Tung T'ing Lake, going as far as Nanking and Yangchow, and finally returning upstream to Yunmeng (云梦) in Hupeh for a rest. His days of apprenticeship were done, and his days of wandering had begun. Although in Yunmeng he was married to a granddaughter of a retired Prime Minister by the name of Hsü Yü-shih (许圉师), yet even marriage could not domesticate this wild bird; for in 735 we find him in Shansi, where one of the most important events of his life happened. He met Kuo Tzǔ-i (郭子仪) there, still serving in the ranks as a humble soldier, and saved him from a court-martial by speaking to the commander. Little did he know that Kuo was later to become the savior of the Empire and of his own life. But for this chivalrous act of his, the course of the history of T'ang would have been different. Might it not be that Li Po intuitively saw even then some of the potentialities of this great soldier?

A little later, we find him, in Shantung, entering into a warm friendship with five other men of letters. The six gentlemen, lovers of wine all, called themselves "Six Idlers of the Bamboo Brook" (竹溪六逸).

But his wanderlust was insatiable. He went down to the South, roaming on the hills and floating on the rivers and lakes of Chekiang and Kiangsu.

> 敏捷诗千首，飘零酒一杯。
>
> 匡山读书处，头白好归来。 （英译：李德兰）

匡山在哪儿？在成都附近。

他都读些什么书呢？儒家经典，比如《诗》《书》自然在其所爱之列。但是他似乎更偏爱天文和玄学书，诸如《六甲》《太玄经》。李白兴趣广泛，除了书本，还学习驯养野禽。像浮士德一样，他如饥似渴地进行各种尝试。在一封自荐信里李白写道，"十五好剑术，遍干诸侯"。到二十岁时，他路见不平，已亲手杀了几个人。诚然，李白一生放荡不羁，但是他天性慷慨，出手大方，有侠客精神。

二十五六岁的时候，李白离开四川，乘船沿长江而下，经洞庭湖到达南京和扬州，最后又折回云梦小憩。学徒生涯结束，他开始游历四方。在云梦他与前宰相许圉师的孙女结婚，但是婚姻也无法驯服这只野鸟。735 年，他来到山西，遇到当时还是一名小卒的郭子仪正要被军法处置，李白请求为其开脱刑罚。这可是他人生的一个重大事件。彼时他哪里知道，此人将成为唐朝和他自己的救星。若不是他的侠义之举，唐朝的历史将是另一番景象了。或许，李白早在当时就已觉察到此人将来大有作为？

不久，李白又去到山东，结交了五位文人朋友。这六位君子，无一例外都爱酒，自称"竹溪六逸"。

他游兴大发，又一路南下，游历江浙的山川河湖。在绍兴，

While in Shaohsing he became friends with the famous Taoist priest Wu Yun (吴筠). In 742, it happened Wu Yun was summoned by Ming Huang to his Court, and he spoke of Li Po very highly, so that His Majesty was moved to invite the latter also to come up to the Capital. There Li Po met another Taoist, Ho Chih-chang, who was then serving in the Court as a Guest of the Crown Prince (太子宾客). On the very first meeting, Ho exclaimed, "Why, you do not belong to this world. You are an angel banished from Heaven!" For this recognition Li Po remained grateful to Chih-chang throughout his life. If, as Emerson said, "next to the originator of a good sentence is the first quoter of it," we can also say that next to a man of genius is the first man who recognizes him to the fullest extent. "An angel banished from Heaven!" That was exactly what Li Po thought himself to be! Had his mother not dreamed, on the eve of his birth, of a star falling from the skies? At any rate, the two poets took to each other at first sight. Chih-chang took down a gold tortoise that he was wearing around the waist, as a badge of official honor, and had it exchanged for wine, and the two new friends had a jolly time of it. Some days later, Li Po was given an audience in the Palace of Golden Bells, and expounded his views on current politics fluently and, we may believe, sensibly too; for Ming Huang was so delighted with him that he treated him to a grand banquet, "seasoning the soup for him personally," as history says. It is also recorded in history that Li Po had knowledge of some "barbarian language"—I am sure it was not English, as it was almost three centuries before *Beowulf* saw the light—and drafted for Ming Huang some diplomatic documents in that language. History stops with this meagre information, but it is the foundation upon which an interesting story is built, which has been translated by E. R. Howell as "The Diplomacy of Li T'ai-po."

Everything seemed to bid fair to start Li Po on a great political career. But he liked wine more than anything else in the world. For very soon we find him a prominent member of a group called "The Eight Immortals of the Wine-cup," including among others his bosom friend Chih-chang. If

Chih-chang was topsy-turvy, Li Po was inside outwards. Of him Tu Fu says:

> Li Po produces a hundred poems before he has finished a peck of wine;
> He sleeps in a wine shop at Ch'ang-an market-place.
> When the Son of Heaven summons him, he does not board the boat;
> "Does His Majesty know," he says, "that his humble servant is a drunken angel?"

In reality he was not so bad as Tu Fu caricatured him, but he was bad enough. Once (in 744) Ming Huang wanted him to draft some imperial edicts, and sent someone to fetch him. He did come, but he was soddenly

他结交了著名的道士吴筠。742 年，明皇召见吴筠，在吴筠的力荐下，明皇召李白进京。随后，李白遇到了时任太子宾客的道士朋友贺知章。他们初次见面，知章便叹道："子谪仙人也！"由此，李白对知章的知遇之恩一直念念不忘。爱默生说："堪比佳句的创造者的，是第一个引用这个句子的人。"我们也可以说，堪比天才的，是第一个慧眼识天才的人。"谪仙人"！这正是李白心里所想啊！他的母亲在他出生前夜，不就曾梦见太白金星入怀吗？不管怎样，两位诗人一见如故。知章更是"金龟换酒"，与李白开怀畅饮。数日后，李白被召上殿，高谈阔论，对答如流，在情在理。明皇大为赞赏，并"御手调羹"。史书记载李白通"蛮语"——我确信不是英语，《贝奥武甫》三个世纪之后才得问世——并用蛮语为明皇草拟外交文书。依据史书提供的仅有信息，后人撰写了《李谪仙醉草吓蛮书》，E. R. 豪厄尔将其译成了英文。

　　一切似乎都预示着李白的辉煌仕途。然而他爱酒胜过一切，很快就位列"酒中八仙"，"八仙"中也有他的挚友贺知章。一个山公倒载，一个烂醉如泥。杜甫有诗云：

> 李白一斗诗百篇，长安市上酒家眠。
> 天子呼来不上船，自称臣是酒中仙。

杜甫的诗或有夸张，但李白也足够不羁了。744 年，唐明皇召李白进宫起草诏书。李白倒是去了，却酩酊大醉，凉水洒在脸上他才清

drunk, so that cold water had to be sprinkled on his face before he became aware of what he was about. As soon as he held the brush, he wrote without interruption and finished the writing at one stretch. On another occasion, he was requested to write some songs in praise of the beauty, Yang Kuei-fei, to be set to music by the famous musician Li Kuei-nien. At the suggestion of the Emperor that he might take off his heavy boots and use light shoes, he stretched out his feet to the powerful eunuch Kao Lih-shih, who, by the way, was attending on His Majesty and not on Li Po, and bade him pull off his boots. Kao, of course, had to do it, but he never forgave him for this insult. And no one can blame Kao for being offended, because eunuchs as a rule are preys to inferiority complex. It happened that in one of the three songs Li Po wrote on that occasion, he compared Yang Kuei-fei to "Flying Swallow Chao," one of the most beautiful but unscrupulous queens in the Han Dynasty, who suffered a tragic end. He might have done it with or without malice. At any rate, Kao, who was still writhing under a fresh insult, readily saw the innuendo, and called Kuei-fei's attention to it. Kuei-fei who at first was overjoyed at the praise, as a fat lady must be when she was made to believe that she was as light as "Flying Swallow," was at last convinced that it was a covered dig at her, and thenceforth did her best to prevent any further promotion of the haughty poet. A poet is a poet, a eunuch is a eunuch, and a woman is a woman; and that is all there is to it. But I only wonder whether Kuei-fei thought of that poetic prophecy when twelve years later she met her tragic death.

Anyway, Li Po, with all his political ambitions, was not a man meant for the Court. Ming Huang, who wavered for a time between the love of genius and the love of beauty, finally yielded to the claims of the latter, and decided to get rid of the unruly horse by politely sending him away with generous gifts of gold and silver. The wild horse went away, and formally became a Taoist (授道箓). He made his home in Shantung, but he traveled far and wide in the next ten years, covering almost all the provinces, and I suspect that most of his Nature-poems were written during this period. But in 755, An Lu-shan rebelled; Ming Huang had to escape into Szechuen; in the next year, the Crown Prince assumed the reins of government without the consent of Ming Huang; and Prince Lin of Yung (永王璘), Ming Huang's sixteenth son, contemplating a declaration of independence from the new monarch, invited Li Po to join him as an advisor. Unfortunately for Li Po, the troops of Prince Lin were routed in 757, and our poet had to escape to P'engtse (彭泽) in Kiangsi, but was caught and put in prison. He was sentenced to death, but Kuo Tzǔ-i, whom he had saved twenty years before, and who was by this time

醒过来。待他提笔,一挥而就。又有一次,明皇命他为杨贵妃写诗,由乐师李龟年谱曲。明皇让李白脱掉靴子穿上便鞋,于是他便把脚伸到高力士面前让他给脱靴子。要知道,高力士是伺候皇帝的,可不是伺候李白的!他当然不得不照做,却对此耿耿于怀。高力士的心情常人都能理解,宦官通常都有自卑情结。李白为杨贵妃写了三首诗,其中一首将她比作赵飞燕。赵飞燕是一位美貌而失德的汉代皇后,结局甚惨。李白这样写或有意,或无意。受辱不久的高力士却发现了其中的影射,并向贵妃进言。贵妃体态丰腴,李白夸她"身轻如燕",刚开始她还很高兴,后来也深信这是对她的暗讽,自此以后竭力阻止这位傲慢诗人晋升。诗人就是诗人,宦官就是宦官,女人就是女人,事情就是这样。我只想知道,十二年后贵妃被赐死的那一刻,她是否回想起当初的这一诗意预言。

无论如何,尽管李白胸怀大志,却注定不属于朝廷。明皇在天才和美人之间摇摆不定,最终还是听顺于后者,决定"赐金放还",赶走这批烈马。野马走了,受箓入道。他在山东安家,接下来的十年周游四方,遍访天下,由此我怀疑他的自然诗都是在这个阶段写的。755 年,安禄山叛变,明皇幸蜀。第二年,皇太子李亨私自登基;明皇的第十六子永王璘打算割据一方,邀请李白加入自己的阵营,"辟为僚佐"。不幸的是,两年后,永王的军队被打败,李白被迫逃往江西彭泽,终被捕入狱判死刑。幸运的是,二十年前李白救下的郭子仪,此时已是统领大军的兵部

the Minister of War and the Commander-in-Chief of all the imperial troops, remonstrated strongly with the new Emperor and offered to ransom the life of Li Po by giving up his own official rank which he had so well earned. Incidentally, I may mention that Kuo Tzǔ-i, the greatest soldier-statesman of T'ang, was a Nestorian, and in this he certainly showed the spirit of Christ. As a result of his intercession, the death sentence was remitted, and instead our poet was banished to Yehlang (夜郎). Before he reached Yehlang, however, he was pardoned and returned to Kiangsi. In his last years, his travels were confined mainly to Nanking and two cities in Anhui: Hsüanch'eng (宣城) and Liyang (历阳).

According to a story, which Herbert Giles took for history, Li Po "was drowned on a journey, from leaning one night too far over the edge of a boat in a drunken effort to embrace the reflection of the moon." The story is beautiful, but not true. For in 762, his friend Li Yang-ping (李阳冰) became magistrate of Tangtu (当涂) in Szechuen, and he went to join him there. He was appointed by Tai Tsung (代宗), who had just ascended the Throne, to be a Censor (拾遗), the first time he was ever appointed to a governmental office. But when the order of appointment reached Szechuen, Li Po had already died.

Many critics have said that Li Po led an easy life and that his poetry is mostly hedonist stuff. As if it were not enough of a tragedy to be a man of genius! In the first place, to be a man of genius is to be hyper-sensitive. I think Li Po would agree with Chesterton that "Death is more tragic even than death by starvation," and that "Having a nose is more comic than having a Mormon nose." In the second place, to be a man of genius is to be a possessed man. Li Po was possessed by the Muse, but he also possessed a strong desire for action, which was bound to be frustrated in spite of his ambitions along practical lines. In this connection, some remarks by Walter Raleigh on Shakespeare seem to be so relevant to the case of Li Po that I am tempted to quote them at some length:

But the central drama of his mind is the tragedy of the life of imagination. He was a lover of clear decisive action, and of the deed done. He knew and condemned the sentiment which fondly nurses itself and is without issue. Yet, on the other hand, the gift of imagination with which he was so richly dowered, the wide, restless, curious searchings of the intelligence and the sympathies—these faculties, strong in him by nature, and strengthened every day by the exercise of his profession, bade fair at times to take sole possession, and to paralyze the will. Then he revolted

尚书，他在新皇面前力保，不惜以自己辛苦换来的权位换取李白的性命。顺便一提，郭子仪这位唐代伟大的军事政治家也是位景教信徒，这件事充分体现了他的博爱精神。在他的求情之下，李白免于死刑，改判流放夜郎。去往夜郎的途中，肃宗又下令大赦，于是李白回到了江西。晚年，他的活动范围主要在南京、安徽的宣城和历阳。

相传李白"游采石江中……因醉入水中，捉月而死"，翟理思信以为真。传说固然凄美，却不真实。762 年，李白的友人李阳冰升任为当涂县令，于是李白前往四川投奔。新继位的代宗任命李白为左拾遗，这是李白第一次被委以官职。然而，任命书抵达四川时，李白已经与世长辞了。

许多评论家认为李白生活安逸，他的诗歌主旨大多是及时行乐。似乎生为天才还不足够可悲！首先，生为天才意味着高度敏感。切斯特顿说，"死亡，甚至比饿死更悲惨"，"拥有鼻子比拥有一个摩门教徒的鼻子更可笑"。我想，李白对此会深表赞同。其二，生为天才意味着是一个被附体的人。李白被缪斯附体，同时又是鲜明的行动派，但是不论行动多么切实，注定要失败。在这一点上，沃尔特·雷利关于莎士比亚的评论似乎可以用在李白身上，详录如下：

　　但是他心目中的中心戏剧是想象的悲剧。他热爱明确果断的行动，热爱这一行动的结果。对呵护自我爱怜、却不付诸行动的情感，他非常了解并加以诅咒。另一方面，他丰富的想象力，对心智与同理心广泛却从不停息、满怀好奇的探索——这些与生具有的才能，经由他的职业而日益强化，常常将他占有，使他无法行动。于是他开始与自己对抗，几乎

against himself, and was almost inclined to bless that dark, misfeatured messenger called the angel of this life, "whose care is lest men see too much at once." If for the outlook of a God the seer must neglect the opportunities and duties of a man, may not the price paid be too high? It is a dilemma known to all poets,—to all men, indeed, who live the exhausting life of the imagination, and grapple hour by hour, in solitude and silence, with the creatures of their mind, while the passing invitations of humanity, which never recur, are ignored or repelled. Keats knew the position well, and has commented on it, though not tragically, in some passages of his letters. "Men of Genius," he says, "are great as certain ethereal Chemicals operating on the Mass of neutral intellect—but they have not any individuality, any determined Character." And again: "A poet is the most unpoetical of anything in existence, because he has no Identity—he is continually in for and filling some other body." Keats also recognized, as well as Shakespeare, that man cannot escape the call to action, and it was he who said—"I am convinced more and more, every day, that fine writing is, next to fine doing, the top thing in the world." But what if this highest call come suddenly, as it always does, and find the man unnerved and unready, given over to "sensations and day-nightmares," absorbed in speculation, out of himself, and unable to respond? A famous English painter was once, at his own request, bound to the mast during a storm at sea, in order that he might study the pictorial effects of sky and water. His help was not wanted in the working of the ship; he was not one of the crew. Who among men, in the conduct of his own life, dare claim a like exemption?

要赞美那个被称为人间天使的黑暗、变态的信使，"惟恐人类一下子知道太多"。如果为了拥有神的预见力，先知必须忽略作为人的机会和义务，这个代价是否太高了？所有诗人都知道这是进退两难的事——事实上，对所有活在令人疲惫的想象中、在孤独和寂寞中时刻与头脑的产物搏斗的人而言都是如此。人性的邀请被漠视或厌恶，稍纵即逝，不会再现。济慈深知这一处境，在信件中有所论述，但他并不觉得多么可悲。他说，"天才，就像作用于中性智力群体的虚无缥缈的化学物质一样伟大，但是他们毫无个性，缺乏坚毅的性格"，"而诗人又是所有存在中最没有想象力的，因为他没有身份——他总在不断地存在于并且填充着其他身体"。和莎士比亚一样，济慈也意识到人类无法逃避行动，正是他说，"每一天我都越来越确信，除了好的行动，好的写作是世界上最重要的事情"。但是，如果这一最高使命突然来临——事实上它常常如此——此时这个人正灰心沮丧、毫无准备，沉溺于"情感和白日梦"，专注于思考，完全忘我而无法回应，那该怎么办？在一次海上暴风雨中，一位著名的英国画家让人将他绑在桅杆上，这样他就可以观察天空和水面的画面效果。他不是船员，所以不需要在船上工作。而在我们的人生中，有谁敢说自己也可以像这位画家一样被免除义务呢？】

IV.   THE PRINCE OF SPRING: HIS POETRY

If Wang Wei is melodious, Li Po is symphonic. It seems as though the Spring of T'ang poetry would not come to a close without having an appropriate finishing canter, without having someone to recapitulate all its phases. For Li Po is as full of gladness and free of heaven as Wang Fan-chih; almost as boastful and self-confident as Tu Shen-yen, only more justifiably so; as strong in creative impulse and cosmic emotion as Ch'en Tzǔ-ang and Chang Jo-hsu, only with better results; as keen and subtle in his understanding of the psychology of women as Wang Ch'ang-ling or any other "chamber poets": and finally he has produced word-pictures comparable in beauty, though of a different kind, to those of Wang Wei and Meng Hao-jan. Let us follow him in all these phases roughly in the order mentioned.

Don't the following lines recall to your mind the voice of Fan-chih:

> We drank continuously and finished a hundred jugs,
>
> Till our minds were rinsed clean of ageless sorrows.
>
> An ideal night it was to engage in transcendental talks,
>
> For the clear moonlight would not let us go to bed.
>
> Feeling drowsy at last, we slept in the open hills,
>
> With the sky for blanket and the earth for pillow.

Li Po's haughtiness is well-known. He was conscious of it himself, and he suffered a great deal for it. As he said:

> Men of the world all sneer at my high talks,
>
> Which are not attuned to their ears.

How unpopular he became in his lifetime is testified to by Tu Fu:

> All the world wants to kill him:
>
> I alone dote on his genius.

"To be great is to be misunderstood," as Emerson puts it, and Li Po forms no exception to the rule. Probably, the chief reason why he was misunderstood lies in the fact that in his mind this world, which we ordinary folks take so seriously, is nothing but an empty dream. As he says:

I am haughty to the world, and slight its transient glories.
Not that I harbor no practical plans in my bosom;

肆 春之骄子：其诗

王维是像一支悦耳的音调，李白是像一曲交响乐。唐诗之春在未消逝之前还有一段雄壮的结尾，总括先前不同的景色。李白像王梵志那么快乐活跃；像杜审言那么夜郎自大（当然较审言更有资格自大）；像陈子昂、张若虚那么富于创造力和宇宙的感怀，只是较陈张的货色更道地；像王昌龄和其他善咏春情的诗人那么了解女人心理；最后，他描写大自然之动人，虽然和王维、孟浩然的不同，却也不弱于他们。我们现在就概括地依次序谈这几点。

下面几行可不使你想起王梵志的声音？

涤荡千古愁，流连百壶饮。
良宵宜清淡，皓月未能寝。
醉来卧空山，天地即衾枕。

李白不可一世的气概是尽人皆知的，为了它他吃了很多苦，他也很有自知之明：

世人见我恒殊调，闻余大言皆冷笑。

一州笑我为狂客，少年往往来相讥。

（《醉后答丁十八以诗讥余槌碎黄鹤楼》）[1]

杜甫也曾说起世人对他的态度：

世人皆欲杀，吾意独怜才。

爱默生说过，"伟大的人是一定要被人误会的"，李白也不能例外。他被误会的原因大概是因为，他把人世间当作梦幻泡影或过眼云烟，所以不免有些玩世不恭。他说（《赠友人》）：

慢世薄功业，非无胸中画。

But that I make a jest of all the heroes in history,

And regard all their deeds as children's plays.

Even the Universe itself will not stay forever:

The sun and the moon will eventually pass away;

Heaven and Earth will some day rot and decay.

The insects that nest in a green pine and sing

Think this tree must be an immutable thing.

An insect himself, he looks at the world with the eyes of an angel. When he was in Huchow, a magistrate asked who he was, and he blurted out these lines:

I call myself the Green Lotus Man;

I am a spirit exiled from the upper blue;

For thirty years I've hid my fame in wine shops.

Warrior of Lake Province, why must you ask about me?

Behold me, a reincarnation of the Buddha of Golden Grains!

(Obata's version)

That he doesn't regard himself as belonging to this world is revealed by another poem:

You ask what my soul does away in the sky,

I inwardly smile but cannot reply;

Like the peach-blossom carried away by the stream,

I soar to a world of which you cannot dream.

(Giles' version)

I should imagine that Li Po sometimes felt as Shakespeare did:

...man, proud man,

Drest in a little brief authority,

Most ignorant of what he is most assur'd,

His glassy essence, like an angry ape,

Plays such fantastic tricks before high heaven

As make the angels weep.

In fact, one of the reasons I like Li Po so much is the iconoclastic tendency that I find in him; for one has to tear down all the idols before one can worship the living God!

But the pathetic thing about Li Po is that, since he doesn't belong to this world, he must find some other world to belong to. His plight is,

谑浪万古贤，以为儿童剧。

这宇宙也不是永不腐朽：

日月终销毁，天地同枯槁。
蟪蛄啼青松，安见此树老。

他自己只是一只小虫，可是他用了一副天神的眼睛来看这世界。他在湖州的时候，有一位司马询问他的来历，他就不耐烦地回答：

青莲居士谪仙人，酒肆藏名三十春。
湖州司马何须问，金粟如来是后身。 （英译：小畑薰良）

下面这首诗也证明，他不承认自己是属于这世界的：

问余何意栖碧山，笑而不答心自闲。
桃花流水窅然去，别有天地非人间。 （英译：翟理思）

我想他有时也不免像莎士比亚那样地想：

……人，骄傲的人，
带了半瓶醋的学问，脆弱的气质，
不知以为知，
像一只癫狂的猴子，
在天堂前翻弄把戏，
弄得天神辈啼笑皆非。

我喜爱李白的理由之一是，因为他有打倒偶像的精神。在没有打倒偶像之前，我们怎能崇拜真神？

李白生命的悲剧也就在这里：他既然不属这个世界，他一定要找寻出他自己的世界。他是像"一只住在陆上的海兽，要想一飞冲

indeed, like that of "a sea animal living on land, wanting to fly in the air." Like Ch'en Tzǔ-ang, he wanted to enter the Gate of Immortality on the Chariot of Mutation! This explains his insatiable wanderlust and cosmic yearnings. This explains also his incessant effort to seek for the happiness of insensibility by getting soddenly drunk.

Some poems of Li Po remind me of the drawing by William Blake called *I Want! I Want!* in which, as the reader will recall, a man is just beginning to climb a long ladder spanning between the earth and the moon. Take for instance these lines:

Let me lay down my cup for a moment and ask:
O Sky! Since how long did you have the moon?
I want to climb up to the bright moon, but I can't;
And yet the moon never ceases to follow me as I walk!

...

The ancients didn't see the moon of tonight,
But the moon did shine upon the ancients.
The past and the present form a flowing stream,
Upon whose endless ripples the moon reflects its light eternally.

In this connection, I beg to reproduce a piece as translated by L. Cranmer-Byng:

DRIFTING (宣州谢朓楼饯别校书叔云)

We cannot keep the gold of yesterday;
Today's dun clouds we cannot roll away.
Now the long, wailing flight of geese brings autumn in its train,
So to the view-tower cup in hand to fill and drink again.

And dream of the great singers of the past,
Their fadeless lines of fire and beauty cast.
I too have felt the wild-bird thrill of song behind the bars,
But these have brushed the world aside and walked amid the stars.

In vain we cleave the torrent's thread with steel,
In vain we drink to drown the grief we feel,

When man's desire with fate doth war this, this avails alone
To hoist the sail and let the gale and the waters bear us on.

On rare occasions, he got a temporary illusion of having flown beyond
this stifling Universe, as in this:

天"！像陈子昂一样，他也想"乘化入无穷"！因此他对宇宙有无限的感怀。他一生好游名山大川也是他要逃出人间的一个表现。他的爱酒，也是因为酒能暂时消他"宇宙渴"的缘故。[2] 他不说么，"三杯通大道，一斗合自然"。可是凭酒的力量，要想"乘化入无穷"，这何异饮鸩止渴，怪不得要"举杯消愁愁更愁"了。李白的悲哀即在这里，他的可爱也在这里。

李白有几首诗使我想起布莱克名为《我要，我要！》的一幅名画，画中一个人正在开始爬上一座跨于地球和月亮间的梯子。试读下面几行：

青天有月来几时？我今停杯一问之。
人攀明月不可得，月行却与人相随。
……
今人不见古时月，今月曾经照古人。
古人今人若流水，共看明月皆如此。

说到这里，我要援引他的《宣州谢朓楼饯别校书叔云》（英译：克莱默·宾）：

弃我去者，昨日之日不可留；
乱我心者，今日之日多烦忧。
长风万里送秋雁，对此可以酣高楼。
蓬莱文章建安骨，中间小谢又清发。
俱怀逸兴壮思飞，欲上青天揽明月。
抽刀断水水更流，举杯消愁愁更愁。
人生在世不称意，明朝散发弄扁舟。

有时，他幻想自己飞出这宇宙的牢笼：

> In early morn I climb up the mountain-top,
> I lift my hands to open the gate of clouds.
> My spirit soars, expanding itself into the air,
> Until it's gone beyond the sky and earth.

But most of the time he was aware that this endeavor to enter the Gate of Immutability on the Chariot of Mutation was doomed to failure, and so he took to wine in order to dull the edge of sensibility.

> No long rope can tie the running sun—
> All ages share this great sorrow in common.
> Had I the yellow metal piled up to the stars,
> I should use it to buy youth and fun.

> A little spark of fire from the stone—
> That is life in this world.
> A moment past is a dream done;
> What will become of us later is known to none.

> Tell me not that you are too poor to drink,
> Let us get wine and call our neighbors to our feast.
> I doubt if there are immortals in the world.
> But we can find sure happiness in the wine at least.

Probably, no one has drunk more cups of wine than Li Po. Assuredly, no one has written more poems on wine than he has. Here is a charming defense of drinking:

> If Heaven does not love wine,
> Then the Star of Wine would not be in Heaven.
> If Earth does not love wine,
> Then the Fountain of Wine ought not to be on Earth.
> Since Heaven and Earth both love wine,
> Then to love wine is worthy of God.
> When clear, wine is comparable to a saint:
> When turgid, a learned savant.

Since you can drink and still remain a saint or a savant,

Then what is the use of becoming a god or a fairy?

Three cups open the door to the Great Way;

A peck brings you back to the bosom of Nature.

O, what infinite charms I find in wine!

To impart them to the sober is to cast pearls before swine.

I remember Thomas Fuller has said that "wine turns a man inside outwards." But everything depends upon the quality of what is inside the man. If he is at bottom a fool, then it would be wiser for him not

平明登日观，举手开云关。

精神四飞扬，如出天地间。

可是他知道，要想"乘化入无穷"只是空中筑楼阁而已，结果必失败，所以他就沉湎于酒中以逃世：

长绳难系日，自古共悲辛。黄金高北斗，不惜买阳春。

石火无留光，还如世中人。即事已如梦，后来我谁身。

提壶莫辞贫，取酒会四邻。仙人殊恍惚，未若醉中真。

大概没有人比李白喝过更多的酒，同时也没有人像他在诗中反复地论酒。这是多么可爱的《月下独酌·其二》：

天若不爱酒，酒星不在天。

地若不爱酒，地应无酒泉。

天地既爱酒，爱酒不愧天。

已闻清比圣，复道浊如贤。

贤圣既已饮，何必求神仙。

三杯通大道，一斗合自然。

但得酒中趣，勿为醒者传。

记得托马斯·富勒曾说："酒能使一个人露出他的真面目。"【然而一切还是由人内在的品质决定。】倘若这人是一个蠢汉的话，他还是不吃酒的好，因为他的真面目是丑陋的；倘使他是

to drink. But if he happens to be a man of genius, wine helps to evoke the best out of him. In fact, one of the most famous songs of Li Po is "The Song of Wine," to whose throbbing music and yeasty madness no translation can ever do full justice:

Don't you see the waters of the Yellow River come from the skies,
And run endlessly toward the Ocean, ne'er to return?
Don't you see in the bright mirror in the high hall our white hairs make
a sorry scene?
In the morning they look like black silk: in the evening they become
snow!
In life, when you are happy, you must drink your joy to the last drop,
And don't let your gold goblets face the moon without wine!
Heaven has endowed me with genius, and will find a use for it:
As for money, a thousand pieces of gold scattered away will return some
day.
Let us roast a lamb and slay an ox and start the music!
We shall drink, each of us, three hundred cups of wine.

You Master Ts'en, and you Tan-ch'iu dear!
To you I offer wine, and refuse me not!
I'll sing a song for you. Please incline your ears and listen!
Bells and drums and choice dishes are not what I prize:
My only wish—to remain drunk and ne'er to be sober.
The sages and savants of old, who remember them now?
But the names of drunkards have resounded throughout all times.
Don't you remember the Prince of Ch'en, how he used to feast in his
Palace of Peace and Pleasure?
What jolly and riotous times they had over endless measures of
precious liquors!
Why should my host worry about his poverty?
Let us order more wine, and I'll drink to you.
Look! What nice roan horses and costly furs you have!

Ask the boy to take them away and barter them for sweet wine!

Let us drown in wine the sorrows of ten thousand ages!

And what sober man could have hit off things like this:

ON THE SHIP OF SPICE-WOOD (江上吟)

My ship is built of spice-wood and has a rudder of *mulan*;

Musicians sit at the two ends with jeweled bamboo flutes and pipes of
gold.

What a pleasure it is, with a cask of sweet wine

And singing girls beside me,

To drift on the water hither and thither with the waves!

一个得天独厚的奇才，那么多喝也无伤大雅，因为他的真面目是可爱的。李白最著名的诗中有一首是《将进酒》，它的跳跃的音韵和飞扬跋扈的气概，不是任何译文所能传达的：

君不见黄河之水天上来，奔流到海不复回。

君不见高堂明镜悲白发，朝如青丝暮成雪。

人生得意须尽欢，莫使金樽空对月。

天生我材必有用，千金散尽还复来。

烹羊宰牛且为乐，会须一饮三百杯。

岑夫子，丹丘生，将进酒，杯莫停。

与君歌一曲，请君为我倾耳听。

钟鼓馔玉不足贵，但愿长醉不复醒。

古来圣贤皆寂寞，惟有饮者留其名。

陈王昔时宴平乐，斗酒十千恣欢谑。

主人何为言少钱，径须沽取对君酌。

五花马，千金裘，呼儿将出换美酒，与尔同销万古愁。

试问，不醉的诗人能够写得出《江上吟》吗？

木兰之枻沙棠舟，玉箫金管坐两头。

美酒樽中置千斛，载妓随波任去留。

I am happier than the fairy of the air, who rode on his yellow crane,

And free as the merman who followed the sea-gulls aimlessly.

Now with the strokes of my inspired pen I shake the Five Mountains.

My poem is done, I laugh and my delight is vaster than the sea.

Oh, deathless poetry! The songs of Chu-ping are ever glorious as the
sun and moon,

While the palaces and towers of the Chu kings have vanished from the hills.

Yea, if worldly fame and riches were things to last forever,

The waters of the River Han would flow north-westward, too.

(Obata's version)

From the foregoing specimens, it might seem that Li Po is an expressionist. He is that, but at times he can be extremely impressionistic, as in this:

TEARS (怨情)

A fair girl draws the blind aside

And sadly sits with drooping head;

I see her burning tear-drops glide

But know not why those tears are shed.

(Giles' version)

This little piece has drawn a very sensible comment from Lytton Strachey: "The blind is drawn aside for a moment, and we catch a glimpse of a vision which starts us off on a mysterious voyage down the widening river of imagination." In fact, all his descriptions of women are impressionistic. Here is another lovely snapshot:

A little maiden is gathering lotus on the brook of Yah.

Spying a passer-by, she turns her boat around, still continuing her song.

She disappears giggling into the thicket of lotus.

Pretending to be bashful, she hides herself among the flowers.

He even wrote some charming lines for his wife meant to be presented to himself:

I am like a peach flower in a well,

Blowing and smiling unseen.

My lord is like the moon on the sky—

When will he turn his gaze into this hidden place?

Incidentally, we see what a negligent husband Li Po must have been. To be the wife of a poet is bad enough, but when the poet happens to be also a drunkard, I should imagine it's Hell. But our poet is not entirely without conscience. He is at least capable of laughing at himself. In a poem to his wife, he confessed his sins of omission:

> 仙人有待乘黄鹤，海客无心随白鸥。
> 屈平词赋悬日月，楚王台榭空山丘。
> 兴酣落笔摇五岳，诗成笑傲凌沧洲。
> 功名富贵若长在，汉水亦应西北流。　　（英译：小畑薰良）

从上面几段诗看来，他是一个表现主义者，不过有时他能转得很印象主义，像这四行（《怨情》）：

> 美人卷珠帘，深坐颦蛾眉。
> 但见泪痕湿，不知心恨谁。　　　　　　（英译：翟理思）

利顿·斯特雷奇曾给这首小诗一句很中肯的评语，"珠帘是卷起了，我们瞥见一个幻梦，在想象的河上神秘地航行"。他描摹女人的笔调都是属于印象主义的。这里又是一张可爱的照片：

> 耶溪采莲女，见客棹歌回。
> 笑入荷花去，佯羞不出来。

他用了他妻子口吻写了几行颇具风韵的诗，算是赠给他自己的：

> 妾似井底桃，开花向谁笑。
> 君如天上月，不肯一回照。

在这四行诗里，我们能看出李白是一个多么疏忽夫道的人。嫁给一个诗人是已够倒霉了，倘使这诗人是个酒鬼的话，那简直是人间地狱。可是李白不是完全无动于衷、不受良心责备的，至少他能笑他自己，也肯承认自己的罪愆：

Throughout all the days of the years,

I am drunk as the mud.

Ah! To be T'ai-po's wife

Is to taste single blessedness to the full!

His snapshots of Nature have some illusive quality about them. He just reproduces his immediate impressions, in which the objective and the subjective are mingled together like chemical compounds. Take this one:

A dog barks through the crooning of the waters.

The peach blossoms are deep dyed in the rain.

Among the thick woods I catch occasional glimpses of deer.

The brooklet seems to slumber in the noontide, and no bells are heard.

The wild bamboos nick and notch the azure sky.

A fall hangs from a green cliff.

Nobody knows where the Taoist has gone.

I lean against one pine after another with my heart full of longings.

Some of his word-pictures almost seem to anticipate the theory of relativity for they make you feel as though the earth were constantly falling to the apples instead of the other way round.

Above the man's face arise the hills;

Besides the horse's head emerge the clouds.

(Lin Yu-tang's version)

*　　*　　*

The wild swans beckon the sorrowing heart away.

The mountain, bird-like, picks up the lovely moon in its beak.

(Wen Yuan-ning's version)

But I like this best of all:

Fragrant mists ooze all over the mountain.

Showers of flowers fall from the sky.

For it transforms the earth into Heaven, making me think of St. Teresa's sweet *plui de fleurs*!

Some Chinese critics have regarded Li Po as an egoist, as a man of genius with little human feeling. This does not strike me as a fair judgment. No one can deny his remarkable capacity for friendship. Who could, for instance, be more generous than he was:

TO A FRIEND IN DISTRESS (君马黄)
Your horse was yellow,
And mine was white.

三百六十日，日日醉如泥。
虽为李白妇，何异太常妻。

他的自然诗颇有些幻觉在内。他只写下他当时的印象，主观的和客观的也就像化学物般地彼此混合。像这几行：

犬吠水声中，桃花带雨浓。
树深时见鹿，溪午不闻钟。
野竹分青霭，飞泉挂碧峰。
无人知所去，愁倚两三松。

有时候他写景的技巧使我想起爱因斯坦相对论，因为它使你觉得地球跌落在苹果上：

山从人面起，云傍马头生。　　　　　　　　　（英译：林语堂）

*　　*　　*

雁引愁心去，山衔好月来。　　　　　　　　　（英译：温源宁）

我最爱的是这两句：

香云遍山起，花雨从天来。

这顿时将世界转成天堂，使我想起圣女小德兰的玫瑰雨！

有些评论家说李白是一个自我主义者，富有奇才而缺乏同情。这是很欠公允的，因为他对待朋友的诚恳是无可否认的。《君马黄》显出他是多么地慷慨：

君马黄，我马白。

But our hearts were equally mellow,

Differ as the colors of our horses might!

What a grand time we had together,

Racing around the suburbs of Loyang,

Wearing a dazzling sword each like the other,

Flaunting our head-gears all along.

Guests of the great, and not meanly dressed either,

Our life was like a long care-free song.

Now like a tiger you writhe entrapped—

A fate common to the heroic and strong.

When my bosom friend in distress is enwrapped,

I feel like a lost sheep not knowing where to belong.

(Teresa Li's version)

His profound sympathy for the oppressed is revealed by some of his songs exalting the virtues of the gallant people who would take others' injuries as personal insults and avenge them of their own accord. In this connection, I may mention that the cult of chivalry is of a long standing one in China. The idea that we should only bow to the humble and soft, and never to the proud and oppressive, is bred in the bone of our people. Long before Confucius was born, songs had been sung in praise of chivalrous persons. Read this from *The Book of Songs*:

There is a saying among men:

"If soft, chew it;

If hard, spit it out."

But Chung Shan Fu

Neither chews the soft,

Nor spits out the hard;

He neither oppresses the solitary and the widow,

Nor fears the truculent and strong.

(Waley's version)

But the interesting thing is that this tradition of chivalry has been kept alive throughout the ages, not by the so-called "gentlemen," but principally by simple folks unspoiled by bookish learning. This seems to be the burden of one of Li Po's best known ballads:

THE ROVER OF CHAO (侠客行)

Oh, the Rover of Chao with his Tartar-fashioned cap,
A scimitar on his side, gleaming bright like the snow,
The silver saddle glittering on his white horse,
Behold, he comes and is gone like a shooting star;

马色虽不同，人心本无隔。
共作游冶盘，双行洛阳陌。
长剑既照曜，高冠何赩赫。
各有千金裘，俱为五侯客。
猛虎落陷阱，壮士时屈厄。
相知在急难，独好亦何益。 （英译：李德兰）

他对受压迫的弱者有深挚热烈的同情，他歌颂见义勇为的侠行。在中国，崇拜侠士是根深蒂固的一回事，我们都牢记"威武不能屈"的箴言，对谦逊的人我们却情愿欠身鞠躬。孔子以前，我们已经有颂赞侠义精神的诗歌，像《诗经》中的这段：

人亦有言：柔则茹之，刚则吐之。维仲山甫，柔亦不茹，刚亦不吐。不侮矜寡，不畏强御。（《烝民》）
（英译：韦利）

值得注意的是，世代以来保存这侠士精神的不是冠冕堂皇的君子，而是未曾受过书本玷污的乡村野人。这便是李白《侠客行》的题旨：

赵客缦胡缨，吴钩霜雪明。
银鞍照白马，飒沓如流星。

Kills a man at every ten paces as he goes,

And goes he a thousand miles without stopping.

The deed done, he shakes his raiment and departs—

None knows whither, nor even his name.

He stops at leisure and drinks with Prince Hsin-ling,

Laying his drawn sword across his knee;

Picks up a piece of roast meat for Chu-hai to eat;

Offers a goblet of wine to Hou-ying to drink;

After three rounds gives a pledge of fealty,

And weightier is his vow even than the Five Mountains.

When his ears are hot and his eyes burn,

His heroic soul blazes forth like a rainbow.

A hammer in his hand saved the kingdom of Chao,

And the whole city of Han-tan shook with terror.

How the glory of two such strong men shines

For a thousand autumns over the ramparts of Tai-Liang!

Sweet honor perfumes their heroic bones,

Putting to shame the literati of the world,

Who can only recline in the study

And whiten their heads over books like the *Tai-hsüan Ching*.

(Obata's version)

No, Li Po was no cock-eyed pacifist. But he did not approve of wars of aggression either.

In the battlefield men grapple each other and die;

The horses of the vanquished utter lamentable cries to heaven,

While ravens and kites peck at human entrails,

Carry them up in their flight, and hang them on the branches of dead
trees.

So, men are scattered and smeared over the desert grass,

And the generals have accomplished nothing.

Oh, nefarious war! I see why the sages of old

Only resorted to it when they were forced to it.

(Obata's version: The last two lines are my rendering,

which accords better with the original.)

After reading this, the reader will agree with me that it is unfair to charge Li Po with callousness to human suffering. It should, however, be admitted that his sympathy with mankind is not so warm and intimate as that of Tu Fu, and that there is always a barrier between this man of genius and the world at large. Somehow, Li Po looks at the human world as an ant-hill, whereas Tu Fu looks at an ant-hill as a human world. Li Po

十步杀一人，千里不留行。
事了拂衣去，深藏身与名。
闲过信陵饮，脱剑膝前横。
将炙啖朱亥，持觞劝侯嬴。
三杯吐然诺，五岳倒为轻。
眼花耳热后，意气素霓生。
救赵挥金槌，邯郸先震惊。
千秋二壮士，烜赫大梁城。
纵死侠骨香，不惭世上英。
谁能书阁下，白首太玄经。　　　　　　　（英译：小畑薰良）

李白反对侵略战争，可是他绝非苟安图存之流。

野战格斗死，败马号鸣向天悲。
乌鸢啄人肠，衔飞上挂枯树枝。
士卒涂草莽，将军空尔为。
乃知兵者是凶器，圣人不得已而用之。

（英译：小畑薰良；最后两行是我的翻译，更贴合原文。）

读完这首诗后，读者一定能够同意我说，李白对人类的痛苦不是漠视无关的。我们承认，他对人类的同情没有杜甫的那么热烈深切；可是我们还须知道，奇才和整个的人类总是有隔膜的。李白将这人类的世界看作一座蚁穴，杜甫却将一座蚁穴看作人类的世界。

wrote, for instance:

> How dim the battlefield, as yellow dusk!
>
> The fighting men are like a swarm of ants.
>
> (Ayscough and Lowell's version)

But Tu Fu wrote:

> I want to build a farm, but I pity the ants in the holes.
>
> I wink at the poor village boys picking up the ears of grain.

In other words, when Li Po deals with human subjects, I miss "the fierce electric high light"—to use an expression of Holmes—that I find in some of Tu Fu's poems.

It has always seemed to me Li Po is cosmically-minded, while Tu Fu is historically-minded. If I may be allowed to use some pompous terms in philosophy, I would say that the former is *transcendental*, while the latter is *immanent*. To take a homely instance, Li Po wrote the following poem "To a Firefly" when he was a mere child:

> Rain cannot quench thy lantern's light,
>
> Wind makes it shine more brightly bright;
>
> Once thou fly to heaven afar,
>
> Thou'lt twinkle near the moon—a star!
>
> (Giles' version)

So he attributed cosmic yearnings even to a firefly! Compare this with Tu Fu's lines on the same subject:

> Dancing round the well, each firefly calls forth a new partner from the deep;
>
> Flying by the flowers, they send sudden flashes into the glories hidden in the dark.

In one case, the firefly has to fly to heaven in order to acquire significance. In the other case, it can be significant even on earth. To my mind, unless we make our earth heavenly, Heaven itself will remain earthy.

Wherein, then, does the significance of Li Po reside? What entitles him to be ranked with the greatest poets, not only of China, but of the world? If, as he said, Heaven had given him genius and would find some use for it, we may be allowed to inquire what type of genius he is and what is its use.

To my mind, Li Po's significance lies in this: he is the most perfect embodiment of the spirit of romanticism. In life as well as in letters, he is a great romantic. Imaginative, passionate, contemptuous of form and convention, grandiose and picturesque in thought and language, remote

李白说，"战地何昏昏，战士如群蚁"（艾思柯、洛威尔英译）。杜甫说，"筑场怜穴蚁，拾穗许村童"。

换句话说，李白摹写人类的事情时，他缺少霍姆斯说的"猛烈的电光"，而杜甫则不然。

李白是以整个宇宙为念，而杜甫是以人类历史为念。倘使读者允许我用两个哲学术语，我说李白是超然的，而杜甫是内在的。李白少时写的《咏萤火》已足为证：

> 雨打灯难灭，风吹色更明。
> 若飞天上去，定作月边星。　　　　　　（英译：翟理思）

在他看来，萤火也是不无宇宙之感怀的！看杜甫怎样描写萤火虫：

> 却绕井栏添个个，偶经花蕊弄辉辉。

在李白看来，萤火虫倘使不能飞冲入空中就不足为奇；在杜甫看来，只能鼓翅于地面的萤火虫已足为我们重视了。在我看来，除非我们在这世界里发现天堂，不然天堂也会变成像地球那般地平淡无味。

李白的重要在哪里？凭什么他被我们认为不但是中国，并且是全球闻名的大诗人？倘若照他说的"天生我材必有用"，让我们问问老天爷给他的是什么"材"，有什么"用"。

在我看来，他的重要就在这里：他是浪漫精神最完美的表现。不论是指人还是指诗，他都是一个雄伟的浪漫天才。他有丰富的想象、激昂的情感、巍峨华瞻的思想和文字；他藐视世习俗套，不事

from experience, and visionary—there is no romantic quality that he lacks. Whether you like him or not depends a great deal upon your own temperament. Being realistically inclined, I cannot help preferring Tu Fu to Li Po both as a man and as a poet; but it would be worse than silly to deny that romanticism has its uses, especially for the present world. In his fine book on *The Decline and Fall of the Romantic Ideal*, F. L. Lucas says: "In this factory-world, whose walls we are daily building higher and higher round us, we are in danger of feeling more and more like mice in some vast generating-station; of forgetting that men remain more remarkable than anything men have made... The individual needs new armor against the world; new foundations for the Ivory Tower of his own thought, the one sure reality, among these vibrations of a million wheels." In fact, the Universe itself is apparently a big factory, with an infinite number of wheels eternally running and revolving, and producing all forms of living beings that make their appearance and struggle with one another for a brief moment and go their way. Our earth itself is but a mouse in a vast generating-station, and we are all microscopic parasites. To relieve ourselves a little from the crushing sense of inferiority, it is good to be able to feel at times as Li Po did:

> When I am inspired, I shake the Five Mountains with my pen!
> I challenge the earth and laugh it to scorn, as I rise on the wings of Poesy!
>
> *   *   *
>
> In the midst of wine the cup of my joy is running over;
>> I hardly know it's midnight.
> I drink to your health, Emperor Yao, do you hear me?
>> Why don't you order Kao Yao to take up a comet,
> To make a clean sweep of the eight corners of the Cosmos,
>> And rid us once for all of these brooding clouds?

In the meantime, clouds are still brooding, and the world is not to be improved by an angel beating ineffectually against the void. But it would be worse to allow vacant-minded persons to beat effectually against an angel. For romanticism can at least impart a ferment, although it furnishes no program for action.

It is because Li Po is a great romantic that in his hands everything becomes so fast moving and quickened with life. One imagines that even his white hair grows rampant like the wild grass in Spring:

世务，时常神往遐远的幻想！总之，他体会浪漫精神，透辟无比。你欢喜或不欢喜他，全看你个人的气质如何。我是倾向于现实的，所以我也就较爱杜甫的为人和诗。可是要否认浪漫主义的功用，尤其是在目今，那简直是连愚笨都不及。在《浪漫观念的衰落》一书内，F. L. 卢卡斯说："我们逐日在添高这机械世界的围墙，住在其中的我们也有日益酷似关在大机器中的老鼠而忘却我们人类是万物之灵的危险……我们个人需要新的甲胄来反抗这世界，需要新的基础以期建立我们个人思想的象牙塔，因为个人的思想是万千环轮中一个实体。"这宇宙确是一个巨大的工厂，无数的轮轴于其中永恒不息地环转，制造各种不同的生物。这些生物问世后就彼此争斗，转瞬即杳。我们的地球不过是一只巨大的机器里的老鼠，我们都是显微镜下的寄生虫，所以要拯救被自卑感觉低压的自己，我们不妨跟李白说：

兴酣落笔摇五岳，诗成笑傲凌沧洲。

* * *

酒中乐酣宵向分，举觞醉尧尧可闻。

何不令皋繇拥篲横八极，直上青天挥浮云。

同时，浮云仍笼罩着穹苍，无效果地用翅膀攻击空间的天使对这世界是没有贡献的，可是让无头脑的蠢汉攻击一个天使简直是更糟。浪漫主义对我们虽然没有积极的辅助，却能激动我们。

李白的浪漫精神使他的作品活跃得像生龙活虎，给人印象极深，我们觉得他的白发也长得像春季的蒙茸那么繁茂（《秋浦吟》之一）：

ON HIS WHITE HAIR (秋浦吟之一)

Methinks my white hair has grown ten thousand feet long!

For it grows alongside of my sorrow.

I only wonder how all this autumn frost

Has entered into the bright mirror in front of me.

And take this description of a journey:

I LEFT THE CITY OF PO TI AT DAWN

At early dawn I left Po Ti among the many-colored clouds.

Now I find myself back in Chiang-ling—a thousand *li* in the course of a day!

The monkeys had hardly done with their continuous howlings on the shores

Before ten thousand ranges of hills had rolled away from my light skiff!

If the reader compares this with Wang Wei's

Following the hills, making ten thousand turnings;

We go rapidly, but advance scarcely a hundred *li*,

he will find how very different the temperaments of the two poets are. Li Po is glad to have covered a great distance in a short time, but Wang Wei is glad to have advanced only a short distance in a long time. It seems to me that Li is at his best in painting Nature in her dynamic aspects, while Wang is at his best in painting her in her restful and calm moods.

Some of Li Po's word-pictures possess a sweep peculiarly his own; for instance, here is what he says about the fall at Lushan:

Flying straight down three thousand feet,

It looks as if the Milky Way had fallen from the sky!

And I don't remember either Wang Wei or Tu Fu has ever written this way:

THE SUMMIT TEMPLE (题峰顶寺)

To-night I stay at the Summit Temple.

Here I could pluck the stars with my hand.

I dare not speak aloud in the silence,

For fear of disturbing the dwellers of heaven.

(Obata's version)

*　　*　　*

The sea does not fill up my retina;

How can its waves satisfy my heart?

*　　*　　*

The Yellow River falls from the skies and runs eastward into the seas.

Ten thousand *li* of water pours itself into my bosom!

*　　*　　*

> 白发三千丈，缘愁似个长。
> 不知明镜里，何处得秋霜！

再看他怎样描写航行（《早发白帝城》）：

> 朝辞白帝彩云间，千里江陵一日还。
> 两岸猿声啼不住，轻舟已过万重山。

倘使读者将王维的"随山将万转，趣途无百里"和李白的前几行比较一下，他就能看出这两位诗人气质的不同：李白以动为乐，而王维以静为乐。我以为李白描摹大自然的活动最为可人，而王维以描摹大自然的宁静见称。

李白的诗艺时常自创一格、别具风味，像描写庐山瀑布的这两句：

> 飞流直下三千尺，疑是银河落九天。

我不相信王维或杜甫曾这样写过（《题峰顶寺》）：

> 夜宿峰顶寺，举手扪星辰。
> 不敢高声语，恐惊天上人。　　　　（英译：小畑薰良）

*　　*　　*

> 海水不满眼，观涛难称心。

*　　*　　*

> 黄河落天走东海，万里写入胸怀间。

*　　*　　*

God the Supreme Artist painted the City of Chengtu,

And all the houses and gates enter into His canvas!

* * *

Like a silken thread, the Yellow River flows at the border of heaven.

* * *

The two rivers look like a pair of bright mirrors inlaid in the land.

The twin bridges hang before us like a gorgeous rainbow.

* * *

My sorrow follows the stream till it lengthens into ten thousand *li*!

* * *

Look, look! How lovely, yonder River of Han, green as a duck's head!

Exactly like grape-wine in its first stage of fermentation!

* * *

Men are walking in a bright mirror.

Birds pass in and out through a beautiful screen.

(From a "Song on a Crystal Brook": 清溪行)

In other words, Li Po looks at Nature as an endless scroll of pictures. On the other hand, he looks at a picture as a natural scene:

The great artist has spun his subtle thoughts and brandished his gorgeous brush,

Driving the mountains and whipping the oceans to come before our eyes!

* * *

It looks as though the twelve peaks of Wu-shan

Had flown from Heaven's border into your silken screen!

Sometimes, even the feathered songsters wish to chime in with human music:

Our music has thrilled the hearts of new nightingales.

They have flown over to the trees in the Royal Park.

Hark! They too have begun to pipe, mingling their notes

With the glorious concert of flutes and fifes!

Anyone who has heard a caged bird burst into song even in the evening when you open the radio cannot fail to feel the fundamental unity of God's creation. One Heart is throbbing throughout the expanding Universe! Li Po even goes as far as to say:

九天开出一成都，万户千门入画图。

* * *

黄河如丝天际来。

* * *

两水夹明镜，双桥落彩虹。

* * *

一水牵愁万里长。

* * *

遥看汉水鸭头绿，恰似葡萄初酸醅。

* * *

人行明镜中，鸟度屏风里。 （《清溪行》）

换句话说，李白将大自然看作一卷无穷的图画，一幅图画所以也只是大自然的一段景色而已：

名公绎思挥彩笔，驱山走海置眼前。

* * *

疑是天边十二峰，飞入君家彩屏里。

有时候，飞鸟也来同人们共同歌唱：

新莺飞绕上林苑，愿入箫韶杂凤笙。

在深夜中你静听无线电播出的音乐，倘使笼中的小鸟突然地鸣啭，你一定会觉得上苍所创造的万物的和谐。这泛大的宇宙内只有一个心在跳跃着！李白甚至曾说（《古意》）：

> If you know the heart of the dodder and the vine,
>
> You would be able to measure the tides of the sea!

How this flash of insight reminds me of a few lines from Tennyson, otherwise so different from Li Po:

> Flower in the crannied wall,
>
> I pluck you out of the crannies,
>
> I hold you here, root and all, in my hand,
>
> Little flower—but if I could understand,
>
> What you are, root and all, and all in all,
>
> I should know what God and man is.

The web of life is so closely interwoven that all things are but the modes of one Substance:

> Chuang Chow dreamed of a Butterfly,
>
> And the Butterfly *was* Chuang Chow!
>
> One Reality is constantly changing its forms;
>
> Endless events are flowing into Eternity![3]

Is it not because of this wonderful inter-relatedness of God's creation that even now, as I am writing this, tears have suddenly gushed into my eyes again when I think of the soldiers at the front? Their blood has changed into my tears! In the meantime, Summer has arrived. So goodbye, Reader, I can write no more!

若识一草心，海潮亦可量。

这深刻的认识使我想起丁尼生的几句话：

围墙罅隙中的花，

我将你从罅隙中采出，

我将你的全身握在手中；

细小的花，倘使我知道你的一切，

我也能懂得天主和人类。

生活的网丝是细密的，万物都是一体的变易：

庄周梦胡蝶，胡蝶为庄周。

一体更变易，万事良悠悠。[3]

是不是为了万物神奇的相互关系，泪珠才夺眶而出，当我想到在前线卫国的战士？他们的血已转成了我的眼泪！同时，夏季已到。读者们，再会，我不能再写了！

V. SUMMER: ITS BLAZING HEAT AND FIRE

A good heart is better than all the heads in the world.

—*Bulwer-Lytton*

Toothless, yes, but heartless I am not!

A tongue to vent my anger, not to wail my fate!

—*Tu Fu*

The art of letters is as old as history,

And yet this inch-long heart knows its hits and misses!

—*Tu Fu*

I am not one of those who would measure God's omnipotence by narrow thoughts and who would fancy that the reason moths seek after the light is because God wants to enable us to catch them on the windows. But the more I study the poetry of T'ang and follow its stages of growth, the more I am convinced that God's finger was in it. In the first place, while it was the poets who wrote the poems, it was God who wrote the poets. He wrote Meng Hao-jan in 689, Wang Wei in 699, Li Po in 701; and as if it were not enough to have created these lovely characters, He produced a real masterpiece in 712 in the person of Tu Fu. In the second place, seeing that the possibilities of Spring had been exhausted, He introduced Summer with thunder and lightning in the political sky, and jerked his dreamy children into wakefulness and brought them face to face with reality by letting them see the marvelous tragedy of T'ang Ming Huang. For the poetry of T'ang was just one organism, and the organism must not be allowed to remain in the stage of infancy and youth, but must be made to grow into manhood; and no one can shed off infantile ways of thinking and feeling without having come into contact and conflict with life and learned lessons from bitter experiences. How monotonous it would be if we always had to listen to such sweet music as this:

What is life after all but a dream?

And why should such pother be made?

Better far to be tipsy, I deem,

    And doze all day long in the shade.

When I wake and look out on the lawn,

    I hear midst the flowers a bird sing;

I ask, "Is it evening or dawn?"

    The mango-bird whistles, "'Tis spring."

伍 夏之烈焰

> 一颗善良的心胜过世上所有智慧。　　——布尔沃-利顿

> 齿落未是无心人，舌存耻作穷途哭。　　——杜甫

> 文章千古事，得失寸心知。　　——杜甫

　　有人说飞蛾扑向光明之处的缘故，是因为上苍要我们在窗前捉住它们。我不是这种以个人狭仄的眼光来度衡上苍的万能之流，可是愈研究唐诗的发展，我也愈相信上苍确曾参与其事。第一，这些名诗的作者固然是这些诗人，但这些诗人的作者却是上苍：689 年他造出孟浩然，十年后他造出王维，701 年他再造出李白。这些可爱的人才好似还不够助兴，所以在 712 年他再添造一个真正的杰作——杜甫。第二，看见春季已经消逝，他便引进了夏季，雷声和闪电在政治穹苍下打醒了在酣梦中的孩子，使他们目睹唐明皇的惨剧而与现实接触。唐朝的诗就是一个有机体，这有机体不会永远幼稚，必定会慢慢地长大成年。当然，在未尝到生活的苦味前，稚气是难脱掉的。倘使我们一直惯听这种甜蜜的音乐，势必觉得发腻：

> 处世若大梦，胡为劳其生？
> 所以终日醉，颓然卧前楹。
> 觉来盼庭前，一鸟花间鸣。
> 借问此何时，春风语流莺。

Overpower'd with the beautiful sight,

Another full goblet I pour,

And would sing till the moon rises bright—

But soon I'm as drunk as before.

(Gile's version)

I can tell you that sometimes I am so fed up with this kind of music that I would cry out, "Come, come, T'ai Po!

That strain again! it had a dying fall:

O! it came o'er my ear like the sweet sound

That breathes upon a bank of violets,

Stealing and giving odor. Enough! no more:

'Tis not so sweet now as it was before."

One of the most curious facts in the history of Chinese literature is that Li Po and Tu Fu, dear friends as they were, never understood each other's temperaments. Li regarded Tu as of the earth, earthy, while Tu regarded Li as of the moon, moony. Tu wrote to Li:

Autumn comes,

We meet each other,

You still whirl about as a thistledown in the wind.

Your Elixir of Immortality is not yet perfected

And, remembering Ko Hung, you are ashamed.

You drink a great deal,

You sing wild songs,

Your days pass in emptiness.

Your nature is a spreading fire,

It is swift and *restless*.

But what does all this bravery amount to?

(Ayscough and Lowell's version)

This sounds more like a man chiding a boy than a young fellow addressing a friend eleven years his senior! On the other hand, Li Po presented an equally impolite poem to Tu Fu:

> I met Tu Fu on the tops of the Rice Hill,
>
> Wearing a big bamboo hat under the noontide sun.
>
> How is it you have grown so very thin?
>
> You must have put too much bitter efforts into the making of poetry!

This sounds like a precocious boy having a naughty dig at an elder. A friend of mine has given a delightfully idiomatic turn to the two lines:

> 感之欲叹息，对酒还自倾。
>
> 浩歌待明月，曲尽已忘情。 　　　　　（英译：翟理思）

老实说，对这种歌调我颇有倦意，时常情不自禁地说：

> 又是那支歌调，它的下降是低冈的，
>
> 它飘到我的耳旁，
>
> 像向岸旁紫罗兰吐气的甜蜜的音乐，
>
> 吸进，又吐出馥郁。够了，不要了，
>
> 它已不像先前那样地可人了。

李白和杜甫虽然是很好的朋友，却不能彼此谅解，这可说是中国文学史上趣事之一。李白当杜甫是尘世中人，枯燥乏味；杜甫却以为李白行动恍惚，耽于梦想。杜甫写给李白：

> 秋来相顾尚飘蓬，未就丹砂愧葛洪。
>
> 痛饮狂歌空度日，飞扬跋扈为谁雄？
>
> 　　　　　　　　　　　　（英译：艾思柯、洛威尔）

这不像一个少年赠给长他十一年的朋友的话，却有些像大人叱责小孩。礼尚往来，李白也赠了杜甫一首同样不客气的诗：

> 饭颗山头逢杜甫，头戴笠子日卓午。
>
> 借问别来太瘦生，总为从前作诗苦。

这有些像一个少年老成的孩子挖苦长者的样子。我有一个朋友将这末两行译成可人的英文，颇具英人土风：

> Gee! you are losing weight terribly!
>
> Maybe your poems have got all the weight you have lost!

Neither Li nor Tu seemed to be aware that they belonged to different seasons, that Spring, newly liberated as it was from the grip of death into a new being, was bound to suffer a dizzy agony in its sheer metempsychosis, while Summer was bound to be heavy with the luxuriant process of aestivation and ripening. The truth is Li Po's lyrics are delightful, but their tantalizing effect is momentary. Tu Fu's are not so light at the first reading, but they sink deep down in your psyche. To me Tu Fu was decidedly the greater genius of the two. He possessed the highest artistic talent without the drawback of an artistic temperament.

In fact, the poetry of T'ang was so much of an organism and followed its stages of development so inevitably that the poets in its first stage look like little children in comparison with a man like Tu Fu. For instance, Tu Shen-yen was the grandfather of Tu Fu, but from the standpoint of poetic maturity Tu Fu may be regarded as the grandfather. Shen-yen died in his sixties, and his last words were: "That little kid the Creator is doing his best to harass me! What more can I say?" Tu Fu died in his fifties, and his last poem, written after an attack of paralysis, contains these significant lines:

> Like a clear level mirror, I have been a fool who knows not how to flatter.
>
> Verily, the light of God has illumined and guided me in my journey through life.

Shen-yen was trying to be funny like a naughty boy, but Tu Fu achieved real humor through a high seriousness. And who was the grandfather?

At any rate, we have to thank Spring for all its charms and all its innocent prattles, but the year would not be complete without the other seasons, and just now we have to deal with Summer. For reasons of time and space I shall confine myself to Tu Fu, the Soul of Summer. But that's exactly where my trouble comes in. For I have to make myself clear as to what I mean by Summer and what qualities I would attribute to it, especially in view of the fact that this particular Summer in this particular place, Hong Kong, leaves much to be desired. If the Summer of T'ang poetry were like the one here, then all the poems of this period would be very awful, and the reader would do well to skip over these pages.

> Gee! you are losing weight terribly,
>
> Maybe your poems have got all the weight you have lost.

李白和杜甫似乎都不曾觉到，他们是属于不同的季候的。他们不曾感觉到那刚从死神掌握中解放出来的春季，在它诞生的过程中，一定要感受到晕眩的痛苦的，更不知道夏季的炎热和成熟的气味会将空气转得沉重。李白的抒情诗是轻松活泼的，它的激动力也只是暂时的；杜甫的诗初读时虽不觉得怎样轻松，却能钻到你灵魂的深处。在我看来，杜甫毫无疑问是较李白来得伟大，他具有最高的艺术天才，却无艺术家执拗怪僻和玩世不恭的脾气。

　　诚然，唐诗是一个有机体，它的滋长是自然的、按部就班的：第一期的诗人和第二期的杜甫比来简直像孩子一样。例如，依家系而言，杜审言是杜甫的祖父；但是在造诣上看来，杜甫较审言成熟得多了，简直可以反做他的祖父。审言死时已六十多岁，他临末的话是，"此刻甚为造物小儿所苦，尚复何言"！杜甫五十多岁时即死，他最末的一首诗，是患麻痹症后写的，有如下面很宝贵的几行：

　　　朗鉴存愚直，皇天实照临。

审言只学孩子们的天真胡闹，杜甫却在严肃中达到幽默。到底谁是谁的祖父！

　　春季的媚态和浑沌始终是值得爱恋的，可是没有别的季候，这年份就不会完全。我们现在就要谈夏季，为了篇幅和时间的关系，我们的范围只限于杜甫——夏之灵魂。可是问题就在这里。我们要弄清楚到底夏季的特点是怎么。倘使唐诗的夏季是像此地香港的夏季的话，这一期的出品一定欠满人意，读者们也可忽

Indeed, my present predicament is very much like that of the fisherman who, as the story goes, was caught in the meshes of his own net. There is no dodging the impossible task of defining Summer. But whenever I am at my wits' end, I draw upon my experience. I will put all my cards on the table. So far, I have passed through forty Summers; one of them I spent in my mother's womb; many of them I spent in Ningpo; a few of them I spent in Hangchow; ten of them in Shanghai; one in Ann Arbor, Michigan; another in Cambridge, Massachusetts; another in Yellowstone Park; another in Paris; another in Wernigerode, Germany; another in Soochow; and another in Tsingtao; another in Peiping; another in Tientsin; another in Lushan; and this one in a little apartment among the books, cudgelling my brains, if any, over the nature of Summer. In fact, my flat is so small that a good friend of mine, Mr. Yeh Ch'iu-yuan, wrote a poem to me containing two Tufuishly tender lines which I beg to render into English:

> A lonely guest, where is your old home now?
> A whole family packed like sardines in such a small flat!

To this I replied in a Tufuish humor (if I may flatter myself):

> Having a guest like yourself, I am no longer a guest!
> Don't call this a small flat,—it's a cozy nest!

But that's not the humor of it. The humor of it is that the more Summers I have known, the less I know about Summer in general. I have to warn the reader, therefore, that in what follows I shall not try to describe Summer but to do a bit of legislation about it. I may even draw a Constitution for Summer! This understood, let me begin.

I daresay that the most prominent quality of Summer is its heat. Corresponding to this aspect of the season is the intense fire of love burning incessantly in the heart of Tu Fu. He loves God and all His creatures except the vultures preying upon others. The scope of his never-dying sympathy ranges from the Emperor to the commonest grass on the wayside. He writes scathing satires against the perpetrators of social injustice and heartless cruelty precisely because he has so much affection for their innocent victims. In other words, his very hate gathers momentum from his all-embracing love. For it is not beyond human possibilities to love one's personal enemies, but who can ever help hating the enemies of God? Among the worst enemies of God are the war-makers,

过这几页。我现在的苦况是像故事上说的,被他自己的罗网套住的渔人,因为我不能解释夏季的定义。可是每到智尽力竭时,我就凭经验说话。我的总账就在这里:我经历过了四十个夏季,在母亲的腹中一年,在宁波多年,在杭州几年,在上海十年,在美国密歇根一年,麻省一年,黄石公园一年,巴黎一年,德国一年,苏州一年,青岛一年,北平一年,天津一年,庐山一年。今年在香港一间小公寓内,为了唐诗的夏在书堆中苦心思索、绞尽脑汁。真的,我的房间实在是小得可以,我的好朋友叶秋原君送了首诗给我,其中有二句颇有杜甫之温柔(我将其译成英文):

　　　　故里今何在?合家住小楼。

我亦答以杜甫之幽默(倘使我可以阿谀自己的话):

　　　　有客便非客,小楼亦是楼。

可是这并不幽默。好笑的是,愈多过夏季,则愈不懂夏季。所以我要声明,在以下的篇幅里,我并不想形容夏季的一切,不过想为它立点法而已,或许我可以替夏季草拟一部宪法!懂得这点,我们就可以前进。

　　我敢说夏季最醒目的特点是炎热,同炎热相应的是杜甫赤心中焚着的烈火。他喜爱上苍和上苍的万物,厌恶掠夺弱者的贪得之徒。他的怜悯是无边的:上达君王,下至街夫。他深怜无辜的牺牲者,他广泛的热情使他加倍地厌恶社会的不公和人类的残忍。所以他写了剧烈的讽刺文,攻击社会。【换句话说,他的恨源自他的博爱。】爱我们的仇敌固然是可以的,可是谁能爱上苍的仇敌?上苍最大的敌人就是那辈幸灾乐祸、引起战争的魔鬼,

whom Tu Fu hates with the intensity of his love for humanity. Here is how he paints a recruiting scene:

> Chariots rumble! Horses neigh!
> Each with a bow and arrows at his girdle, the footmen are ready to go
>> their way!
>
> Their fathers, mothers, wives and children have come to bid them adieu;
> The crowd has raised a confusion of dust, till the bridge is shut off from view.
>
> They clutch at the men's clothes; they stamp their feet; they cry on the roads,
> Till the echoes of their piteous wailings rise to the clouds.

To Tu Fu's mind, all this misery which turned the earth into hell was uncalled for. He laid the blame at the door of the Emperor, whose lust for territories knew no bounds.

> The frontiers have become an ocean of blood.
> But the war-minded Emperor is still bent upon expanding the Empire.
> Does His Majesty know that two hundred districts east of the Mountain
>> are lying waste,
> And all the villages, big and small, are overgrown with briars and thorns?

The earth exists to feed men with its fruits, but when things are not what they ought to be, men exist to feed the earth with their blood. Ming Huang already possessed more land than he had men to cultivate; but he continued to draw the farmers from their fields to the remote frontiers. That was what Tu Fu could not understand.

> Is His Majesty not rich enough in territories?
> Why open up still more frontiers?

And as if it were not enough to deprive wives of their husbands, fathers of their sons, and children of their fathers, the government continued to levy all sorts of taxes, duties and rents upon the poverty-stricken families. "Where," Tu Fu asks without waiting for an answer, "where can they get money to meet these exactions?"

The following specimens will give a glimpse into the social conditions brought about directly or indirectly by the wars:

(1) THE SONG OF SILKWORMS AND COWS

In the world, there are nearly ten thousand cities,

But ah! what a pity

That weapons of war and soldiers fill up

Each and every city!

杜甫爱人类的天性使他咬牙切齿地痛恨他们。下面他摹描军队出发前的惨状：

车辚辚，马萧萧，行人弓箭各在腰。

爷娘妻子走相送，尘埃不见咸阳桥。

牵衣顿足拦道哭，哭声直上干云霄。

在杜甫看来，这些惨不忍睹的苦况不是不可免的，错就在贪得无厌的皇帝一人身上：

边庭流血成海水，武皇开边意未已。

君不闻汉家山东二百州，千村万落生荆杞。

泥土的用途原是供给人类食物，但是倘若万物不循着老天定下的轨道行走，人类的鲜血就只能充作泥土的饮料。明皇疆土之广，已非他的臣民所能耕种完的，还要送他们到千里之外的战场去做什么？这不是杜甫所能理解的：

君已富土境，开边一何多？

夺了人家的丈夫妻子还不够，还要征收捐税，搜刮贫无立锥地的人家。杜甫疑问道："租税从何出？"

下面几段足以显示社会内因战争直接或间接而引起的状态：

（一）蚕谷行

天下郡国向万城，无有一城无甲兵。

When will the swords and shields be beaten
    Into hoes and ploughs,
So every inch of waste land may be tilled
    By the patient cows?

    Cows till the *mow*,
    And silkworms grow!
Farmers and silk-maids sing as they go!
Tears of passionate scholars cease to flow!

(2)

Last year the price of rice was high,
    And the soldiers had not enough to eat.
This year the price of rice is low,
    And the farmers can't make both ends meet.
The great officials, riding high horses,
    Are overfed with wine and meat;
In the farmers' barns no grain is left,
    And on their looms, of silk there's not a sheet!
...
Everywhere the poor are selling their children
    In order to pay their rents and taxes.

(3)

Over the earth so wide and waste,
I see few men, but many vultures!

(4) THE PRESSGANG

There, where at eve I sought a bed,
    A pressgang came, recruits to hunt;
Over the wall the goodman sped,
    And left his wife to bear the brunt.

Ah me! the cruel serjeant's rage!
    Ah me! how sadly she anon

Told all her story's mournful page,—

How three sons to the war had gone;

How one had sent a line to say

That two had been in battle slain:

He, from the fight had run away,

But they could ne'er come back again.

She swore 'twas all the family—

Except a grandson at the breast;

His mother too was there, but she

Was all in rags and tatters drest.

焉得铸甲作农器，一寸荒田牛得耕。

牛尽耕，蚕亦成，

不劳烈士泪滂沱，男谷女丝行复歌。

（二）岁晏行

去年米贵阙军食，今年米贱大伤农。

高马达官厌酒肉，此辈杼轴茅茨空。

……

况闻处处鬻男女，割慈忍爱还租庸。

（三）

萧条四海内，人少豺虎多。

（四）石壕吏

暮投石壕村，有吏夜捉人。

老翁逾墙走，老妇出门看。

吏呼一何怒！妇啼一何苦！

听妇前致词：三男邺城戍。

一男附书至，二男新战死。

存者且偷生，死者长已矣！

室中更无人，惟有乳下孙。

有孙母未去，出入无完裙。

The crone with age was troubled sore,

But for herself she'd not think twice

To journey to the seat of war

And help to cook the soldiers' rice.

The night wore on and stopped her talk;

Then sobs upon my hearing fell...

At dawn when I set forth to walk,

Only the goodman cried Farewell!

(Giles' version)

(5) DREAMING IN DAYTIME

My sleeping in broad daylight is not solely because of the shortness of
the night:

There is something in the air of March that makes me drowsy and dozy.

How the warm breath of the peach-blossoms intoxicates my eyes!

The sun has set but my dreams are rising still.

I dream of my native town, now overgrown with thistles and thorns.

I dream of His Majesty and his entourage, so near the beasts of prey.

When will the war cease and farmers return to their fields?

And when will the petty officials cease to fleece the poor?

(6)

How heartless are the overfed ones!

Cannibals they are, the eaters of choice foods!

In the rich families' kitchens meats stink:

On the battlefield there are white bones!

(7)

Behind the red-painted doors, wine turns sour, and meat stinks:

On the roads lie corpses of people frozen to death.

A hair-breadth divides opulence and dire penury!

This strange contrast fills me with unutterable anguish!

The last quoted stanza is, perhaps, the most widely known of all his
lines. I have heard it recited even by politicians who are otherwise not

Interested in poetry. There is no question that these four lines are beautiful. But the question is, where does the beauty lie? Does it lie in the soured wine and stinking meat? Not for me! Does it lie in the frozen bodies on the roads? *Non plus!* Does it then lie in the contrast? No, I should rather think that it makes the whole phenomenon all the more emphatically ugly. To my mind, the beauty lies in the fact that the strange contrast calls forth such unutterable anguish. In other words, a glaring injustice is exposed and denounced in adequate terms. When injustice is denounced, the negation

老妪力虽衰，请从吏夜归。
急应河阳役，犹得备晨炊。
夜久语声绝，如闻泣幽咽。
天明登前途，独与老翁别。　　　（英译：翟理思）

（五）昼梦
二月饶睡昏昏然，不独夜短昼分眠。
桃花气暖眼自醉，春渚日落梦相牵。
故乡门巷荆棘底，中原君臣豺虎边。
安得务农息战斗，普天无吏横索钱？

（六）
饱食复何心，荒哉膏粱客。
富家厨肉臭，战地骸骨白。

（七）
朱门酒肉臭，路有冻死骨。
荣枯咫尺异，惆怅难再述。

最后的一段可说是最脍炙人口的了。我曾听见不学无术的政客背诵它。毫无疑问的，这四行是极美的上品。但是问题是：它的美在哪里？是不是在"酒""肉"中？我说不。是不是在"冻死骨"中？也不是。是不是在贫富不平的比较中？不，我说这只会使它变得丑不入目。在我看来，这四行的美就在能唤起我们的无名火。狞恶的不平赤裸裸地站在面前，受我们的指斥，一切邪恶都隐灭无踪。看，

is negated, and behold! there appears justice in its full effulgence.

I have always thought that justice is beauty as applied to human relations. When we see an innocent person acquitted, we exclaim, "What a fair judgment!" All fair dealings between man and man are beautiful, and all unfair dealings are ugly. And any writings that are strong enough to evoke the sense of justice dormant in our minds are beautiful. I confess I am thoroughly enthralled by the beauty of these lines in St. Mary's "Song of Joy":

> He hath showed strength with his arm;
>
> He hath scattered the proud in the imagination of their heart.
>
> He hath put down princes from their thrones,
>
> And hath exalted them of low degree.
>
> The hungry He hath filled with good things;
>
> And the rich He hath sent empty away.

I also find superb beauty in these words of St. John:

> Flourish, therefore, that ye may fade: be rich for the time, that ye may be beggars for ever... For it is out of reason that for one belly there should be laid up so much food as would suffice a thousand, and for one body so many garments as would furnish clothing for a thousand men... But wretched and unhappy is the man who would have something more than sufficeth him: for of this come heats of fevers, rigors of cold, diverse pains in all the members of the body, and he can neither be fed with food nor sated with drink; that covetousness may learn that money will not profit it, which being laid up bringeth to the keepers thereof anxiety by day and night, and suffereth them not even for an hour to be quiet and secure. (From *The Apocryphal New Testament*)

It is said that Tu Fu used to boast, in a good-humored way, that his poetry could cure malaria. I don't know about that. But it does serve to vent our pent up feelings against the violent contrast between "heats of fevers" and "rigors of cold" in human society. What "rigors of cold" he himself suffered is vividly described in the following song:

It is the Eighth Moon, when the Autumn skies are high, the wind howls
    angrily.

It sweeps away three layers of grass-roof on my house.

The thatch flies in scattered bits until the shores of the river are strewn
    with them.

Some of them fly high and hang themselves on the tops of tall trees.

The low-flying ones whirl down into the hollows of the marsh.

A swarm of small boys from the South Village, taking advantage of my
    feeble age,

光耀的正义就在我们眼前。

    我常想，在人类的关系中，正义就是美。当我们看见一个无辜者被释放时，我们就说："这是一个多么公正的判断！"人类一切公正的往来都是美的，一切不公平的往来是丑的。任何作品能唤起我们脑海内潜伏的爱公平的天性也是美的。我承认圣玛丽《快乐歌》的美使我出神多久：

> 主但一举手，傲者顿挫抑。
> 王侯失其位，贫民蒙拔识。
> 富人空手归，饿者坐得食。

圣约翰的这几句话里也有崇高的美：

> 现在你兴旺，可是凋谢就在目前；现在你丰足，你就要永远沦为乞丐……你没有理由食千人之食，衣千人之衣……贪图财产者必有忧愁，因为财产要使他发热、发寒、周体不适、不能进食、不能饮水，他也就会知道金钱不能给他帮助，只能使他日夜焦虑不安，无一时一刻的安息。（《新约外传》）

    传说杜甫时常幽默自夸，说他的诗可以医愈疟疾。医病的事确否则不得而知，他反抗社会极端不平的诗确能替我出一口气。他自己不幸的遭遇可在下面这首诗里看到：

> 八月秋高风怒号，卷我屋上三重茅。茅飞渡江洒江郊：高者挂罥长林梢，下者飘转沉塘坳。南村群童欺我老无力，忍能

Seize the bits under my very nose and run into the bamboo groves.

I shout at them until my lips are scorched and throat dry, but they turn
a deaf ear to me.

I return home, leaning on my staff, sighing and musing on my fate.

After awhile, the wind stops, but the clouds become inkish,

Until the Autumn skies are blackened all over and hang above our heads
like a brooding gloom.

Our cloth blankets, worn out and stiffened, are as cold as iron.

My spoiled kid, whose bed manners are bad, kicks hard at the blanket
until his toes peep out from the holes.

Under the leaking roof, there is not a single dry spot in our beds.

The rain, as thick-set as hemp, never ceases to pour.

Ever since the rebellion and disorder, I have never been able to sleep well;

And tonight, with my body soaked all over, how could I enjoy a single wink?

Ah for a big mansion of a thousand, or ten thousand rooms

To give shelter and cheer to all the poor scholars of the world!

Safe from the ravages of wind and rain, they will feel as calm as a mountain.

Ah me! The day on which I shall see such a mansion rise before my eyes,

I shall be happy to live in a broken hut by myself and be frozen to death
all alone.

But of all Tu Fu's "social poems," I like the following one best:

A BRIDE'S FAREWELL TO HER GROOM

A vine should intertwine itself with an evergreen.

Entangled with the weeds, how could it creep high?

To marry a girl to a soldier

Is to cast her away by the side of a road.

Only yesterday were our hairs knotted together.

Hardly has our nuptial bed been warmed,

This morning you will take leave of me;

Is it not a bit too soon?

Although your destination is not far,

As you are going to stand guard on this side of the river,

Yet my humble body being still a virgin's,

How can I serve your mother as my mother-in-law?

When my parents brought me up,

They kept me day and night in the house.

But a girl must have someone to cling to,—

Even a cock or a dog is better than none.[1]

Now you are going to live in the neighborhood of death!

I feel my heart has sunk under the weight of intense pain.

How I wish to go with you!

But what's the use of wishing the impossible?

Don't let any thought of me distract you

From your heavy duties among the ranks!

The presence of a woman in the camp

Would wreck the morale of the soldiers.

对面为盗贼。公然抱茅入竹去，唇焦口燥呼不得，归来倚杖自叹息。俄顷风定云墨色，秋天漠漠向昏黑。布衾多年冷似铁，娇儿恶卧踏里裂。床头屋漏无干处，雨脚如麻未断绝。自经丧乱少睡眠，长夜沾湿何由彻。安得广厦千万间，大庇天下寒士俱欢颜，风雨不动安如山。呜呼！何时眼前突兀见此屋，吾庐独破受冻死亦足。

杜甫的"社会诗"中，我最喜欢这一首（《新婚别》）：

兔丝附蓬麻，引蔓故不长。嫁女与征夫，不如弃路旁。结发为君妻，席不暖君床。暮婚晨告别，无乃太匆忙！君行虽远，守边赴河阳。妾身未分明，何以拜姑嫜？父母养我时，日夜令我藏。生女有所归，鸡狗亦得将。[1] 君今往死地，沉痛迫中肠。誓欲随君去，形势反苍黄。勿为新婚念，努力事戎行！

Ah me! A daughter of a poor family,

It took me long to acquire these clothes of gauze and silk.

I shall no longer wear them in your absence.

Even before you go, let me wash away the powder and rouge from my face.

Behold the birds flying in the sky!

Big and small, they all soar in pairs.

Only the human world goes awry,

Rending apart what Love has joined together!

This poem is, in its original language, so beautiful and full of enchanting music that I cannot help wishing that I had the pen of Shakespeare to do it full justice in English. As it is, a great part of its fragrance has evaporated in the process of translation. But I hope the reader will get something of the tender sentiments with which the poem is saturated. And I wish also to point out at this juncture some of the similarities that seem to me to exist between Tu Fu and Shakespeare. (I had called Shakespeare a Spring bird; now I am convinced he belongs to Summer.) In the first place, both of them seem to possess the happy knack of entering into the soul of another person and identifying themselves with him. Secondly, like Shakespeare, Tu Fu could introduce comedy into a tragical situation, and mingle the real and commonplace with poetry. Thirdly, both seem to believe in a moral order in the universe to which the human world must try to conform if it doesn't want to go awry. They hold their mirrors up to Nature not only in the sense that their descriptions are life-like, but also in the more important sense that they measure things human by the standard of a higher Law. Finally, the Singer-Saint of China seems to share with the Singer-Saint of England a heart on fire with love,—"a heart burning with compassion for every phase of human misery, physical or moral, and wonderful in its sympathy with the lowly and the poor." (These words I have taken from a truly remarkable book, *Saint Thérèse of Lisieux, The Little Flower of Jesus*.) As a result of these qualities which they have in common, they are at once fiery and watery. As Tu Fu would put it,

A hidden fire is constantly cooking a jade spring,

Which bubbles forth its waters to swell a quiet crevice.

Is it not remarkable that in his last sonnet, Shakespeare should have used exactly the same image? There he spoke of "a cool Well,"

Which from Love's fire took heat perpetual,

Growing a bath and healthful remedy

For men diseas'd.

妇人在军中，兵气恐不扬。自嗟贫家女，久致罗襦裳。罗襦不复施，对君洗红妆。仰视百鸟飞，大小必双翔。人事多错迕，与君永相望！

这首诗的美，其感情之温柔，只有莎士比亚才比得上。【事实上，在翻译的过程中，大部分韵味都消失了，希望读者仍能感受到原诗透出的些许柔情。】说到这里，我要顺便略谈这二位大诗人的共同点。先前我曾叫莎士比亚为春鸟（见序幕），现在我想他是属于夏季的。第一，他和少陵似乎都有钻入第三者的灵魂、体会他的精神的本领。第二，像莎士比亚一样，杜甫能将幽默的插科引入悲惨的景况中，能将日常的生活充满诗意。第三，他们颇信任宇宙的道德律，都以为人类的世界若要不陷入黑暗的话，必须遵守这规律。他们将他们的明镜对照着大自然，这不仅是说他们的摹描生动可爱，而且更重要的是，他们以崇高的眼光来衡评世事。第四，中国的歌圣和英国的歌圣都有一个被热情和爱之火燃烧的心——"对人类身体或精神上的苦难满怀悲悯，对贫困和卑微的人们深表同情"（摘自《耶稣的小花》一书）。这几个共同点使他们同时有像火那样的热烈，又有像水那样的清澈。例如，杜甫就这样说：

阴火煮玉泉，喷薄涨岩幽。

很巧，莎士比亚在最后一首商籁内也用了同样的影像。谈起"冷井"，他说：

爱情的火给它永久的热，

变成能医愈疾病的沐浴水。

And he concluded with a line which fits Tu Fu as well as himself:

> Love's fire heats water, water cools not love.

Other poets, so far as I know, have either more fire than water or more water than fire. Dante belongs to the former, while Goethe belongs to the latter. But in Tu Fu and Shakespeare they have attained a perfect balance. I hope the reader will see my point as we go along.

While Tu Fu was opposed point-blank to all wars of aggression and self-aggrandizement, he was too much of a patriot to bear with equanimity the invasions of his country by other peoples. I wonder if any human being could feel more happy than he did when he heard that some lost territories had been re-taken by the royal troops from the hands of the rebels:

> Happy news has just reached this remote part of the world!
> The royal troops have re-taken the territories along the Yellow River!
> I was so overjoyed on hearing it that warm tears gushed from my eyes,
> Until my clothes were drenched all over.
> All traces of sadness have left the faces of my wife and children.
> I pack up my books hurriedly, and I am maddened by joy.
> I sing loudly in the broad daylight and abandon myself to wine.
> Isn't it heavenly to return to our village in the company of green Spring?

God knows how many times I have recited this poem and how many times I have cried "Amen!" The happiness that Tu Fu felt when he wrote the poem was more than the silvery gladness of Spring. It was much warmer and denser. There is something aestival about it. It reminds me of the first of the thirty-three moments of happiness that Chin Sheng-t'an knew in his life:

> It is a hot day in June when the sun hangs still in the sky and there is
> not a whiff of wind or air, nor a trace of clouds; the front and back yards are
> hot like an oven and not a single bird dares to fly about. Perspiration flows
> down my whole body in little rivulets. There is the noon-day meal before

me, but I cannot take it for the sheer heat. I ask for a mat to spread on the ground and lie down, but the mat is wet with moisture and flies swarm about to rest on my nose and refuse to be driven away. Just at this moment when I am completely helpless, suddenly there is a rumbling of thunder and big sheets of black clouds over-cast the sky and come majestically on like a great army advancing to battle. Rain water begins to pour down from the eaves like a cataract. The perspiration stops. The clamminess of the ground is gone. All flies disappear to hide themselves and I can eat my rice.

这首诗末尾的几行很适合杜甫和他自己：

爱情的火将水烧热，
水却不能使爱情变冷。

在我所知道的，别的诗人或者是火多于水，或者是水多于火。但丁是属于第一例者，歌德是属于第二例者，只有杜甫和莎士比亚才有平衡的发展。我希望读者从下面几页里能会意我的观点。

杜甫绝对反对侵略他人以自肥，他爱国的热忱使他不能漠视其他民族的侵略。当官军从叛逆手里收复了失地的时候，我知道没有一个人能有像他那样兴高采烈的：

剑外忽传收蓟北，初闻涕泪满衣裳。
却看妻子愁何在，漫卷诗书喜欲狂。
白日放歌须纵酒，青春作伴好还乡。

只有天主知道我将这首诗念过多少次数，说了多少遍数"阿门"！杜甫写这首诗时的心境不是春季轻飘的快乐所能及到的，他的快乐较春季的快乐更温暖、更浓厚，它有夏季的特性在内。这使我想起金圣叹"三十三乐"的第一则：

夏七月，赤日停天，亦无风，亦无云；前后庭赫然如洪炉，无一鸟敢来飞。汗出遍身，纵横成渠。置饭于前，不可得吃。呼簟欲卧地上，则地湿如膏，苍蝇又来缘颈附鼻，驱之不去。正莫可如何，忽然大黑车轴，疾澍澎湃之声，如数百万金鼓。檐溜浩于瀑布。身汗顿收，地燥如扫，苍蝇尽去，饭便得

Ah, is this not happiness?

(From Lin Yu-tang's The Importance of Living)

But even in prosecuting a war of defense, Tu Fu held that it would be utterly unpardonable to kill more men than absolutely necessary. This is the burden of the following song:

> Bows should be drawn with a firm hand and strong,
>
> And the arrows you use should be sharp and long.
>
> In shooting men, shoot first the horses they ride;
>
> In taking prisoners, first capture the Wang[2].
>
> In killing men, be sure to keep within the limits of necessity!
>
> In defending a nation, to go beyond your borders would be wrong.
>
> For the object is to ward off aggression and invasion,
>
> And not to indulge in massacres and devastation!

What a noble voice we are hearing here! And what an interfusion of strength and tenderness! The refined aesthetes may object to this kind of poem as a bit of moralizing, but what do they know about beauty? Beauty is like happiness in that when it comes at all, it comes like a thief. But if you make it the object of pursuit, it runs away from you like a shy maiden. To my mind, nothing can be more beautiful than flashes of moral insight coming directly and spontaneously from the heart. To go a step farther, I would say all genuine beauty is a byproduct of bringing our souls nearer to God; and the reason why war is so ugly is because it makes the earth, which ought to be the playground of the children of God, so much like Hell. Only the other day, I read in the *China Mail* (July 14) a graphic account of the savage bombing of Canton. It is only necessary to quote the opening paragraph:

> From the ruins of a house, a child wailed pitifully. Her whimpering suddenly ceased. Another name has been added to the death list. All the horror and tragedy of this morning's savage bombing of the crowded areas of Canton and Honam is exemplified in that isolated example of similarly

distressing incidents.

What man with a heart can read this without hating the war-makers and without asking himself how long this kind of thing will be allowed to happen in this supposedly civilized world? Who can deny that "there is a terrible slump in the market of human values," as Mr. Wen Yuan-

吃。不亦快哉！　　　　　　　　　（林语堂《生活的艺术》）

　　就是在进行着防御战的时候，杜甫也以为过分的杀戮是不可饶恕的罪愆。在下面一首诗中可以看出他的主张：

> 挽弓当挽强，用箭当用长。
> 射人先射马，擒贼先擒王 [2]。
> 杀人亦有限，列国自有疆。
> 苟能制侵陵，岂在多杀伤。

我们听见的是一个多么高尚的声音！怎样的一种刚强与温柔的融和！一般审美家或许会睥睨这首诗的道学色彩，可是他们懂得什么美？美是像快乐一样，不来则已，来则必像梁上君子那般地神不知鬼不觉。倘使你一心一意要追寻它的话，它就要像一个怕羞的少女那样逃走。在我看来，天下实在没有较从内心中自然地涌出的道德见识更美的东西。进一步说，一切真纯的美都是我们的心灵顺天乐道的副产品。战争是多么地丑恶，因为它将这世界——上苍的孩子的游嬉场——弄得像暗无天日的地狱。日前香港《德臣西报》（7 月 14 日）载有一篇大轰炸后惨不忍睹的广州的描写，它的第一段已够令人酸鼻：

> 一个小孩子在倾坍的废墟旁呜咽，她微弱的声音未几即中断。死亡的名单又多了一个名字。今晨在广州河南一带人口稠密的地方，所遭遇到的轰炸的恐怖和悲惨，可以在这一桩单独的例子中看出来。

哪一个有心肠的人看了这段之后不会痛恨那些引起战争的人，不会疑问道这种惨无人道的暴行在这算是文明的世界上能够继续多久？【谁会不同意温源宁先生所说，"人类的道德水准大跌"？谁不跟全

ning puts it? And who can help feeling as Mr. T. K. Chuan does, "I hate war, but I hate the war-makers even more"? And what man with any grain of sense and conscience in him can disagree with the verdict of Pearl S. Buck, "If Japan wins, let the world prepare for further strife and aggression or, if not these, at least for constant conflict. If China wins, we may hope for peace"? But Tu Fu assures us:

> The butchers of men in this world
> Will soon receive the wages of their sin.

One great quality of Tu Fu is that while he would never bow to the powerful and haughty, he never kicked anybody who was already down. For instance, we have seen how critical he was of Ming Huang in the heyday of his glory, and on Yang Kuei-fei and her sisters and their cousin Yang Kuo-chung the rotten Prime Minister, he could write such satirical lines as:

> Full of coquettish charms and high-flown notions,—
> Ah! What veritable embodiments of chastity and virtue!
>
> ...
>
> The *yang* flowers fall like snowflakes,
> And mingle with the white frogbit.
> The blue bird flies away,
> Holding a rose-red handkerchief in its beak.

This is Tu Fu's symbolic way of describing the widely rumored promiscuous union between Yang Kuo-chung and one of the Yang sisters. He compares the latter to the *yang* flowers (Chinese name for the willow catkins), and Kuo-chung to the frogbit. That they are both white in color symbolizes their coming from the same family. As to the "blue bird" business, an old commentator, Ho Yi-meng (何义门), subtly hinted that it reminded him of these lines from *The Book of Songs*:

> Heigh, not so hasty, not so rough;
> Heigh, do not touch my handkerchief.

Take care, or the dog will bark.

(Waley's version)

The only difference is that in the present case, the handkerchief *was* touched, and the dog, the faithful watch-dog of the common decencies of life, *did* bark, and how musically he barked! But the point is that the poem was written when the Yang family was actually the power behind the throne, when as Tu Fu put it:

增皲先生感同身受，"我厌恨战争，可是我厌恨引起战争者更甚"？哪一个有良心的人会不同意赛珍珠女士的话，"倘使日本战胜的话，这世界就该未雨绸缪，准备应对杀戮和侵略。哪怕不是这些，也至少该为永久的冲突做准备。倘使中国战胜的话，那么我们还可以期望和平"？】杜甫曾替我保证：

> 杀人红尘里，报答在斯须。

杜甫的伟大不但在富贵不能淫，威武不能屈，他并且绝对不打落水狗。我们知道，在明皇极盛时代他曾痛讥这位风流皇帝，下面几行是他讽刺杨贵妃姊妹和当时秉掌大权的杨国忠的话：

> 态浓意远淑且真，肌理细腻骨肉匀。
> ⋯⋯
> 杨花雪落覆白苹，青鸟飞去衔红巾。

这是杜甫所用的象征方法来描述外间所盛传的杨国忠和杨氏姊妹不名誉的苟合。他将杨女比拟"杨花"，将杨国忠比拟"白苹"，他们所共有白色象征他们的出自一家。至于"青鸟"，批评家何义门说，这使他想起《诗经》中的这二行：

> 舒而脱脱兮，无感我帨兮，无使尨也吠。　（英译：韦利）

不同的是，在这里，"帨"已被"感"，"尨"（日常礼节忠实的看门狗）也已"吠"了，吠得又多么悦耳！我们须记牢，杜甫写这首诗的时候，杨氏一家正是气焰万丈、不可一世，像杜甫所说的：

Their light dazzles one's eyes, their heat scorches one's hands,

Their power and influence, how extraordinary!

Take care! Don't come near them!

Are you not afraid of the Prime Minister's ire?

One feels that there must be something in the atmosphere that caused our poet to sneeze so loudly. But such extraordinary influence could never last long, for as P. G. Wodehouse would put it, "it's always just when a chappie is feeling particularly top-hole, and more than usually braced with things in general that Fate sneaks up behind him with a bit of lead piping." And sure enough, the lead piping did come. For soon afterwards, An Lu-shan rebelled, and the Emperor had to escape to Szechuen, and Yang Kuei-fei was executed on the way. Our poet himself was hiding somewhere in the Capital (Ch'ang-an) which had fallen to the hands of the rebels. It was then that he wrote "A Lamentation" in which, as the reader will see, he no longer carps upon the faults of Ming Huang and Kuei-fei, but simply bewails their Fate. The very fire of love that he bore in his belly which had flared forth into furious flames when he saw the Empire being misdirected and heading toward a catastrophe melted him into tears when he saw how the culpables suffered from their own failings. There is a Chinese proverb that you must not throw a stone at somebody down in a well, and Tu Fu would not be a worthy representative of our people if he did. Moreover, when one sees before one's very eyes a concrete illustration of the terrible truth that *the mills of God grind slowly, yet they grind exceeding small,* one is awestruck and has no time to celebrate the downfall of even one's enemies. After all, with all his failings, Ming Huang was one of the most lovable monarchs in the history of China.

A LAMENTATION

A wild old man from Shaoling, I weep silently, gulping down my tears,

As I saunter stealthily along the meandering banks of the Ch'u River.

The Spring is in its full splendor, but the Palaces and Temples are all bolted—

For whom then do the tender willows and new iris don their lovely green?

I remember, in the old days, when the rainbow-banners fluttered in the
    South Park,

Everything basking in the sun of royal favor brightened up its countenance.

The First Lady of the Chao Yang Court,

She used to sit in the royal chariot by the side of the Monarch.

Before the chariot a group of pretty courtiers rode forth with bows and
    arrows in their hands,

Their white horses champing proudly at their gold bits.

炙手可热势绝伦，慎莫近前丞相嗔！

我们感觉到，在氛围中一定有些东西使我们的诗人大声打嚏，可是这种异乎寻常的势力决不能持久。【正如 P. G. 沃德豪斯所言，"正当一个风流浪子趾高气昂得意忘形的时候，命运就从后面鬼鬼祟祟地带了一根铅管钻出来"。这根铅管确实来了。】不久安禄山即叛，明皇避难四川，杨贵妃也就在途中受诛。杜甫那时尚隐藏于已陷落贼手之长安，他的《哀江头》是那时候写成的。读者们念这首诗时一定能看出，他已不再非难明皇和贵妃之短处，而只哀悼他们悲惨的命运。当他看到大权旁落在狐群狗党手里时，他知道灾难即在目前，他腹中之火也就射出无数暴怒的火星；现在明皇贵妃遭遇患难，这热烈的火只发出不断的泪珠。俗语道，"好汉不打落水狗"，杜甫倘使打落水狗的话，决不能作值得我们效法的模范。当我们目睹那句西方格言"天主的磨子磨得极慢，却磨得极细"得到具体的证明时，我们只能仰天叹息，哪还有心肠来庆祝我们敌人的颠覆？明皇的短处固然无可讳言，可是他不失为中国历史上最可爱的皇帝之一。

哀江头

少陵野老吞声哭，春日潜行曲江曲。
江头宫殿锁千门，细柳新蒲为谁绿？
忆昔霓旌下南苑，苑中万物生颜色。
昭阳殿里第一人，同辇随君侍君侧。
辇前才人带弓箭，白马嚼啮黄金勒。

Bending back agilely, with their faces to the sky, they shot into the clouds;

With a smile they brought down a pair of winged creatures.

Now where is the Lady with such bright eyes and pearly teeth?

The poor Wandering Soul, defiled by blood, she is doomed to remain homeless forever!

The clear Wei River flowing eternally toward the east, the road through the Sword Tower penetrating deep into the west,

The dead remained behind, the living journeyed on, between them an ever widening gulf!

What man with a heart can help wetting his breast with tears?

O grass and flowers, when will you cease to grow on the shores of this river?

At dusk, the Hu cavalry filled the city with dust.

I have to return to the southern suburb, but I gaze far into the North.

It was Su Tung-po who said, "Among all the poets ancient and modern, Tu Fu holds the superlative place. Is it not because, although a castaway for life and steeped in hunger and cold, he never took a single meal without thinking of his Sovereign?" I agree, of course, that Tu Fu is the greatest poet of China. No critic worthy of his salt has ever doubted it. But I think the reason that Su gave is wide of the mark. Tu himself had said:

I remonstrated so fearlessly before the Court,

Because I wanted to requite my Creator.

So, even in Court he was thinking more of the Creator than of the Emperor, and it was because he always wanted to requite the love of the Creator that he loved all His creatures. Among the latter he loved the common people above all; and he loved his sovereign only as a potential ally of God:

I have heard the wise sovereigns of old

Governed their states by lenient laws.

They melted weapons of war into hoes and ploughs.

Indeed, this is the sure way to peace and tranquility.

*　　*　　*

A common scholar from Tu Lin,

My stupidity has grown with age.

...

Sorrowing for the people throughout the seasons,

My bosom is burning and sighing like a furnace.

...

Not that the rivers and seas hold no attraction for me,

Not that I don't know how to enjoy myself and play with the sun and
　　the moon:

翻身向天仰射云，一笑正坠双飞翼。
明眸皓齿今何在？血污游魂归不得。
清渭东流剑阁深，去住彼此无消息！
人生有情泪沾臆，江草江花岂终极？
黄昏胡骑尘满城，欲往城南望城北。

　　苏东坡曾说杜甫的伟大在于"古今诗人众矣，而子美独为首者，岂非以其流落饥寒，终身不用，而一饭不忘君也欤"！我当然同意，杜甫是中国最伟大的诗人。能懂他的人、替他表同情者，绝未怀疑过他的伟大。可是东坡的话还有些欠妥。杜甫自己说过，"廷争酬造化"。就是在朝廷里，他怀念"上苍"较他怀念皇帝更深切，他要报答"上苍"广泛的爱，所以他也就爱世人，尤其是贫苦之流。他爱他的君王，因为君王是上苍有力的助手：

吾闻聪明主，治国用轻刑。
销兵铸农器，今古岁方宁。

*　　*　　*

杜陵有布衣，老大意转拙。
……
穷年忧黎元，叹息肠内热。
……
非无江海志，潇洒送日月。

> But that being born in the reign of a sage Emperor,
> I was loath to leave him for good so soon!

Like all Chinese scholars of lofty ideals, Tu Fu's ambition was above all to be a great statesman, a practical benefactor of the people. He saw that the root of all troubles in human society was the divorce of goodness and power. He said so frankly,

> I want to turn His Majesty into a greater man than Yao and Shun!

But God had other plans. He wanted to turn Tu Fu into the greatest poet of China, and make him the throat and tongue of the poor. He paved his ways with thorns in order that he might feel the more intimately and keenly the sufferings of others in the same boat with him. I know of no other poet who suffered so much as he did.

> To dull the edge of hunger I have often lain in bed ten days at a stretch;
> My ragged clothes are patched up and knit over more than a hundred
>   times.
> You don't see, when twilight drenches these empty walls,
> How I weep silent tears of blood—silent tears of blood!

These silent tears of blood quickened his eyes to such an extent that he could see things which would not be observed by the happier ones, who do not see because they do not feel. For instance, he found a hungry eagle pecking at mud, he found a throng of crows pecking at the ulcers of an ownerless lean horse, he found in a recruiting scene that the fat boys had mothers to see them off while the lean ones were standing all alone, he found that the Universe was stinking with the blood of men, and he found nothing but snuffles and tears in the stream of time. To him, history was a brewery of pathos, and he was in such familiar terms with the spirit of history that it became his willing collaborator in the making of his poems. Some of his poems are like window-screens through which the river of time is continually glittering. Far from getting stale, they grow richer in meaning and poignancy with the passing of time. Take this pair of lines:

I evoke all the romance of the past,

While I gaze at the city of Kiukiang.

What a gaze! He poured the whole stream of time into it. In the meantime, twelve centuries have passed since he gazed, and history has brewed more pathos. Indeed, no one knows so well as Tu Fu how to borrow from history. For instance, in one of his quatrains he seems to have caught all that was floating in the air when momentous events were happening. It was a poem to the great court-musician Li Kuei-nien, who

生逢尧舜君，不忍便永诀。

像一切胸襟宽博的士人一样，杜甫曾希望做一个为民服务的大政治家。他以为社会一切不安的根本是善与力的分离。他说得多么恳切，"致君尧舜上"。但是上苍却另有他意。他要杜甫成为中国最伟大的诗人、贫苦者的喉舌，他要使杜甫吃尽人间之苦，因而能体会别人的苦楚。他吃的苦较任何别的诗人来得多：

饥卧动即向一旬，弊裘何啻联百结。
君不见空墙日色晚，此老无声泪垂血。

这无声的血泪张开了他的眼睛，他能看见一班没有感觉的人所看不见的：他看见一只饿鹰啄食泥土，他看见一群乌鸦啄吮一匹瘦瘠的野马的脓疮，新军出发时他看见"肥男有母送，瘦男独伶俜"，他发现整个宇宙是满溢着血腥气，他发现时间的涌流里只有叹息和血泪。他熟悉历史的精神，他的诗得力于历史不少。在他看来，历史只是悲哀的酿造厂。他有几首诗是像幕帘，在它的背后，时间的河流不断地闪耀。这幕帘不会破烂，反有愈老愈形崭新愈有意义之势。像这行：

都将百年兴，一望九江城。

他将时间整个的涌流灌注在这"望"内！同时，自从他写这首诗以来，十二个世纪已经消逝，历史又酿造了不少悲哀。诚然，没有人较杜甫更善用历史。他有一首诗，虽然只有短短四行，却好像已收进国家存亡千钧一发时空中一切的声音。这首诗是赠给明

had flourished in the heyday of Ming Huang, and whom he met at Kiang-nan fifteen years later. Many things had happened in the interim, and all these events were recalled to life in just four lines:

> Just at this time, when Spring has reached its meridian,
> And flowers are beginning to fall here in Kiang-nan,
> I meet you again—you, whose music I used to enjoy years ago
> At the houses of the late Prince Chi and Ts'ui Chiu at Ch'ang-an!

Yes, grief made him see and feel. His sympathies were not confined to the human world. There is, for instance, a touching poem on a sick horse which he had ridden for many years:

> For a long time I have ridden on you.
> How you carried me through the frontier-passes in cold weather!
> Your energies have been spent on the dusty roads.
> You are old and sick now—what a pain I feel in my heart!
> Your mane and bones are not inferior to any of your kind,
> Nor have your tameness and decency declined with age.
> A humble creature, yes; but who can measure your feelings?
> Tender emotions are rising and humming within me.

There is a cordial warmth in his attitude toward Nature. Like a true democrat, he treats all his fellow-beings as his equals, as members of one big family. Animals, birds, fish, insects and flowers, all of them seem to confide their secret sorrows to him, because they know that he is their sympathizer and brother in suffering. Does he attribute human feelings to them? No, to him their feeling hearts are palpable realities. Even the earth has it:

> Rumbling, rumbling, the thunder is feeling the pulse of the earth.

And who is more affectionate than the dog:

> My old dog senses my sorrows,
> And stands beside my bed with drooping head.

My old friend the dog, overjoyed at my return,

Whirls around me and disappears into the skirts of my gown.

Even a little thing like the cricket seems to possess a soul:

皇兴旺时极负盛名的李龟年的，十五年后杜甫在江南遇见他。
这十五年中变迁良多，一切好像都由这四行说出：

> 岐王宅里寻常见，崔九堂前几度闻。
> 正是江南好风景，落花时节又逢君。

忧愁使他的目力达到深远处，使他感觉灵敏。他的同情心不只
限于人类。例如，他有一首诗，赠给他骑过多年的病马的，是
很动人的：

> 乘尔亦已久，天寒关塞深。
> 尘中老尽力，岁晚病伤心。
> 毛骨岂殊众，驯良犹至今。
> 物微意不浅，感动一沉吟。

他对大自然的态度是有一种极诚挚的热情。像一个真正提倡民
治主义者，他看待世人一律平等，像一个大家庭里的人待他的
亲人一样。就是飞禽、走兽、鱼介、昆虫、花卉之类，也都好
像对他叹吐心事，因为它们知道杜甫是它们的患难兄弟，是它
们的同情者。杜甫并不以为它们有人类之灵性，在他看来，它
们多感情的心乃是我们五官所能接触的现实。例如，地球：

> 殷殷寻地脉。

谁较狗更多义气：

> 旧犬知愁恨，垂头傍我床。

＊　　＊　　＊

> 旧犬喜我归，低徊入衣裾。

即使就是一个小小的促织好像也有灵魂：

ON THE CRICKET

The cricket is a tiny little thing,

And yet how touching are its melancholy notes!

Feeling too chilly to sing under the roots of grass,

It comes indoors to keep you company under the bed.

Its music can melt a lonely traveler into tears,

And make a widow feel as though the dawn would never come.

What silk-strings and bamboo-pipes are half as moving

As this simple music of Nature?

On a withering orange-tree he observed feelingly:

Seared, half-dead leaves

Still cling on to the withered branches:

For it would break their hearts

To bid goodbye to their old homes.

To him, the hearts of these half-dead leaves have just as much objective reality as his own heart, of which he wrote after an attack of paralysis:

My heart is half-dead, with the other half still feeling the wounds of life.

促织甚微细，哀音何动人。

草根吟不稳，床下意相亲。

久客得无泪，故妻难及晨。

悲丝与急管，感激异天真。

对于一枝干枯的橘树，他也会观察得很动人：

萧萧半死叶，未忍别故枝。

在他看来，这些半枯的黄叶，像他自己的心一样，也有客观的现实。在他患了麻痹症后，关于他自己的心，曾有这样一句：

犹伤半死心。

VI. SUMMER: ITS PLEASANT SHADES

Fair, kind, and true, have often liv'd alone,

Which three till now, never kept seat in one.

—*Shakespeare*

When sorrow comes, read Tu Fu and Han Yu,

And you will feel as though a fairy hand were scratching at your itch!

—*Tu Mu*

In motion, it was like thunder and lightning boiling with intense anger:

At rest, it was like a calm ocean crystallized into serene light.

—*Tu Fu on a "Sword Dance"*

So far, we have only seen Summer in its dinner jacket, as it were. Now we want to see it in slippers and dressing gown. Who has not known some gracious hours of a breezy Summer afternoon, when the air is filled with the warm aroma of roses and the lulling drone of insects, when the cows drowse lazily in the wide meadows, when Nature itself seems to unbutton its waistcoat and put its feet up? In fact, Su Shun-ching, a great poet of the Sung Dynasty, seems to regard this aspect of Summer as its very essence; for in a poem on "The Idea of Summer," he says:

In a secluded summer house, I sleep supinely on a cool mat of fine bamboo.

The pomegranate is in full bloom and glitters through the screens.

The ground is full of shades cast by the leafy trees in the noontide sun.

Between my dreams I catch some intermittent notes of the darting orioles.

Nobody can appreciate and enjoy such moments of lassitude more than Tu Fu himself:

A gentle breeze is blowing, butterflies are frolicking.

Flowers are blazing, and honey bees buzzing.

I sip wine leisurely to enjoy its fine flavors deeply,

I compose a poem and weigh its merits on the delicate scales of my
  mind.

And nobody can know more intimately the diligent indolence of a
Summer day:

HOME JOYS

My home is girdled by a limpid stream,
  And there in summer days life's movements pause,

陆　夏之清光

> 真、善、美，各居一方，直到现在，尚未联系。
>
> ——莎士比亚
>
> 杜诗韩集愁来读，似倩麻姑痒处抓。　　——杜牧
>
> 来如雷霆收震怒，罢如江海凝清光。
>
> ——杜甫《观公孙大娘弟子舞剑器行》

我们只看了夏季的正面，现在我们要看夏季的侧影。谁不欢喜清风徐来的夏暮，空气中荡漾着玫瑰花的馥郁，小虫们慢慢地歌唱，母牛在无边的草地上懒洋洋地躺着，大自然好像也解开她的胸衣，跷起足来休息？诚然，宋朝大诗人苏舜钦认为懒洋洋的闲适是夏季的精粹，在《夏意》那首诗里他说：

> 别院深深夏簟清，石榴开遍透帘明。
> 树阴满地日当午，梦觉流莺时一声。

没有人较杜甫更善欣赏这种舒适的懒倦：

> 风轻粉蝶喜，花暖蜜蜂喧。
> 把酒宜深酌，题诗好细论。

也没有人较他更熟悉夏日勤力的怠惰（《江村》）：

> 清江一曲抱村流，长夏江村事事幽。

Save where some swallow flits from beam to beam,

    And the wild sea-gull near and nearer draws.

The good wife rules a paper board for chess;

    The children beat a fish-hook out of wire;

My ailments call for physic more or less,

    What else should this poor frame of mine require?

(Giles' version)

If we remember that there were days in Summer when Tu Fu was simply maddened by the heat and felt like uttering a loud cry, we cannot help wondering what various qualities are contained in Summer's bosom. The same holds for the poetry of Tu Fu. We have already heard some of his loud cries. Now we shall address ourselves to those charming poems which he hit off in a light mood, when he took life easy and his high-strung nerves had lapsed into a sort of sweet torpor. For Tu Fu is not only a nightingale who sings so loud that the hawthorn seems too frail for the vigor of his song, but also a blackbird whose whistle, as Richard Jefferies knew so well, is very human, like someone playing the flute, who strives to express his keen appreciation of the loveliness of the days, the golden glory of the meadow, the light, and the luxurious shadows.

First let us take up some of his delectable Nature poems, which present a veritable riot of roses. We have to content ourselves with a few specimens here:

(1) BEAUTIES OF NATURE

Sprinkling a footpath, aspen flowers spread a white carpet.

Floating on a brooklet, the lotus-leaves overlap like green coins.

Amidst bamboo-shoots baby-pheasants lie hidden from the human eye.

On the sand young wild ducks nestle quietly 'neath their mothers' wings.

(2) A COMPLAINT TO SPRING

The sorrows of an exile fill my eyes and inebriate my heart.

The vagabond Spring Genie has arrived around the river-bower.

He sends all the buds into flowering—rash enough on his part!

And what is more, he teaches the nightingales to sing with such

persistent power!

(3) THE THIEVERY OF THE SPRING WIND

The peaches and pears planted with my own hands are not without owner.

My walls are low, 'tis true, but they enclose a humble home.

The East Wind apparently took me for a fool!

Like a burglar in the night he broke down some sprays of my flowers!

自去自来梁上燕，相亲相近水中鸥。

老妻画纸为棋局，稚子敲针作钓钩。

多病所需惟药物，微躯此外更何求？　（英译：翟理思）

倘使我们记得杜甫有时候被炎热所烦扰，暴躁嘶喊，我们不禁奇怪夏季的胸怀中有多少不同的特质。杜甫的诗也是如此。我们已听见他竭力大叫，现在我们来看看他心境宽逸、乐天知命时的作品。他不仅是一头不顾喉中刺荆而泣血鸣啭的夜莺，并且还是一只山鸟。这山鸟的歌声是有人性的，像玉箫那般地悦耳（理查德·杰弗里斯对此相当熟稔），表象它欣赏这天气的可爱，这青草、阳光、深荫的美丽。

现在我们先看他愉快的自然诗——一群可爱玫瑰花——我们能这样称呼它。因为篇幅关系，我们只能录下数行：

（一）绝句漫兴九首·其七

糁径杨花铺白毡，点溪荷叶叠青钱。

笋根雉子无人见，沙上凫雏傍母眠。

（二）绝句漫兴九首·其一

眼见客愁愁不醒，无赖春色到江亭。

即遣花开深造次，便教莺语太丁宁。

（三）绝句漫兴九首·其二

手种桃李非无主，野老墙低还是家。

恰似春风相欺得，夜来吹折数枝花。

(4) THE LAVISH HOSPITALITY OF SPRING

The river deep, the bamboos quiet,

Only a couple of homes around here.

The fussy flowers, red and white,

Vie with one another in beauty and charm.

Now I have found the place to requite

The lavish hospitality of Spring!

All that I need is sweet wine

To sweeten the rest of my days.

(5) MADAM HUANG'S GARDEN

Rows upon rows of flowers

In the little garden of Madam Huang!

All the branches are heavy-laden

With countless clusters of flowers.

The carefree butterflies loiter around them,

And start dancing from time to time.

The lovely orioles are intoxicated with freedom.

"Cheerio, cheerio!" they sing.

(6) THE RIOT OF FLOWERS

The endless flowers on the river bank,

How they crash the gates of my eyes and irritate my soul!

I have no place to complain of their nuisance,

I am simply maddened by their colors.

I called on my southern neighbor.

Who, like myself, has a great liking for wine.

For ten days I have drunk with him,

Leaving an empty bed at home!

(7) AN INVITATION TO THE HERONS

The herons used to come to the front of our door,

But for reasons unknown to me they have ceased to visit us.

Today I chanced upon them on the sandy beach.

They looked at me with suspicious eyes.

From now on they should know I have nothing in my sleeves,

And come as many times as they wish in the course of a day.

(8) THE SWALLOWS

My thatched studio is small and low,

And yet the swallows have taken a fancy to it.

See, my little friends, how you have soiled my harp and books!

Hey! Don't drive the insects to slap my face!

(9) TAKE IT EASY!

From the court every eve to the pawnshop I pass,

To come back from the river the drunkest of men;

As often as not I'm in debt for my glass;—

Well, few of us live to be three score and ten.

（四）江畔独步寻花·其三
江深竹静两三家，多事红花映白花。
报答春光知有处，应须美酒送生涯。

（五）江畔独步寻花·其六
黄四娘家花满蹊，千朵万朵压枝低。
留连戏蝶时时舞，自在娇莺恰恰啼。

（六）江畔独步寻花·其一
江上被花恼不彻，无处告诉只颠狂。
走觅南邻爱酒伴，经旬出饮独空床。

（七）三绝句·其二
门外鸬鹚去不来，沙头忽见眼相猜。
自今已后知人意，一日须来一百回。

（八）绝句漫兴九首·其三
熟知茅斋绝低小，江上燕子故来频。
衔泥点污琴书内，更接飞虫打着人。

（九）曲江二首·其二
朝回日日典春衣，每日江头尽醉归。
酒债寻常行处有，人生七十古来稀。

The butterfly flutters from flower to flower,

    The dragonfly sips and springs lightly away,

Each creature is merry its brief little hour,

    So let us enjoy our short life while we may.

                        (Giles' version)

(10) SOME SELECTED LINES AND STANZAS

A quiet temple thick-set with flowers;

A sequestered lake hidden in the fine bamboos.

Oh where come the passionate songs of the nightingale?

All alone he has been singing his heart out for hours.

             *   *   *

What a lovely patch of green!

I know it's grass on the other side of the lake.

What a glorious stretch of crimson!

I see it's the clouds beyond the eastern sea.

             *   *   *

Patches of green have whirled away from us:

We have just passed by some lovely ridges.

Look! There is something yellow in front of us!

I see the orange trees are coming toward us.

                  ("Things Seen on a Boat Trip")

             *   *   *

A cluster of red spottings—

The flowers in the corner of the house!

A patch of green loveliness—

The grass by the side of the wall!

             *   *   *

A tortoise leaves a watery path behind it,

As it sails slowly through the duckweeds.

             *   *   *

Kingfishers are chirping on a clothes-line.

A dragonfly rests motionless on the silken cord of a fishing rod.

                    *　　*　　*

Entering into the peach blossoms,

Redness grows soft and tender.

Returning to the willow leaves,

Greenness becomes fresh and new.

                    *　　*　　*

The water being calm, the shadow of the tower stands motionless.

                    *　　*　　*

穿花蛱蝶深深见，点水蜻蜓款款飞。

传语风光共流转，暂时相赏莫相违。（英译：翟理思）

（十）选句

花浓春寺静，竹细野池幽。

何处莺啼切，移时独未休。

                    *　　*　　*

碧知湖外草，红见海东云。

                    *　　*　　*

青惜峰峦过，黄知橘柚来。　　　　　　　　　　　　（《放船》）

                    *　　*　　*

红绽屋角花，碧委墙隅草。

                    *　　*　　*

龟开萍叶过。

                    *　　*　　*

翡翠鸣衣桁，蜻蜓立钓丝。

                    *　　*　　*

红入桃花嫩，青归柳叶新。

                    *　　*　　*

水静楼阴直。

                    *　　*　　*

The dark ravine oozes with the music of silence.

The bright moonlight is being sifted through the thick foliage.

*　　*　　*

Ting, ting goes the woodman's axe,

And the mountain becomes the more solitary and silent for the sound.

*　　*　　*

A tiny rivulet trickles like a hidden thread through a flower-path.

Spring stars girdle my grass hut like a necklace of pearls.

*　　*　　*

The emeraldine fine bamboos, in the gentle caress of the wind,

Are as coy and quiet as a little maiden.

The red water-lilies, bathed in the rain,

Send forth whiffs after whiffs of invisible incense.

*　　*　　*

A petal falls! The oriole chases after it,

Taking it for a butterfly.

What is that noise on the brooklet?

Oh I see, a mink has caught a poor fish!

*　　*　　*

Countless dragonflies are darting up and down in a group.

A pair of wild ducks float and dive together.

*　　*　　*

White sandy beaches and emerald bamboos

Embrace the river village in eventide.

The wooden door of my humble house

Seems to hold a hearty *tête-à-tête* with the new moon.

*　　*　　*

The Autumn water is clear and fathomless.

It cleanses and refreshes the heart of a lonely traveler.

*　　*　　*

The nice rain knows its season,

It is born of Spring.

It follows the wind secretly into the night,

And showers its blessings, silently and softly, upon everything.

*   *   *

The peach-blossoms and the pear-blossoms

Follow closely upon one another's heels to the ground.

The yellow birds and the white birds

Sometimes mingle together in their flight.

*   *   *

阴壑生虚籁，月林散清影。
*   *   *
伐木丁丁山更幽。
*   *   *
暗水流花径，春星带草堂。
*   *   *
风含翠筱娟娟静，雨裛红蕖冉冉香。
*   *   *
花妥莺捎蝶，溪喧獭趁鱼。
*   *   *
无数蜻蜓齐上下，一双鸂鶒对沉浮。
*   *   *
白沙翠竹江村暮，相送柴门月色新。
*   *   *
秋水清无底，萧然净客心。
*   *   *
好雨知时节，当春乃发生。
随风潜入夜，润物细无声。
*   *   *
桃花细逐杨花落，黄鸟时兼白鸟飞。
*   *   *

The birds are the whiter for the blue of the river;

The flowers almost burn on the green hills.

*　　*　　*

A lamp glimmers upon my sleeplessness.

Inwardly calm, I begin to smell the ethereal scent of incense.

In the depth of the night the temple strikes me with a sudden awe.

The tinkling of the golden bells by the wind brings silence to the fore.

Blackness has enveloped the courtyard with all its Spring colors.

Dark fragrance is haunting this stainless spot on earth.

*　　*　　*

Darting upward, a bee gets entangled in a falling catkin.

Forming a queue, the ants are crawling up to a withered pear.

*　　*　　*

I seem to see Lightness itself!

Some stray feathers are sailing before the wind.

Recovering from a state of self-forgetfulness,

I have caught myself counting the stamens of a flower!

*　　*　　*

Aboating in a Spring river, I fell into a trance,

And felt as though I were sitting in Heaven!

Looking at the flowers through my old eyes,

I thought the air must have been very foggy!

*　　*　　*

A gentle shower, and the little fish come to the surface;

A little breeze, and the swallows are darting with slanting wings.

*　　*　　*

The bees and butterflies are all instinct with life;

A beautiful dragonfly looks stealthily at a passing shrike.

*　　*　　*

The maples and orange trees are playing for us a wonderful orchestra of
colors!

*　　*　　*

The evening sun is smoking the fine grass.
The luminous river is sparkling through the screen.

    *   *   *

But for the moon hanging above the green cliff,
Sorrow would have killed a white-headed man!

    *   *   *

I get up late and everything is quiet at home.
Indolence makes the place doubly cozy.

江碧鸟逾白，山青花欲燃。

    *   *   *

灯影照无睡，心清闻妙香。
夜深殿突兀，风动金银铛。
天黑闭春院，地清栖暗芳。

    *   *   *

仰蜂黏落絮，行蚁上枯梨。

    *   *   *

见轻吹鸟毳，随意数花须。

    *   *   *

春水船如天上坐，老年花似雾中看。

    *   *   *

细雨鱼儿出，微风燕子斜。

    *   *   *

蜜蜂蝴蝶生情性，偷眼蜻蜓避伯劳。

    *   *   *

枫林橘树丹青合。

    *   *   *

夕阳薰细草，江色映疏帘。

    *   *   *

若无青嶂月，愁杀白头人。

    *   *   *

晚起家何事，无营地转幽。

*   *   *

The waters being deep, the fish are extremely happy.

The forest being thick, the birds feel quite at home.

*   *   *

Unable to move about freely,

I looked up at the feathered ones shame-facedly.

Before we proceed further with our promenade in the garden of Tu Fu, let us pause awhile to examine the little posy of flowers we have already gathered together, and, if possible, to count their stamens and pistils just for the sheer pleasure of it. To drop metaphor and to speak plainly, what are some of the qualities that have revealed themselves to us in reading over the above specimens? I wish I could have a hearty *tête-à-tête* with the reader over a glass of beer, and sort out patiently between us one quality after another until everything is straightened out. But as this is impossible in the nature of things, I have to play solitaire. The first thing that impresses me is the remarkable power of observation with which our poet seems to be endowed. His mind is microscopic in intensity. It seems nothing is too small for it to record graphically. I am reminded of some of our artists, now too few, who could carve a wonderful landscape upon the very tiny kernel of a fruit. Among poets, John Keats seems to possess the same quality to a similar degree. I can never forget the thrill that went through my mind when, reading his "Endymion," I came upon such a passage as this:

> ...Hereat the youth
>
> Look'd up: a conflicting of shame and ruth
>
> Was in his plaited brow: yet, his eyelids
>
> Widened a little, as when Zephyr bids
>
> A little breeze to creep between the fans
>
> Of careless butterflies...

Another noteworthy thing about Tu Fu is that he is a past master of the chiaroscuro, who likes to put things in black and white. He sees contrasts in colors, and in other things for that matter. The white birds look whiter against the background of the blue waters, and the red flowers seems to pop out from the green hills and burn like candles. He pits a white-headed man against a green cliff, a grass hut against a necklace of stars, a grey wooden door against the new moon, maples against orange trees, and so on and so forth. I have found him using the same trick a thousand times, and every time he seems to attain the

*   *   *

水深鱼极乐，林茂鸟知归。

*   *   *

伫立东城隅，怅望高飞禽。

在杜甫的诗园中走得更远前，我们应该细察我们已经收集的小花，倘使可能的话，数计它们的心蕊。不用隐喻，就坦白地说，在上面的几行里，我们能发现些什么特点？我希望能同读者们面面晤谈，手握啤酒一杯，耐心地研究每首诗的特点。可是这在事实上是不可能的，我也只能唱独脚戏。杜甫给我最深的印象是老天赐给他的观察力，其深刻独到之处，实非他人所可及。他的热情是无微不至的，看上来天下好像没有东西不足他的记述。这使我想起我们几个能在水果核心上雕刻风景的手艺家。在别的诗人中，济慈好似也有这种特才。我永远不会忘记读他的《恩底弥翁》这几行时，透过我脑海那种因快乐而致的震颤：

……这少年

举首仰视：他的眉辫画出

羞耻和怜悯的冲突：

当西风微微闪过蝴蝶的翅翼时，

他的眼睛也睁大了一点……

另一件值得注意的是，杜甫擅长阴阳画法，喜以浓淡衬配。【他看到颜色里的相互映衬，也看到其他事物里类似的对比。】有了碧水作背景，白鸟就愈形洁白；在青山上，红花就像蜡烛燃烧。他将一座青崖衬托一个白发老翁，将一串星珠衬配茅屋，将新月衬托陈旧的木屋，将枫树衬托橘树等等。这技巧我发现他重复了不下千余

effect he wants to achieve. For instance, in a poem on the great general Li Kwang-pi, we find a most touching line:

> His head white, his heart as red as ever.

Here again the effect is enhanced by means of a deliberate contrast. As a matter of fact, he makes no secret of his deliberate and patient labor. He confesses it:

> If my words fail to thrill and please,
> I should not die in peace!

It seems to me what he says of the silk-maid is equally true of himself:

> With a loving solicitude, a pretty girl
> Has ironed the silk till it's perfectly smooth;
> And made it into a nice cloth,
> Which appears a seamless whole.

Perhaps, it may be said (as Dr. Sun Fo once pointed out to me a few years ago) that his descriptions of Nature are not so spontaneous as those of Wang Wei and Li Po, but what he loses in spontaneity he gains in emphasis. And we should remember that they belong to different seasons, and Summer cannot reproduce the virginal freshness of Spring, any more than Spring could have attained to the wide awareness, incisive clarity and white-hot concentration of Summer. The other day I ran across in James Joyce's *Ulysses* a quaint expression: *Poetical idea pink, then golden, then grey, then black. Still true to life also.* I find it somewhat true also of the Poetry of T'ang. For while the Spring poets were pink, Tu Fu is golden, and there can be no reversal of the seasons. As to whether Autumn and Winter will be grey and black, we shall see later.

But what makes this little posy of flowers and petals especially lovely is the sweet perfume of sympathy emanating constantly from them.

> The rose looks fair, but fairer we it deem,
> For that sweet odor which doth in it live.

For our poet has a genuine love for the little things in Nature. When the herons ceased to come to him, he really missed them. When he saw the birds moving freely about among the woods, he really felt a sense of shame within him, because he had lost his freedom at that time. On the other hand, when he called the flowers "a nuisance" and the Spring Genie "a vagabond," and complained about the swallows soiling his harp and books and driving the insects to slap his face, he really loved them

次，每次都能成功。在他歌颂大将军李光弼那首诗内有如此动人的一句，"白头虽老赤心存"，这里胜人之处就在物色的衬配。他并不否认他勤孜的工作，他干脆地说"语不惊人死不休"！他描摹一个织女的话，对他自己也极适合，"美人细意熨帖平，裁缝灭尽针线迹"（《白丝行》）。

或像孙哲生博士数年前对我说的，杜甫描摹大自然的诗不及李白、王维的来得活泼自然；但是讲到表情力量，却不是李白、王维所能及的。我们不能忘却他们属于不同的季候：夏季缺乏春季纯洁的活跃，春季没有夏季的醒觉、锐利、明晰和专心。日前，在乔伊斯的《尤利西斯》看到很奇怪的一句，"诗意先红，后黄金色，再后灰，末了黑。生活也是如此"。我想唐诗也是如此。春季诗人的颜色是红的，杜甫是黄金色的，这是不能颠倒更换的。秋冬是不是灰黑，以后我们就能看到。

这一小群花朵的特别可爱处就在它不单是美丽，而且不断地射发出同情的芬芳：

> 这玫瑰花是美丽的，
> 但是为了其中的馥郁，
> 我们说它是更美。

杜甫真挚地怜爱大自然的一切，鸬鹚不飞到他的视线内，他就觉得若有所失；当他看见鸟雀在丛林中欢乐跳跃，他就觉得羞耻，因为他自己没有自由。反之，当他说"江上被花恼不彻"、叫春色"无赖"时，当他怨恨玷污他书琴、驱使飞虫吵烦他的轻燕时，他只深爱它

so much that he wanted to hide it, just as a fond mother would say to her guests what a naughty boy her little Johnnie is. Once he invited some friends to his house, and complained to them about the deafening noise made by the cicadas:

> Who says my home is quiet?
> Listen, what a row the cicada makes!

Maybe, that time he was truly annoyed, but who can blame him for that little aberration from his usual good humor, seeing that no less a lover of the cicada than J. H. Fabre has felt the same:

> Ah! Creature possessed, the plague of my dwelling, which I hoped would be so peaceful!—the Athenians, they say, used to hang you up in a little cage, the better to enjoy your song. One were well enough, during the drowsiness of digestion; but hundreds, roaring all at once, assaulting the hearing until thought recoils—this indeed is torture! You put forward, as excuse, your rights as the first occupant. Before my arrival the two plane-trees were yours without reserve; it is I who have intruded, have thrust myself into their shade. I confess it: yet muffle your cymbals, moderate your arpeggio, for the sake of your historian!

At any rate, Tu Fu is one of the most humorous poets I have ever read. It would seem that his dire poverty made him extremely rich in humor. Here are some lines from "The Song of an Empty Pouch":

> Let others take part in the mad hunt for riches;
> *My* way leads through difficulties and straits!
> ...
> To spare my pouch the shame of complete emptiness,
> I leave my last cash in it to keep it company.

On another occasion, he sang about a fish-shaped pouch of red silk, given to him by the Emperor as a kind of badge:

> I am still wearing the fish-shaped pouch,

Awarded to me by His Majesty.

What if I am old and poor!

The pouch contains at least an echo!

The jolly old man not only derived much fun from poverty, but also enjoyed other misfortunes of life, such as having his hat blown off by the wind:

们，不过不直说罢了，正如一个慈母对客人说她的爱儿是多么地会胡闹一样。有一次他邀请几位朋友到他家里叙谈，听了知了震耳之声，就说"叶密鸣蝉稠……孰谓吾庐幽"。这次，我们的幽默诗人真正地觉得烦恼了，但是谁能责怪他一时的脾气？法布尔也极爱好知了，但有时也不免说：

> 疯狂的小东西，你是我的烦恼，你弄得我的住所多么吵闹不安！有人说雅典人将你禁闭在一只小笼内，然后欣赏你的歌唱。饭后闲坐时，听你一个的声音正好，几百个一起大叫，妨害我的听觉，扰乱我的思想——那真是苦楚！你说你较我先到这里，应有优先权；在我没来之前，这二棵筱悬木全是你的；我闯入其间，强占它的绿荫。我承认一切，但是为了你的历史家，我请求你抑制你的乐器，减轻你弦线的声音。

总之，杜甫是我所知悉的诗人中最幽默的一位，物质的贫穷使他特别富于幽默。下面四行录自《空囊》：

> 世人共卤莽，吾道属艰难。
> ……
> 囊空恐羞涩，留得一钱看。

另一次，他吟一首诗关于明皇赐给他的绯鱼袋：

> 病减诗仍拙，吟多意有余。
> 莫看江总老，犹被赏时鱼。

这善谑老人不但在贫穷中找到快乐，并且还将一切的不幸引以为乐。帽子被风吹落，他说：

What a shame! The wind blew off my hat,

Exposing to the full light a bald head!

I had a good laugh and requested a bystander

To put the hat on my head with special care.

Even more serious misfortunes than this didn't dampen his good spirits. When he became deaf he sang:

Deaf have my ears been since last month.

My eyes—ah, when will they be blind?

Monkey howlings no autumn tears will call forth from me.

Nor will the noisy chirps of sparrows breed my evening sorrows.

Just now I saw yellow leaves fall from the mountain trees,

And I asked my son, "The wind is roaring, isn't it?"

(Wen Yuan-ning's version)

Here is another delightful piece of self-mockery:

With my face turned upward, I gazed and gazed at the birds.

When I heard someone call somebody else, I answered, "Yes, I am coming!"

In reading books I skip over difficult words.

In drinking wine one bottle is not enough.

This kind of humor, that is, making jokes at the expense of oneself, is what I should like to call a typically Chinese humor. Su Tung-po seems to be a worthy follower of Tu Fu, since he too could make fun of himself:

I am an old man, and yet I wear a flower in my hair!

I am not ashamed, because I have a thick-skinned face!

But I see the flower is blushing on my head,

To find itself in such an unfitting place!

I am drunk, and need someone to lean upon as I walk home;

It will give the pedestrians a pleasant surprise.

At least half of the window-curtains will be lifted up,

And pretty girls will peep at me with admiring eyes!

The reason why this type of humor is particularly valuable to us is because it is a corrective to our excessive fear of losing face. When we are poor, we pretend to be rich. When we are bald-headed, we pretend to be as hairy as a Pekinese. When we are deaf, we pretend to hear. When we are fools, we pretend to know a great deal by keeping a sage-like silence. And even when we are dead, we pretend to be very much alive by making our funeral procession as pompous an affair as a military parade. When we are humbugs, we pretend to be big bugs. In one word, we are afraid to be laughed at, or looked down upon. When, therefore, we see real big

> 羞将短发还吹帽，笑倩旁人为正冠。

就是再严重些的不幸也不能扫他的兴，耳聋时他说：

> 眼复几时暗，耳从前月聋。
> 猿鸣秋泪缺，雀噪晚愁空。
> 黄落惊山树，呼儿问朔风。　　　　（英译：温源宁）

这里又是一首可人的自嘲诗：

> 仰面贪看鸟，回头错应人。
> 读书难字过，对酒满壶频。

这种自嘲幽默，我认为是标准中国幽默。苏东坡好像也是杜甫的信徒，因为他也能取笑自己（《吉祥寺赏牡丹》）：

> 人老簪花不自羞，花应羞上老人头。
> 醉归扶路人应笑，十里珠帘半上钩。

这种幽默对我们特别有益，因为它能矫正我们怕丢脸的心理。穷的时候，我们装像有钱；秃顶的时候，我们装得像多毛的小狮狗；聋的时候，我们装作听觉锐敏；不知的时候，我们就缄口不言，装出一副哲人样子，使别人以为我们满腹经纶；就是我们死的时候，我们也要丧仪排仗弄得像军事会操那般炫人眼目。其实我们是骗子，却装出大亨的样子。一言蔽之，我们怕别人取笑我们、蔑视我

bugs like Tu Fu and Su Tung-po enjoying such a good laugh over their own follies, we feel that after all our face is not such a precious thing. I would call the Tufuish humor our national humor, precisely because it helps to expose the most prevailing humbug among us. For if we want to save our soul, we must first be prepared to lose our face.

But the question is, where did Tu Fu get all his humor? My answer is that it was partly due to natural endowment, but mostly due to suffering. For one thing, suffering makes the prospect of life brighter by lessening the fear of death. The evanescence of life which to the happy ones is such a tragic idea is a source of happiness to the sufferer. As Tu Fu says:

> My path is paved with thorns all through.
> Thank God, my days are numbered too!

This is exactly what St. Thérèse of Lisieux says in a letter to her sister: "Thought of the shortness of life gives me courage, and helps me to put up with the weariness of the journey. What matters a little toil upon earth?" For another thing, anyone who has experienced great sorrows and emerged from them without a nervous breakdown will be able to stand the little annoyances of life and even regard them as sweetmeats. But before I ride my hobby horse of philosophizing, let us first listen to his own story:

> After a whole year's journey, I arrived at my thatched hut,
> And found my wife in rags and tatters.
> Deeply touched, our loud cries were echoed by the sighing pines,
> And our stifled sobs blended with the sad music of the flowing brook.
> My little son whom I used to fondle so much looked paler than the snow.
> Seeing his father, he turned away his face and wept silently.
> Dirty and greasy, he wore no socks on his feet.
> In front of the bed stood my two little girls, with their seamy dresses
>> barely covering their knees:
> I saw the embroidered sea-waves were all broken and disconnected.
> And the purple phoenixes and water-sprites dismembered beyond
>> recognition.

For several days, preyed upon by depression and illness,

I had lain in bed, vomiting and purging.

With no money in my purse,

How can I save my family from being frozen?

But my wife has taken out some old silk quilts,

And opened the cosmetics she had laid away during my absence.

I see beauty gradually returning to her emaciated face;

And the girls, idiotic little things, are combing their own hair.

They ape their mother in every way:

In their morning coiffeur, they help themselves to the cosmetics;

们。所以，当我们看见杜甫、苏东坡那辈"大亨"取笑他们自己时，我们就觉得我们的面子并不十分可贵。我说杜甫的幽默是我们民族幽默，因它能帮助我们揭穿我们自欺欺人的心理。倘使我们要拯救我们灵魂的话，我们首先要预备失脸。

但是问题来了，杜甫的幽默是从哪里来的？一半固然是天赋的，大半却是从患难中得来的。苦难能减轻我们对死亡的恐惧，因此我们也就能欣赏生活。在养尊处优辈看来，生命之短促是悲惨的；但是在患难者看来，它却是快乐的泉源。杜甫说：

> 世路虽多梗，吾生亦有涯。

这也就是圣女小德兰给她姐姐那封信里的话："想到生活之短促，我就勇气百倍，忍受这旅程的厌倦。这地球上的一点小事有什么了不得？"凡经历过重大的悲痛而神经不受影响者，一定能忍受生活片段的烦恼而反视之为乐事。在我没有穷究哲理前，让我们先听杜甫自己的话（《北征》）：

> 经年至茅屋，妻子衣百结。恸哭松声回，悲泉共幽咽。
> 平生所娇儿，颜色白胜雪。见爷背面啼，垢腻脚不袜。
> 床前两小女，补绽才过膝。海图坼波涛，旧绣移曲折。
> 天吴及紫凤，颠倒在裋褐。老夫情怀恶，呕泄卧数日。
> 那无囊中帛，救汝寒凛栗。粉黛亦解包，衾裯稍罗列。
> 瘦妻面复光，痴女头自栉。学母无不为，晓妆随手抹。

> They paint their faces haphazardly with vermillion and white powder,
>
> And draw their eye-brows so broad that they look like comic masks.
>
> Coming back alive, and looking fondly at my kids, I almost forget our dire penury.
>
> And what naughty kids they are! They storm me with endless questions, and even pull my beard!
>
> But who can be angry with them just now?
>
> When I remember how miserable I was in the hands of the brigands,
>
> I find it very sweet indeed to be pestered by the noise and clamor of my little ones.
>
> Newly reunited, it is for us to be nice to each other and make the best of life,
>
> Before we think of the problem of livelihood.

Anybody who has had any dealings at all with children will sympathize with our poet. Even Confucius knew that the kids were not easy things to handle. "When you treat them too intimately, they would throw all your dignity to the winds." For instance, they pull your beard. I am sure Confucius must have had some unpleasant experience of that sort, before he could utter such a pungent truth. But I am not thinking so much of the dignity factor as the mental wear-and-tear one has to undergo in living with lots of children. Just at the time when you sit down at your desk rolling up your sleeves as if you were going to produce a real masterpiece, you hear a noise in the next room which sounds very much like a hurdy-gurdy. Just when you are not in a talking mood, they pester you with questions, some of which are not particularly easy to answer. "Daddy, how high is the sky?" Not wanting to show the seamy side of your knowledge, you take down from the shelves such books as Jeans' *The Mysterious Universe*, Eddington's *The Expanding Universe* and even Einstein's *The Theory of Relativity*, and after a few feverish searchings in their pages, you find no answer and try to save your face by corking their mouths with some candies. And what is even worse, when you are in a talking mood and feel like telling them a nice Christmas story, they call you down by "Aw, nuts!" and announce the end of your story even before you have started, and you would be a very lucky man indeed if you happen to grow no beard or moustache, although, it is true, your nose is always there to attract the unwelcome attention of the little fingers. Old Benchley knows very well what a trying thing it is to travel with a kiddie of three. And so did our poet, when he and his family, as refugees of war, had to travel on foot through rough roads and wild mountains:

My idiotic little girl, feeling the gnawing pangs of hunger, hit at my body;
She wailed loudly, and I was afraid the tigers and wolves might hear,
So I held her close to my bosom to stop her crying,
But she struggled hard and wailed even more furiously than before.

移时施朱铅，狼藉画眉阔。生还对童稚，似欲忘饥渴。
问事竟挽须，谁能即嗔喝？翻思在贼愁，甘受杂乱聒。
新归且慰意，生理焉得说！

同孩子们有过接触的人，一定会同情杜甫。【孔子也知道孩子不好对付，"近之则不逊"。他们可能会扯你的胡子，我敢肯定孔子一定有过这样的经历，才会有此论断。相较于自尊，和孩子在一起时精神上所遭受的损耗更甚。你刚刚坐到桌前，卷起袖子准备写就一篇辉煌巨著，隔壁房间传来手摇风琴的响声。你没心情讲话时，他们向你抛来一堆问题，有些问题还真不好回答——"爸爸，天有多高？"不想让他们知道你在知识上有所欠缺，你从书架上取下天文学家金斯爵士的《神秘的宇宙》、埃丁顿的《膨胀的宇宙》、爱因斯坦的《相对论》。疯狂翻找，未果，你只好用糖果堵他们的嘴来挽救颜面。还有更糟糕的：你心情不错，想给他们讲一个好听的圣诞故事，他们却说："哦，去你的吧！"你还没开始讲，故事就结束了。如果你碰巧没留胡子，那你真的很幸运。不过，你的鼻子总会吸引到那些小手指。】年老的本奇利知道，同三尺童子一起旅行是多么讨厌的事，杜甫亦然。他同他的家眷因兵燹步行避难，迂回峻山崎路：

痴女饥咬我，啼畏虎狼闻。
怀中掩其口，反侧声愈嗔。

There are innumerable accounts of his travels in his poems, but he has presented them in a nutshell in just two lines:

> For ten years, I have been tossed to and fro like a silken ball,
> And I had to carry my chicks along to the farthest ends of the earth.

All this may sound a little melancholy and not particularly humorous, but Tu Fu could very well answer in the words of Shakespeare, "I have neither the scholar's melancholy, which is emulation; nor the musician's, which is fantastical; nor the courtier's, which is proud; nor the soldier's, which is ambitious; nor the lawyer's, which is politic; nor the lady's, which is nice; nor the lover's, which is all these; but it is the melancholy of mine own, compounded of many simples, extracted from many objects, and indeed, the sundry contemplation of my travels; which, by often rumination, wraps me in a most humorous sadness." But you ask how one could be sad and humorous at the same time. As to this, Tu Fu himself has given us a clue to the answer:

> When I remember how miserable I was in the hands of the brigands,
> I find it very sweet indeed to be pestered by the noise and clamor of my little ones.

In suffering he has found the key to happiness. For happiness, like the boiling point, is relative. A given situation in life would pass unnoticed or even prove annoying if worse circumstances had not been experienced. In passing through sad circumstances to better ones, one feels the external pressure lightened, while the mind still retains the power of resistance called forth by the former situation; and there arises the boiling point of happiness. In order to be happy most of your days, you must always remember the blackest days of your life. Otherwise happiness will lead you a wild-goose chase. When a man is on the point of drowning, all he cares for is his life. But as soon as he gets ashore, he asks, "Where is my umbrella?" The wisdom of life consists in not asking for the lost umbrella. And herein lies the secret of Tu Fu's invincible cheerfulness of spirit. But of course, I don't mean to say that it is a very pleasant thing to lose your umbrella. No, it is a sad thing, especially to a poor man. What I mean is that since you are not drowned in water, that sadness at least ought to be drowned in humor, and when this happens you get what Shakespeare calls a humorous sadness.

Li Po was humorsome, because, the poor man, he remembered his happiest days. Tu Fu was humorous, because, the happy man, he remembered his darkest days. The former was like a speculator in Wall

他记述旅行的作品可说是不少，这里我们只须引证一句就可以见其战时奔波之一斑了，"十年蹀躞将雏远"。【这听上去有些忧郁，也不幽默。】我想杜甫的心境，可以借用莎士比亚的话来说明，"我没有士人好胜的忧郁，没有音乐家怪诞的忧郁，没有朝臣骄傲的忧郁，没有战士雄心的忧郁，没有律师机敏的忧郁，没有贵妇妩媚的忧郁，也没有情人包罗一切的忧郁。我的忧郁是我自己的，是多种从各式物体中提炼出来的药草合成的，其中有旅途中的沉思，时常将我笼罩在幽默的悲哀中"。你会疑问怎样一个人可以同时悲哀幽默，杜甫能给你这答案的线索：

> 翻思在贼愁，甘受杂乱聒。

在患难中他找到了快乐之门。快乐之沸点，我们知道，是相对的。俗语道："不知高山，焉知平地？"从一个凄惨的境况转到一个较好的境况，我们就觉得外面的压力自动减轻，可是我们的内心却仍旧保持先前凄惨境地所练成的忍受痛苦的力量，这样，快乐就达到了沸点。倘使你要终年快乐的话，必须记住你先前的惨况，否则快乐只能驱使你空中筑楼阁而已。一个人失足落水，他只要性命，别的在所不顾；挣扎了上岸以后，就问旁人说："我的雨伞在哪里？"人生的智慧就在不寻找这雨伞，这也就是杜甫终年常乐的秘密。当然，我绝不以为失掉雨伞是一件值得欢唱的事。不，这是一件不幸的事，尤其是在穷人。我意思你没在水中溺毙，你的悲哀应该在幽默中溺毙。这就是莎士比亚所说的幽默的悲哀。

李白是暴躁不安的，因为他这个可怜的人，记住他过去的黄金时代；杜甫是幽默的，因为他这个快乐的人，记住他最不幸的日子。

Street who bought at the highest quotation and watched the price go down every day until he found himself a bankrupt; but the latter was like one who sold short and watched himself growing richer every day until he became the biggest shareholder in the Bank of Happiness. For the fact is, Li Po regarded himself as an angel exiled, for reasons that mystified him, from Heaven; while Tu Fu regarded himself as a dead man miraculously come back home alive, and finding his wife and his little ones miraculously spared from the ravages of war. Here is another touching poem which the reader cannot afford to miss:

> The crimson clouds on the west
> Spread before me like a gorgeous panorama.
> The foot of the sun has just gone down
> Below the level of the earth.
> On arriving at the door of my thatched hut,
> I hear sparrows and other birds sing a chorus.
> At last, I am at home again
> After traveling a thousand *li*.
> My wife and my children marvel
> That I am still alive.
> Recovering from their first shock,
> They weep and wipe tears from their eyes.
> The world is still in a broil,
> And human life is like dust in the wind.
> Have I really returned alive?
> How precarious an event it looks!
> Our neighbors have come in crowds
> To peer at me over the walls.
> Moved by sympathy,
> They sigh and snivel.
> In the depth of the night.
> Under a glimmering candlelight,
> My wife and I sit silently face to face,—

It seems as though we had met in a dream.

And the interesting thing is that he had hardly expected his family to survive the horrible massacres perpetrated around his home of which he had learned. The following poem is too deservedly famous to omit even in such a casual survey as this:

Last year the T'ung Pass was broken through
By the rebel troops.
I was separated for a long time
From my wife and children.
In the summer of this year,
When grass and trees were growing thick,
I managed to run away from the brigands
And came here westward.

【前者就像华尔街的投资人，以最高的报价买进，看着价格逐日下跌，直到最后破产；后者则卖空，看着自己一天天变富，直到成为幸福银行的最大股东。】李白当他自己是天仙，不知为了什么缘故被谪下凡；杜甫当他自己是死后复活的人，他妻子儿女能逃出兵燹在他看来就是神迹。这里又是一首动人的诗，读者不能错过：

峥嵘赤云西，日脚下平地。
柴门鸟雀噪，归客千里至。
妻孥怪我在，惊定还拭泪。
世乱遭飘荡，生还偶然遂。
邻人满墙头，感叹亦歔欷。
夜阑更秉烛，相对如梦寐。

有趣的是，他并未料到他的家眷能避免可怕的屠杀。下面这首是名副其实地脍炙人口，就是像这种没有次序的研究也不能放过它：

去年潼关破，妻子隔绝久。
今夏草木长，脱身得西走。

Wearing hemp shoes,

I saw the Son of Heaven;

My sleeves were in rags and holes,

From which my two elbows peeped at His Majesty!

The court was touched by my return alive,

And my old friends pitied my ugly features.

In tears I accepted the censorship,

So grateful I was to the kind Emperor.

Though I was homesick,

I could not bring myself to broach the subject.

I sent a letter to San Ch'uan,

To ascertain whether my family was still there.

Later I heard that the whole village

Fell a prey to the barbarians;

Not a single life was spared,

Not even the dogs and cocks.

...

After such a wholesale massacre,

How can I expect my family to have survived alone?

I look at yonder precipitous mountains,

The whole earth seems to have become a den of tigers.

My sorrows form into a hard knot,

Which nobody can untie.

Since I sent the letter,

Ten months have elapsed.

Now I am no longer expecting any news.

On the contrary, I sorely fear lest any news should come.

I don't know why this sudden change from expectation to fear,—

This inch-long heart within me, what a mystery it is!

So, at the end of our journey, we find ourselves again at the threshold of mystery. Indeed, all roads seem to lead to it, provided they are long enough. We already saw how Li Po soared and soared until a limit was reached:

Let me lay down my cup for a moment and ask:
O Sky! Since how long did you have the moon?

Now we have watched Tu Fu diving like a bucket in a concealed well and exploring the penetralia of his heart and finally discovering its unfathomableness:

This inch-long heart within me, what a mystery it is!

It would seem the universe is a mystery in and out and whether you gauge it horizontally or perpendicularly. Then what have we got from our

麻鞋见天子，衣袖露两肘。
朝廷愍生还，亲故伤老丑。
涕泪授拾遗，流离主恩厚。
柴门虽得去，未忍即开口。
寄书问三川，不知家在否。
比闻同罹祸，杀戮到鸡狗。
……
几人全性命，尽室岂相偶。
嵚岑猛虎场，郁结回我首。
自寄一封书，今已十月后。
反畏消息来，寸心亦何有！

旅程的终点到了，我们仍旧站在玄妙之门的前面。诚然，任何道路，倘使够长的话，好像都通到玄妙之门。我们已看见李白向天飞冲，直到他碰到了顶点：

青天有月来几时？我今停杯一问之。

现在我们看见杜甫像一只深入隐井的水桶，探测他自己内心的深度，最后发现它的无底，"寸心亦何有"！

不论系纵地或横地衡量它，这宇宙看上来终是一个玄妙。我们

arduous pilgrimage to the shrine of Tu Fu? Nothing except that he has made us more aware of our ignorance and littleness. As he puts it explicitly:

Saints and sages regard themselves as little or nothing.

This humility is no false modesty, but is born of a true insight into the mystery of life. As Einstein says, "The most beautiful thing we can experience is the mysterious. It is the source of all true art and science. He to whom this emotion is a stranger, who can no longer pause to wonder and stand rapt in awe is as good as dead: his eyes are closed." And Tu Fu is such a great poet, precisely because he opens our eyes to the mystery that we carry within us, and thus bring us nearer to God who is the source of all mysteries.

向杜甫的圣庙进香，得到了些什么？除了他使我们明悉我们自己的无知和渺小，没有别的。他明坦地说"圣哲为心小一身"。

这种谦仰并不是假冒的虚逊，却是对生命之玄妙的认识。爱因斯坦说过，"我们经历中最美的是玄妙，它是一切真正科学、文艺的泉源。谁不会欣赏玄妙，不会对它惊叹神往，就等于死亡，因为他的眼睛是关闭的"。杜甫是一个伟大的诗人，正因为他睁开我们的眼睛，使我们看见自己的玄妙，就此将自己带近一切玄妙之源的上苍。

VII.   AN INTERLUDE

Salamander

Happy, happy glowing fire!

Zephyr

Fragrant air! delicious light!

Dusketha

Let me to my glooms retire!

Breama

I to green-weed rivers bright!

—*Keats, "Song of Four Faeries"*

The tendinous part of the mind, so to speak, is more developed in winter; the fleshy, in summer. I should say winter had given the bone and sinew to literature, summer the tissues and blood.

—*John Burroughs*

All sorts of things and weather

Must be taken in together

To make up a year.

—*Emerson*

"Sporadic great men," says William James, "come everywhere. But for a community to get vibrating through and through with intensely active life, many geniuses coming together and in rapid succession are required. This is why great epochs are so rare—why the sudden bloom of a Greece, an early Rome, a Renaissance, is such a mystery. Blow must follow blow so fast that no cooling can occur in the intervals. Then the mass of the nation grows incandescent, and may continue to glow by pure inertia long after the originators of its internal movement have passed away."

In this James has hit upon the first requisite, the *sine qua non*, of any vital movement in the cultural history of mankind. How well the poetry of T'ang fulfilled this condition can, among other evidences, be substantiated by the fact that around the date of Tu Fu's death there were born no less than three literary lions, each supreme in his own field. Tu

柒 夏秋之插曲

火神
快活、闪烁之火。
　和风
芬芳的气氛，愉快的兴奋。
　黄昏
让我在忧郁中退歇。
　鲫鱼
我到长满青草、活泼的河流中去。　　　——济慈《四仙歌》

脑中的腱在冬季比较来得发达，
脑中的肉在夏季比较来得发达。
我以为冬季供给文学的骨和腱，
夏季供给文学的纤维和血。　　　　　　——约翰·伯勒斯

各种景色，各种季候，
并在一起，方成为一年。　　　　　　　——爱默生

　　哲学家詹姆斯说："巨人在各处可以发现，可是整个社会的绝端活动的生活要是继续不断地在跳动，那么必须有大群的天才聚集在一起，连续不断地出现。因此，大时代就如此稀有了——这是为此，为什么有希腊、罗马文化的勃兴，以及文艺复兴的崛起，会变成这样难以解释的谜。槌击必须紧急相连，使其间没有冷下来的机会。必须如此，一个民族的文化才能白热化，即使就是在他们的先锋早已逝世了的时候，也能继续发扬光大。"

　　在这寥寥数语间，詹姆斯讲到了人类历史中任何文化运动的必具条件。唐诗发展之合乎条件（除了别的以外），可以在这里看到：大约在杜甫瞑目的时候，先后有三位巨人出世，每位都在他自己的

Fu passed away in 770. Two years before that date Han Yu had seen the light. Two years after that Po Chü-i came, accompanied by a lesser poet, Liu Yu-hsi, who was to be one of his life-long friends. And then the next year saw the birth of the last of the mighty triumvirate, Liu Chung-yuan.

There are also some interesting anecdotes which help us to visualize how popular a thing poetry had come to be in the whole period of T'ang. Once three poets, Wang Chih-huan, Kao Shih, and Wang Ch'ang-ling were having a *petit souper* together in a wine shop. There came later a group of actors from the Imperial Theater to attend a banquet that was being offered upstairs. Then a few sing-song girls also arrived one after another. A brilliant party it was, and music was soon started. The three poets, in a *jeu d'esprit*, agreed privately among themselves that they would determine their relative merits by the number of their songs that would be sung by the actors and sing-song girls on that occasion. By and by they heard an actor sing a song by Wang Ch'ang-ling, which contained these well-known lines:

> If my friends in Loyang should ask about me,
> Tell them that my heart is pure as the ice in a jade cup.

Thereupon Ch'ang-ling marked it down and said airily, "So friends, I have scored one." Then another actor took up a song by Kao Shih, which had these lines:

> On opening my handbag, tears wetted my breast;
> For I saw my sweetheart's letter of the other day.

With equal elation he marked it down and said, "So I too have scored one." Sometime later, another actor sang, and it was again a poem by Wang Ch'ang-ling. You can imagine how exalted he must have felt, having scored a second time. But think of poor Wang Chih-huan, who had none whatever to his credit! He certainly was greatly exasperated by the humiliation, but he did not give up hope. "These vulgar things, the actors, what do they know?" he blurted out. "It's in their nature to prefer the familiar to the exquisite. But I am quite confident that when it comes to the turn of the sing-song girls, the most beautiful one will sing one of my songs. I'll stake my life and honor upon it!" Curiously enough, it came off exactly as he had expected. For the most beautiful girl did pick up his song, which has been on the lips of every student of Chinese poetry for more than a millennium:

境界内称雄。杜甫死于 770 年，二年前韩愈出世，二年后白居易和他终身知友刘禹锡出世；再隔一年，柳宗元出世，凑成了一个庞大的三人团。

终唐之世，诗变成如何一样普遍的东西，是可以引几件有趣的故事来帮助我们想象的。有一次，王之涣、高适、王昌龄三人在酒楼小酌，刚巧对面来了一群伶人到楼座宴会上献技，接着又陆续来了一些歌妓。这是一个盛大的宴会，音乐不久即从上面悠悠传出。这三位诗人兴致正好，所以就彼此议定，以伶妓们歌诵他们作品次数的多寡断定他们天赋的高下。不久他们听见一个歌伶诵唱王昌龄的一首诗，其中有如此驰名的二行：

洛阳亲友如相问，一片冰心在玉壶。

昌龄随即画了一笔，就兴高采烈地说："朋友，我已有了一次了。"接着，另一位伶人高唱高适的一首诗，其中有如此二句：

开箧泪沾臆，见君前日书。

他的得意当然也不减于昌龄，也画了一笔，说："我也有了一次了。"须臾，歌声又从上面飘出，却又是王昌龄的一首。这时他的得意忘形是可想而知的了。可是看那个可怜的之涣，到现在还没有人诵唱他的作品！他的气馁是不容怀疑的，可是他并不绝望。"这辈俗人，"他突说，"懂些什么？他们原是那些舍雅而取俗的庸人。到歌妓们献技的时候，我深信，其中最美的一定会唱我的作品，我愿以性命名誉作赌。"说也奇怪，歌妓中最美的那个，果然选了他的一首诗，千年来我们不断地争诵它（《凉州词》）：

The Yellow River climbs up far into the white clouds;

The Great Wall runs through all the ridges like a continuous thread.

Why should the western pipe "complain about the willows"?

The breath of Spring has never passed beyond the Gate of Jade.

What a relief it must have given to Chih-huan! "You country boys," he said to his friends triumphantly, "did you think I was bragging?"

But, perhaps, no poet in the world, as Arthur Waley has assured us, has ever enjoyed greater contemporary popularity than Po Chü-i. Waley has put it so neatly that I want to borrow a passage from him:

His poems were "on the mouths of kings, princes, concubines, ladies, plough-boys, and grooms." They were inscribed "on the walls of village schools, temples, and ship-cabins." "A certain Captain Kao Hsia-yu was courting a dancing-girl. 'You must not think I am an ordinary dancing-girl,' she said to him, 'I can recite Master Po's "Everlasting Wrong."'" And she put up her price."

These anecdotes, which I have selected out of a great number, ought to be sufficient to show how community in the time of T'ang was actually vibrating through and through with the pulse of poetry. If William James had known Chinese and made a study of T'ang poetry, I am sure he would have mentioned it alongside the other great movements. But what would probably have surprised him most was the strange phenomenon that one group of singers after another came upon the scene and each group sang almost like a pre-arranged chorus to give full expression to the spirit of the particular season to which it belonged. A great variety of voices participated in each chorus, but together they formed a superb harmony. "Distinct as the billows, yet one as the sea."

I have not followed closely the stages of the other great movements that James mentioned. I am only slightly acquainted with the evolution of Roman Law. It too had four periods, namely, *ius civile, ius gentium, ius naturale*, and finally codification by Justinian. But I hardly can see a succession of seasons in that movement, but only a progressive liberalization. On the other hand, the poetry of T'ang forms such a *living* year that I cannot explain its stages otherwise than in terms of the seasons. It is really a grand symphony, with its opening, development, change, and conclusion. Integral parts as they are of a whole, they are yet so differentiated from each other that one can without much difficulty tell

> 黄河远上白云间，一片孤城万仞山。
> 羌笛何须怨杨柳，春风不度玉门关。

这是一个多大的抚慰！"你们这两个乡下孩子，"他胜利地说，"你想我难道是信口雌黄不是？"

不过，正如韦利所说的，没有人像白居易那样享受过盛誉。韦利说得甚为简洁中肯，我就录一段在下面：

> 他的诗是在帝皇、太子、官姬、贵妇、农人、马夫的口唇上，镌刻在乡塾、庙宇、船舱的墙壁上。"有军使高霞寓者，欲聘娼妓。妓大夸曰：'我诵得白学士《长恨歌》，岂同他妓哉！'由是增价。"

这两则轶事是我在一大群诗话中挑选出来的，足以显示当时诗歌的盛况，由此可见唐代人士的生命的确是同诗歌的心脉一起跳跃。倘使詹姆斯熟悉中国史事，曾经研究过唐诗的发展的话，我相信他一定会将唐诗和希腊、罗马文化运动并列。要使他惊奇的大概是，怎样一群一群诗人接踵而至，像事先有练习的歌唱班一样。这歌唱班中有高低不同的声音，像狂风下的大海的皱纹，可是合在一起，却是一段超越的和音，像平静的大海那么整齐，奏出他们所代表的季候的精神。

我不曾仔细研究詹姆斯所提起的文化运动，关于罗马法我倒略知一些，它也有四个时期：市民法，万民法，自然法，最后是查士丁尼法典。每一期的内容都较前一期来得进步，可是里面没有季候性；反之，唐诗却是一个整整的年份，它的发展除了以季候解释外，我实在想不出更好的办法。它是一曲伟大的交响乐：有序，有发展，有变化，最后有结尾。其中的段落是属于一个总系的，可是每段却

to what part a particular poem belongs! Reserving my explanation of this wonderful phenomenon to a later stage, I would like to introduce here some concrete illustrations.

Take for example these lines:

> On the ocean, the sun is born out of the entrails of the night.
> Around the river, Spring has overtaken the closing year.

This makes you feel as though the sun were impatient of the night and wanted to anticipate the dawn, as though Spring were racing like a spirited pony with the New Year and came off with flying colors, I humbly submit that such images would not have occurred, and even if they did, would not have *appealed*, to any but a poet of the Spring period. And indeed it was written by Wang Wan (王湾), an elder contemporary of Li Po. On the other hand, take these lines:

> I pity the plum-blossoms,
> For they are always the flowers of a yester-year!

The plum-blossoms burst in the twelfth month of the Lunar calendar and continue to blow in the New Year. They may very well be regarded as the heralds of Spring, and yet to Li Shang-yin, a typical wintry poet, they are always the relics from the last Winter. Don't you see how the poets create Nature in their own image?

Tu Fu wrote:

> A gentle breeze is blowing, butterflies are frolicking.
> Flowers are blazing, and honey bees buzzing.

You feel some cordial warmth in these lines. But you are in an entirely different world when you come across such sentiments as these:

> All day, I have asked the flowers without getting an answer,
> "For whom do you bloom and for whom do you fade?"

(Yen Yün: 严恽)

✱ ✱ ✱

After you have gathered your honey from all the flowers,

What have you got for all your bitter sweetness?

(Lo Yin: "On the bees")

I leave the reader to guess for himself to what season Yen Yün and Lo Yin belong.

Ch'en Tzǔ-ang sang hilariously of the Master of Dark Truth, who "saw the wide world in a jade cup." But Li Shang-yin feels differently, for, as he says:

能独立，我们很容易能看出它是属于哪一季的。下面，我要更进一步地解释这稀有的现象，现在先举几个例子，看这两行：

海日生残夜，江春入旧年。

这可不使你觉得太阳有些不耐烦这残夜，而先宣布破晓？或新春像一匹小骏马飞扬跹屣地同新年赛跑？在我看来，这种影像，除了春季诗人，别人是决想不出的（哪怕想到了，也不会被打动）。果然，这两行的作者是较李白更早的王湾。反之，看这两行（《忆梅》）：

寒梅最堪恨，长作去年花。

梅花开放的时间是旧历十二月和正月间，可以视为春季之先声。可是在李商隐这位标准冬季诗人看来，它是已消逝的冬季的残迹。现在你可知道诗人怎样在他们自己的影像中创造宇宙？杜甫说：

风轻粉蝶喜，花暖蜜蜂喧。

我们觉得其中有可亲的热诚。可是你读这四行时，你的感受又是多么地不同：

尽日问花花不语，为谁零落为谁开。 （严恽）

＊　　＊　　＊

采得百花成蜜后，为谁辛苦为谁甜。 （罗隐《蜂》）

我让读者们自己决定严恽和罗隐是属于哪一季的。

陈子昂兴高采烈地歌颂"观世玉壶中"的玄真子，可是李商隐的情绪又不同了：

If the wide world is contained in the jade cup,

We should still have to wail our separation within the cup!

Li Po wrote about the waterfall of Lushan:

Flying straight down three thousand feet,

It looks as if the Milky Way had fallen from the sky!

The same waterfall evokes a different image in the mind of an autumnal poet, Hsu Ning (徐凝):

Eternally wafting like a long sheet of white silk,—

A line that divides once for all the mountain into two.

There is something neat and clear-cut about Autumn. I don't know how a summer poet would describe the same phenomenon, as I have not succeeded in finding an example among the works of Tu Fu and his friends Kao Shih (高适) and Tseng Ts'an (岑参); but I should imagine they would fall in for the rough-hewn grandeur of this from Keats:

... for the solid roar

Of thunderous waterfalls and torrents hoarse,

Pouring a constant bulk, uncertain where.

One of the most popular themes with the T'ang poets throughout the seasons is the sorrows of the maids-of-honor waiting in the Imperial Harem for the uncertain favors of the Monarch. Here is how a springy poet, Wang Ch'ang-ling, describes their feelings:

I rose at the peep of dawn, and swept the ground.

I have watched the gates of the Gold Temple swing open one by one.

With the moon-like fan in my hand,

Let me rest awhile and loiter around.

Ah that my fair features should prove no match

For the black feathers of yon cold raven!

See how it brings the sunlight along

As it wings its way over the Court of Chao Yang!

This is one of the most famous songs of its *genre*. How springy it is! It is full of longing, and yet full of hope. The sunlight that the cold raven bears on its back symbolizes the coming of the Emperor.

Now let us listen to Tseng Ts'an, who was six years Tu Fu's junior:

His Majesty, displeased with my jealous nature,

Shut me up in this lonely Seraglio.

Fresh favors must now be hanging proudly from the dancing sleeves;

But the memory of the old love is locked between my knit eye-brows.

壶中若是有天地，又向壶中伤别离。

李白说起庐山的瀑布：

飞流直下三千尺，疑是银河落九天。

同一的瀑布却唤起了一位秋季诗人（徐凝）绝对不同的影像：

千古长如白练飞，一条界破青山色。

秋季总是清静明晰的。我不知道一个夏季诗人怎样摹描瀑布，因为我不曾在杜甫、高适或岑参的诗里找出例子，可是我相信他们一定会欣赏济慈暴烈的壮丽：

……因为这雷响似的瀑布，

和汹涌的激流的怒吼

泻成了一条方向不定的大流。

唐朝四季诗人都不断地以宫院中等待天子宠幸的宫女的怨愁为题旨。在这一首诗中，春季诗人王昌龄描摹她们的情绪：

奉帚平明金殿开，且将团扇共徘徊。

玉颜不及寒鸦色，犹带昭阳日影来。

这是这一类诗中最脍炙人口的一首了，每一行都荡漾着春气，充满了渴念和希望。这里寒鸦带着的"昭阳日影"象征天子的宠幸。

现在让我们听较杜甫小六岁的岑参的歌声（《长门怨》）：

君王嫌妾妒，闭妾在长门。

舞袖垂新宠，愁眉结旧恩。

The green coin-like leaves are growing on the fading foot-prints before my door.

The rouge on my face melts with my tears and form furrows upon my cheeks.

The peach-blossoms seem to be laughing at me.

In sullen silence, I look wistfully at the bright colors of Spring.

I find something Tufuish about this song. The denseness and poignancy of the feeling, and the vivid contrasts between fresh favors and old love, between sullen silence and bright Spring, are characteristic of Summer. If our first specimen be called a song of innocence, this one may be called a song of experience.

For the period of Autumn, I will give two samples, one by Li Yi (李益: *circa* 746–829), and the other by Po Chü-i, both of which are so well-known that most of the anthologies include them.

A CAST-OFF FAVORITE

The dewdrops gleam on bright spring flowers whose scent is borne along;

Beneath the moon the palace rings with sounds of lute and song.

It seems that the clepsydra has been filled with the sea,

To make the long long night appear an endless night to me!

(Li Yi in Giles' version)

DESERTED

Soaked in her kerchief with tears, yet slumber will not come;

In the deep dead of night she hears the song and beat of drum.

Alas, although his love has gone, her beauty lingers yet;

Sadly she sits till early dawn, but never can forget.

(Po Chü-i in Giles' version)

It is noteworthy that longing here has not the impetuosity of Spring nor the density of Summer. It is thinning and toning down; but at the same time it has acquired a tenacity and an elasticity peculiar to Autumn. The longing seems to become longer and longer until it appears endless. In fact, I find in all the autumnal poets a tendency, more or less marked, to brood over their sorrows world without end. As Po Chü-i would say:

Heaven and earth will pass away someday,
But this Sorrow will linger on through all eternity!

I am glad that I am not the only one to find in Autumn "a cadence, lingeringly long."

When we come to the last Season, we are confronted again with a different sentiment altogether:

绿钱侵履迹，红粉湿啼痕。
羞被夭桃笑，看春独不言。

这首诗的口吻有些像杜甫。其感情之深刻和浓厚，新宠旧恩、抑郁欢乐的比较，都是夏季的特色。倘使王昌龄的那首诗是天真歌的话，岑参这一首可以称为经验歌。

秋季的精神和特质可以在李益、白居易的这二首驰名古今的诗里窥见一斑：

宫怨
露湿晴花宫殿香，月明歌吹在昭阳。
似将海水添宫漏，共滴长门一夜长。

（李益；英译：翟理思）

后宫词
泪湿罗巾梦不成，夜深前殿按歌声。
红颜未老恩先断，斜倚熏笼坐到明。

（白居易；英译：翟理思）

值得注意的是，这里的渴念不复有春季的骚动力，也没有夏季浓厚的色彩。它渐渐转得稀淡沉寂，同时却富于持久性和伸缩性，这是秋季的特色。这种渴念能以"绵绵无尽期"五字形容之。诚然，大多数秋季诗人都有无尽期地哀悼他们忧郁的趋势。白居易说得好：

天长地久有时尽，此恨绵绵无绝期。

发现秋季是"一支绵绵无尽的歌曲"的，不只我一人，这颇足以高兴。
到了冬季，我们又遇到了不同的情绪（《宫怨》）：

The willows grow in profuse confusion,

Screening off a secluded mansion.

The wails of the mango-bird in the morning

Fill the whole Seraglio with sorrows.

From year to year, the flowers fall unseen,

And silently follow the Spring stream out of the moat.

(Sze-ma Tse: 司马札)

Not a trace of hope is to be found here. The heart is too faint even to yearn. What is the use of struggling when you are in the grip of ruthless Fate? All the wintry poets seem to wear taciturnity like an armor. Each of them seems to have made for himself a shelter to creep into, as a tortoise would withdraw into its impenetrable carapace in the face of a hostile world. Even when they were singing of the pleasures of life, as they occasionally did:

Today we have wine, today let us drink!

To-morrow will take care of its own sorrow!

they remind me all too much of "the fowls of heaven," which, as James Thomson says:

Tamed by the cruel season, crowd around

The winnowing store, and claim the little boon

Which Providence assigns them.

On the whole, Fatalism is the common philosophy of the wintry poets:

When time comes, all the forces of the Universe are united to back you up.

When luck is gone, even a hero cannot remain his own master.

Another popular theme with the poets of T'ang is the war. The following representative pieces, all of equal fame, will speak for themselves:

(1)

Sweet grape-wine filled in a cup of luminous jade!

I want to drink on, but the cavalier's *p'i-p'a* is bidding me speed.

Don't laugh, my friend, if I lie topsy-turvy on the sand!

How many have ever returned from the battle-ground?

(Wang Han: 王翰)

(2)

The Commander-in-Chief holds the banner in his hands,

And starts out for the western front.

The bugle blows at dawn,

And a great army marches on!

柳色参差掩画楼，晓莺啼送满宫愁。

年年花落无人见，空逐春泉出御沟。 （司马札）

这里没有一丝的希望，诗人的内心已是衰弱得不能再有所渴念了。一个人到了命运的铁腕中，挣扎还有什么用？一切冬季诗人都以沉默为甲胄，他们好像都已造好了退隐之所，预备过遁世不问的生活，正像一只乌龟看见形势不佳时缩到背壳内一样。即使他们歌颂生活的逸乐时，像这两行：

今朝有酒今朝醉，明日愁来明日愁。

他们也难免使我想起汤姆森所说的"飞禽"：

它们经过了凶残的季候的驯良后，

飞集到打糠场旁。

领取天主规定给它们的食物。

总之，命运论是冬季诗人的人生观：

时来天地皆同力，运去英雄不自由。

战争也是唐朝诗人爱好题旨之一。下面录的几首都是相当地闻名，足以称为诸家的代表作：

（一）

葡萄美酒夜光杯，欲饮琵琶马上催。

醉卧沙场君莫笑，古来征战几人回。 （王翰）

（二）

上将拥旄西出征，平明吹笛大军行。

On all sides drums rumble like thunder,

Arousing billows in the sea of snow;

The troops howl in one voice,

Causing the dark hills to tremble with fear.

On the frontiers the martial spirit

Rises to camp with the clouds,

While on the battle-ground white bones

Cling tenaciously to the roots of grass.

Over the Sword River, blasts rage,

And clouds roll in big masses.

The stones on the desert are frozen;

Even the horses sometimes slip to the ground.

But the great general is dauntless in spirit,

To him bitter hardships taste like sweetmeat.

For he is sworn to requite the Sovereign

By quelling the rebellious borders.

Who doesn't see the glorious history of the past?

But today we see a more glorious history in the making!

(Tseng Ts'an)

*   *   *

On horseback you will snatch fame and honor,—

A true Hero you, and worthy of your Manhood!

(Tseng Ts'an)

*   *   *

The old general of Kuan-hsi,

A good fighter he!

At seventy he is stout

As any youth could be!

(Tseng Ts'an)

*   *   *

Ten thousand drums sound like thunder,

 Making the earth rumble.

A myriad cavaliers hail forth like fire,

 Giving birth to a warm blast.

(Kao Shih)

(3)

In front of the Peak of Happy Return

Lies a sandy desert, gleaming like snow.

Beneath the City of Victory

The moon spreads a frosty rug.

Hark! The notes of a reed-pipe!

Ah! Where comes the music?

In one night it fills a myriad hearts

With infinite yearnings for home!

(Li Yi)

四边伐鼓雪海涌，三军大呼阴山动。

虏塞兵气连云屯，战场白骨缠草根。

剑河风急云片阔，沙口石冻马蹄脱。

亚相勤王甘苦辛，誓将报主静边尘。

古来青史谁不见，今见功名胜古人。　　　（岑参）

＊　　＊　　＊

功名只向马上取，真是英雄一丈夫。　　　（岑参）

＊　　＊　　＊

关西老将能苦战，七十行兵仍未休。　　　（岑参）

＊　　＊　　＊

万鼓雷殷地，千旗火生风。　　　（高适）

（三）

回乐烽前沙似雪，受降城外月如霜。

不知何处吹芦管，一夜征人尽望乡。　　　（李益）

(4)

They swore to make a clean sweep of the Huns.

They started out with a will to die.

Five thousand men in furs and silk

Were all buried in a hostile desert land.

Ah, the pity of it! The skeletons

On the shores of the Inconstant River

Still live as darlings in the dreams

Of their brides in their nuptial beds!

(Ch'en T'ao: 陈陶)

*　　*　　*

The hills and rivers of the lowland country

　　You have made your battle-ground.

How do you suppose the people who live there

　　Will procure "firewood and hay"?

Do not let me hear you talking together

　　About titles and promotions;

For a single general's reputation

　　Is made out of ten thousand corpses.

(Ts'ao Sung in Waley's version)

Parting from our friends and dear ones is always a sad experience, especially in old China when the means of communication were very poor and the world seemed to be very wide indeed. Even Napoleon has said, "The moment which separates us from the object of our affections is terrible, it severs us from all the earth." And yet even this sadness has its seasonal modulations and nuances. In the first period, we find such sentiments as:

The existence of a single bosom friend on earth

Turns the wide, wide world into a cordial neighborhood.

(Wang Po)

*　　*　　*

My friend took leave of me here at the Yellow Crane Tower,

And went down eastward to Yangchow amidst the April vapors and
   flowers.

I strained my eyes and watched the shadow of the lonely sail vanish into
   the blue hills.

Now I see only the River flowing along the border of heaven.

                        (Li Po: "On Seeing Off Meng Hao-jan")

In the second period, the sentiments are even more manly. Here are some
typical lines from Kao Shih:

Cheer up, dear friend!

The present Emperor is full of "rain and dew." [1]

He will recall you soon from your temporary exile.

Don't let our parting dishearten you too much!

(四)

誓扫匈奴不顾身，五千貂锦丧胡尘。

可怜无定河边骨，犹是春闺梦里人。　　　　　　　（陈陶）

＊　　　＊　　　＊

泽国江山入战图，生民何计乐樵苏。

凭君莫话封侯事，一将功成万骨枯。（曹松；英译：韦利）

同至亲密友分手是一件难受的事，尤其是在交通不便的古时，世界
显得尤为宽广。拿破仑也说过，"同我们亲爱的人物分手时，我们
就觉得整个的世界已离弃了我们"。可是这离别的哀愁也随季候而
异。在第一期内，我们看见这种感情：

海内存知己，天涯若比邻。　　　　　　　　　　（王勃）

＊　　　＊　　　＊

故人西辞黄鹤楼，烟花三月下扬州。

孤帆远影碧空尽，惟见长江天际流。

                        （李白《黄鹤楼送孟浩然之广陵》）

第二期诗人的感情更有丈夫气，这里是高适的话：

圣代即今多雨露，暂时分手莫踟蹰。

*   *   *

Don't feel sorry to be temporarily away from home.

I know a man like you will find welcome wherever you go.

In the third period, one feels a feminine touch and also a rather pale attempt to rationalize away the sorrows of parting. Here is what Yuan Chen said to his friend Po Chü-i:

Last time we parted, it took us five years to meet again.

This time we part, who knows when I shall see my old pal?

Stay at peace, Lot'ien dear, don't miss me too much.

Just suppose I had not come to the Capital at all.

If Autumn is feminine, Winter is effeminate:

True love looks like no love.

I only feel I cannot smile before the cup.

Even the wax-candle has a heart and pities our parting,—

It drops silent tears for us until the dawn.

(Tu Mu)

The third line needs some explanation. We call the wick "candle-heart." In this respect, our language is very much like Old English, which calls thought "breast-hoard," man "earth-dweller," jaundice "gall-disease," and the body "flesh-coat."

Even the dream-life of the poets seems to retain the qualities of the Season to which they happen to belong. What did Li Po dream? He tells us:

One night I flew across the Mirror Lake in the bright moonlight!

What did Tu Fu dream? He tells us:

I dream of my native town, now overgrown with thistles and thorns;

I dream of His Majesty and his entourage, so near the beasts of prey.

Another summery poet writes:

On the pillow I had a wink and dreamed:

I *walked* all over the land south of the River.

The dreams of the wintry poets are apt to be nightmares. As Li Shang-yin has it:

> I dreamed I was setting out upon a long journey,
> And was on the verge of being wrung from you.
> I wept so hard that it was with difficulty

*　*　*

莫怨他乡暂离别，知君到处有逢迎。

在第三期里，我们感觉到一种柔性的风味，一种以理智的清水来冲淡离别之痛的尝试，这里是元稹对白居易说的话：

> 前回一去五年别，此别又知何日回。
> 好住乐天休怅望，匹如元不到京来。

秋季倘是柔性的话，冬季则是弱不禁风、愁不胜愁的了：

> 多情却似总无情，惟觉樽前笑不成。
> 蜡烛有心还惜别，替人垂泪到天明。　　　　（杜牧）

【第三句英文需要做一些解释。我们称灯芯为 candle-heart，这一点，我们的语言很像古英语。古英语称思想为 breast-hoard，称人为 earth-dweller，称黄疸病为 gall-disease，称身体为 flesh-coat。】

就是诗人的梦，好像也含蕴着他们所隶属的季候的特性。李白做的是什么梦？他说：

> 一夜飞度镜湖月。

杜甫做的什么梦？他说：

> 故乡门巷荆棘底，中原君臣豺虎边。　　　（《昼梦》）

另一位夏季诗人说：

> 枕上片时春梦中，行尽江南数千里。　　　　（岑参）

冬季诗人做的大多是梦魇，像李商隐：

> 梦为远别啼难唤。

People succceded to wake me up.

As for the autumnal period, I can find no better illustration than Yuan Chen's "Dreaming of a Well," which has been so well translated by Arthur Waley under the title of "The Pitcher":

I dreamt I climbed to a high, high plain;

And on the plain I found a deep well.

My throat was dry with climbing and I longed to drink,

And my eyes were eager to look into the cool shaft.

I walked round it; I looked right down;

I saw my image mirrored on the face of the pool.

An earthen pitcher was sinking into the black depths;

There was no rope to pull it to the well-head.

I was strangely troubled lest the pitcher should be lost,

And started wildly running to look for help.

From village to village I scoured that high plain;

The men were gone: the dogs leapt at my throat.

I came back and walked weeping round the well;

Faster and faster the blinding tears flowed—

Till my own sobbing suddenly woke me up;

My room was silent, no one in the house stirred;

The flame of my candle flickered with a green smoke.

The tears I had shed glittered in the candlelight.

I sat up in bed and tried to arrange my thoughts:

The plain in my dream was the graveyard at Ch'ang-an,

Those hundred acres of untilled land.

The soil heavy and the mounds heaped high;

And the dead below them laid in deep troughs.

Deep are the troughs, yet sometimes dead men

Find their way to the world above the grave.

And to-night my love who died long ago

Came into my dream as the pitcher sunk in the well.

That was why the tears suddenly streamed from my eyes,
Streamed from my eyes and fell on the collar of my dress.

I can prolong this pageant of the Seasons indefinitely. For on all conceivable subjects the poets seem to reflect the *Zeitgeist* of their particular period. It would, however, take a whole volume by itself to explain with some adequacy the causes of this phenomenon. One would have to look for them among the political, social, economic, literary-historical, biological, and psychological factors which all conspired together to make such a perfect year possible. But here I can only give some hints.

至于秋季，元稹的《梦井》是最好也不过的：

> 梦上高高原，原上有深井。
> 登高意枯渴，愿见深泉冷。
> 徘徊绕井顾，自照泉中影。
> 沉浮落井瓶，井上无悬绠。
> 念此瓶欲沉，荒忙为求请。
> 遍入原上村，村空犬仍猛。
> 还来绕井哭，哭声通复哽。
> 哽噎梦忽惊，觉来房舍静。
> 灯焰碧胧胧，泪光疑囧囧。
> 钟声夜方半，坐卧心难整。
> 忽忆咸阳原，荒田万余顷。
> 土厚圹亦深，埋魂在深埂。
> 埂深安可越，魂通有时逞。
> 今宵泉下人，化作瓶相憬。
> 感此涕汍澜，汍澜涕沾领。　　　　　　（英译：韦利）

我能无限止地延长这季候的迎会，因为诗人在任何题目上都能发扬时代的精神，所谓 *Zeitgeist* 者。倘使要穷究这奇特的现象的根源，那非洋洋大文不可：我们要研究这年份的政治、社会、经济、文史、生物、心理等背景，它们共同作用打造出如此完美的一年。这里我只能略谈其大概。

Ordinarily any movement in art and culture follows its own seasons. Some men of genius give the original impetus to it; then others come along and bring it to its fullest development; then a third batch arrives upon the scene, curbing its exuberance and shaving off, with Occam's razor in their hands, all its superfluities, while preserving its beauties in neat form; and finally come the aesthetes who, seized with the spirit of forms, give a finishing touch to the whole movement. But only on rare occasions do the internal seasons of such a movement run parallel with the seasons of life. And this is exactly what happened in the case of T'ang poetry. Its Spring coincided with the happiest day of the Dynasty. Its Summer, while it did not see the fullest development of the Dynasty, nevertheless saw its days of the most intensive and hectic activities. Rebellions had arisen and the centrifugal forces had been set loose, but then the centripedal forces were just as strong, and great military geniuses like Kuo Tzǔ-i and Li Kwang-pi were leading the armies. It was an age in which Tseng Ts'an could exclaim: "Today we see a more glorious history in the making!" The poets were rather strengthened than disheartened by the great trials and hardships that they went through. That age is somewhat like the present age, with only this difference: now even greater leaders than Kuo Tzǔ-i and Li Kwang-pi are walking the earth, and now a mightier breath of patriotism is sweeping through the nation. As Dr. Sun Fo once said to me, "A New Golden Age is ahead of us, in which we shall see the combination of the joyous faith of Spring with the ripe wisdom of Autumn." That will indeed be an ideal Summer! But in the Autumn of T'ang poetry we feel an entirely different atmosphere. The troublous days had lasted too long for any candid optimism, and a sense of disintegration had entered the souls of the poets. As to its Winter, it happened to coincide with the fall of the great Dynasty. So for once Life and Art seem to walk hand in hand, so much so that it almost looks like a lone instance of poor Leibnitz's "harmonie pré-établie"! Let us now proceed to Autumn.

大致说来，任何文艺运动的发展都是极自然的。一群天才先出现，播下种子；然后另一群天才出来培植这种子，使它开花结果；第三群接踵而至，节制它的繁茂，修剪它的过盛部分，保存它的整齐和美；最后一群是审美家，他们都饱享了先人的作品，出来完成最后的工作。大半文艺运动内部的季候性极少有同生活的季候相应合的，唐诗便是难得可贵的一个。唐诗的春是和初唐之盛相应合的。唐诗的夏虽然没有看见唐朝最光荣的日子，却曾目历其最激昂、令人叹为观止的时际：那时候叛军蜂起，离心力人物已东西分散，向心力人物却坚强如昔，大将郭子仪、李光弼等仍统率大军作战。这时岑参大叫"今见功名胜古人"！

　　诗人们非但不为这一切痛苦的磨损所气馁，反有再接再厉之势。那时候同目前的情形有些相同，不过现在我们的军事领袖较郭子仪、李光弼高明多多，举国人民的抗战热忱也不是任何别的时代所够得上的。【正如孙哲生博士所言，"一个新的黄金时代就在我们面前，我们将看到春季愉快的信仰和秋季成熟的智慧相结合"。】这就是一个理想的夏季！可是唐诗的秋是不同了："国不泰""民不安"的日子是太长了，我们已不能乐观地过活，一种畏惧瓦解的心理渗透了诗人的心灵。唐诗之冬同唐朝之冬完全应合，"生活"同"艺术"也就手牵手地退隐，正像莱布尼茨所说的"天定的和谐"。【下面我们就谈谈秋季。】

VIII.   AUTUMN: PO CHÜ-I

The weather is cooling down, but not yet cold.

—*Han Wu*

Where are the songs of Spring? Ay, where are they?

—*Keats*

New Philosophy calls all in doubt;
The element of fire is quite put out.

—*John Donne*

But now the mystic tale that pleas'd of yore
Can charm an understanding age no more.

—*Addison*

Outwardly conforming to the ways of the world,
Inwardly emancipated from all the ties of life.

—*Po Chü-i*

Writing about the pine-trees, Po Chü-i (772–846) says:

In Autumn they whisper a soothing tune;
In Summer they yield a cooling shade;
In the depth of Spring the fine evening rain
Fills their leaves with little sparkling pearls;
At the close of the year heavy snowfalls
Adorn their branches with unsullied jade.
From each season they derive a peculiar charm,
And this the reason why they are peerless among trees.

I venture to think that the same is in some senses true also of the four seasons of T'ang poetry, and no one represents Autumn better than Po Chü-i himself. Like the pine-trees in Autumn, his poems, at least a great number of them, do whisper a *soothing tune*. But at this point, I must note down at once that the original word which I have rendered as "soothing" is *su* (疏), which is very rich in meanings. In the first place, it means "sparse," as in Lao Tzǔ's well-known sentence:

> All-embracing is heaven's net;
>
> Sparse-meshed it is, and yet
>
> Nothing can slip through it.

Secondly, it also conveys the idea of being "detached" and "remote." When for example the relations between two persons are not very thick, we

捌 秋之灵魂——白居易

已凉天气未寒时。	——韩偓
啊，春日的歌哪里去了？	——济慈
新哲学怀疑一切， 火星已被扑灭。	——约翰·多恩

从前引人入胜的神秘故事，不能取悦于这智力的时代。

——艾迪生

外顺世间法，内脱区中缘。　　　　　　　　——白居易

讲起庭前的松树，白居易说：

> 疏韵秋槭槭，凉阴夏凄凄。
>
> 春深微雨夕，满叶珠㴋㴋。
>
> 岁暮大雪天，压枝玉皅皅。
>
> 四时各有趣，万物非其侪。

这几句话也很适合唐诗的四季，同时也没有人较白居易更完美地代表秋季的精神。像深秋的松树一样，他的诗，至少大部分，都是"疏韵槭槭"。这"疏"字的意义很是晦涩广泛，不易断定。第一，它可以当作"稀疏"解，像《老子》这句里的用法，"天网恢恢，疏而不漏"。第二，它有分离之意，譬如我们说某某人同某某

say that they are rather *su* to each other. Thirdly, as Dr. Lin Yu-tang has pointed out, it is closely connected with the idea of *tan* (淡), which he translates as "mildness," but I would translate as "flavorlessness." Fourthly, it has the meaning of "getting rid of impediments." When a tube is stopped up, we say we must *su* it. Lastly, it means "relieving the tension of your nerves," as when an old-fashioned Chinese doctor says to a patient, "Your case requires more *su* than *pu* (nourishment)." We Chinese use words more intuitively than logically. When we use the word *su*, all these meanings are more or less present in our minds. Some of them may float in the upper parts of our psyche while others may lurk just below the threshold of consciousness, but the point is that they are all stubbornly there. My English vocabulary is so limited that I cannot find any equivalent for this word. To put it clearly, a "*su* tune" is one that is sparse and thin of texture, mild or flavorless in its tones, detached and remote in its motif, fluent and unimpeded in its flow, and, finally, soothing in its effects. I am rather surprised to find that Arthur Waley, whom I regard as the best translator of Chinese poems, and who is especially happy in his translations of Po Chü-i, should have rendered the phrase as "a vague tune." Its meanings are indeed rather vague, but it does not mean "vague." I thought of the word "airy," which comes near to it, but it may also mean "sprightly" and "superficial," and you can say nothing of that sort about Autumn. I must confess that this word *su* has been haunting me for years, because it seems to me to furnish one of the keys to the understanding not merely of the poetry of Po Chü-i, but of the spirit of Chinese culture since the T'ang Dynasty. I am not satisfied with my own translation, but let me tell you the interesting story of my arriving at it. Some time ago, I had a dream in which I was lying in a hospital and quite unexpectedly my old friend Justice Holmes called upon me, taking a seat by my bedside. He said that he was sorry to see China in war. "I just wonder," said I, "why America should have been so reluctant in helping my country to ward off an aggression which has become a veritable danger to the international community." "Well," he said, "the peculiar thing about America is that the individuals move very fast, but the nation as a whole moves very slowly. But I assure you, my dear boy, that it is moving steadily and will pretty soon rally to your side." "But when will that be? When?" I asked with a show of impatience. "I see you still bear the fire in your belly," he smiled affably, "but be patient, for Time is your greatest ally. In the meantime,

人很疏远。第三，像语堂先生说的，它同"淡"有密切的相似点，此时他译作 mildness，我会译作 flavorlessness。第四，它有"出清"之意，譬如说我们疏通一根塞没的管子。最后，"疏"可以当作"宽心"解，老法郎中时常对病人说："你的病需要疏补疏补"，就是这意思。我们中国人用字时以直觉为主，逻辑仅居次要。当我们用"疏"这字时，它不同的意义就自动在我们脑海中出现，有些浮在我们脑子上部，有些逗留在意识的门前。【我的英文词汇有限，将"疏"字译作英文时，找不到一个适当的字包括它的全意，所以就用了 soothing（抚慰）】。总之，"疏"的质地是稀薄的，气调是和淡的，命意是消极的，动作是从容的，效果是抚慰的。韦利我认为是最好的一位译中国诗的人，他对自己译的白居易十分满意。莫测得很，他竟将"疏"字译作 vague（晦涩）。"疏"的意义的确很晦涩，可是决不能当作"晦涩"解。我想起 airy 这字，可是它含有轻飘和浮而不入的意义，当然不适合于秋季。关于"疏"这字，我已萦思多年，因为它是启开不仅白居易的诗，并且唐朝以后中国文化精神的秘门的钥匙。【Soothing 这个翻译我自己也不满意，不过它的来历倒是挺有意思的。不久前，我梦见自己生病住院，老友霍姆斯来看我，出乎我的意外。他坐在我的床边，说他很为中国的战祸痛心。我问他："我只是想知道，为什么美国不愿帮助中国抵抗这威胁国际和平的侵略呢？"他答道："美国之奇就在于，国民个人都行动得很快，可是整个国家却行动得很慢。但我向你保证，我的孩子，美国目今正在行动，不久就可以助作一臂之力。""可是要等到什么时候？什么时候？"我有些不耐烦。他和蔼地笑着说："我看你腹中仍旧有火，不要心急，时间对你

take good care of your health, your nerves seem to need a great deal of soothing!" Our conversation was interrupted, because the loud noise I was making had awakened my wife, who in turn woke me up. Next morning, as I was reading the poems of Po Chü-i, I came across this word *su*. A sudden flash came across my mind: *su* means "soothing"! But I want my reader to bear in mind the other meanings as well.

I feel that Po Chü-i would have agreed with me that he belongs to Autumn. For the qualities he ascribed to his own poetry all fall under the definition of *su* as I have given above, and therefore may by his own consent be called autumnal. Here is what he says about his poetry:

> Illness and idleness give me much leisure.
>
> What do I do with my leisure when it comes?
>
> I cannot bring myself to discard inkstone and brush;
>
> Now and then I make a new poem.
>
> When the poem is made it is slight and flavorless,
>
> A thing of derision almost to everyone.
>
> Superior people will be pained at the flatness of the meter;
>
> Common people will hate the plainness of the words.
>
> (Waley's version)

In other words, his poetry is anything but thick and dense, anything but gorgeous and loud, anything but flowery and highfalutin, anything but enthusiastic and keen. It is akin to the old harp, which he says:

> Of cord and cassia-wood is the harp compounded:
>
> Within it lie ancient melodies.
>
> Ancient melodies—weak and savorless,
>
> Not appealing to present men's taste.
>
> Light and color are faded from the jade stops;
>
> Dust has covered the rose-red strings.
>
> Decay and ruin came to it long ago.
>
> But the sound that is left is still cold and clear.
>
> I do not refuse to play it, if you want me to:

But even if I play, people will not listen.

(Waley's version)

He has not the rapturousness of Li Po nor the breathless intensity of Tu Fu; but he is full of subdued charm and mellow wisdom. On the whole, no poet seems to embody more perfectly than Po the spirit of Autumn, at least Autumn as Keats describes it so *su-ishly* in his "The

们是莫大的帮助。同时，当心你的身体，你的神经需要大量的 soothing！"我们的谈话就此中断，因为我的动静太大，惊醒了妻子，她就将我推醒。次日早晨读白居易的诗，看见这"疏"字，顿时大有所悟，想起"疏"就是 soothing 的关系。可是我希望读者也能牢记"疏"的其他意义。】

我深信白居易同意我将他列入秋季，因为他在《自吟拙什，因有所怀》那首诗里的话都同"疏"的意义吻合，我们或许可以说他将他自己列入秋季：

> 懒病每多暇，暇来何所为？
> 未能抛笔砚，时作一篇诗。
> 诗成淡无味，多被众人嗤。
> 上怪落声韵，下嫌拙言词。 　　　（英译：韦利）

换句话说，他的诗既不浓厚深刻，也不炫耀夺目，既不巍峨华瞻，也不趾高气扬，只是像他所说的"旧琴"：

> 丝桐合为琴，中有太古声。
> 古声淡无味，不称今人情。
> 玉徽光彩灭，朱弦尘土生。
> 废弃来已久，遗音尚泠泠。
> 不辞为君弹，纵弹人不听。 　　　（英译：韦利）

他没有李白的混沌狂乐，也没有杜甫令人窒息的热情；但是他充满了幽隐的风韵和成熟的智慧。总之，没有人较白居易更精当地体会秋季的精神，至少在浪漫诗人济慈眼光里的秋季。他

Human Seasons." The sonnet is so appropriate to my present theme that it is worth quoting in its entirety:

> Four seasons fill the measure of the year;
>> There are four seasons in the mind of man:
> He has his lusty Spring, when fancy clear
>> Takes in all beauty with an easy span;
> He has his Summer, when luxuriously
>> Spring's honied cud of youthful thought he loves
> To ruminate, and by such dreaming nigh
>> His nearest unto heaven: quiet coves
> His soul has in its Autumn, when his wings
>> He furleth close; contented so to look
> On mists in idleness—to let fair things
>> Pass by unheeded as a threshold brook.
> He has his Winter, too, of pale misfeature,
>> Or else he would forego his mortal nature.

What quiet coves Po Chü-i has in his soul can be gathered from the following lines:

> For restful thoughts one does not need space;
> The room where I lie is ten foot square.

(Waley's version)

*　　*　　*

> Can the single cup of wine
> We drank this morning have made my heart so glad?
> This is a joy that comes only from within,
> Which those who witness will never understand.

(Waley's version)

As to furling his wings, why, he even thinks his feet unnecessary:

> All that matters is an active mind, what is the use of feet?

(Waley's version)

Addressing himself to a crane, he says:

People love to see you dance,

But I like you better standing still.

His philosophy of contentment and his love of idleness are well known. Out of

的《人类季候》这首商籁同我的题旨极有关系，值得录于下面：

一年有四季，
人的心灵也有四季：
他有生气勃勃的春，当明洁的幻想
轻易地抓住了天下的美；
他有夏季，他喜爱奢侈地反刍
春季吞进的甜蜜的思想，这种梦
使他紧紧靠近了天国；在秋季，
他的灵魂有幽静的荫蔽所，
他卷起他的肢翼，懒洋洋地，知足地，
他对烟雾凝视，让各样美物
像溪流般不受人注意而流过。
他也有灰白、破相的冬季，
否则是有违天性了。

白居易灵魂中幽静的荫蔽所可以在这几行内看到：

闲意不在远，小亭方丈间。　　　　　　（英译：韦利）

* 　* 　*

今旦一尊酒，欢畅何怡怡。
此乐从中来，他人安得知。　　　　　　（英译：韦利）

白居易不但卷起他的羽翼，他根本连二足都认为是可有可无的：

但有心情何用脚？　　　　　　　　　　（英译：韦利）

对一只鹤，他说：

谁谓尔能舞，不如闲立时。

他知足的人生观和喜爱懒惰的天性是尽人皆知的，他遗留下的

193

over three thousand and six hundred poems he has left behind him, two-thirds of them seem to harp upon the same string. But here we must content ourselves with a few typical specimens:

(1) A MAD POEM ADDRESSED TO MY NEPHEWS AND NIECES

The World cheats those who cannot read;

I, happily, have mastered script and pen.

The World cheats those who hold no office;

I am blessed with high official rank.

The old are often ill;

I, at this day have not an ache or pain.

They are often burdened with ties;

But I have finished with marriage and giving in marriage.

No changes happen to jar the quiet of my mind;

No business comes to impair the vigor of my limbs.

Hence it is that now for ten years

Body and soul have rested in hermit peace.

And all the more, in the last lingering years

What I shall need are very few things.

A single rug to warm me through the winter;

One meal to last me the whole day.

It does not matter that my house is rather small;

One cannot sleep in more than one room!

It does not matter that I have not many horses;

One cannot ride in two coaches at once!

As fortunate as me among the people of the world

Possibly one would find seven out of ten.

As contented as me among a hundred men

Look as you may, you will not find one.

In the affairs of others even fools are wise;

In their own business even sages err.

To no one else would I dare to speak my heart,

So my wild words are addressed to my nephews and nieces.

(Waley's version)

(2) LAZY MAN'S SONG

I have got patronage, but am too lazy to use it;

I have got land, but am too lazy to farm it.

My house leaks; I am too lazy to mend it.

My clothes are torn; I am too lazy to darn them.

I have got wine, but I am too lazy to drink;

So it's just the same as if my cellar were empty.

I have got a harp, but am too lazy to play;

So it's just the same as if it had no strings.

My wife tells me there is no more bread in the house;

I want to bake, but am too lazy to grind.

My friends and relatives write me long letters;

I should like to read them, but they're such a bother to open.

三千六百首中有三分之二都述及这二点，我们只能录下下面寥寥几首：

（一）狂言示诸侄

世欺不识字，我忝攻文笔。世欺不得官，我忝居班秩。

人老多病苦，我今幸无疾。人老多忧累，我今婚嫁毕。

心安不移转，身泰无牵率。所以十年来，形神闲且逸。

况当垂老岁，所要无多物。一裘暖过冬，一饭饱终日。

勿言舍宅小，不过寝一室。何用鞍马多，不能骑两匹。

如我优幸身，人中十有七。如我知足心，人中百无一。

傍观愚亦见，当己贤多失。不敢论他人，狂言示诸侄。

（英译：韦利）

（二）咏慵

有官慵不选，有田慵不农。屋穿慵不葺，衣裂慵不缝。

有酒慵不酌，无异樽常空。有琴慵不弹，亦与无弦同。

家人告饭尽，欲炊慵不舂。亲朋寄书至，欲读慵开封。

I have always been told that Chi Shu Yeh

Passed his whole life in absolute idleness.

But he played the harp and sometimes transmuted metals.

So even *he* was not so lazy as I.

(Waley's version)

(3) RESIGNATION

Keep off your thoughts from things that are past and done;

For thinking of the past wakes regret and pain.

Keep off your thoughts from thinking what will happen;

To think of the future fills one with dismay.

Better by day to sit like a sack in your chair;

Better by night to lie like a stone in your bed.

When food comes, then open your mouth;

When sleep comes, then close your eyes.

(Waley's version)

(4) A MIDDLE-CLASS RECLUSE

High-class recluses stay in the government and market-place.

Low-class recluses enter into hills and woods.

Hills and woods are too lonely and isolated.

The Court and the market are too much of a hustle and bustle.

I prefer to be a middle-class recluse,

Hiding myself in a sinecure!

Somewhere between society and solitude,

Neither busy nor idle.

No onerous work, mental or physical;

And yet no danger of hunger or of cold.

Throughout the year, no duties arise;

From month to month, salaries come.

If you want to roam and climb,

There are the Autumn hills on the southern suburb.

If you want to promenade and picnic,

There is the Spring garden east of the City.

If you are inclined to drinking,

You can go to the parties from time to time.

There are many scholars in Loyang,

With whom you can pass your time in pleasant chats.

If you are inclined to enjoy solitude and sleep,

You can shut yourself in as long as you want.

I can assure you no office-seekers or job-hunters

Will ever come to disturb your peace.

During our brief sojourn in this world,

It's hard to have everything to our heart's satisfaction.

If you are humble and poor,

You suffer hunger and cold.

If you are too high up and well off,

You will be eaten up by worries and cares.

常闻嵇叔夜，一生在慵中。弹琴复锻铁，比我未为慵。

（英译：韦利）

（三）有感

往事勿追思，追思多悲怆。来事勿相迎，相迎已惆怅。

不如兀然坐，不如塌然卧。食来即开口，睡来即合眼。

（英译：韦利）

（四）中隐

大隐住朝市，小隐入丘樊。丘樊太冷落，朝市太嚣喧。

不如作中隐，隐在留司官。似出复似处，非忙亦非闲。

不劳心与力，又免饥与寒。终岁无公事，随月有俸钱。

君若好登临，城南有秋山。君若爱游荡，城东有春园。

君若欲一醉，时出赴宾筵。洛中多君子，可以恣欢言。

君若欲高卧，但自深掩关。亦无车马客，造次到门前。

人生处一世，其道难两全。贱即苦冻馁，贵则多忧患。

Between adversity and prosperity,

Between opulence and penury,

A middle-class recluse

Steers safely through the channel of life.

Of his willingness to let the fair things of life pass by unheeded, the evidence is just as overwhelming:

(1)

The willows are aging.

Spring is past its prime.

The sun is slanting.

What if the catkins are flying over the walls

To our neighbors' homes?

Who can always play the children's game

Of pursuing the catkins wafted in the Spring wind?

(2) LOSING A SLAVE-GIRL

Around my garden the little wall is low;

In the bailiff's lodge the lists are seldom checked.

I am ashamed to think we were not always kind;

I regret your labors, that will never be repaid.

The caged bird owes no allegiance;

The wind-tossed flower does not cling to the tree.

Where to-night she lies none can give us news;

Nor any knows, save the bright watching moon.

(Waley's version)

(3) THE SPRING RIVER

Heat and cold, dusk and dawn have crowded one upon the other;

Suddenly I find it is two years since I came to Chungchou.

Through my closed doors I hear nothing but the morning and evening drum;

From my upper windows all I see is the ships that come and go.

In vain the orioles tempt me with their song to stray beneath the

flowering trees;

In vain the grasses lure me by their color to sit beside the pond.
There is one thing and one alone I never tire of watching—
The spring river as it trickles over the stone and babbles past the rocks.
(Waley's version)

All this may lead us into thinking that Po is a real optimist. Here, you will say, is a man who has set himself completely in tune with life. Here we have at last found a philosopher who "could endure the toothache patiently." Doesn't he style himself as "Lot'ien" (乐天) or The Optimist? But wait! The matter is not half so simple as this. The fact that the moon always shows its bright side does not mean that it has not also got a dark side. In the case of Po, moreover, he has not succeeded so well as the

惟此中隐士，致身吉且安。穷通与丰约，正在四者间。

证明他让各样生活之美物不受注意地过逝的诗也不胜枚举：

（一）杨柳枝

柳老春深日又斜，任他飞向别人家。
谁能更学孩童戏，寻逐春风捉柳花。

（二）失婢

宅院小墙庳，坊门帖榜迟。
旧恩惭自薄，前事悔难追。
笼鸟无常主，风花不恋枝。
今宵在何处，惟有月明知。

（三）春江

炎凉昏晓苦推迁，不觉忠州已二年。
闭阁只听朝暮鼓，上楼空望往来船。
莺声诱引来花下，草色句留坐水边。
惟有春江看未厌，萦砂绕石渌潺湲。（英译：韦利）

这一切或能使我们想白居易是一个乐观主义者，因为他个人和生活完全和谐，至少我们发现了一个哲人“能忍受他的牙痛”。他可不曾自号“乐天”？可是事件并不这样简单。月亮时常显露光明的一面，这并不是说它没有黝黯的一面。可是白居易并没有像月亮

moon in hiding the less pleasant aspects. The very fact that he calls himself an optimist shows how pessimistic he really is. The long and short of it is that neither the word *su* nor Keats' lines constitutes a complete picture of Autumn. I would go so far as to say that they have only given us the more superficial aspects of Autumn, but have not touched its heart-strings. For Autumn is the saddest of the seasons. As Ou-yang Hsiu puts it so well: "Her breath is shivering and raw, pricking men's skin and bones; her thoughts are desolate, bringing emptiness and silence to the rivers and hills." It is rightly called "the doom-spirit of heaven and earth," or, as Horace would have it, "the harvest-season of the Goddess of Death." Never do life and death come so near as in Autumn. Its very fruitfulness hastens death. Its very fairness breeds sadness. One feels with William Watson:

> O be less beautiful, or be less brief!

In one word, it is the season in which the Dialectical Process of Nature comes to a head. It is the Clearing-House of the year, in which balances must be made up in cash, for the debt has ripened beyond cavil and its payment can no longer be deferred.

Yes, Desolation is the soul of Autumn, and the door through which Po Chü-i enters into it is his awareness of the Dialectical Process of Nature. The very first poem preserved in his complete works, which was written when he was fifteen, marks him down as an autumnal poet:

> Thick, thick, the grass on the plain!
> Each year, it has its season of growth and season of decay.
> No prairie fire can destroy it root and all;
> For when the Spring wind blows, it grows again.
> Its fresh smell, wafted from afar, invades an old road.
> Its bright emerald borders upon a desolate city.
> Once again it has come to see the Genie of Spring off,
> With its heart seething with parting sorrows.

The second line reminds me of that wonderful passage of the Preacher which begins with "For everything there is a season, and a time for every purpose under heaven." And the tone of the whole poem makes me think of Wordsworth's:

The clouds that gather round the setting sun
Do take a sober coloring from an eye
That hath kept watch o'er man's mortality;
Another race hath been, other palms are won.

那么成功掩没他的黝黯，他叫自己"乐天"，这足以显出他是多么地悲观。问题是，白居易的"疏"和济慈的诗都不能显呈秋的全景。进一步说，它们只是秋季的外表而已，距它的"心弦"尚远。秋季是最伤感的时候，欧阳修说得好，"其气凛冽，砭人肌骨；其意萧条，山川寂寥"。我们或可以说它是"天地的死运"，或像贺拉斯所说的"死神的收获期"。生与死在这时候最为接近，它的丰熟催促死亡，它的温柔酝酿伤感。【正如威廉·沃森所说，"不要这样美，也不要这样短"！】一言蔽之，在秋季大自然的辩证法到达了顶点。秋季是一年的总清算期，账目都须算清，债务都已到期，不得再拖延。

是的，萧条是秋季的灵魂。白居易就穿过了大自然辩证法的门而钻进了去。他的全集的第一首已注定他为秋季诗人，写那首诗时他只有十五岁：

离离原上草，一岁一枯荣。
野火烧不尽，春风吹又生。
远芳侵古道，晴翠接荒城。
又送王孙去，萋萋满别情。

这里的第二句使我想起《旧约·传道书》的一段惊语，它的第一句是，"万物皆有其期，天下各物皆有定期"。这首诗的口吻使我想起诗人华兹华斯：

夕阳旁的云彩，
从那看守人类死生的眼睛，
得多一些庄严的色彩；
又有一圈赛跑完了，
又有棕枝赢得了。

The more I follow the seasons in T'ang poetry, the more I am convinced that, while the ages of life do influence an individual to some extent, yet the individual as a whole is destined to belong to a particular season. A springy spirit will remain springy even on his deathbed, and likewise an autumnal spirit begins to see and feel Autumn pretty early, if he is really not born autumnal. The child, as people say, is father to the man. In this connection, Alfred de Vigny has thrown out one of the keenest insights into human nature: "I have observed that everyone has naturally the character of one of the ages of life, and retains it always."

It seems to me that the vision of the interpenetration of opposites permeates the poetry of Po. He is by nature a Taoist. It's all very true that he "utilized Confucianism to order his conduct, utilized Buddhism to cleanse his mind, and then utilized history, paintings, mountains, rivers, wine, music and song to soothe his spirit." But this is exactly what only a thorough-going Taoist could have done. At any rate, the *Tao Teh Ching* and *The Book of Changes* seem to furnish the very sinews to the philosophy of Po. He expressed it very clearly:

> As the ancient sages have said,
> Good and ill follow in endless chain.

> (Waley's version)

And here is a song of opposites:

GOOD AND EVIL

We plant the orchids, but not the weeds;
And yet where the orchids grow, there grow the weeds.
Their roots and seeds are inseparably mingled;
Their stalks and leaves are inextricably entangled.
The sweet scent of the one and the bad smell of the other
Are undistinguishably mixed together.
To cut off the weeds would cause the orchids to perish:
To water the orchids is the weeds to nourish.
My mind is held in suspense between the two possibilities,

For both of them are attended with undesirabilities.

You are a wise man, my dear friend,

You may be able to solve this puzzle of my mind.

This vision of the permeation of good and ill in life haunts him so persistently that it would crop up even in the most unexpected places:

愈研究唐诗之季候，我则愈相信时代在某种程度下固然能影响个人，但是大致说来，个人却是隶属于某特一季候的。一个春季诗人，就是到了死期，也有物我皆春之意。一个秋季诗人，倘使他真真属于秋季的话，不待老成，便会觉得老气横秋。正像诗人所说的，孩子是成人的父亲。阿尔弗雷德·德·维尼曾说了一句对人类天性的认识最尖刻独到之语，"我的观察是，每个人都天然地代表某时代的精神，他也始终保持这精神"。

照我看来，白居易的诗是浸沉在万物对向通彻的哲学里。他天生是迫近道家的。不错，他"以儒家伦理为做人标准，以佛教净洗他的内心，以历史、书画、山水、美酒、乐曲和诗歌抚慰他的心灵"，可是这一切都是一个道家中人所要做的事。总之，《道德经》和《易经》这二部书是白居易人生哲学的骨髓。他说得很清楚：

常闻古人语，损益周必复。　　　　　　　　　（英译：韦利）

这里是一首善恶对向歌：

问友

种兰不种艾，兰生艾亦生。

根荄相交长，茎叶相附荣。

香茎与臭叶，日夜俱长大。

锄艾恐伤兰，溉兰恐滋艾。

兰亦未能溉，艾亦未能除。

沉吟意不决，问君合何如。

白居易深觉生活是充满了善与恶，就是他最闲散的时候，这种感觉也会从他的笔尖下漏出来：

CHILDREN

My niece, who is six years old, is called "Miss Tortoise";

My daughter of three,—little "Summer Dress."

One is beginning to learn to joke and talk;

The other can already recite poems and songs.

At morning they play clinging about my feet;

At night they sleep pillowed against my dress.

Why, children, did you reach the world so late,

Coming to me just when my years are spent?

Young things draw our feelings to them;

Old people easily give their hearts.

The sweetest vintage at last turns sour;

The full moon in the end begins to wane.

And so with men the bonds of love and affection

Soon may change to a load of sorrow and care.

But all the world is bound by love's ties;

Why did I think that I alone should escape?

(Waley's version)

This calls to mind a stanza which I have found in Shakespeare's *The Rape of Lucrece*:

Unruly blasts wait on the tender spring;

Unwholesome weeds take root with precious flowers;

The adder hisses where the sweet birds sing;

What virtue breeds iniquity devours:

We have no good that we can say is ours,

But ill-annexed Opportunity

Or kills his life or else his quality.

At this point I must make an explanation. I had said that Shakespeare was springy, and then dealing with Tu Fu I said that Shakespeare was summery. Now I find myself comparing him with an autumnal poet! Furthermore, did I not write the essay on "Shakespeare as a Taoist"? The conclusion seems to be unescapable that Shakespeare belongs to Autumn! *Mais non*! My present view is that he is springy in his heart, but autumnal in his head, and that's why he is so perfectly summery. As to Po Chü-i, it's an entirely different story. He is autumnal through and through, in his heart as well as in his head. For the Dialectical Process has two ends to it. One end leads to Heaven, the other to Hell. Shakespeare sees more of the bright side, and Po Chü-i more of the dark. The dark moments of

弄龟罗

有侄始六岁，字之为阿龟。有女生三年，其名曰罗儿。
一始学笑语，一能诵歌诗。朝戏抱我足，夜眠枕我衣。
汝生何其晚，我年行已衰。物情小可念，人意老多慈。
酒美竟须坏，月圆终有亏。亦如恩爱缘，乃是忧恼资。
举世同此累，吾安能去之。

（英译：韦利）

这使我想起莎士比亚《鲁克丽丝受辱记》中的一段：

狂飙侍立在温柔的春季旁；
患害的莠荑参杂在美花间；
德节所抚养的，被邪恶吞没；
小鸟婉歌，小蛇却嘻嘻不休；
我们不能声称我们有什么好东西，
除了不无瑕疵的"机会"，
或使美好事物夭折，或使其变味。

　　说到这里，我又要替自己解释了。我在序幕里说莎士比亚是春季的鸣禽，在论杜甫的时候我又说莎士比亚是属于夏季的。现在，好像矛盾得很，我竟将他同白居易比较！我可不曾写过《莎士比亚是道家论》那篇东西？最好的结论好像他是属于秋季的！可是事情并不如此简单！我现在的解释是，他的心灵是活跃如春，他的头脑却稳重如秋，所以他是一个极完美的夏季诗人。白居易又不同了。他从头到尾，不论心灵头脑，都是属于秋季的。我们须注意，大自然的辩证法有二个头，一个通到天堂，一个通到地狱。莎士比亚趋近天堂，白居易退缩到黑暗的一面去。莎士比亚的黑暗时期是像日

Shakespeare are like the eclipses of the sun, which will finally shine forth again in all its effulgence. His best Sonnets all testify to this eloquently. I wish especially to refer the reader to Sonnets XXX and XXXIII; and I cannot refrain from quoting this one in full:

> When, in disgrace with fortune and men's eyes,
> I all alone beweep my outcast state
> And trouble deaf heaven with my bootless cries
> And look upon myself and curse my fate,
> Wishing me like to one more rich in hope,
> Featured like him, like him with friends possess'd,
> Desiring this man's art and that man's scope,
> With what I most enjoy contented least;
> Yet in these thoughts myself almost despising,
> Haply I think on thee, and then my state,
> Like to the lark at break of day arising
> From sullen earth, sings hymns at heaven's gate;
> > For thy sweet love remember'd such wealth brings
> > That then I scorn to change my state with kings.

Love is his idol and prop. It is very significant that while he despises himself for his low spirits, Po is ashamed of his emotions! Here is a typical poem:

AWAKENED FROM THE DREAM OF LIFE

In the morning I weep over the death of a friend,
In the evening I weep over the death of a relative.
Friends and dear ones having passed away,
What is the use of my surviving alone?
The infinite ties of flesh and bone
Have raveled up my bowels into a knot of pain.
The accumulated affections of a life-time
Are turned into sour snuffles at the tip of my nose.
Griefs have enervated my limbs,

Weeping has dizzled my eyes.

In age I am only forty,

But at heart I am like a man of seventy.

I hear that in Buddhism they have a doctrine

Called "the Door of Emancipation":

Turn your heart into a still water,

Regard your body as a floating cloud;

蚀，不久即会全部出现，灿烂如昔。他最得意的十四行诗都证明这一点。我希望读者能参考他的商籁第三十和三十三两首。下面这一首尤其是可人：

> 在失意、命运不佳、遭人冷眼的时候，
> 我独自一人为自己不幸的遭遇悲泣，
> 对那片没有感情的天我枉然呼喊，
> 望着自己，只能诅咒自己的命运；
> 情愿自己是另一个人，有着更多的希望，
> 长得像他，像他一样地交友众多，
> 愿望有这个人的本领、那个人的地位，
> 对自己最喜欢的东西，最不满意。
> 可是在这近于自暴自弃的意念中，
> 忽然有想起你，于是我的心
> 就像一只黎明时的百灵，从昏暗的地面，
> 飞升。在天门旁唱着赞美的歌；
> 关于你蜜爱的回忆带给我那么多财产，
> 即使给我帝王的尊贵我也不愿意交换。

爱是他的偶像，他的倚赖。很值得注意，莎士比亚蔑视他自己的沮丧抑郁，白居易却以自己的情感为耻。这一首诗足以证明：

自觉二首·其二
> 朝哭心所爱，暮哭心所亲。亲爱零落尽，安用身独存。
> 几许平生欢，无限骨肉恩。结为肠间痛，聚作鼻头辛。
> 悲来四支缓，泣尽双眸昏。所以年四十，心如七十人。
> 我闻浮屠教，中有解脱门。置心为止水，视身如浮云。

Strip off your dust-stained clothes,

And tear yourself from the Whirl of Life and Death.

Ah, why should one cling to the love of bitterness?

Why linger and loiter in the labyrinths of the world?

Upon deliberation, I make a solemn vow:

I vow that this temporary body of mine

Shall only receive the consequences of my past *karma*,

But I shall never sow any seeds for future crops of woe!

I swear I shall wash away the annoying dust

With the waters of wisdom and grace,

So that I may be spared from reaping sorrows and griefs

From the seeds of affection and love!

Herein lies the difference between Christianity and Buddhism: Christ suffered in order to reap a crop of Love, whereas the Buddhists, at least those of the type of Po Chü-i, dare not even love for fear of reaping a crop of Sorrow. This also constitutes the difference between the West and the East. They espouse life whole-heartedly, but we try to play truant to it.

Where Keats would say:

Welcome joy, and welcome sorrow,

Lethe's weed and Hermes' feather;

Come today, and come tomorrow,

I love you both together!

Po Chü-i would say:

Those who are happy regret the shortness of the day;

Those who are sad tire of the year's sloth.

But those whose hearts are devoid of joy and sadness

Just go on living, regardless of "short" or "long."

(Waley's version)

Where Keats says:

Fair and foul I love together.

Po Chü-1 answers:

Black and white I have ignored together.

Where Keats asserts:

        ... let me slake

All my thirst for sweet heart-ache!

        斗擞垢秽衣，度脱生死轮。胡为恋此苦，不去犹逡巡。
        回念发弘愿，愿此见在身。但受过去报，不结将来因。
        誓以智慧水，永洗烦恼尘。不将恩爱子，更种悲忧根。

这里也就是基督教同佛教的区别：基督教因欲收获爱之丰稔而受难；佛教徒，至少白居易，因怕收获罪果而不敢放胆爱人。这也是东西之不同。西方人倾心钟爱生活，我们却想逃避它。

    济慈说：

        我喜爱欢乐，我喜爱忧愁，
        我喜爱迷魂河 [1] 的灵草
        和黑梅斯 [2] 的羽毛，
        今天，明天，你来，
        我一样欢喜你们。

    白居易说：

        乐人惜日促，忧人厌年赊。
        无忧无乐者，长短任生涯。   （英译：韦利）

【济慈说：

        美丑我同爱。

    白居易回答说：

        白黑无分别。

    济慈说：

        ……让我满足
        我对甜蜜心痛之渴念。

Po would pour his cold waters upon this enthusiasm:

> The Unicorn will be made into hash,
>
> And the Dragon into dried flesh.
>
> After all, the tortoise is not a fool:
>
> See how comfortably he trails his tail in the muddy pool!

*   *   *

REALIZING THE FUTILITY OF LIFE

> Ever since the time when I was a lusty boy
>
> Down till now when I am ill and old,
>
> The things I have cared for have been different at different times.
>
> But my being *busy*, *that* has never changed.
>
> *Then*, on the shore,—building sand-pagodas;
>
> *Now*, at Court, covered with tinkling jade.
>
> This and that,—equally childish games,
>
> Things whose substance passes in a moment of time!
>
> When there are no Scriptures, then Doctrine is sound.
>
> Even should one zealously strive to learn the Tao,
>
> That very striving will make one's error more.

(Waley's version)

A passionate nature preyed upon by the sense of Desolation—that is Po Chü-i. He is most akin to Matthew Arnold, who, with all smokescreen of "Sweetness and Light," is capable of occasional sincerity in thought and expression, as in this:

> Ah, love, let us be true
>
> To one another! for the world, which seems
>
> To lie before us like a land of dreams,
>
> So various, so beautiful, so new,
>
> Hath really neither joy, nor love, nor light,
>
> Nor certitude, nor peace, nor help for pain;
>
> And we are here as on a darkling plain
>
> Swept with confused alarms of struggle and flight,

To both Arnold and Po Chü-i, poetry ought in theory to be a criticism of life, but the best of their poems betray their precious theory, for they tell us in effect that life is not even worth criticizing! They seem to ask, *A quoi bon*? It is no accident that the very poem which all the competent anthologists regard as the best of Po, "The Song of the Lute-Girl," should

白居易会将冷水浇在这热忱上：

> 麒麟作脯龙为醢，何似泥中曳尾龟。

*　　*　　*

感悟妄缘，题如上人壁
自从为稚童，直至作衰翁。
所好随年异，为忙终日同。
弄沙成佛塔，锵玉谒王宫。
彼此皆儿戏，须臾即色空。
有营非了义，无著是真宗。
兼恐勤修道，犹应在妄中。　　　　　　　　（英译：韦利）

一个激昂的灵魂牺牲在萧条的冷手下——这是白居易。他最像善于施放《甜蜜与光明》的烟幕而时或寄情诗歌的阿诺德。阿诺德有时的确很诚恳，像这里：

> 啊，爱人，让我们真心对待彼此！
> 因为这卧在我们面前梦地似的世界，
> 看上来多么地五花八门，美丽、新鲜，
> 其实没有欢乐、爱情、光明、真诚、平安，
> 也没有急难之助。我们是像在黑暗的平原上，
> 那里斗杀溃逃的惊慌交错，
> 无知的军队在晚中互相杀戮。

在阿诺德和白居易看来，诗应该是生活之批评，可是他们最好的诗句都否认这话，因为他们都深觉生活是不值得批评的！他们好像都问："有什么用？"现在我们都以为《琵琶行》是白居易最好的作品，

have been spurned upon by himself as a merely occasional piece. For there we hear a cry of the outcasts in the air. There he is saturated through and through with the spirit of Autumn, and thus he is completely denuded. The denudation hurts his sense of dignity and self-respect. A Stoic is caught crying like a child for a little toothache! No, no, he would protest, this is not my real mood, I am beside myself! But posterity has judged differently. Let us listen to the voice of Autumn:

THE SONG OF THE LUTE-GIRL

The other night I went down to the riverside
To bid my friends farewell.
Maples and rushes all around,
Enchanted by Autumn's ghostly spell.

Dismounting from my horse, I found
My friends in the boat on the point of starting.
We drank some cups of wine in a cheerless mood,
For no music was there to soothe our parting.

The more we drank, the deeper we sank in despair,
For every cup brought our parting nearer.
At last, as I rose to say goodbye,
I saw the pale face of the moon in the river.

Suddenly we heard the sound of a lute on the waters,
Which gave us such a thrill in the heart
That I forgot to return,
And my friends were loath to start.

We traced the sound and called out aloud,
"Hey, who is playing the lute?"
The music stopped at once,
But the musician remained for a long time mute.

At last, the voice of a lady answered,

And we moved our boat nearer hers.
We invited her to come over to our boat
In the hope that she would play for us.

We relit the lamps,
We called for more wine,
We renewed our feast,
In a more cheerful state of mind.

But she was so modest and shy
That we had a hard time getting her to play.
Even then she still held her lute like a screen,
Behind which her pretty face was half hidden away.

可是他自己却认它为不足重视的草作。这并不是没有原因的。在那首诗里，我们听见一个已被奚落的人的泣声。我们发现白居易完全浸沉在秋季的空气内，没有掩饰，没有隐蔽，赤裸裸地站在前面。他颇觉得难为情，他觉得这有关尊严，有伤威风。一个稳健的老人，为了区区牙痛而像小孩子们破涕大哭！不不，他要声辩，这并不是我的真我，我有些发狂。可是后人并不这样说。现在让我们听秋季之声：

琵琶行
浔阳江头夜送客，枫叶荻花秋瑟瑟。
主人下马客在船，举酒欲饮无管弦。
醉不成欢惨将别，别时茫茫江浸月。
忽闻水上琵琶声，主人忘归客不发。
寻声暗问弹者谁，琵琶声停欲语迟。
移船相近邀相见，添酒回灯重开宴。
千呼万唤始出来，犹抱琵琶半遮面。

Then tuning up, she deftly turned the nuts,

And gave the strings a flying touch here and there.

The few scattered notes already had atmosphere,

Though they had not formed into an air.

Every string was charged with subdued emotion,

And every sound pregnant with past feelings,

As if she had breathed her soul into the lute,

Until it vibrated in unison with her heartstrings.

With bent head and nimble fingers,

She played on with such gusto and fire

That the infinite hoard of her breast

Seemed to be all laid bare.

Now a light skirmish, now a long-drawn dash;

Now a flying skip, now a violent snatch.

After "Robes of Clouds" she played a popular tune;

In her hands, the old and the new seemed well to match.

The base tones grumbled like a sudden storm.

The trebles murmured like the whisper of a lover.

Then hoarse and shrill at once, Oh, what a shower

Of pearls and pearlets upon a marble laver!

Anon an oriole, intoxicated with the flowers,

Pouring out the melody of her carefree soul!

Anon a streamlet sobbing stifledly

As it trickled down to the shoal!

Then the flow stopped as if it had crystallized into ice,

And there ensued a pause oozing with hidden sorrows,

Sorrows that lie too deep for music to score.

Ah! Divine Silence from which all music its meaning borrows!

Suddenly we were roused from our trance.

A silver vase had burst abruptly into bits,

And the pent-up waters gushed out with all their force!
Or was it the mailed horsemen giving each other deadly hits?

A deadening peal of diapason ended all,
Like the ruthless ripping of silk out of boiling spite!
Silence on all sides: not a sound stirred the air.
In the bosom of the river the Autumn moon was shining white.

The song is a long one. At this point, it is followed up with a story of the girl's life as told by herself. I beg to insert here a neat prose translation of this part by Herbert Giles:

"My childhood," said she, "was spent at the capital, in my home near the hills. At thirteen, I learned the guitar, and my name was enrolled among the *primas* of the day. The *maestro* himself acknowledged my skill; the most beauteous of women envied my lovely face. The youths of the neighborhood

转轴拨弦三两声，未成曲调先有情。
弦弦掩抑声声思，似诉平生不得志。
低眉信手续续弹，说尽心中无限事。
轻拢慢捻抹复挑，初为霓裳后六幺。
大弦嘈嘈如急雨，小弦切切如私语。
嘈嘈切切错杂弹，大珠小珠落玉盘。
间关莺语花底滑，幽咽泉流冰下难。
冰泉冷涩弦凝绝，凝绝不通声暂歇。
别有幽愁暗恨生，此时无声胜有声。
银瓶乍破水浆迸，铁骑突出刀枪鸣。
曲终收拨当心画，四弦一声如裂帛。
东船西舫悄无言，惟见江心秋月白。

【这首诗很长。接下来，女子讲述了她的故事（引用翟理思一段简洁的英译文）。】

自言本是京城女，家在虾蟆陵下住。
十三学得琵琶成，名属教坊第一部。
曲罢曾教善才伏，妆成每被秋娘妒。

vied with each other to do me honor: a single song brought me I know not how many costly bales. Golden ornaments and silver pins were smashed, blood-red shirts of silk were stained with wine, in oft-times echoing applause. And so I laughed from year to year, while the spring breeze and autumn moon swept over my careless head. Then my brother went away to the wars; my mother died. Nights passed and mornings came; and with them my beauty began to fade. My doors were no longer thronged; but few cavaliers remained. So I took a husband and became a trader's wife. He was all for gain, and little recked of separation from me. Last month he went off to buy tea, and I remained behind, to wander in my lonely boat on moon-lit nights over the cold wave, thinking of the happy days gone by, my reddened eyes telling of tearful dreams."

Frankness invites frankness, and our poet too opens himself up and tells his story:

> "I was already moved by your music,
> And your story has made me doubly sorry for your lot.
> For we are both castaways on the sea of life,
> And a casual meeting has found us in the same boat.

> "Since I left the Capital last year,
> I have lived in the city of Hsünyang.
> Illness and depression have taken hold of me,
> And throughout the year I have not heard a song.

> "I have made my home by the marshy river-bank
> Surrounded by yellow reeds and stunted bamboos.
> I have heard nothing but the gibbons' wailings,
> And the heart-rending notes of the cuckoos.

> "In the fine days of spring and moon-lit nights of Autumn,
> I drank all alone without the slightest feeling of cheer.
> And the hill songs and rural pipes
> Conveyed no meaning to my ear.

"But tonight your heavenly music
Has enlivened me through and through.
Refuse not to play one more tune for me,
And I will write a song for you."

Touched by my words, she resumed her seat,
And hit upon a minor key so desolate and forlorn
That all the hearers wept, and I most bitterly of all,
Until there was not a dry stitch on my gown.

五陵年少争缠头，一曲红绡不知数。
钿头云篦击节碎，血色罗裙翻酒污。
今年欢笑复明年，秋月春风等闲度。
弟走从军阿姨死，暮去朝来颜色故。
门前冷落车马稀，老大嫁作商人妇。
商人重利轻别离，前月浮梁买茶去。
去来江口守空船，绕船月明江水寒。
夜深忽梦少年事，梦啼妆泪红阑干。

【女子推心置腹，我们的诗人亦坦诚相待，讲述自己的故事：】

我闻琵琶已叹息，又闻此语重唧唧。
同是天涯沦落人，相逢何必曾相识！
我从去年辞帝京，谪居卧病浔阳城。
浔阳地僻无音乐，终岁不闻丝竹声。
住近湓江地低湿，黄芦苦竹绕宅生。
其间旦暮闻何物，杜鹃啼血猿哀鸣。
春江花朝秋月夜，往往取酒还独倾。
岂无山歌与村笛，呕哑嘲哳难为听。
今夜闻君琵琶语，如听仙乐耳暂明。
莫辞更坐弹一曲，为君翻作琵琶行。
感我此言良久立，却坐促弦弦转急。
凄凄不似向前声，满座重闻皆掩泣。
座中泣下谁最多？江州司马青衫湿。

217

IX.   AUTUMN: OTHER POETS

I wonder where on the desolate sea of life
The Muse is wailing the Autumn wind from year to year.

—Li Ho

I sing because my sorrows lie too deep for tears.

—Liu Chung-yuan

My drunken features are like the leaves of maples:
Though they are red, they are not Spring.

—Po Chü-i

Autumn wins you best by this, its mute
Appeal to sympathy for its decay.

—Robert Browning

Deep thoughts are decked by clearness.

—Vauvenargues

It is significant that the music of the lute-girl should have ended in a minor key. If we compare Po Chü-i's song with Crashaw's version of "Musick's Duell," it would look very anaemic indeed. But just here lies the secret charm of the autumnal poets, for they have a way of turning an anti-climax into a real climax! To them the sauce, not the fish, is the thing.

The truth is, poets are like sensitive barometers that reflect the slightest changes of the weather. The poets of this Season were living in an age of decline, and it would not be sincere for them to sing in a major key. The age was rotten to the core. Po Chü-i saw no less than eight Emperors on the throne; two of them were assassinated by their trusted eunuchs; one died in consequence of taking the Elixir of Life; another was a usurper who had killed his brother, the rightful Heir Apparent; and the rest were all wretched middlings. Political intrigues were rife, and border troubles and internal disorders became the order of the day.

In his "Song of the Bitter Cold," Han Yu (韩愈: 768- 824), consciously or unconsciously, seems to have reflected pretty faithfully the atmosphere of his age:

Sinister blasts are disturbing the Universe,
They are as sharp as a knife.
The sun and the moon, powerful as they are,
Are unable to breathe life into a dead toad.

玖 秋之余音

不见年年辽海上，文章何处哭秋风?	——李贺
我歌诚自恸。	——柳宗元
醉貌如霜叶，虽红不是春。	——白居易
秋季最胜人处，就是 它无声地乞人怜恤它的衰落。	——勃朗宁
清澈时常点缀深刻的思想。	——沃弗纳尔格

琵琶女之歌的结尾是凄凉的，这也就是它的重要。倘若我们将它同克拉肖的《音乐之斗》比较，它就显得孱弱无力得多了。可是秋季诗人的娟媚也就在这里，他们有方法在渐弱的笔调中，达到真正的峰顶。在他们看来，菜盆中的酱油较鱼来得重要。

事情是这样的，诗人们是像锐敏的气候表，反映出空气中最微小的变迁。这季的诗人活在国不泰、民不安的时代，当然不能兴奋地歌唱。这时代糟透了，白居易总共看见了不下八位天子，其中二个被他们亲信太监所暗杀，一个食长生药而死，一个是杀死亲兄的篡位者，其余四个都是无耻的庸物。政治阴谋层出不穷，国家内外都闹得暗无天日。

在《苦寒》那首诗里，故意或者无意，韩愈很忠实地反映出这时代的形势：

凶飙搅宇宙，铓刃甚割砭。
日月虽云尊，不能活乌蟾。

...

Ch'iu, Ch'iu, chirp the sparrows around the windows.

They don't know their own smallness and insignificance.

They lift up their heads to heaven and sing pleadingly.

They want to live for a few more moments.

It would be far better for you to be shot to death,

Then at least you will have a taste of fire when you are roasted!

I cannot imagine either Li Po or Tu Fu writing in this vein. Nor would they have produced the following lines:

The sky is jumping.

The earth is stumbling.

The cosmos has returned to Chaos.

*   *   *

The thunder-god chops

The mountains into chips.

The oceans are turned upside down.

*   *   *

With my face smeared with blood,

I went to God in the dreamland.

But at the gate of Heaven,

I was scolded by the gate-keeper.

*   *   *

My heart is cold like ice,

My sword white as snow.

But unable to run my sword

Through my slanderers,

My heart has rotted,

And my sword has snapped.

I do not regard Han Yu as a good poet. I agree entirely with an old Chinese critic, Shen Kua (沈括) that "Han Yu's poetry is prose in rhymes," although I must add that some of his prose writings, for example, that famous elegy on his nephew, may be called poetry without rhymes. This curious phenomenon is due to the fact that he does not seem to have taken poetry so seriously as he did prose. It appears to me that whenever he took to versification, he was in a frivolous mood, and regarded it only as a kind of literary acrobatics. He would sometimes, as in the "Song of the Stone-Drum," take in hand a dictionary of rhymes and try to show his resourcefulness by using almost all the words, however recondite and out of the way, of the same rhyme. He aims at "steepness" in language. To read his poetry is like watching a tight-rope dancer doing perilous feats over a yawning abyss. But

......

> 啾啾窗间雀，不知已微纤。
> 举头仰天鸣，所愿晷刻淹。
> 不如弹射死，却得亲鼎烊。

李白、杜甫当然说不出这种话：

> 天跳地踔颠乾坤。

＊　　＊　　＊

> 雷公擘山海水翻。

＊　　＊　　＊

> 梦通上帝血面论，侧身欲进叱于阍。

＊　　＊　　＊

> 我心如冰剑如雪，不能刺谗夫，使我心腐剑锋折。

韩愈我不认为是一个大诗人，我同意沈括说的"韩退之诗乃押韵之文耳"。不过话还得说回来，他的散文，若《祭十二郎文》等，反而可认为是不押韵的诗。这奇怪的现象也不难解释：写诗的时候，他总不像写文章时那么认真罢了。在他看来，诗只是一种文艺消遣品，所以不值得重视。有时候，像在《石鼓歌》里面，他手持韵文字典一册，选了其中最深奥的字，以期显示他的博学。他惟求文字上的"险奇"，读他的诗同看一个人在深崖上走绳索没有什么分别。

poetry is no circus. Was he thinking of his art of poesy when he said:

> I draw a snake and give it legs, to find I've wasted skill?

(Giles' version)

But one thing is significant. As some keen critic has pointed out, Han Yu fed himself upon "the beauty of ugliness." It seems that he deliberately and with malice aforethought, as the lawyers would say, used words which are almost disgusting, such as "vomiting," "purging," "lice," "ulcer," "a rotten frog," and even "ordure." All this reflects the dirty age. "Where all is rotten," says the English philosopher F. H. Bradley, "it is a man's work to cry stinking fish."

But this is a *man's* work, not a *woman's* work; and Han Yu is the only masculine writer in this period of Autumn. All the other men respond to the same environment in a more or less *feminine* way. They shied away from life, and found in art their only consolation, and their only shield against the sordid perils of actual existence. Disgusted with life, they withdrew into themselves, and poetry became their dominant passion and remained their lifelong infatuation. Even as many-sided and moderate a man as Po Chü-i confesses to his weakness:

> There is no one among men that has not a special failing:
> And my failing consists in writing verses.
> I have broken away from the thousand ties of life:
> But this infirmity still remains behind.
> Each time that I look at a fine landscape,
> Each time that I meet a loved friend,
> I raise my voice and recite a stanza of poetry
> And am glad as though a God had crossed my path.
>
> *   *   *
>
> My mad singing startles the valleys and hills:
> The apes and birds all come to peep.
> Fearing to become a laughing-stock to the world,

I choose a place that is unfrequented by men.

(Waley's version)

He was madly in love with the Muse, and he was afraid of becoming a laughing-stock to the world. This is perhaps why he laid so much emphasis on the practical utility of poetry, just as a man who loves a girl for her sheer beauty would explain to his friends that she is a very able house-keeper as well. As a matter of fact, Po is a futilitarian masquerading as a utilitarian. But as we shall see, with most of the other poets in this period,

但是我们知道，诗并不是马戏。他可想到诗的艺术，当他说"画蛇著足无处用（翟理思英译）"这句话的时候？

【有一点很重要。】某批评家曾指出，韩愈喜欢"丑物之美"。他好像故意（或像律师常说——蓄意）用令人厌恶的字，若"啰""涤""虱""疮""蛤蟆"，甚至于"粪丸"。这一切都反映出时代的污秽。英国哲学家 F. H. 布拉德利说："一切都糟糕的时候，即使去叫卖臭鱼，亦不足为耻。"

不过，这是男人的工作，不是女人的工作，韩愈也就是秋季仅有的刚性诗人。别人对社会环境的反响都是柔性的：他们逃避生活，在艺术找到了安慰，找到了抵御生命危险的盾牌。或许，他们都已厌倦生活，所以就向内心中退缩，诗歌于是变成了他们惟一的伴侣、终身的爱物。就是多才虚逊的白居易，也承认他的弱点：

> 人各有一癖，我癖在章句。
> 万缘皆已消，此病独未去。
> 每逢美风景，或对好亲故。
> 高声咏一篇，恍若与神遇。
>
> ＊　　＊　　＊
>
> 狂吟惊林壑，猿鸟皆窥觑。
> 恐为世所嗤，故就无人处。

（英译：韦利）

他在恋"文艺女神"，但他又怕世人取笑。这足以解释他为什么如此着重诗的实用，正像一个人痛爱一个女子的美，而对他朋友说她很善操家事。其实，白居易是一个虚无论者矫饰一个功利论者。但

their love for their Mistress was much more open and unashamed. They would even kiss her in public! Let us see how they did it.

Chia Tao (贾岛: 779–843) brooded for three years over the wording of just these two lines:

> A lonely shadow walking at the bottom of the pond,
> A body that hath often lodged amidst the woods.

As a foot-note to these lines, he wrote a quatrain:

> Two lines of poetry in three years!
> Each time I sing, two streams of tears!
> If the understanding reader fails to smile and praise,
> I'll to the hills and sleep away the rest of my days!
>
> (Teresa Li's version)

Here is a man who ploughs his lonely furrow alone. But he was soon to meet his friend Han Yu. Once he was riding on a donkey in the streets of Chang-an, and suddenly two lines flashed across his mind:

> The birds nestle quietly in the trees by the side of a lake.
> A monk is knocking on a moon-lit door.

Then he thought of changing "knocking" into "pushing," making unconscious gestures with his hands. He was so absorbed that he was not aware that his donkey, apparently nonplussed by the unexpected knocks, had stopped and was standing in the way of an officer's carriage. He was arrested before the officer, who was none other than Han Yu. Han asked him what he was doing with his funny gestures, and Chia told him the whole story. Instead of punishing him, Han suggested that he should retain the original word "knocking." That was the beginning of their friendship. More than a millennium has passed since then, but even today I have just received a letter from a Chinese poet of the old school, enclosing two poems and asking me politely to "knock-push" them! Such is the continuity of the cultural life of China!

Meng Chiao (孟郊: 751–814), another friend of Han Yu, whose

position among his friends, by the way, reminds me of that of Dr. Johnson, wrote of himself:

I hum my poems all night long.

Ghosts seem to be hovering around me and wailing with me.

I wonder why I take poetry so seriously and will have no rest.

My soul seems to be bent upon wearing out my body like a bitter
    enemy.

是这时期别几位诗人都公开地表示他们对"情妇"的爱。他们要在大庭广众前拥吻她！现在让我们看吧。

　　贾岛（779—843）费了三年工夫的苦心思索，才写了下面二行：

　　　　独行潭底影，数息树边身。

他又写了一首四行小诗，当作注解：

　　　　两句三年得，一吟双泪流。
　　　　知音如不赏，归卧故山秋。　　　　　　　　　　（英译：李德兰）

他耿介地耕耘他的田，但是不久他便遇见韩愈。有一次他在长安一条街上骑着一匹驴子，忽然诗性勃发，口中念出如下二句：

　　　　鸟宿池边树，僧敲月下门。

这时候他想将"敲"字改作"推"，手中便不觉地做起手势来。他过于专注，没意识到他骑的驴子，因受了震动的关系，突然停在一个官吏的车子面前，阻了它的路。贾岛早已被人拖下，揪到这官的面前，这位官就是韩愈。韩愈问他为什么做出如此好笑的傻样子，他便将事实说出来。韩愈非但不罚他，反而对他说应该用"敲"字。这是他们友谊的开始。从那时到现在，一千多年已经消逝了。可是今日我还收到一位旧派诗人的一封信，附了两首诗，很谦逊地叫我"推敲推敲"。我们中国的文化生命便这样绵延下去。

　　孟郊（751—814）也是韩愈的朋友，他的地位使我想起英国十八世纪大文豪约翰逊博士：

　　　　夜学晓未休，苦吟神鬼愁。
　　　　如何不自闲，心与身为仇。

Meng was not happy with the examiners, for he did not even succeed in taking his first degree. A failure in life, he is, however, quite a success in poetry. He sings of his poverty and adversity all the time. But what else could he sing? Su Tung-po compares him to a hedge-cricket shivering in the cold. But the Autumn of T'ang poetry would not be complete without such mournful singers. The following are some of his characteristic lines:

> A man shivering in the cold
> Wishes to be turned into a moth;
> For then he can fly to the luscious wax
> To burn himself to death!

> *　　*　　*

> When the cold air enters the ulcers,
> What a gnawing pain I feel in the night!

> *　　*　　*

> Too poor to get candles for the night,
> I read my books in the bright moonlight.

> *　　*　　*

> When the rich take leave of each other,
> There is sorrow in their faces.
> But when poor people part,
> Sorrows penetrate into their bones.

> *　　*　　*

> Always feeding on cheap vegetables,
> My very viscera are bitter,
> I force myself to sing,
> But my song is without joy.
> I meet obstacles wherever I go,
> And yet people say that the Universe is wide!

But it is on the strength of just one song that he has lived throughout all the generations and will continue to live in all the generations to come, "The Song of a Wandering Son":

Thread in the hands of a doting mother:

Clothes on the body of a far-journeying son.

Upon his leaving, she adds one stitch after another,

Lest haply he may not return so soon.

Ah! How could the heart of an inch-long grass

Requite a whole Spring's infinite love and grace?

I cannot imagine any anthology of Chinese poetry that does not include this simple hymn to motherly love. It introduces one to the Fifteen Mysteries of the Rosary:

他在考场内的运气很不佳，连初试都不曾遭取。他的生活可说是失败的，但是他的诗却是成功的。他不断地唱述他自己的贫苦不幸，因为，除此以外，他还能唱些什么？苏东坡将他比拟在寒冷中抖栗的蟋蟀，这很对。唐诗之秋，倘若没有这种悲哀的音调，便不会完全。下面数行很足以代表他的面目：

> 寒者愿为蛾，烧死彼华膏。
>   *　　*　　*
> 冷气入疮痛，夜来痛如何。
>   *　　*　　*
> 夜贫灯烛绝，明月照吾书。
>   *　　*　　*
> 富别愁在颜，贫别愁销骨。
>   *　　*　　*
> 食荠肠亦苦，强歌声无欢。
> 出门即有碍，谁谓天地宽。

但是仅《游子吟》这一首诗，已足使他永垂不朽：

> 慈母手中线，游子身上衣。
> 临行密密缝，意恐迟迟归。
> 谁言寸草心，报得三春晖！

在中国，倘若一本诗选不将这首歌颂母爱的诗选进，那真要闹笑话了。它使我们想起《玫瑰经》中的"十五玄妙"：

> We are seeking for a mother
>
> O'er the earth so waste and wide.

It was not for nothing that William Cowper, another autumnal poet, who wrote "The Castaway," should also have written such tender lines about his mother. When the world is treating you like a step-mother, what is more natural for a child then to wish, with Alexander Pope (who is no less autumnal):

> To rock the cradle of declining age?

But how many persons possess such a privilege?

Another fanatical lover of the Muse is Chang Chieh (张籍: *circa* 767–830), who is said to have burned a scroll of Tu Fu's poems, and, mixing the ashes with honey, taken a mouthful of it from time to time, saying, "This will change my viscera!" I don't know whether it had *changed* him, but it certainly had *cleansed* him in and out. It is always a delight to read his poems, or even to look at them. They are so very neat and pure. Every word in them is as clear as crystal, as lovely as pearl, and as unsullied as a white jade. Of all colors he likes whiteness best, if we may judge by the frequency with which he uses the word "white." He never tires of speaking of the "white sun," "white silk," "white bones," "white hairs," "white atmosphere," "white China-grass," "white sand," "white waters," "white silver," "white water-lily," "white cloud," "white stork," "white stone," "white goblet," "white stamens," "white feathers," "white dew," "white iguana," "white dragon," and finally the "White Star." If he has not got the soul of Autumn, he has at least got its color. For according to a deep-rooted folklore of our country, Spring is green, Summer red, Winter black, and Autumn white. Autumn is like a middle-aged man who has seen so many colors in life that all of them begin to merge into whiteness, if not into colorlessness, as the colors of the rainbow vanish into nothing on "Newton's disc" when it is set a-rolling. And we must keep in mind that in Chang Chieh's time, the world was so muddy and bloody that one had only to look at it long enough to see a spontaneous vision of a quite different color arise before one's eyes, as in the case of crystal gazing. The same subtle reaction was at work when Tao Yuan-ming dreamed of the "Peach-Blossom Fountain"—T'ao Yuan-ming who lived in a time when, as he testified:

在这荒凉、广泛的地球上，
我们寻找一个母亲。

另一位秋季诗人威廉·柯珀——《流浪者》的作者，写了如此温柔动人的思母诗，这并不是不无原因的。当这整个世界都像一个后母那样处待你时，一个小孩，除了随诗人蒲柏（也很秋季的一位诗人）愿望，"一摇这衰落时代的睡床"外，还有什么话可说？可是有多少人有这种福气？

张籍（约767—830）也狂恋诗神。据说他焚烧了一卷杜甫的诗，将烧剩下的灰拌了蜜糖，不时飨腹，并说"改易肝肠"！内脏可曾改换则不得而知，但是他整个身体的里外，确被洗干净了。读他的诗，不，只要看他的诗，我们就觉得高兴，因为它是多么地清纯！每一个字都像水晶那样澄澈，像珍珠那样可爱，像白玉那样雅洁。从他用"白"这字的次数看来，在各种颜色中他最爱"白"。他始终不倦地说起"白日""白练""白骨""白发""白气""白草""白沙""白水""白银""白荷""白云""白鹤""白石""白杯""白蕊""白毛""白露""白鼍""白龙"，最后"白星"。假使他没有抓住秋季的灵魂的话，他至少抓住了秋季的颜色。照我们古时传下的一则故事说来，春季的颜色是绿的，夏季是红的，冬季是黑的，秋季是白的。秋季是像一个中年人，他曾看见生活不同的颜色，现在一切都转成白色（或无色），正像虹光不同的色彩射在旋转的"牛顿盘"上，便倏然不见一样。我们须记牢，在张籍的时代，这世界正闹得乌烟瘴气，我们只要对它凝视少息，便会看见一个色彩不同的幻象，像看圆光镜一样。陶渊明梦见"桃花源"，也就是这种幻象，因为他的时代，像他自己说的：

Darkening clouds hang over our heads;

The showers of the season pour without cease.

Not a streak of light in the skies above;

Not a smooth road on the earth below!

But I just wonder why George Meredith should have used "white" no less than thirteen times in his "Love in the Valley," which contains two hundred and eight lines in all. Was his time as dirty as the age of Chang Chieh? Or was it due to the queer *fin de siècle* feeling? I leave this little query to the students of English literature. In the meantime, let me give a specimen from Chang Chieh.

THE CHASTE WIFE'S REPLY

Knowing well that I am a married woman,

You sent me as a gift a pair of bright pearls.

Moved by your tenacious love and devotion,

I fixed them on to my red silken vest.

But fair sir, I belong to a household of high honor,

My dear husband being a bulwark to the Royal Throne.

I know your love is as bright as the sun and the moon;

But I am sworn to serve my lord and my lord alone.

With tears flowing from eyes, I return you the pearls.

Wish I had met you before the day of my wedding!

Now what was the occasion of this poem? At that time, Chang Chieh was serving in the camp of a warlord, who was loyal to the Emperor. Another warlord of doubtful fidelity sent him a letter and tried to entice him to his camp by a generous gift of money. He sent back the money and wrote him a letter enclosing this poem. A keen contemporary critic, commenting upon it, has observed that while this poem has two sides to it, the outer side and the inner, it can be enjoyed even without knowing the inner side. But what I want to point out here is that the desire to keep himself pure and chaste in the midst of a muddy world, so nicely expressed in this poem, seems to chime in perfectly with his preference for the white color.

Now we come to the greatest of the minor poets in the whole of T'ang, Li Ho (李贺), who was born in 790 and died in his twenty-sixth year in 816. It is said that he began to write poems as early as six years old, and very soon won the recognition of Han Yu. When still under twenty he went to the Capital to take the examination leading to the first degree of *chin-shih*. But those who were jealous of his talents objected to his being a candidate for *chin-shih* on the flimsy ground that his father's name was

> 霭霭停云，濛濛时雨。
> 八表同昏，平路伊阻。

我又奇怪，为什么乔治·梅瑞狄斯在《爱在山谷》的二百零八行诗内用了不下十三次"白"字？难道他的时代也和张籍的一样糟？还是为了"世纪末"的感觉？这个小问题我留给研究英国文学的人回答。现在让我引一首张籍的作品（《节妇吟·寄东平李司空师道》）：

> 君知妾有夫，赠妾双明珠。
> 感君缠绵意，系在红罗襦。
> 妾家高楼连苑起，良人执戟明光里。
> 知君用心如日月，事夫誓拟同生死。
> 还君明珠双泪垂，恨不相逢未嫁时。

张籍为什么写这首诗？那时候，他在一个军阀手下做事，这军阀对皇帝还忠诚。另一个态度可疑的军阀以重金赠他，意欲招他入幕，张籍将礼金退还，并附了这首诗。近来有一个很有见地的批评家，他说这诗的意义固然是双关的，但是即使我们不知作者的原意，也能一样欣赏它。可是我要指出的只是另外一点：他在这首诗内所表示要保持自己清白无疵的意思，同他偏爱"白"字的性情完全符合。

现在我们谈李贺。他不仅是唐诗秋季，并且是整个唐朝最伟大的次要诗人。他生于790年，二十六岁即死。据说他六岁时便开始写诗，不久就为韩愈所赏识。不到二十他便进京考试，但是嫉忌他才能的人却卑鄙地从中作梗，说他不能取得进士荣衔，因为他父亲

"Chin Su." It's extremely absurd, isn't it? How would you feel if people object to your taking the Bachelor of Arts degree because your mother comes from a family of Batchelders? Han Yu took up his cudgels for his friend, and wrote a very eloquent defense. "If a son cannot be a *chin-shih* because his father is called 'Chin Su'," he argues, "then it would follow that a son cannot be a man if his father is called 'Humanity'." Logically the argument is unanswerable, but it did not convince the examiners. It was an age of literary taboos, superstitions, inhibitions, and frustrations.

But Li Ho was a poetry-intoxicated boy. Every morning he went out on horse-back, carrying his stationeries with him, and followed by a little slave with a silken bag on his back. Whenever the inspiration came, he would immediately jot down the lines on a slip of paper and throw it into the bag. In the evening, when he returned, he looked into the bag as a fisherman would look into his basket at eventide, and took out all the slips, arranging the isolated lines into stanzas and poems. It is said that he did this every day except when he was drunk or had to attend some funeral service in the neighborhood. Whenever his mother saw the bag packed full with slips, she would say tenderly but not without pain at heart, "This boy will not be satisfied until he will have exhausted himself by pouring out his very heart into poetry!" Indeed, it is much easier to cut off the habit of opium-smoking than to tear oneself away from the grip of the Muse. The Muse is a jealous mistress, and no one can ever hope to win her heart, unless one pours out one's heart to her. In the case of Li Ho, the Muse eats him up as the ferocious female mantis does her mate! He died in his twenties, but he had completed the mission of his life. He had produced a type of poetry which has cut an indelible impression on the river of Time. And our consolation is that he would have died more than two hundred years ago, even if he had lived as long as the fabulous P'eng Chu. After all, we must remember that a poet is only a detour of nature to arrive at a few poems of lasting value.

Old critics of the highest standing have compared Li Ho with Li Po.

Li Po, they say, is a fairy-like genius; while Li Ho is a ghostly genius. I endorse their judgment with all my heart, but nobody has ever pointed out that it is as impossible for Spring to produce a Li Ho as it is for Autumn to produce a Li Po.

Another race has been, and other palms are won.

Let us see what kind of poems he writes:

的名字是"晋肃"。这可笑不可笑?【假如有人反对你取得文学学士学位,就因为你母亲姓巴彻尔德,你作何感想?】韩愈替他抱不平,写了一篇《讳辩》。他说:"父名晋肃,子不得举进士;若父名仁,子不得为人乎?"在逻辑上说来,这是解释不通的,考官们置之不理。这是一个文学禁忌、迷信、挫抑、阻挠的时期。

李贺沉溺于诗中。每天早晨他骑了马出外,带了笔墨文具,令一个小厮背了一个锦囊跟在后面。灵感来时,他就拿一条纸写下数行,随后投入囊中。晚上回家后,像一个渔夫在黄昏时收集他的鱼一样,整理囊内的纸条,然后将它们排成整首的诗。他每天如此做,未尝间断,除了酒醉或赴邻人丧礼的时候。当他母亲看见他的锦囊内塞满了纸条时,心中当然不免痛苦,便温柔地说:"是儿要当呕出心乃始已尔。"诚然,要逃脱"文艺女神"的手掌,简直比解根深的烟瘾还难!她是一个多妒的情妇,我们不能博得她的欢心,除非我们将整个的心都献给她。李贺怎样呢?"文艺女神"将他消磨尽了,正像一只凶猛的雌螳螂吞食它的伴侣一样。他只活了二十多年,但是他已完成了他的使命。他产生了一种诗,在时间的河流上刻下不可磨灭的印迹。天下没有不死的人,就是他能像传说中的彭祖活到八百岁,也终不免一死。我们须记牢,诗人不过是大自然的一段迂回,用以写出一二首不朽的诗而已。

古时有名的批评家曾将李白和李贺比较。李白,他们说是仙才,李贺是鬼才。我完全嘉纳他们的话,可是没有人指出春季不能产生一个李贺,正像秋季不能产生李白一样。诗人华兹华斯说:"又有一圈赛跑完了,又有棕枝赢得了。"

现在让我们看他写的是哪一类的诗:

233

Glazed goblets
Of rich-colored ambers.
From the little plume
Wine flows in drops
Like dainty crimson pearls.

Dragons are cooked,
Phoenixes roasted.
Their grease and fat, jade-white,
Weep tears clean and bright.

Let's blow the dragon-flute!
Let's beat the iguana-drum!
Let the pearly teeth sing!
Let the slender waists dance!

Don't you see green Spring is near its sunset,
And peach-blossoms are falling like a shower of red rain?

Let's drink for a whole day!
Wine does not go down to the grave of Liu Ling.

*　　*　　*

Autumn wolds bright.
Autumn wind white.
The pool clear and deep.
Tsê, tsê, the insects chirp.

At the root of the clouds grows lichen,
Lending colors to the rocks on the hill.
The flowers are coldly red, weeping tears of dew,
Shedding around them an atmosphere of delicate sadness.

On the fields, wild and desolate,
Sprouts of rice are just shooting out like little forks.
Ah, it's Double Nine! Why have you come so late?

Somnolent glow-worms flit low
Across the dilapidated dykes.

Water flows in the veins of stone,
Washing out the sands one by one.

Goethe has said that everything that is alive forms an atmosphere around itself. And what a ghostly atmosphere these poems shed! They send an eerie sensation down your spine.

The corpse-candles look as if painted on the pine-trees,
Setting them afire with flowers!

These flowers, blazing and gorgeous as they are, remind you of the bright silver linings on a black coffin. A borrowed glory, yes; but the very "borrowedness" is the property of Autumn. Sometime ago I had a hunch

琉璃钟，琥珀浓，小槽酒滴真珠红。
烹龙炮凤玉脂泣，罗帏绣幕围香风。
吹龙笛，击鼍鼓；皓齿歌，细腰舞。
况是青春日将暮，桃花乱落如红雨。
劝君终日酩酊醉，酒不到刘伶坟上土！

       *   *   *

秋野明，秋风白，塘水漻漻虫啧啧。
云根苔藓山上石，冷红泣露娇啼色。
荒畦九月稻叉牙，蛰萤低飞陇径斜。
石脉水流泉滴沙，

歌德曾说，一切有生命的东西，都发生出一种空气。李贺的诗产生的空气是多么地阴森！一种鬼怪的感觉直伸到你背脊骨的深处——

鬼灯如漆点松花。

这些松花，华丽炫目固然是不必怀疑的，却使你想起黑漆灵柩上放光的白银边。这美不是本有的，乃是借来的。不错，这特

which I have set down in verse:

>Spring challenges, Summer fights,
>
>Autumn borrows, Winter steals.

I have found that the works of Li Ho have confirmed my hunch so far as Autumn is concerned.

I shall now give some lines from Li Ho:

>Under the bright moonlight,
>
>Autumn drops tears of white dew.

*   *   *

>Through the prism of tears, the lamp
>
>Now brightens up, now flickers out.

*   *   *

>If heaven had the feelings of man,
>
>Heaven itself would have grown old.

*   *   *

>The moon-lit dew drops crystal tears.

*   *   *

>My poetry envelopes two strings of tears.

*   *   *

>The day is warm, but desolate is my heart.

*   *   *

>I am twenty but not happy,
>
>My heart has decayed like a withered orchid.

*   *   *

>Can youth be always young?
>
>Even the sea may someday be turned into a mulberry field.

*   *   *

>All over the Autumn hillsides,
>
>The mothers of the ghosts are wailing aloud.

*   *   *

>Ghostly rains are sprinkling an empty field.

*   *   *

The ghosts are weeping, but *a quoi bon*?

*   *   *

The marble stones on the hills
Are weeping transparent tears.

点就是秋季的精神。不久前我曾说过，"春激夏战，秋借冬偷"。关于秋季，我发现李贺证实了我的怀疑。现在让我举几个例子：

月明白露秋泪滴。

*   *   *

泪眼看灯乍明灭。

*   *   *

天若有情天亦老。

*   *   *

光露泣幽泪。

诗封两条泪。

*   *   *

日暖自萧条。

*   *   *

我当二十不得意，一心愁谢如枯兰。

*   *   *

少年安得长少年？海波尚变为桑田。

*   *   *

嗷嗷鬼母秋郊哭。

*   *   *

鬼雨洒空草。

*   *   *

鬼哭复何益。

*   *   *

山罍泣清漏。

*   *   *

Let the peach-blossoms of Hsi Wang Mu

Bloom a thousand times,

And how many times P'eng Chu and Wu Yen

Would have died?

*   *   *

Life is like a candlelight in a breeze.

*   *   *

Today the flag has burst into flowers:

Tomorrow will see the maple-leaves wither.

How all these lines remind me of Shelley's "Omens":

Hark! the owlet flaps his wings

In the pathless dell beneath;

Hark! 'tis the night-raven sings

Tidings of approaching death.

It may surprise my readers, but I have found much affinity between Li Ho and Shelley. Chinese critics have pointed to the fact that Li Ho is so fascinated by the pale ghost of Death that he often writes his poems in the very rhyme of the word "death." I have found the same true of Shelley. But how is it that the total impressions of these two poets are so different from each other? My tentative answer is that Shelley is an autumnal spirit born in an age of Summer, in an age in which he could absorb such hot stuff as the philosophy of Godwin; while Li Ho is autumnal in and out—both in his own heart and in his external environment, the future stretched out before him in desolate emptiness.

This period has so many poets—"teeming with rich increase," as Shakespeare would say—that I have to skip over many of them and give only a passing glance at a few others whom I cannot possibly omit. First of all there is Liu Chung-yuan (柳宗元: 773–819), who, together with Han Yu, did for Chinese prose what men like Dryden, Swift, Addison and Goldsmith did for English prose, but who is also no mean poet. See how he writes:

Myriad mountains   not a bird flying.

Endless roads—not a trace of men.

Only an old fisherman in a lonely boat,

Angling silently in the river covered with snow.

＊　＊　＊

王母桃花千遍红，彭祖巫咸几回死？

＊　＊　＊

风吹盘上烛。

＊　＊　＊

今日菖蒲花，明朝枫树老。

这数行还使我想起雪莱的《预兆》：

听！在下面无径的林谷中，
　　这幼枭鼓拍它的翅翼。
听，这是夜鸦，报唱
　　将临的死亡。

　　读者们听了或会觉奇怪，我的确发现雪莱同李贺有很多的相似点。有人说，李贺迷醉死亡的黯淡的鬼灵，就是他用的韵也同"死"字相合。我说雪莱也是如此。但是问题来了，为什么这二位诗人给我们的印象如此绝对不同？我的意思是，雪莱是一个生在夏季的秋季幽灵，所以他能不怕炎热而吸收戈德温的哲学；李贺的里外都是秋季的——在他的内心中，照他的环境看来——将来只是一片萧寥的空虚。

　　这一时期产生了许多诗人，正如莎翁所说"硕果累累"。为了篇幅关系，有许多人我们只能忽过不提；不能忽过的，我们也只能窥其大概。第一个是柳宗元（773—819），他和韩愈在中国散文界的地位，正像德莱顿、斯威夫特、艾迪生和哥尔德斯密斯在英国散文界的地位一样，但是他写的诗也不坏。这里是一首（《江雪》）：

千山鸟飞绝，万径人踪灭。
孤舟蓑笠翁，独钓寒江雪。

You cannot have a better picture of the soul of Autumn than this. And the language is an embodiment of steeliness. If Li Po wrote with a swan's feather, Tu Fu with a pen of gold, and Po Chü-i with a simple brush, Liu Chung-yuan, in prose as well as in poetry, wrote with a bronzed stiletto.

Then we have Wei Yin-wu (韦应物: *circa* 737–791), whom Chu Hsi has rated even above Wang Wei, being "more limpid, colorless, flavorless, and savorless" than the latter. Chu Hsi ought to have said that he is autumnal while Wang Wei is springy. Who but a child of Autumn could have written a political allegory like this:

> Alas for the lonely plant that grows beside the riverbed,
> While the mango-bird screams loud and long from the tall tree overhead!
> Full with the freshets of the spring, the torrent rushes on;
> The ferry-boat swings idly, for the ferryman is gone.
>
> (Giles' version)

A ferry-boat without a ferryman! That was the plight in which the ship of state found itself in his age. To a friend, he wrote:

> Last year when parted the flowers were blooming.
> Today I see the same flowers blooming again.
> The events of the world are becoming more and more vague and
>   unpredictable.
> The sorrows of Spring have so darkened my spirit that I only want to
>   sleep.

Nor can we omit Liu Yu-hsi (刘禹锡: 772–842), who still lives by half a dozen of his poems. The best-known is also the most typically autumnal:

> By the side of the Red-Sparrow Bridge,
> The wild grasses are bursting into flowers.
> At the mouth of the Black-Clothes Lane
> Are shining the slanting beams of the evening sun.
> The swallows that used to frequent
> The towering mansions of the erstwhile great men,

Now are flying into the humble homes

Of the ordinary people.

Poetry is entering into a reminiscent mood, isn't it? But the most reminiscent of all is Yuan Chen (元稹: 779–831), who has won immortality by his elegies on his wife, which contain these unforgettable lines:

I remember how you fumbled in the suitcases

In order to find more clothes for me.

I remember how I impelled you to pawn

Your golden hairpin to change for more wine.

这样秋季的灵魂的描写，可说是天衣无缝、精确无比的了，这首诗的文字也可以说是刚硬的代表。倘若我们说李白用的是雁毛笔，杜甫用的是金笔，白居易用的是普通毛笔的话，那么无论写文还是作诗，柳宗元用的当然是一根钢针了。

其次，我们谈韦应物（约737—791）。朱熹将他列在王维之上，因为他较王维来得"更清澄、更疏淡"。朱熹应该说他属于秋季，而王维属于春季。除了秋季的孩子，谁会写出这种政治寓言：

独怜幽草涧边生，上有黄鹂深树鸣。

春潮带雨晚来急，野渡无人舟自横。 （英译：翟理思）

一条没有船夫的船，这是唐朝那时的惨况。下面是一首他赠友人的诗：

去年花里逢君别，今日花开已一年。

世事茫茫难自料，春愁黯黯独成眠。

此外，我们也不能忽过刘禹锡（772—842），到现在他还靠了六七首诗而在我们的脑海浮现，其中最驰名的一首也就是最"秋季的"：

朱雀桥边野草花，乌衣巷口夕阳斜。

旧时王谢堂前燕，飞入寻常百姓家。

诗走进了回忆的境界中，是不是？但是最能引起回忆的是元稹（779—831），他吊妻的那首诗使他永垂不朽，其中有如此不可忘却的数行：

顾我无衣搜荩箧，泥他沽酒拔金钗。

...

I have nothing but a winkless night
Of memories and sighs to requite,
A lifetime of hardships
And ever-knit eyebrows.

Henry King in his "Exequy on His Wife" concluded with a hope:

... I am content to live
Divided, with but half a heart,
Till we shall meet and never part.

But Yuan was not so sanguine:

To lie together in the cold grave,
What does that amount to anyway?
To meet you in our after life again
Is a hope I dare not even entertain.

If Yuan Chen were living today, he would wonder why some young people are so anxious to divorce their wives when there is in store for them an Eternity of separation.

There are many poems on the tragedy of Ming Huang and Kuei-fei. The longest is from the hands of Po Chü-i, the shortest is by Yuan Chen. I like the latter even more than the former:

A desolate old Traveling Palace.
The flowers in utter loneliness blush.
A white-headed maid-of-honor is there,
Sitting idly and telling stories about Hsüan Tsung.

But I cannot bid goodbye to Autumn without mentioning an elder contemporary of Po Chü-i, Chang Chi (张继), who introduced Autumn and set the tone to it by this remarkable poem which he wrote in a boat temporarily moored in Soochow:

The moon has gone down.

The crows are crying.
The air is filled with frost.

The maples on the river-banks
And the fishermen's lanterns
Breed somber thoughts in me,
As I lie sleepless in bed.

From the Cold Hill Temple outside the City of Wusu
Come the echoes of a midnight bell to a passing boat.

......

惟将终夜长开眼，报答平生未展眉。

亨利·金的《葬妻曲》的结了是希望：

......我满意现在的分离；

带了半颗心，

期望着我们再遇，永不分离的时候。

元稹天性并不如此富于热望：

同穴窅冥何所望？他生缘会更难期！

倘使他今日还活着的话，他会奇怪，当永久的分离就近在目前的时候，为什么有些青年还急于要离婚？

我们有许多诗关于明皇贵妃的事，其中最长的是白居易的，最短的是元稹的。两者比较起来，我还是欢喜元稹的《行宫》：

寥落古行宫，宫花寂寞红。

白头宫女在，闲坐说玄宗。

未同秋季告别之前，我不能不提起较白居易年长的张继（懿孙），他将秋季引进来，又配之以这段暂泊苏州船上的音乐：

月落乌啼霜满天，江枫渔火对愁眠。

姑苏城外寒山寺，夜半钟声到客船。

For twelve centuries the echoes of the bell have kept ringing in the ears of successive generations, and will keep on ringing still after this generation has become a mere memory. This "solemn midnight's tingling silentness" will continue to beat on heaven's shore, when all the boisterous war-makers of the present age will be groaning and gnashing their teeth at the bottom of hell!

十二世纪以来，这钟声的回音不断地在我们的耳旁震荡，就是目今这时代变成无形的回忆时，也永远不会消灭。这"沉萧的深夜的静寂"，当这时代一切可恶的魔鬼都在地狱中咬牙呻痛时，还会继续向天岸冲击。

X. THE WINTER: THE ANATOMY OF A MOOD

One must have passed through the tunnel to understand how black is its darkness.

—*Saint Thérèse of Lisieux*

... Parting day
Dies like the dolphin, whom each pang imbues
With a new color as it gasps away,
The last still loveliest, ...

—*Byron*

Drag on, long night of winter, in whose heart,
Nurse of regret, the dead spring yet has part!

—*William Morris*

How infinitely charming is the setting sun!
Only it is so near the yellow dusk.

—*Li Shang-yin*

The more I mumble my verses,
The fainter grows my voice.

—*Chang Ch'iao* (张乔)

In James Thomson's "The City of Dreadful Night" I have run across two lines that are very much to my liking:

O desolation moving with such grace!
O anguish with such beauty in thy face!

The first line gives us a snapshot of the autumnal poetry we have just dealt with; the second forms a studied portrait of the soul of Winter. Autumn is desolate at heart but graceful in its motion: Winter is pent up with anguish within, but its external aspects are stunningly beautiful. Its blood is warm, but it assumes the appearance of a grandsire cut in alabaster. It is as angry as Summer, if not more so; but its anger is afraid to show itself,—"an impotent fury conscious of its impotence." It is like

Vesuvius swallowing its own lava. In a season like this, one no longer wishes to

拾 冬之心理分析

> 一个人须经过地下的隧道后，方会知道
> 里面的阴暗是多么黑。　　　　　——圣女小德兰

> 离逝的日子
> 像海豚那样死去，每一阵剧痛都
> 给它加上一层新的颜色，
> 当它深喘不息的时候；
> 最后一层也就是最美的一层……　　——拜伦

> 拖下去，冗长的冬夜，在它的心中——
> 悔恨的保姆，已死的春还未离去。　　——威廉·莫里斯

> 夕阳无限好，只是近黄昏。　　　　　——李商隐

> 长吟语力微。　　　　　　　　　　　——张乔

在詹姆斯·汤姆森的《恐怖之夜的城市》内，这二行我极其欢喜：

> 萧条的动态是多么地娟媚！
> 惨痛，你的脸上有这样的美！

第一行可以说是我们刚才讨论过的秋季的速照，第二行是冬季灵魂的一幅惟妙惟肖的画。秋季的心是萧条的，但是它的动态却是娟媚的；冬季的内心是充满了惨痛，但是它的外貌却美得迷人。它的血是热的，但是它的外表却像石膏雕成的老人。它的怒恨较夏季是有过之无不及，但是却不敢显露出来——"一种无力的忿怒，深知它自己的无力"。它是维苏威火山，吞没它自己的岩石。在这种季候

Rock the cradle of declining age.

On the contrary, one begins to lay blame at the door of one's parents:

> Ai, ai poor mother,
> your birth-pangs were fruitless.[1]

One is so disgusted with life that one could wish one's father had been a monk and one's mother a nun, or at least that they had been thoughtful enough to practice birth control:

> I wedded not in my life.
> Would my father had taken no wife![2]

One becomes a prey to suicidal thoughts:

> At the beginning of my life
> All was still quiet;
> In my latter days
> I have met these hundred woes.
> Would that I might sleep and never stir![3]

This was how a poet felt during the last days of the Western Chou Dynasty, and this was how Sophocles must have felt when he indited these lines in his "Ajax":

> Oh! when the pride of Græcia's noblest race
> Wanders, as now, in darkness and disgrace,
> When Reason's day
> Sets rayless—joyless—quenched in old decay,
> Better to die, and sleep
> The never-waking sleep, than linger on,
> And dare to live, when the soul's life is gone.

To such a spirit, Spring, the life-giver, is the most unendurable season:

> April is the cruelest month, breeding
> Lilacs out of the dead land, mixing

Memory and desire, stirring

Dull roots with spring rain.[4]

内，我们不再希望"一摇这衰落时代的睡床"；反之，我们只埋怨我们自己父母：

> 唉，唉！可怜的母亲，
> 你生产的痛苦是徒然的。[1]

我们厌恶现在的生活，竟希望我们的父亲是一个和尚，或我们母亲是一个尼姑，至少他们须有些脑子而履行节育：

> 我此生不结婚，
> 我希望我的父亲也不曾娶妻。[2]

我们就变成自杀之念的牺牲：

> 我生之初，尚无为，
> 我生之后，逢此百罹。
> 尚寐无吪。[3]

这是西周末日时一位诗人的感觉，这也一定是索福克勒斯写他《埃阿斯》内这数行时的感觉：

> 哦！当希腊最高贵的民族的自尊
> 像目今那般在黑暗、耻辱中徘徊，
> 　　当"理智"的日子
> 西落时没有光彩——没有快乐——浸沉在陈旧的朽腐中，
> 　　那还是死好，还是睡得永远不醒的好，
> 比生命的灵魂在离逝后仍苟延残喘终好。

在这种人看来，春季——那生命的泉源，是最不可容忍的一季：

> 四月是残酷的日子，
> 使紫丁香从死地下萌出，
> 将回忆和希望渗淆，
> 以春雨激动枯根。[4]

When one finds within oneself nothing but

Blown buds of barren flowers,

how the bright colors stab the heart!

Oh, the flowers of the bignonia,

Gorgeous is their yellow!

The sorrows of my heart,

How they stab![5]

The poets of different ages and different countries seem to feel the same way if they belong to the same season. Here is how Li Ch'ün-yu (李群玉) of the last period of T'ang describes Spring:

Who can depict the soul of Spring?

Its brilliant colors breed vertigo in me.

The evening waters reflect the green sorrows of the poplars.

Behind a deep window one senses the sadness of the fallen flowers.

I think of the lonely harems, where the weather is warming up,

And the ocean swallows coming flying in pairs.

My autumnal thoughts bedim the radiant vapors;

A boundless fog fills the cup of the universe.

When a gale is blowing, it brings profound trouble to the soul; and the greater the soul, the more intensely it suffers. As Pascal says, "Great men and insignificant men have like accidents, like vexations, and like passions; but the former are on the outside of the wheel, and the latter near the center, and are therefore less agitated by the same movements." And I should imagine that of all great men the poets are the most agitated, precisely because they live in a garret, if not in an ivory tower. Who has not occasionally felt as Goethe did, "What a time it is when we must envy the dead in their graves!" Or as Pushkin did:

I've lived to bury my desires,

And see my dreams corrode with rust;

Now all that's left are fruitless fires

That burn my empty heart to dust.

Fortunately, at such moments a poet would feel with a sense of relief that he has not long to wait

当你发现自己内心只剩下

残花落蕾，

这些鲜艳的颜色多易断人心肠！

苕之华，芸其黄矣。

心之忧矣，维其伤矣。[5]

异国异时的诗人的感觉都是同样的，倘若他们属于同一季候的话。这里是唐末李群玉描写春季的话：

春情不可状，艳艳令人醉。

暮水绿杨愁，深窗落花思。

吴官新暖日，海燕双飞至。

秋思逐烟光，空濛满天地。

当大风在吹啸的时候，灵魂就受到极大的痛苦；这灵魂愈大，这痛苦也愈深。帕斯卡说得好，"大人物与庸才有相同的意外之事，相同的困扰的环境，相同的感情；但是前者是处在车轮的外圈，后者却逼近其中心，所以少受到些环转所致的扰乱"。我说在大人物中，诗人最为其扰乱而感痛苦，就因为他们居住在阁楼上，倘若不在象牙之塔内的话。谁不有时跟歌德那样说，"这种时候！我们还妒嫉在坟中的死人"？或如普希金所说：

我活着埋葬我欲望，

看我的幻梦腐朽生锈；

现在所剩的只是无用的火，

将我的空心烧成灰末。

很幸运地，在这种时候一个诗人会有一些慰藉，因为他会想到不久

> Till suddenly, Eternity
>
> Drowns all the houses like a sea.[6]

This thought alone saves him from committing suicide.

In Spring body and soul are undifferentiated; in Summer they are differentiated but live in perfect wedlock; in Autumn they begin to quarrel; and finally in Winter they are divorced or, if not divorced, one of them dies, leaving the other as its widow. If the body has died and the soul lives on, one achieves a real resignation of which the mellow wisdom of Autumn is but a pale shadow. The grapes are no longer sour, but the celestial fruits are infinitely sweeter. The soul has found its home, and all that it desires is to spend its heaven in doing good upon earth. Such a soul is a poem in itself and finds no particular urge to write verses. It becomes a note in the Grand Symphony of God. Its only wish is to see His Kingdom come, to see Reality turned into Poetry. It is so consumed by the flame of living Love that it can at most utter an ecstatic cry as did Saint John of the Cross:

> O burn that burns to heal!
>
> O more than pleasant wound!
>
> And O soft hand, O touch most delicate,
>
> That dost new life reveal,
>
> That dost in grace abound,
>
> And, slaying, dost from death to life translate!

But such poets are rare and not necessarily of the highest order, for when one really feels ecstatic, when one's heart throbs in unison with the Heart of the Universe, Silence becomes more musical than any song, and Shakespeare himself appears like a poor bird who sings in such profuse strains simply because he has not found his ideal mate.

In one sense, a poet like Saint John of the Cross belongs to no season; for, while he, too, has experienced Winter, the obscure night of the soul, as he calls it, he has passed through the dark tunnel and finds himself in a realm where the whirligig of time has stopped. Most poets of Winter remain in the *cul-de-sac* of the world. They feel as Li Shan-fu (李山甫) did:

> 忽然地，永常
> 将这一切房屋都淹没，
> 像大海一样。 **⁶**

这念头就使他不致走自杀的那一条路。

在春季，身体和灵魂是不分开的；在夏季它们虽已分离，仍过着美满的婚姻生活；在秋季它们开始争吵；在冬季它们便离婚分居，或一人先死，剩下另一个人做寡妇。倘若身体死亡而灵魂继续生活下去的话，我们就达到了真真修养的程度，秋季成熟的智慧只是它黯淡的影子而已。这些葡萄已是不酸了，但是天堂间的水果却是更甜。这灵魂已找到了它的老家，它惟一的愿望便是为了这世界做好事。这样的一个灵魂，其本身便是一首诗，没有再写诗的必要。它是上苍伟大交响曲内的音符，它的希望是天堂的到临，现实转成真理。它为爱的火焰所消磨得竟只能像圣十字若望那般兴奋而已：

> 哦，焚烧，所以能医病！
> 不仅高兴的伤痕！
> 温柔的手，细软的感触，
> 显示新的生命，富于妩媚，
> 斗杀后将死亡转成生命！

但是这类的诗人很鲜罕，也不一定是超等，因为倘若一个人真真感到兴奋狂乐的时候，当他的心同宇宙的心一起跳跃的时候，静寂就较任何诗歌都来得悦耳，莎士比亚看上去也只像一头可怜的小鸟，因为不曾找到一个理想的伴侣而诵唱不同的歌调。

从某点看来，像圣十字若望这样的诗人不属于任何季候。因为一方面，他固然经历过冬季——他所称为灵魂之黑夜的，但他却已穿越那黝黑的地道而到达了另一境界，在其中时间已不复转运。大部分冬季诗人都端居在这世界的死巷内，他们都像李山甫般觉得：

> I faint from grief, but no tears come from my eyes;
>
> Demented and maddened, I feel like one who has lost his soul.

Their souls have died in agony or wandered away from them, but their bodies still linger on like guests who have out-stayed their welcome. Their problem is how to flirt with life and keep up their spirits during the interval between their spiritual death and their physical death. The problem belongs to the body exclusively, and the body reasons—for it is a great logician—in this way:

> The wheel of life no less will stay
>
> In a smooth than rugged way:
>
> Since it equally doth flee,
>
> Let the motion pleasant be.[7]

The conclusion seems to be unescapable:

> Crown me with roses whilst I live,—
>
> Now your wines and ointments give;
>
> After death I nothing crave,
>
> Let me alive my pleasures have,
>
> All are Stoics in the grave.[8]

Indeed, no one clings to life with such tenacity as an old man:

> But this I know, without being told,
>
> 'Tis time to live, if I grow old;
>
> 'Tis time short pleasures now to take,
>
> Of little life the best to make,
>
> And manage wisely the last stake.[9]

The epicureans have a way of making all Stoics look like fools:

> There grows an elm-tree on the hill,
>
> And by the mere an alder-tree—
>
> You have a coat, but do not wear it,
>
> You have a gown, but do not trail it,

You have a horse, but do not drive it,

And so it will be when you are dead

恸哭翻无泪，颠狂觉少魂。

他们的灵魂都或已在痛苦中死去，或已离开他们；但是他们的躯壳却继续存在，像等留过久受主人讨厌的客人一样。他们的问题是，在精神与肉体的死亡间，怎么同生活逗情，怎样支持他们的兴。这问题只同肉体有关，肉体便运用理智——因为它是一个伟大的逻辑家——作如此着想：

生活的环轮，
在崎岖光滑的路上都不停留：
既然它终是前进，
还是选令人高兴的旋转好。[7]

这结果似乎是不可避免的：

当我活在的时候，给我玫瑰花的冕——
给我你的美酒和香膏；
死了以后我不要求任何东西；
让我享受我的逸乐！
在坟墓里我们都是"斯多葛"。[8]

诚然，没有人像老人那般紧抓住生命：

这我知道，即使没有人告诉我：
倘若我到老时，便是生活的时候；
现在是享受片刻逸乐的时候，
尽量利用这短短的生命，
然后智慧地安排那最后的一注。[9]

"伊壁鸠鲁"享乐派能将一切"斯多噶"都显得像呆子（毛诗《山有枢》章）：

山有枢，隰有榆。
子有衣裳，弗曳弗娄。
子有车马，弗驰弗驱。

And others can enjoy them!

…

There grows a gum-tree on the hill,

And by the mere a chestnut-tree.

You have wine and food, why do you forget

Sometimes to play your lute,

Sometimes to laugh and sing,

Sometimes to steal new playtime from the night?

Shall it be so when you are dead

And others have your house?[10]

Perhaps, if you have still got some scraps of conscience in you, you will ask, "What heart have I to play the fiddle while Rome burns?" To which the Devil will answer, "But what else can you do, my sophomoric friend?" And by and by you may find yourself singing:

Hey nonny no!

Men are fools that wish to die!

Is't not fine to dance and sing

When the bells of death do ring?

Is't not fine to swim in wine,

And turn upon the toe,

And sing hey nonny no!

When the winds blow and the seas flow?

Hey nonny no!

This is how a poet would feel in any decadent period, when the world is hopelessly at sixes and sevens. Tu Ch'iu-niang (杜秋娘), whom we may regard as the mother of the Winter of T'ang poetry, seems to have set the key to it in the following song:

I would not have thee grudge those robes

which gleam in rich array,

But I would have thee grudge the hours

of youth which glide away.

Go pluck the blooming flower betimes,

lest when thou com'st again

Alas, upon the withered stem

no blooming flowers remain!

宛其死矣，他人是愉。

……

山有漆，隰有栗。

子有酒食，何不日鼓瑟？

且以喜乐，且以永日。

宛其死矣，他人入室。**10**

或许，倘若你有些良心的话，你会问："罗马在大火的时候，我还有什么心肠来奏琴？"魔鬼就回答："除此以外，我的糊涂朋友，你还能做些什么？"不久你便发现你自己歌唱：

嗳哎哎嗥！

希望死的人都是蠢汉！

当死亡的钟还在响时，

唱歌跳舞还不好吗？

在酒中游泳，然后提起脚尖，

在风吼浪飞的时候，

唱歌嗳哎哎嗥，那岂不好？

嗳哎哎嗥！

这是一个诗人在世界乱七八糟、世风日下的时候的感觉。我们认为是冬季之母的杜秋娘在下面这首诗内似乎也有同样的感觉：

劝君莫惜金缕衣，劝君惜取少年时。

花开堪折直须折，莫待无花空折枝。（英译：翟理思）

257

It seems to me that Walter Pater sums up the wintry philosophy of life when he says, "Well! we are all *condamnés*, as Victor Hugo says: we are all under sentence of death but with a sort of indefinite reprieve—*les hommes sont tous condamnés à mort avec des sursis indéfinis*: we have an interval, and then our place knows us no more. Some spend this interval in listlessness, some in high passions, the wisest, at least among 'the children of this world,' in art and song. For our one chance lies in expending that interval, in getting as many pulsations as possible into the given time."

It is very odd that the exponent of such a dead man's philosophy of life should also be so very wintry in point of style. As Samuel Butler puts it, "Mr. Walter Pater's style is, to me, like the face of some old woman who has been to Madame Rachel and had herself enameled. The bloom is nothing but powder and paint and the odor is cherry blossom." I feel the same about it, for it reminds me of a stanza in Lucianus' "Artificial Beauty":

> You give your cheeks a rosy stain,
>> With washes dye your hair,
> But paint and washes both are vain
>> To give a youthful air.

I have often thought that Spring is cosmically-minded, Summer historically-minded, Autumn philosophically-minded, and Winter *cosmetically-minded*. Lady Blessington has somewhere said that the best cosmetic for beauty is happiness. But the point is that happiness is not to be had for a song, and where it is entirely lacking, powder and paint are not altogether useless. To congratulate ourselves for not belonging to a decadent moment is one thing; but to declaim against it is quite another. There are times when artificiality is not only natural but inevitable, when Art, tongue-tied by authority, dares not deal with the grand issues of life, and decoration becomes its main activity and sole concern. Such periods deserve as much sympathy from us as the "posthumous coquetry" of a lady:

Let there be laid when I am dead,
Ere 'neath the coffin-lid I lie,
Upon my cheek a little red,
A little black about the eye.[11]

在我看来，沃尔特·佩特在这句话里总括了冬季人生哲学："唉，我们都是定了罪的犯人，像雨果所说的，我们都已被判了死刑，不过在无限期的缓刑下罢了；我们都有一个间歇，以后这世界便不认识我们了。有些人将这间歇花在委顿中；有些人花在激情中；但是最聪明的人，至少'这世界的孩子们'，却花在艺术和歌唱中。因为我们惟一的机会便是去消磨这间歇，尽力将生气灌入所有的时间内。"

很奇怪，解释这样死的人生哲学的人的笔调也竟如此"冬季"。塞缪尔·巴特勒说得好，"沃尔特·佩特先生的笔调，据我看来，是像曾到蕾切尔夫人那里去化妆过的老太太的脸——她的鲜艳只是脂粉，她的馥郁全靠樱花"。我很同意这句话，因为它使我想起卢西亚努斯《人工美》内的一段：

你给你的双颊涂上一层玫瑰红，
又染了你的头发，
但是胭脂和染料都不能
给你青年的生气。

我时常想，春季以宇宙为念，夏季以历史为念，秋季以哲学为念，冬季以化妆为念。布莱辛顿夫人说过，最好的化妆品是快乐。但是问题是，快乐不是廉价所能换来的；但是没有快乐，脂粉也许不无小补。为了我们自己不隶属于衰落时期而额手称幸是一回事，痛斥它当然又是一回事。有时候人工不但是自然的，并且还是不可少的，尤其是当艺术为权力所缄口结舌、不敢研究人生大问题，妆饰便成为它惟一的工作、惟一的使命。这种时期，像女人"身后的妖艳"一样值得我们怜恤：

当我死后，睡在棺材内的时候，
脸上给我涂些胭脂，
眼周给我涂一圈黑。[11]

Since to the wintry spirit everything is posthumous, a craftsman-like solicitude fares no worse than the noble negligences of a genius, and artificiality is no more a house of cards or a fabric of snow than Nature itself. Even a brief recalescence of Spring is not out of place in this season of bitter cold. How nicely George Herbert, who belongs to the "Fantastic School of Poetry," puts it:

> And now in age I bud again;
> After so many deaths I live and write;
> I once more smell the dew and rain,
> And relish versing: O my only light,
>> It cannot be
>> That I am he
> On whom thy tempests fell all night.

If our life on earth is but a dream, as indeed it is, then the whiteness or colorlessness of Autumn is no less shadowy than the bright colors of Spring and Summer. Instead of annihilating all the colors, what about, as Andrew Marvell would have it,

> Annihilating all that's made
> To a green thought in a green shade?

These lines remind me of a beautiful stanza by a wintry poet of T'ang, Liu Teh-jen (刘得仁):

> A pair of white birds, oblivious of
> The endless events of the dusty world,
> Fly side by side and fade gradually
> Into the faint emerald of the hills.

Instead of the emerald dissolving into whiteness, we have here two specks of whiteness fading into the hill-brewed emerald.

It is very significant that the word "emerald," which we so often met in the poems of Tu Fu, but which all but disappeared in the poetry of Autumn, has come back again in this period of T'ang poetry. The variegated and full-blooded world which Autumn had annihilated seems to revive in Winter. And yet it is no longer the same world. The world that Winter has built upon the wrecks of Autumn belongs to an order of

既然在一个冬季诗人看来，每样东西都是属于身后的，匠人的焦虑不见得会比天才的怠慢来得差，人工的作品也不见得会比大自然来得更像纸片搭成的房屋或白雪的细纤。在这冷酷的季候内，就是一次春暖的复现，也不是不适合的。属于"怪僻诗派"的乔治·赫伯特说得多么好：

> 现在上了年纪，我再蓓蕾，
> 经过了多少死亡，我再做人，写作；
> 我重新再嗅着雨露之味，
> 再喜爱诵诗：哦，我惟一的引导，
> 　　不会
> 　　我就是
> 你的风雨整夜吹打的那个人。

倘若我们在世上的生活只是梦幻泡影的话（诚然，它的确是黄粱一梦），那么秋季的白色或清色决不会比春夏鲜艳夺目的色彩来得真实。所以我们不要灭绝这些颜色，反之，如安德鲁·马弗尔说的：

> 灭绝一切，使化成绿荫下的
> 一个嫩绿思想！

这几行使我想起冬季诗人刘得仁很美的二行！

> 不知尘里无穷事，白鸟双飞入翠微。

翠绿不曾化作淡白，反之在这里，二点白色反在山谷的翠色中悠然消失。

这是很重要的，"翠"字——我们在杜甫的诗内时常看见，在秋季的诗内则绝迹不见——现在又出现于冬季。秋季所消灭的多彩多姿的世界在冬季重生了，但是已换了一个面目。冬季在秋季的残

its own, it is bathed in the ether of imagination, it has a hieroglyphic veil of inscrutable mysteries drawn over it. Its symbol is not the sun or even the moon, but the candlelight. As Helen Waddell phrases it so beautifully, "One sees most by candlelight, because one sees little. There is a magic ring, and in it all things shine with a yellow shining, and round it wavers the eager dark. This is the magic of the lyrics of the twelfth century in France, lit candles in 'a casement ope at night,' starring the dusk in Babylon; candles flare and gutter in the meaner streets, Villon's lyrics, these; candles flame in its cathedral-darkness, Latin hymns of the Middle Ages, of Thomas of Celano and Bernard of Morlaix. For if Babylon has its Quartier Latin, it has also its Nôtre Dame. The Middle Ages are the Babylon of the religious heart." Miss Waddell might have added that the Winter of T'ang poetry is the Babylon of the heart of China. It, too, has its Quartier Latin, in which many a "hermit of the green chamber"[12] fritters away his nights. It, too, has its Nôtre Dame: the lonely inn, in which a homeless wayfarer confides his sorrows to an orphanlike candle that listens sympathetically to him and weeps tears of blood over the sad story of his life. Let a few specimens suffice:

(1)

It has been so hard for us to meet,
It will be harder for us to part.
The East Wind is growing feeble;
The flowers are beginning to fade.
But the silkworm in the Spring goes on
Spinning gossamer threads until its death;
And the candle of wax ceases not to weep
Its tears of blood until it burns itself to ashes.

(Li Shang-yin)

(2)

True love looks like no love.
Only I cannot bring myself to smile before the cup.

Even the wax-candle has a heart and pities our parting,—
It drops tears for us until the dawn.

(Tu Mu)

(3)

The wax-candle weeps tears of blood,
Lamenting the coming of the dawn.

(Li Shang-yin)

迹上所建筑的世界是自创一格的，浸沉在想象的以太中，外面
罩了一阵纱幕，印有不可解释的玄妙。它的代表不是太阳，也
不是月亮，乃是烛光。海伦·沃德尔解释得多么好："在烛光
下我们看得最仔细，因为我们看得最少。这里有一个奇妙的圆
圈，在其中万物都发出微黄的光，旁边就是在摇荡的急切的黑
圈。这是法国十二世纪抒情诗的奇妙，'晚上开着的窗扉内'的
火烛，照耀巴比伦的黄昏；烛火在较低鄙的城市内闪烁、涌流，
这是维永的抒情诗；在大教堂的黝暗内的烛光，这是中古时期
塞拉诺的托马斯、莫莱的贝尔纳的拉丁赞美诗。因为，巴比伦
倘若有它的拉丁区的话，也一定有它的圣母院。中古时期乃是
虔诚的心的巴比伦。"沃德尔女士可以说唐诗之冬是中国的心房
的巴比伦，它有它的拉丁区，在其中许多"青楼隐士"[12]消磨
他们的深晚；它也有它的圣母院——在一家孤冷的旅舍内，一
个无家可归的游荡者，向对他表同情因而流血泪的孤儿似的蜡
烛诉叹他的生平。且看这里寥寥数首：

(一)

相见时难别亦难，东风无力百花残。
春蚕到死丝方尽，蜡炬成灰泪始干。　　　(李商隐)

(二)

多情却似总无情，惟觉樽前笑不成。
蜡烛有心还惜别，替人垂泪到天明。　　　(杜牧)

(三)

蜡烛啼红怨天曙。　　　(李商隐)

(4)

A lonely candlelight ushers in

A Spring far away from home.

(Ts'ui T'u: 崔涂)

(5)

I sit and watch

The flower-like moon

And the sparkling stars

Fade from the sky.

The shadows of the mountains

And the far echoes of the tides

Are weaving Sorrow in the gloom.

In the depth of night,

Before the candlelight,

The events of the past decade

Come flooding to my heart

Together with the rain.

(Tu Hsün-hê: 杜荀鹤)

(6)

A flickering candlelight

Accompanies a dissolving dream.

The lands of Ch'u lie dimly

On the borders of heaven.

The moon has gone down,

And the nightingale has ceased its song.

All over the courtyard

Apricot flowers are flying.

(Wen T'ing-yuen)

(7)

At midnight I wake from wine.

The red candle is burned almost to its socket.

Its cold tears have been congealed

Into a coral-reef.

(P'i Jih-hsiu: 皮日休)

(8)

I sit up and watch

The dim, dim flame

Of a lonely, lonely lamp

Flickering out noiselessly

Toward the dawn.

(Ch'i Chi)

We are no longer in the world of flesh and blood. We are in the Dreamland in which the soul glimmers like the flame of a candle. The landscape has been transformed into an "inscape." The world is drowned in the immeasurable ocean of Darkness, and there remains only "an odorous shade."

（四）

孤烛异乡春。 （崔涂）

（五）

月华星彩坐来收，岳色江声暗结愁。

半夜灯前十年事，一时和雨到心头。 （杜荀鹤）

（六）

香灯伴残梦，楚国在天涯。

月落子规歇，满庭山杏花。 （温庭筠）

（七）

夜半醒来红蜡短，一枝寒泪作珊瑚。 （皮日休）

（八）

坐看孤灯焰，微微向晓残。 （齐己）

我们不再是在有血肉的世界内，乃是在梦境中，灵魂像烛光那般闪烁，山水风景也变成一种"内在本质"。这世界已在"黑暗"深不可测的大海中溺毙，所剩的只是一块"有香气的荫地"。

> An odorous shade lingers the fair day's ghost,
>
> And the frail moon now by no wind is tost,
>
> And shadow-laden scents of tree and grass
>
> Build up again a world our eyes have lost.[13]

The most touching type of wintry poetry is where dead Spring comes back to life in a dream. Prince Li Yu, the last monarch of the Southern T'ang, who ended his days in captivity, is a consummate master of this *genre* of lyrics. I shall dedicate a whole section to the study of the life and works of this purest lyricist of China. Two samples will suffice here:

(1) A DREAM

Ah, how sad!

Last night in my dream

I was again roaming in the Royal Park

Like in the old days—

Carriages were rolling like a stream

And horses prancing like dragons—

Moonlight flowers were quivering

In the warm caress of the Spring breeze!

(2) UPON WAKING FROM A DREAM

Outside the window-screen the rain drizzles and drips.

The Spring is gasping away.

Under thin silken quilts I shiver in the cold tide of the morning watch.

In a dream, forgetting my homeless plight,

I feasted myself like a glutton upon the past joys again!

Ah, lean not upon the balcony all alone,

Lest you should see the endless rivers and mountains,

That make separation so easy and meeting so hard!

The stream flows on, the flowers have fallen, and the Spring is gone,

Leaving no trace in Heaven or on earth.

In his dreams he becomes a king again; upon waking, no such matter! He is like a widow dreaming of her hymeneal night. A volcanic cataclysm, a yawning hiatus, lies between the past and the present. Everything is gone, leaving no trace behind, like the ceasing of exquisite music. There seems to be an eternal gash on Time, covered up only in dreams, but in effect cut deeper by them. How these lines remind me of Michael Field's "After Soufrière":

一块有香气的荫地引住了这美日的幽灵，
　这细弱的明月不被什么风所掀动，
花草树木载幽荫的馥郁，
　重新造起我们视觉已失落的世界。[13]

冬季的诗最动人处便是，已死去的春季重新在梦中复活。后主李煜，南唐最好的一个君王，死于俘闭中的，是这种抒情的圣手。我将要费一整段研究中国这位最纯洁的情圣的生平和作品，这里只能录下如下两首：

（一）望江南

多少恨，昨夜梦魂中。还似旧时游上苑，车如流水马如龙，花月正春风。

（二）浪淘沙

帘外雨潺潺，春意阑珊。罗衾不耐五更寒。梦里不知身是客，一晌贪欢。

独自莫凭栏，无限江山。别时容易见时难。流水落花春去也，天上人间！

在梦内，他又重登龙位，醒来没有这回事！他是像一个寡妇梦忆她的婚夜。在过去和现在间躺着一阵火山似的洪水，一条宽大的罅裂。万物都已不留痕迹地过逝，像美妙的音乐一样。时间上似乎有一个永远的伤痕，只有在梦中才会补没，其实却被它割得更深些。后主这二首诗使我想起迈克尔·菲尔德的《苏弗里耶尔之后》：

267

It is not grief or pain;

But like the even dropping of the rain

That thou art gone.

It is not like a grave

To weep upon;

But like the rise and falling of a wave

When the vessel's gone.

It is like the sudden void

When the city is destroyed,

Where the sun shone:

There is neither grief nor pain,

But the wide waste come again.

And yet something is haunting on still, the fair day's ghost. A Ghost! That's what Winter is. Autumn may be ghostly, but it is still a human being. Winter is a Ghost, but what a lovely Ghost! What a beautiful face and a kindly voice the Ghost has! "Vainly you ask yourself:—'Whose voice?—whose face?' It is neither young nor old, the Face: it has a vapory indefinableness that leaves it a riddle; ... yet you cannot ignore it, because of a certain queer power it possesses to make something stir and quiver in your heart,—like an old vague regret,—something buried alive which will not die."[14] And the Voice, though feeble as the hum of a bee, "exhales an exquisite perfume—strange, indistinct, and yet, after the manner of perfume, unforgettable."[15] Spring is like the Pink that buds and blooms so gayly in the arbor; Summer is like the Rose with its damask dyes peering through a thick leafage; Autumn is like the Lily unstained and chaste, or the Violet wrapped in lonely communings; but Winter is like the Forget-Me-Not, whose love alone can feed the lamp of pale existence.[16] Spring is something to be seen; Summer can be tasted and touched; Autumn is to be heard; but Winter, like an odorous shade, can only be smelt. Spring liberates you; Summer inspires you; Autumn soothes you; but Winter captivates you. If the reader will excuse me for resorting to a homely analogy, I would say that T'ang poetry as a whole is like a good dinner, of which Spring is the soup and the fish, Summer the beefsteak or stuffed turkey, Autumn the ice-cream and the fruits, and Winter is the little cup

当你去了以后，
没有忧愁，也没痛苦，
不过像雨水平衡的点滴。
这不是像使人们哭泣的坟墓，
不过是波浪的起伏，
当船只驶过的时候。
不过是忽然的空虚，
当城市被毁灭，
太阳照耀的时候，
这里没有忧愁，也没有痛苦，
不过是荒芜的重临。

但是终有些东西在滋扰，这美日的幽灵。幽灵！这就是冬季。秋季或许有些幽灵色彩，但是终不失为一个人。冬季是一个幽灵，但是多么可爱的一个幽灵！它的面目是多么地美，声音是多么地悦耳！"徒然地你问你自己：'谁的声音？谁的脸孔？'不年轻，也不老，这脸孔：它有烟雾般的不可解处，使它变成一个大谜……但是你不能忽略它，因为它有一种特别的力量，能使某物在你心中震荡——像古老模糊的悔恨——活埋而不肯死的东西。"[14]这声音，虽然只像蜂的吟声那么低，"吐出一层极佳的馥郁！奇怪、混杂，但是像任何馥郁一样，是不会被遗忘的"。[15]春季是像在园亭内蓓蕾、开花的石竹；夏季是像在浓叶中出现的红玫瑰；秋季是像清洁无玷的荷花或孤居一处的紫罗兰；冬季是像不忘草，只有它的爱才能维持生命的暗灯。[16]春季是看得见的；夏季能尝得到、摸得着；秋季可以听得出；但是冬季像有香气的荫地一样，只能被嗅到。春季解放我们，夏季给我们灵感，秋季抚慰我们，但是冬季迷惑我们。倘若读者们肯原谅我用一个不甚体面的比喻的话，我说整个唐诗是一客丰富的西菜：春季是其中的汤和鱼，夏季是牛排或腹中塞满调味物的火鸡，秋季是冰淇淋和水果，冬季是最后的一小杯咖啡。春季或许是很开

of mocha that crowns all. Spring may be appetizing, Summer savory, and Autumn refreshing, but who can ever forget the fine flavors of the mocha?

Who but a wintry poet like George Herbert would have thought of Spring as "A box where sweets compacted lie"? To the children of the other seasons this may look like a fantastic conceit; but Winter, as I have said, is cosmetically minded, and this kind of perfumed image arises spontaneously in its mental eye. In our Father's year there are four seasons; and I have a suspicion that he fondles Winter even more than the others:

> And so a flower bright
> Has bloomed in coldest winter
> E'en in the deepest night.[17]

It may be that Winter is a peacock which, with its splendid plumage and tail, reminds you of a lady "in gloss of satin and glimmer of pearls." But only a shallow critic would say that a peacock is less natural than a skylark. There is a provision in the Universe even for a pair of mandarin ducks in a golden cage. How touchingly Li Shang-yin has put it:

> ON THE MANDARIN DUCKS
> The hen has gone.
> The drake is flying
> All over the boundless sky
> In search of his love.
> He only sees
> The gauzy clouds,
> And his eyes
> Ooze with tears.
> Oh, have done with a life
> Amidst the winds and waves!
> Ah for a golden cage
> In which he and she

Can live together

In sweet thralldom!

To Li Po the Universe is not big enough for his spirit to soar in: to Li Shang-yin a little corner is good enough for his body to live in, provided only that it is safe and secure from the cruel blasts of the North Wind that are making a holocaust of the world. He feels somewhat, though not exactly, as Richard Lovelace does:

胃，夏季或许是很可口，秋季或许很能提神，但是谁能忘记那杯咖啡的美味？

除了像乔治·赫伯特那样的冬季诗人外，谁会将春季认为是"一盒浓缩的芬芳"？在别的季候的孩子看来，这话或许是狂想夸饰罢了；但是冬季，如我所说的，只以化妆为念，这种已加香料的影像在它的灵眼前很自然地升起。在上苍的眼里，一年共有四季，我说他最爱冬季：

一朵鲜花
在严冬中开放，
甚至在深晚中。[17]

冬季我们或可以说是一只羽毛美艳的孔雀，使你想起一位贵妇"身穿锦缎，满戴珠宝"。但是只有一个肤浅的批评家会说孔雀没有云雀来得活泼自然；宇宙内甚至还有在金笼内的鸳鸯呢！李商隐说得多么动人：

鸳鸯
雌去雄飞万里天，云罗满眼泪潸然。
不须长结风波愿，锁向金笼始两全。

在李白看来，宇宙虽大，还不够他心灵冲飞；在李商隐看来，小小的角隅已足够他栖身，只要这地方安全、不被毁坏这世界的暴风雨所吹打。他的感觉有些像理查德·洛夫莱斯，虽然不完全相同：

Stone walls do not a prison make,

    Nor iron bars a cage;

Minds innocent and quiet take

    That for a hermitage.

If I have freedom in my love,

    And in my soul am free,

Angels alone, that soar above,

    Enjoy such liberty.

Perhaps, Li Shang-yin feels more closely with Ovid, whom I regard as his contemporary and next of kin:[18]

I pray you, stay, Aurora; and to your Memnon's[19] shade

A sacrifice—I vow it—shall every year be made.

'Tis now my love is by me, her lips are mine to kiss,

Her arms are twined about me—is any hour like this?

Like Ovid, too, Li Shang-yin, fed up with the Nature of Things as they are, dives into the Nature of Things as they are fancied to be, and deals in occult Metamorphoses:

THE WEB OF LIFE[20]

The precious harp has fifty strings,

    No more, no less.

How every string, every nut, evokes thoughts

    Of my youthful days!

In his morning dreams, Master Chuang was metamorphosed

    Into a butterfly!

The Spring heart of Prince Tu Yu of old still echoes

    In the cuckoo's cry!

When the moon shines brightly on the murky sea,

    Tears come from the pearls.

When the sun is warm, the jades of the Blue Fields

    Send up smokes in curls.

A sudden glimpse into the mystery of mysteries flashed
    Across my mind,
But its meaning escaped immediately, for like lightning
    It struck me blind!

How well William Blake seems to have sized them up, these wintry poets:

> 石墙不一定是监狱，
>   铁栅不一定是笼子；
> 清静无邪的人将它
>   当作隐居之所。
> 倘若我的爱是自由的，
>   在灵魂内我是自由的话，
> 只有天使，翔回于空中的，
>   才能享受这种权利。

或许，李商隐同罗马诗人奥维德较近，奥维德是他的同时代人、最近的亲戚： [18]

> 我求你，留在这里，奥萝拉；
>   对你的门农的阴影 [19]
> 我发誓每年燔祭一次。
>   现在我的爱人是在我身旁，
> 她的口唇是给我吻的，
>   她双手紧围住我——可有别的如此的时候？

像奥维德一样，李商隐对大自然一切的表面都觉得有些腻，所以便耽于超自然的幻想：

锦瑟 [20]

> 锦瑟无端五十弦，一弦一柱思华年。
> 庄生晓梦迷蝴蝶，望帝春心托杜鹃。
> 沧海月明珠有泪，蓝田日暖玉生烟。
> 此情可待成追忆，只是当时已惘然。

威廉·布莱克将这些冬季诗人一言道尽：

> The Door of Death I open found,
>
> And the Worm Weaving in the Ground:
>
> Thou'rt my Mother, from the Womb;
>
> Wife, Sister, Daughter, to the Tomb:
>
> Weaving to Dreams the Sexual strife,
>
> And weeping over the Web of Life.

And yet many a dry-humored critic has said that Li Shang-yin is the most obscure poet of China and the above-quoted poem on "The Web of Life" is the most obscure of his poems. They have even given him a nickname: "an otter offering libations to the fish"! That is, they could not make head or tail of his poems. But what do they know about Poetry, especially when it has reached its stage of Imago? They don't realize that the poems of this stage are like women in that they are made to be loved, not to be understood. I would even go as far as to say that the only way of understanding them is by not trying to understand them. Simply love them, and they will confide their secrets to you; and this usually happens when you are not particularly interested in knowing them, for you want to go to sleep. Oh the charm of the "Ewige Weiblische," the eternal Feminine, the living Embodiment of the Irony of Life which is the very Stuff of Universe! How shallow the Masculine looks beside it! A hairpin on the head of a woman shoots beyond the barriers of the unknown, while all the philosophies of men have only served to mystify Existence. All roads lead in the end to the Cosmos, but cosmetics may be a short-cut. Nature herself seems to me a great coquet.

Winter is a Woman. She lives and moves and has her being in the Realm of Essence. She is emancipated from the phenomenal world. She has her own system of causality, and she has a way of interfusing the senses with one another. At her magic touch even the barriers between matter and mind seem to have crumbled down. What kind of a world she lives in can be gathered from the few glimpses with which the following specimens will furnish us:

A lamp glimmers amidst a choir of crickets.

(Li Ch'ang-fu: 李昌符)

*   *   *

My lingering thoughts have reddened the maple leaves.

(Prince Li Yu)

*   *   *

死亡的门我发现是开的，
蠕虫在地下编织；
你是我的母亲，从胎里开始；
妻、妹、女，到坟内为止，
将性的挣扎织到梦内为止，
对生活的网丝痛哭。

但是有许多枯燥乏味的批评家说，李商隐是中国最晦涩的一位诗人，《锦瑟》又是他作品内最晦涩的一首。他们甚至于替他提一个绰号——"獭祭鱼"。这就是说，他们不懂他的作品。但是，老实说，他们懂些什么诗，尤其是当它到达"意象"（最后一个时期）的地步时？他们不知道，这时代的诗是像女人一样，并不预备给我们了解，只给我们钟爱。我甚至于要说，惟一的了解女人的方法便是不去了解她们。你只要爱她，她便会向你吐谈心事，而这时常是在你不介意她们的时候，因为你正预备要睡觉。哦，"永恒女性"的魅力，永久的女性，生活幽默的活表象，宇宙的本质！在她的旁边，"男性"显得多么浅陋！女人头上的一枚金钗能射到未知之外，但是男人的哲学只能玄化生存。任何道路都通到宇宙，但是化妆是一条近路。大自然本身在我看来就是一个大尤物。

　　冬季是一个女人。她活着，动着，居在事物本质的境界内。她不受外界的束缚，她有自己的因果律，她能沟通各部官觉。在她的神奇的指触下，事物和思维的界限也消失无迹。在下面寥寥数首唐诗内，可以看出她是端居在哪一种世界内：

蟋蟀声中一点灯。 （李昌符）

*   *   *

相思枫叶丹。 （李煜）

*   *   *

The west wind is scattering sorrows among the green ripples.

(Prince Li Chin)

*   *   *

All alone I have been blowing the pipe of jade
Until my little garret freezes with its icy notes.

(Prince Li Chin)

*   *   *

Home-sent letters,

Home-wending dreams,

Between them lies

Gaping Eternity.

An empty bed

And Autumn sere

Vie with each other

On the score of desolation.

The green moss

Below the steps,

The red trees

In the courtyard,

Now mope

In the rain,

Now melt into Sorrow

In the moonlight.

(Li Shang-yin)

*   *   *

The splendid glories of the past
Have been pulverized into fragrant dust.

(Tu Mu)

*   *   *

The roads are long, but my dreams are short.

(Lu Kuei-meng: 陆龟蒙)

＊　＊　＊

This city once rode upon the floating clouds,
And vanished into the emerald of evening.
Now again it accompanies the setting sun,
Splashing the echoes of Autumn.
There are countless painters in the world,
But who can paint this patch of poignant pathos?

(Kao Ch'an: 高蟾)

Ay, who can paint this patch of poignant pathos? This is the "inscape" of Winter, and painters can only paint landscapes. Who can paint a glimmer of light amidst a choir of crickets, or the maple leaves being dyed to crimson by lingering thoughts, or the wind scattering green sorrows among the ripples, or a little garret being frozen out and out by the icy

西风愁起绿波间。　　　　　　　　　　　　（李璟）
　　　　　＊　＊　＊
小楼吹彻玉笙寒。　　　　　　　　　　　　（李璟）
　　　　　＊　＊　＊
远书归梦两悠悠，只有空床敌素秋。
阶下青苔与红树，雨中寥落月中愁。　　　　（李商隐）
　　　　　＊　＊　＊
繁华事散逐香尘。　　　　　　　　　　　　（杜牧）
　　　　　＊　＊　＊
路永魂梦短。　　　　　　　　　　　　　　（陆龟蒙）
　　　　　＊　＊　＊
曾伴浮云归晚翠，犹陪落日泛秋声。
世间无限丹青手，一片伤心画不成。　　　　（高蟾）

唉，谁能画出这一片伤心？这是冬季的本质，但是丹青能手只能画风景。谁能画出蟋蟀声中的一点灯，或被相思染红了的枫叶，或引起绿波间的哀愁的西风，或被玉笙寒冷的音调吹彻了的小楼，或死

notes of a jade pipe, or dead Hope buried in a bloomless bud, or the green moss and red trees moping in the rain and melting into Sorrow in the moonlight, or the splendid glories of the past pulverized into fragrant dust? And above all, who can paint the dreams? And yet there is a subtle seductiveness about all those lines which somehow grapples your heart to them more tightly than any "hoops of steel." They are like pomegranates opening to the night, staining the darkness with their dusk-etherized tints. The tints are not faint in themselves, but they are fainting in the circumambient oblivion.

We may say of the wintry poetry what Li Shang-yin says of the pear-blossom:

> It phosphoresces in the moonless night.
> It forces itself to smile when a storm is brewing in the sky.

What tenderness lies impanate in these lines! Our hearts would be broken, if Shakespeare had not assured us:

> The robb'd that smiles steals something from the thief.

And Li Shang-yin's description of a dying girl seems to fit Winter like a glove:

> Her forlorn soul is flickering out in the maze of life.
> Her gossamer breath is gasping charmingly away.[21]

The whole output of the belated songsters in the last days of T'ang reminds me of a beautiful line by Wen T'ing-yuen:

> The apricot-flowers fall incense-breathing to the ground.

In trying to define the indefinable qualities of Winter, I feel like one suffering from the itch. The more I scratch, the more itchy I feel. Perhaps, Winter can best be studied in relation to the other seasons. In appearance it can be as gay and blithe as Spring. Listen to Prince Li Yu's song, "Let Us Enjoy":

> To welcome Spring, one must come before Spring.

To enjoy the flowers, one must not wait till they are withering.

When such soft ivory hands offer a cup of effervescent wine,

Who has the hardness of heart to decline?

Why not beam in smiles alway?

In this Forbidden Park, Spring finds a cozy place to stay.

Let us drink our fill and talk *ad libitum*!

As for poetry, I find a rhyme in every beat of the drum!

亡了的希望埋葬在不会蓓蕾的花苞中，或在雨中寥落、在月中愁的青苔与红树，或散落在香尘中已往的繁华？最后，谁能画出梦来？但是，在这几行内有一种难于捉摸的引诱力将你抓住，较任何铁环都来得紧。它们是像在夜间开放的石榴花，以暗淡的色彩渲染这黑暗。这些色彩本身并不暗晦，却是在周围的遗忘中变得暗晦。

李商隐关于梨花的话也很适合于冬季的诗：

> 自明无月夜，强笑欲风天。

这样的温柔是多么地伤心！我们的心一定要裂碎，倘若莎士比亚不曾保证我们：

> 被劫后而笑的人，
> 一定已反偷贼子的东西。

李商隐描绘一个临终的小女孩的话，也极适合冬季：

> 怨魂迷恐断，娇喘细疑沈。[21]

唐末这群歌唱者的全部作品，使我想起温庭筠极美的一句：

> 杏花零落香。

要想解释冬季不可解释的特质，我似乎是在吃奇痒之苦，愈搔则愈痒。或许是我只能将冬季同其他季候作比较研究。在表面上看来，它的快乐活跃也不减于春季。且听李煜的《子夜歌》：

> 寻春须是先春早，看花莫待花枝老。
> 缥色玉柔擎，醉浮盏面清。
> 何妨频笑粲，禁苑春归晚。
> 同醉与闲评，诗随羯鼓成。

And yet one cannot help feeling that we have here only a Dionysian in garment, Spring in a minor key. It seems to me that Verlaine knows the mind of Prince Yu:

> Your soul is a sealed garden, and there go
> With masque and bergamasque fair companies
> Playing on lutes and dancing and as though
> Sad under their fantastic fripperies.
>
> Though they in minor keys go caroling
> Of love the conqueror and of live boon
> They seem to doubt the happiness they sing
> And the song melts into the light of the moon.

Prince Li Yu is no more springy at heart than Thomas Hardy:

> Let me enjoy the earth no less
> Because the all-enacting Might
> That fashioned forth its loveliness
> Had other aims than my delight.

We have already pointed out that Winter is as angry as Summer, but not as outspoken. Its satires are more subtle and more pregnant. Tu Fu says:

> Behind the red-painted doors, wine turns sour and meat stinks:
> On the roads lie corpses of people frozen to death.
> A hair-breadth divides opulence and dire penury!
> This strange contrast fills me with unutterable anguish.

But Tu Mu would say:

> In this world only the white hair is just and fair,
> For it does not spare even the heads of the great!

A very naughty friend of mine has given a modernized version of it:

> In this world only the white hair
> Is just and fair:
> For it does not spare

Even the head of a millionaire!

Tu Fu asks openly:

但是我们很自然地觉得，这里只有一件狄俄尼索斯的外罩，一曲郁陶的春季之歌。在我看来，魏尔兰很能懂得李煜：

> 你的灵魂是一座闭锁的花园，
> 那里有戴假面具的美伴
> 弹琵琶、跳舞，好像是在
> 怪诞的虚饰下，很是忧愁。
> 虽然他们在郁陶的音乐下欢颂
> 征服者的爱和活的恩惠，
> 他们好像都怀疑他们的快乐，
> 他们的歌也就融在月光内。

后主不见得比哈代来得更"春季"：

> 我享受这世界，
> 决不因为万能的权力的发扬光彩
> 不是为了我的便利而扫兴。

我们已经说过，冬季是像夏季一样愤怒，不过不如夏季那样显明罢了；它的讽刺较夏季来得更尖锐、更深刻。杜甫说：

> 朱门酒肉臭，路有冻死骨。
> 荣枯咫尺异，惆怅难再述。

但是杜牧说：

> 公道世间惟白发，贵人头上不曾饶。

【我有个调皮的朋友，将上面的二句译成现代英文：

> In this world only the white hair
> Is just and fair:
> For it does not spare
> Even the head of a millionaire! 】

杜甫爽直地问：

When will the war cease and farmers return to their fields?

And when will the petty officials cease to fleece the poor?

But Ts'ao Yeh (曹邺) deals out a more covert blow:

> In the public granaries,
>
> The rats have grown
>
> Almost as big as a cow.
>
> They don't run away
>
> When they see men
>
> Come near them.
>
> The soldiers at the front,
>
> Their food-supplies are running short,
>
> And the people are starving.
>
> Nowadays,
>
> The grain is meant
>
> Only to fatten the rats!

Tu Fu wants "to turn His Majesty into a greater man than Yao and Shun," the sage emperors of old; but Nieh Yi-chung (聂夷中) only wishes the heart of the sovereign to be transformed into a candlelight:

> THE POOR FARMERS
>
> In March they sell out their new silk.
>
> In June they place new grain on the mart.
>
> 'Tis like dressing the wounds of the skin
>
> With slices of flesh torn from the heart!
>
> I wish the heart of the Sovereign
>
> Would soon a bright candlelight become,
>
> To shine not on a splendid feast,
>
> But on a runaway's drear home!

If, as Somerest Maugham says, Michelangelo is the father of baroque, in the same sense we may regard Tu Fu as the father of the latest T'angs. Just

as Tu Mu is called "the little Tu," so we can call Winter "the little Summer."
I think that at heart Winter is more affiliated to Summer than to the other
seasons. Is this not why men like Swinburne and Pater should have been
so much attracted by Victor Hugo?

Winter is as desolate as Autumn, but its desolation has acquired
colors and got a body. The pangs of regret become "red," and sorrows
become "green." Dolors are transmuted into colors. Desolation seems to
beat on like a live heart that has been segregated from the poor mortal
whose heart it used to be. Here is what Li Shang-yin sings about the Lady
in the Moon:

安得务农息战斗，普天无吏横索钱。

但是曹邺的质问却是较隐蔽的：

官仓老鼠大如斗，见人开仓亦不走。
健儿无粮百姓饥，谁遣朝朝入君口。

杜甫欲"致君尧舜上"，但是聂夷中却愿君王的心化作光明之烛：

咏田家
二月卖新丝，五月粜新谷。
医得眼前疮，剜却心头肉。
我愿君王心，化作光明烛。
不照绮罗筵，只照逃亡屋。

倘若，如毛姆所说的，米开朗琪罗是怪诞的祖师的话，那么杜甫我
们可以认为是晚唐诸诗人的祖师。杜牧有人称他"小杜"，所以冬
季可以称作"小夏"。我说在心中，冬季是接近夏季的。这可足以
解释，为什么斯温伯恩和佩特那辈人偏爱雨果。

冬季是像秋季一样萧条，但是它的萧条已有了色彩和身体。悔
恨的痛苦变成了"红"色，忧愁的痛苦变成了"绿"色。【疼痛都
化成颜色。】萧条继续跳跃，像一颗已和它可怜的主人脱离后仍有
生命的心。这里是李商隐的《嫦娥》：

I sit behind the screens of marble

In front of a shaded candlelight.

I have watched the Milky Way

Gradually going down,

And the morning stars sinking.

Ah, you Lady in the Moon!

How you must have repented

Your theft of the Elixir of Life,

For which you have been condemned to live eternally,

With your heart bleeding from night to night

In the loneliness of the murky sea and the blue sky!

The following poem by a contemporary poetess, Yeh Ching-i (叶静宜: 1879–1926), seems to be as wintry can be:

A FAREWELL TO SPRING

The wailing cuckoo has called the Spring away.

Desolation is blowing in the wind!

Desolation is dripping in the rain!

Desolation is filling the air with the flying flowers!

The flower of Time is fading before my eyes.

Sadness rings in the nightingale's song!

Sadness echoes in the swallow's twitter!

Sadness lingers on, when the Spring is gone!

Indeed, to pass from Autumn to Winter is like watching pensive evening deepening into night. I have made a parody of John Gay, which will reveal what I mean:

Life is a jest, and all things show it:

Autumn thought so, but Winter knows it.

To sum up, then, Winter is Spring in a minor key, Summer under cover, Autumn in gloss of satin and glimmer of pearls. But has it got a soul of its own? Has its soul died beyond the possibility of revival? My answer is that, with most of the wintry poets, the soul is only lost in the maddening maze of things, but not actually dead. And deep down in the heart there lurks a mystical censer, which has acquired a spark of life from its very antiquity, and which sends forth intermittently invisible wisps of incense in search of the soul it once possessed. These ethereal wisps of incense rise like silent somnolent prayers to God, whose Heart is easily melted by the aroma of green thoughts and red fancies.

云母屏风烛影深，长河渐落晓星沉。
嫦娥应悔偷灵药，碧海青天夜夜心。

下面近代女诗人叶静宜（1879—1926）这首词极尽冬季之愁：

春归

啼鹃唤了春归去，风也凄凄，雨也凄凄，一任残花落又飞。
韶华在眼轻消遣，莺也依依，燕也依依，几度留春春竟归。

诚然，从秋季到冬季，正像沉思的黄昏转入深夜。我曾拟约翰·盖伊之体而说：

生活原是玩笑，每样东西都证明这点；
秋季以为如此，但冬季确实知道。

总而言之，冬季是郁陶的春季，掩没的夏季，衣穿锦缎、满戴珠宝的秋季。但是它可有它自己的灵魂？它的灵魂可曾死去而不再复活？我的答案是，大部分冬季诗人的灵魂都迷失在事物的昏乱中，并不曾死去。在他们心中隐伏着一具玄妙的香炉，在早期就有火星，现在不时发出看不见的烟圈，企图寻找他们的灵魂。这些缥缈的烟圈升到空中，像在梦中向上苍作静默的祈祷，上苍的心也就很容易地被绿的思索和红的幻想的馥郁所溶冶。

XI. THE WINTER OF T'ANG POETRY

The melancholy notes of the birds are floating on the eventide.

—Szu-k'ung Tu

Trailing along a dying echo,
The cicada flits into a neighboring bough.

—Fang Kan

The day is at its sunset,
The year is in its wrecks.

—Ts'ui Tu

Look in my face; my name is Might-have-been;
I am also called No-more, Too-late, Farewell.

—Dante Gabriel Rossetti

Wandering between two worlds, one dead,
    The other powerless to be born,
With nowhere yet to lay my head,
    Like them, on earth I wait forlorn.

—Matthew Arnold

Around 840 Tu Mu wrote a poem to a Taoist priest who was by that time nearly a centenarian:

Pale and emaciated, you have lived almost a hundred years.
To the weather-beaten temple another Spring has come.
The whole world has long since become a battlefield:
You alone of our contemporaries were born in the days of peace.

The fact is that ever since the rebellion of An Lu-shan in 755, the T'ang Dynasty had not known a single day of peace. Nor was there the slightest ray of hope for the restoration of the body politic to anything like its normal health. On the contrary, things were moving from bad to worse; and more than a century was to elapse before China was united again under a new regime, namely, the Sung Dynasty, which established itself in 960. During that long period, with the exception of twelve years (from 847 to 858, in which a series of victories were effected against some of the bordering tribes, and there was a brief breathing space and a faint promise of a renaissance), the country was writhing under all sorts of

拾壹 冬季之诗

雕声带晚悲。 ——司空图

蝉曳残声过别枝。 ——方干

一日又将暮，一年看即残。 ——崔涂

对我的面孔看；我的名字是"或许是"；
我又叫"没有了""太迟了""再会"。
——但丁·加布里埃尔·罗塞蒂

在两个世界间徘徊，一个已死了，
另一个欲生无力；
我没有地方安置我的头颅，
像它们一样，在这地球上我荒凉地等待。
——马修·阿诺德

大约在 840 那一年，杜牧将下面这一首诗赠给一位年已近百的道士：

清羸已近百年身，古寺风烟又一春。
寰海自成戎马地，惟师曾是太平人。

事实是，唐朝自安禄山 755 年造反以后，便未曾有过一日太平。国家政府要振作恢复，那简直连一线之望都没有；反之，情形是每下愈况，直到宋太宗 960 年平定藩镇各国，建国以后社会方归太平。在这一百多年里，除了 847 年至 858 年这十二年外（在这时间内，官军打了几场胜仗，人民也有了些透气之时，复兴之光

evil, such as intrigues of the eunuchs, brigandage, uprisings, massacres, mutinies, party squabbles, foreign invasions, rebellions of the warlords, famines and plagues. At the wake of the fall of the T'ang Dynasty in 906 China was split into a host of little dominions, like a flower-pot shattered into shards. Among those little states, the Southern T'ang, which was established in 937 with Nanking as its Capital and lasted till 975, is of especial interest to us. For in the first place, its founder was a descendant of T'ang; and secondly, a formidable group of poets, including Princes Li Chin and Li Yu, flourished in it. It may therefore be regarded, in poetry as well as in politics, as the afterglow of the T'ang Dynasty.

In short, the Winter of T'ang poetry covers a period of about one hundred and forty years, that is, from 840 to 978, the latter being the year in which Prince Li Yu died.

There is, of course, no hard and fast line of demarcation between the seasons, especially between Autumn and Winter, as both belong to the shady side of the year. But there is no more appropriate date from 840 to mark the beginning of Winter. It was the year in which the poor Emperor Wen Tsung (文宗) died from neurasthenia. Shortly before his death, chafing under the oppression of the eunuchs, he suffered a nervous breakdown. Sometimes he was found standing waywardly and gazing blankly before him; at other times, he was found muttering and sighing to himself. On one occasion he summoned a minister before him and asked him, "Of all the Emperors of the past, with whom do you think I can compare?" The minister answered, "Your Majesty belongs to the company of Yao and Shun!" But His Majesty did not think so. "How dare I aspire to be Yao and Shun?" he said. "The reason why I asked you is whether I am not inferior to Chow Nan and Han Hsien." The minister was taken aback, and asked, "They were good-for-nothing monarchs at whose hands their respective dynasties were wrecked and finished. How can they compare with Your Majesty?" "But don't you see," Wen Tsung rejoined, "that they were only oppressed by powerful dukes, while I am held in grip by my own family slaves? From this standpoint, I am even worse than they."

Than this there can be no better illustration of the wintry mood. An impotent fury conscious of its impotence, a feeling that the end has come, a pang of regret that finds no words but issues in sighing and whimpering to oneself, a loss of self-confidence, a defeatist attitude toward life, a sense of responsibility for the miseries of the world which one has in no way caused and can in no way remedy, a realization that only a miracle can save the world from another deluge and that there are no miracles,

微露），整个国家是在痛苦不宁下苟延残喘：宦官专权，朋党纷争，盗匪横行，起义频频，残杀无辜，藩镇叛乱迭起，盗贼又乘机而入，加之旱荒鼠疫，诚可谓暗无天日。唐朝于906年覆没以后，便造了五代十国之局面，像敲碎后的花盆一样，零零落落。在这十国中，有南唐者，在937年建都南京，至975年方亡。我们对它特别发生兴趣：因为南唐李氏乃是唐朝的后裔；其次，一大群词人像李璟、李煜等，都生在这时期内。所以不论政治或诗，南唐可以说是唐朝的晚霞。

总之，唐朝之冬，约占一百四十年。自840年到978年后主李煜死的那一年。

在季候之间，当然没有明晰之界线，尤其是秋冬，因为它们都属于一年的幽暗那方面。但是比840这一年再适合冬季之始的，可说没有的了。那时候，文宗受宦官之压迫，患神经衰弱病而死。未死前，时或向空中凝视，时或自语自叹，终有不知所从之感。有一次他问一位大臣："朕可方前代何主？""陛下尧舜之主也！"这位大臣回答。但是文宗并不以为如此，他说："朕岂敢比尧舜，所以问卿者，何如周赧汉献耳。"这位大臣大吃一惊，说："彼亡国之主，岂可比圣德？"文宗道："赧献受制于强诸侯，今朕受制于家奴，以此言之，朕殆不如！"

这最足以表显冬季之境地。无力的忿怒深觉它自己的无力，末日已到的感觉；一种非言语所能表述的痛恨，只能为它叹息流泪；自信力的失落；悲惨消极的人生观；对非人力所造成、也非人力所能补救的悲痛的责任心；只有神迹方能将这世界从灭

an increase of sensitiveness coupled with a failure of nerve, a drowning man's quickened recapitulation of all his past experiences,—these are some of the symptoms of the spirit or rather spiritlessness of the age whose poetry we are now to survey.

Wen Tsung was the author of the well-known poem:

> On the roads grows the Spring grass.
>
> In the park the trees are flowering.
>
> I lean upon a high balcony, musing alone.
>
> Who knows the infinite pathos in my mind?

All nature is blossoming forth, but the heart is shut up within itself like a dead foetus rotting in the womb. This poem sets the tone to the poetry of Winter.

Let me first present a group of poems, which forms a composite picture of Winter both in its external and internal aspects.

亡中救出、而天下又无神迹的明觉；愈转锐敏的感觉，渐趋衰弱的神经；将溺死的人突然回忆他的过去——这就是我们正要讨论的诗的时代精神（或更确切地说是精神萎靡）的表征。

文宗是下面这首著名的诗的作者：

> 辇路生春草，上林花发时。
>
> 凭高何限意，无复侍臣知。

大自然正在萌芽蓓蕾，但是诗人的心却紧闭着，像胚胎在母腹中腐烂。这首诗正合冬季的音调。

让我先介绍几首诗，它们正能显示冬季之内容外貌。

(1) SULLENNESS

Dim, dim the waters of the long river.

Faint, faint the heart of a far wanderer.

The fallen flowers seem to loathe one another,

They drop to the ground without a sound.

(Ts'ui Tao-yung: 崔道融)

（一）寄人二首·其二

澹澹长江水，

悠悠远客情。

落花相与恨，

到地一无声。

（崔道融）

(2) SPRING

A forlorn man in the green Spring,

How I hate to see the flowers!

On the roads I meet a group of drunken fops,

All wearing garlands on their heads.

(Ts'ui Tao-yung)

（二）春题二首·其一

青春未得意，

见花却如仇。

路逢白面郎，

醉插花满头。

（崔道融）

(3) SENDING CLOTHES TO THE SOLDIERS

A battle was raging at night

Amidst a heavy snowfall.

The soldiers from the interior,

Half of them were killed.

In the morning came letters from their homes,

Together with the clothes made by their wives.

(Hsü Hun: 许浑)

（三）塞下

夜战桑干北，

秦兵半不归。

朝来有乡信，

犹自寄征衣。

（许浑）

(4) THE RURAL CONDITIONS

I walk alone among the wild fields.

I see the doors of the farm-houses all closed up.

I ask where the farmers have gone.

I am told they have all gone into business.

The government does not tax the traders,

But only taxes the toil-ridden farmers.

So they leave their farms and travel east and west

On the roads that lie contiguous to the dykes.

Some have gone into the mountains to quarry jade;

Others are diving into the seas to get pearls.

But the soldiers at the frontiers want food and clothing;

（四）庄居野行

客行野田间，

比屋皆闭户。

借问屋中人，

尽去作商贾。

官家不税商，

税农服作苦。

居人尽东西，

道路侵垄亩。

采玉上山颠，

探珠入水府。

边兵索衣食，

To them jade and pearls are as good as soil and mud. 此物同泥上。

In the old days, the labor of one farmer 古来一人耕，

Could barely furnish food to three mouths. 三人食犹饥。

Now out of thousands of families 如今千万家，

Not a single person holds the plough and hoe. 无一把锄犁。

Our granaries are constantly empty, 我仓常空虚，

Our fields are overgrown with thorns and briars. 我田生蒺藜。

Heaven does not rain grains of rice. 上天不雨粟，

How can we keep the teeming masses from starvation? 何由活烝黎。

(Yao Ho: 姚合) （姚合）

(5) A WINTER NIGHT IN THE HILLS （五）山中冬夜

The leaves fall, 寒叶风摇尽，

And shiver in the cold wind. 空林鸟宿稀。

Only a few birds 涧冰妨鹿饮，

Nestle in the bare trees. 山雪阻僧归。

The brooks are frozen, 夜坐尘心定，

And the deer are thirsty. 长吟语力微。

The snows on the hills prevent 人间去多事，

The return of the monks. 何处梦柴扉。

Sitting up in the night, （张乔）

My heart is purged of dust.

Humming my verses,

My voice grows faint.

Enough of loafing!

But where is my home?

(Chang Ch'iao: 张乔)

(6) THE BORDER TROUBLES （六）书边事

On the northern frontiers the clouds of war are looming, 朔野烟尘起，

And our Imperial Government is raising troops again. 天军又举戈。

Sullen blasts rage more fiercely toward the evening; 阴风向晚急，

The killing breath of Autumn is making havoc of the land. 杀气入秋多。

The trees being destroyed, birds are nestling in the grass. 树尽禽栖草，

The ice thickening, people are walking on the rivers,

Since there is no Kuo Tzŭ-i today,

How can we expect the barbarians to sue for peace?

(Li Ch'ang-fu: 李昌符)

冰坚路在河。

汾阳无继者，

羌虏肯先和。

（李昌符）

(7) WAILING

In the glimmering lamplight

My beard looks black.

The green grass mopes

In the shade of gloomy walls.

The year coming to an end,

I bewail the world and myself.

All of us are glow-worms,

In the grip of the frost.

(Szu-k'ung Tu: 司空图)

（七）有感

灯影看须黑，

墙阴惜草青。

岁阑悲物我，

同是冒霜萤。

（司空图）

(8) AUTUMN THOUGHTS

A sick body living in a perilous age,

How often have I fainted from weeping in Autumn!

Blasts and billows are raging and heaving;

Heaven and earth are turning flip-flap.

An orphan-like glow-worm flits on a waste land;

Falling leaves pierce through a shattered house.

The world is getting more snobbish than ever;

Who will call upon a solitary castaway?

(Szu-k'ung Tu)

（八）秋思

身病时亦危，

逢秋多恸哭。

风波一摇荡，

天地几翻覆。

孤萤出荒池，

落叶穿破屋。

势利长草草，

何人访幽独。

（司空图）

(9) ARE WE IN A CUL-DE-SAC?

The sun and the moon

Journey on without cease

Day and night.

They bring to men

Now prosperity,

Now decay.

The righteous ones

（九）世迷

乌兔日夜行，

与人运枯荣。

为善不常缺，

为恶不常盈。

天道无阿党，

人心自覆倾。

所以多迁变，

Are not always

On the wane,

Nor will the wicked

Remain always

Full and bright.

God is impartial;

'Tis man who stumbles

And incurs calamities

By his own wrongs.

Fickle and inconstant,

He goes astray from God.

宁合天地情。

我愿造化手，

莫放狐兔走。

恣海产珍奇，

纵地生花柳。

美者一齐美，

丑者一齐丑。

民心归大朴，

战争亦何有。

（苏拯）

I wish the great Creator

Will hold the wild beasts

At bay;

Fill the seas

With precious things,

And the earth

With flowers and willows;

And separate once for all

The evil and ugly

From the good and beautiful.

Then people's hearts

Will return to Simplicity,

And the wars

Will cease for ever.

(Su Cheng: 苏拯)

(10) PARTING FROM A FRIEND AT AN INN　　（十）南山旅社与故人别

The day is at its sunset,　　一日又将暮，

The year is in its wrecks.　　一年看即残。

Illness forbids me　　病知新事少，

To hope for much new;　　老别旧交难。

Age sharpens the pain　　山尽路犹险，

Of parting from old friends.

The mountains have come to an end,

But the roads are still rugged.

The rain has stopped,

But the Spring is as cold as ever.

How can I bear to look back?

Where the beacons burn is Changan!

(Ts'ui Tu)

雨余春却寒。

那堪试回首，

烽火是长安。

（崔涂）

(11) AT NANKING

The rain is pouring incessantly on the river,

The grass is growing thickly on the banks.

The Six Dynasties have vanished like a dream;

The birds' cries sound hollow.

The most heartless are the willows along the wall:

They still sway carelessly in the midst of smoke and mist.

(Wei Chuang: 韦庄)

（十一）金陵图

江雨霏霏江草齐，

六朝如梦鸟空啼。

无情最是台城柳，

依旧烟笼十里堤。

（韦庄）

(12) A GIRL'S YEARNING FOR HER LOVE

I took out the mirror

From the hibiscus case,

But I have no heart

To look into it.

My waist was slender

Enough as it was,

But I find my gauze girdle

Growing looser than ever.

Ever since you left home,

I have not played the flute;

For my thoughts are as cold as its notes,

Which you alone can warm up.

My heart yearns

To see you in dreamland.

（十二）赠远

芙蓉匣中镜，

欲照心还懒。

本是细腰人，

别来罗带缓。

从君出门后，

不奏云和管。

妾思冷如簧，

时时望君暖。

心期梦中见，

路永魂梦短。

怨坐泣西风，

秋窗月华满。

（陆龟蒙）

295

But the roads are long,

And my dreams are short.

Angry with my fate I sit up

Bewailing the west wind.

The autumn window is filled

With the bright beams of the moon.

(Lu Kuei-meng)

(13) LINES WRITTEN ON A NEW YEAR'S DAY

From month to month,

I look about the same.

From year to year,

I look differently.

This morning, as I peeped

Into the antique mirror,

I found the features of one

Wrecked by years of traveling.

In the bustle of the world,

Quiet leisure is hard to get;

And what one is forced to do

Is mostly much-ado-about-nothing.

My floating life will not last

Much longer anyway.

'Tis time to get drunk

With the winy breath of Spring.

(Hsü T'ang: 许棠)

（十三）新年呈友

一月月相似，

一年年不同。

清晨窥古镜，

旅貌近衰翁。

处世闲难得，

关身事半空。

浮生能几许，

莫惜醉春风。

（许棠）

(14) BOATING ON THE RIVER

The great river holds the city of Wu Chang in its embrace.

Facing the Isle of Parrots live families of staggering wealth.

Some rich fops are sleeping in their painted boats.

（十四）江行

大江横抱武昌斜，

鹦鹉洲前户万家。

画舸春眠朝未足，

In their dreams, they arc transformed into butterflies
　　hunting after the flowers!

　　　　　　　　(Yu Hsüan-chi: 鱼玄机)

梦为蝴蝶也寻花。

　　　　　　　　（鱼玄机）

(15) THINKING OF HIM

I hate you, O water of Chin Huai!

I hate you, O boats on the river!

Years ago you bore him away from me.

But when, O when will you bring him back to me?

…

That year when he took leave of me,

He said he was going to Tung-lu.

Now I don't see the man from T'ung-lu,

But get a letter from Kwangchow!

Yesterday was happier than today.

This year is older than last year.

The turgid Yellow River may some day turn clear:

But blackness will never return to the white hair.

　　　　　　　　(Liu Ts'ai-ch'un: 刘采春)

（十五）啰唝曲六首

不喜秦淮水，

生憎江上船。

载儿夫婿去，

经岁又经年。

……

那年离别日，

只道住桐庐。

桐庐人不见，

今得广州书。

昨日胜今日，

今年老去年。

黄河清有日，

白发黑无缘。

　　　　　　　　（刘采春）

(16) THE NUPTIAL NIGHT

The waiting maid, coming to remove the cosmetic box,

Was surprised to find the bride already in bed.

But really she had not slept.

She was sobbing furtively with her face turned away.

Languorously she took down the phoenix hairpin.

Blushingly she slipped into the nuptial quilts.

From time to time she espied the corn-like candle,
　　burned almost to its end,

Dropping down its golden ear together with smoke.

　　　　　　　　(Han Wu: 韩偓)

（十六）生查子

侍女动妆奁，

故故惊人睡。

那知本未眠，

背面偷垂泪。

懒卸凤凰钗，

羞入鸳鸯被。

时复见残灯，

和烟坠金穗。

　　　　　　　　（韩偓）

(17) LOVE

Lingering, lingering,

Pulsating, pulsating,

Two hearts beat in one.

Fine as gossamer,

Vast as the waves,

Inconstant as the moon,

Frail as a flower,

This strange thing we call love,

What a prolific source of sorrow it is!

(Wu Yung: 吴融)

(18) WAITING FOR A FRIEND AT NIGHT

The bright moon is setting.

The autumn wind is growing chill.

Is he coming tonight, or is he not?

The shadow of the *wut'ung* tree is fading out:

But here I'm standing still!

(Lu T'ung-ping: 吕洞宾)

(19) A SATIRE

How elaborate the beautiful lady's coiffure!

What lovely pearls and emerald jades on her head!

Does she realise that the two specks of cloud she wears

Wear out the taxes of several villages?

(Chen Yun-sou: 郑云叟)

(20) A POOR GIRL

A poor girl, I have never tasted

The perfumed robes of precious gauze.

I try to find a good match-maker,

But what is the use?

Who in this world would appreciate

High romance and pure love?

Who will ever marry a girl

（十七）情

依依脉脉两如何，

细似轻丝渺似波。

月不长圆花易落，

一生惆怅为伊多。

（吴融）

（十八）梧桐影

落日斜，秋风冷。

今夜故人来不来，

教人立尽梧桐影。

（吕洞宾）

（十九）富贵曲

美人梳洗时，

满头间珠翠。

岂知两片云，

戴却数乡税。

（郑云叟）

（二十）贫女

蓬门未识绮罗香，

拟托良媒益自伤。

谁爱风流高格调，

共怜时世俭梳妆。

敢将十指夸针巧，

不把双眉斗画长。

苦恨年年压金线，

Without the attraction of a dowry?

All that I have to offer

Is the skill of my fingers.

I have not even the heart to paint

My eyebrows in appealing arches.

Year in, year out, how I groan

Under the endless heaps of golden threads!

Ah me! When shall I cease to make

The wedding dresses of other girls?

(Ch'in T'ao-yu: 秦韬玉)

为他人作嫁衣裳。

（秦韬玉）

(21) THE SILKMAIDS

Morning and night

They gather the mulberry leaves.

Patiently they toil and moil.

Even in the season of bright flowers

They find no time to enjoy themselves.

If they too knew how to follow

The frivolous fashions of the world,

The fashionable ladies

Of the golden houses

Would be frozen to death.

(Lai Ku: 来鹄)

（廿一）蚕妇

晓夕采桑多苦辛，

好花时节不闲身。

若教解爱繁华事，

冻杀黄金屋里人。

（来鹄）

(22) BUTTERFLIES AND SWALLOWS

When the flowers bloom,

Butterflies cluster around them.

When the flowers wither,

Butterflies take leave of them.

Only the swallows

Return to their old nests

In spite of the poverty

That has befallen their host.

(Wu Kuan: 武瓘)

（廿二）感事

花开蝶满枝，

花谢蝶还稀。

惟有旧巢燕，

主人贫亦归。

（武瓘）

(23) ON THE WRITING OF POETRY

（廿三）苦吟

Don't talk of the craft of poetry!

莫话诗中事，

No other craft is so full of difficulties.

诗中难更无。

Before you can put a single word in the right place,

吟安一个字，

Your moustache will be thinned out by constant twirling.

拈断数茎须。

The exploration for what is new and uncommon

险觅天应闷，

Would wear out the patience of Heaven.

狂搜海亦枯。

The fastidious search for the exquisite and precious

不同文赋易，

Would exhaust the resources of the ocean.

为著者之乎。

For poetry is not like prose

（卢延逊）

Which admits of prepositional makeshifts.

(Lu Yen-sun: 卢延逊)

From these specimens the reader will find one thing about the wintry poets: Whenever they are not weeping, they are flirting. The preoccupation with sex is always a symptom of low vitality. Winter is lustful where Spring is lusty. It is only when one's libido is dying out that one would brag as Baudelaire does:

> My spirit, you move with a pure ardency,
> And, as one who swoons in the senses of sound,
> You furrow furiously the immensity profound
> With an invincible and male sensuality.

Another thing to note is that the language of the poems of this period (I mean of course the original) is refined to the point of agony. When great Poetry is dead, people begin to produce light verses and to write poems on Poetry. The whole movement of the T'ang poetry began as a revolt against rhetoric: it ended as a cult of rhetoric. The style of the Six Dynasties has come back again. This is a concrete illustration of Samuel Butler's insight: *The history of art is the history of revivals.*

Having presented the general atmosphere and features of the age, we are prepared to treat some of the better known poets individually. There is a plethora of poets during the ninth century; but I can only confine myself here to the big three: Tu Mu, Wen T'ing-yuen, and Li Shang-yin.

Tu Mu (杜牧: 803–853) was one of those poets who, disappointed with life, sought refuge in wine, women and song. He wrote a caricature of himself:

A lost soul amidst rivers and lakes,
I never travel without bringing wine along.

Ah, the charm of the slender-waists, so light and slim
That they could almost dance on my palm!

Waking from a dream of ten years in Yangchow,
I find myself famous as a heartless fop!

从这几首诗内，读者们一定会发现一件事：冬季诗人倘不哭泣，便撒娇弄情。性的怀念始终是微弱生活力的表示。冬季是好色淫荡的，但是春季却是壮强有力。只有当一个人的"基力"死亡时，他才会像波德莱尔这样夸言：

我的精灵活动，你活动时有纯洁的热情，
像在声音的感觉晕厥的人，
你恣怒地耕耘深的无限，
仗了不可克服、男性的肉欲。

另一件值得注意的事是：这时期的诗的文字，修饰得有些厌人。当伟大的"诗"死亡后，人们便写些轻松论"诗"的小诗。唐诗在反对词藻的标帜下兴起，现在结尾却崇拜词藻，六朝之死灰复燃。这是塞缪尔·巴特勒卓见的证明，因为他曾说，文艺的历史是复兴的历史。

看见了冬季的大概和面目后，我们便能进一步个别讨论诸较闻名的诗人。第九世纪生了一大群诗人，我在这里只能谈及三位：杜牧、温庭筠和李商隐。

杜牧（803—853）是在生活失意后，在酒、女人、诗歌内寻找安慰的诗人之一，这里是他的一幅自绘：

落魄江湖载酒行，楚腰纤细掌中轻。
十年一觉扬州梦，赢得青楼薄幸名。

But he was really not so heartless as he was reputed. Here is a touching farewell song he wrote to one of his girls:

> True love looks like no love.
>
> I only feel I cannot smile before the cup.
>
> Even the wax-candle has a heart and pities our parting,—
>
> It drops silent tears for us until the dawn!

It seems as though he was too sad to weep and had to borrow tears from the candle. He had too much love for his poor heart to contain.

Of all the girls in the Green Chambers of Yangchow, he seems to have taken a special fancy to one:

> A maid just o'er thirteen,
>
> So graceful and so arch!
>
> A nutmeg bursting into leaf
>
> In the early days of March!
>
> In the streets of Yangchow,
>
> Aquiver with the breath of Spring,
>
> All the pearl-screens are rolled up,
>
> But I see none so ravishing!

I suspect that it was the same girl whom he saw fourteen years later. At that time she was already married and mother of quite a few children. He wrote a symbolic poem, which touches a note of deep pathos:

> SIGHING OVER A FLOWER
>
> Oh! How I hate myself for coming so late
>
> > In search of the flower!
>
> Years ago, I saw her before she had blown,—
>
> > Just a budlet was she!
>
> Now I find the wind has made havoc of her,—
>
> > Her petals strew the ground!
>
> I only see a tree with a thick leafage
>
> > And branches full of fruits!

Not all his poems deal with love; but whatever he sings is charged with wintry forlornness and expressed in a style which has some funereal sleekness about it. Let a few specimens suffice:

(1) AT AN IMPERIAL CEMETERY

The pale boundless space has swallowed
The faint shadow of a lonely bird.
Ah, this is where all the ages of the past
Have been drowned and dissolved into nothing!

其实他并不像人家所说的那样薄幸无心，这里是他同一位情妇分别的痛心语：

多情却似总无情，惟觉樽前笑不成。
蜡烛有心还惜别，替人垂泪到天明。

好像是他已悲伤得欲哭无泪，只得向蜡烛借些泪水。他的爱不是他的心所能包容得下的。

在扬州的青楼妓女中，他好像最痛爱一个：

娉娉袅袅十三余，豆蔻梢头二月初。
春风十里扬州路，卷上珠帘总不如。

我猜疑这就是他十四年后遇见的那一个：那时她已经从良，生了子女多人。他写了一首象征诗，引起无限感慨：

叹花

自恨寻芳到已迟，往年曾见未开时。
如今风摆花狼藉，绿叶成阴子满枝。

他的诗并不是每首都谈儿女之情，但是不论他唱述些什么，总是充满了冬季的绝望，他的笔调又有些死丧的色彩在内。下面数首足以为证：

（一）登乐游原

长空澹澹孤鸟没，万古销沉向此中。

What has remained of the glories of the Han Dynasty?

Only the bare Imperial Tombs swept by the Autumn wind!

(2) THE GARDEN OF GOLDEN VALLEY

The splendid glories of the past

Have been pulverized into fragrant dust.

The stream flows on indifferently,

And the grass keeps Spring to itself.

At sunset, the singing birds

Lament the passing away of the East Wind.

The falling flowers recall the pretty one

Who threw herself from a high balcony.

(3) A NIGHT AT AN INN

A cold lamplight evokes memories of the past.

The broken notes of the wild geese pierce through my sorrow-ridden
   sleep.

My home-wending dreams impinge upon the dawn.

The letters from home cross the boundary of years.

(4) ROAMING IN A MOUNTAIN

Driving up the cold mountain

Along the coils of a rocky path,

I find in the depth of the white clouds

Several families are leading a quiet life.

I halt my carriage and sit awhile

To admire the maples in the eventide.

How the frost has dyed their leaves

To a deeper crimson than the flowers of March!

Wen T'ing-yuen (820–866) was another hermit of the Green
Chambers. Once he met at an inn Emperor Hsuan Tsung (宣宗), who was
traveling incognito. The emperor asked him, "Do you know who I am?"
Wen answered, "I think you are a bodyguard of the emperor." The emperor

never forgave him for that, and Wen was doomed to remain out of office.

Reading his poems makes one feel as though one were in a jeweler's and a draper's shop. The feminine pulchritude is his main concern. The following four pieces will suffice to illustrate his style:

(1) TO A SINGING BIRD

A secluded lane meanders alongside the river.
A little door is on the latch all day.
The crimson pearls grow on the curtains like ripe cherries.
The gold-tailed peacocks stand idly on the marble screens.
Her tresses of cloud enchant the butterflies with their fragrant smell.
The yellow patches on her temples remind one of twilit hills.

看取汉家何事业，五陵无树起秋风。

（二）金谷园

繁华事散逐香尘，流水无情草自春。
日暮东风怨啼鸟，落花犹似坠楼人。

（三）旅宿

寒灯思旧事，断雁警愁眠。
远梦归侵晓，家书到隔年。

（四）山行

远上寒山石径斜，白云生处有人家。
停车坐爱枫林晚，霜叶红于二月花。

温庭筠（820—866）也是一个青楼隐士。有一次，他遇微服出行的宣宗。宣宗问他："你知道我是谁？" 温庭筠回答："得非六参、簿、尉之类。"宣宗因此决不恕他，所以他就不能飞黄腾达。

读他的诗，我们便觉得像处在珠宝或绸缎店内，女性的娇娴是他惟一的目标。下面几首足以显示他的风格：

（一）偶游

曲巷斜临一水间，小门终日不开关。
红珠斗帐樱桃熟，金尾屏风孔雀闲。
云髻几迷芳草蝶，额黄无限夕阳山。

You and I can remain an inseparable pair of golden ducks!

Let us forget the lures of the outside world!

(2) A WEARY NIGHT

The fragrant breath of the jade censer

And the crimson tears of the wax-candle

Fill the Painted Hall with autumnal thoughts.

The emerald on her eyebrows is paling.

The cloud on her temples is fading.

The night is long, and the quilt and pillow cold.

The *wut'ung* tree,

The midnight rain,

They don't know the pang of nostalgia.

Leaf after leaf,

Drop after drop,

On the empty steps they fall till the dawn.

(3) A NOCTURNE

The clear sky

Hangs like a mirror

Upon the hook-like moon.

The endless ripples of the river

Glint sorrows

Into the traveler's heart.

Nocturnal tears

Ooze furtively

From the Song of Bamboo Sprigs.

The distant echoes

Of the Spring Tide are flooding

My little boat of spice wood.

Events pass away

Together with the clouds,

Leaving our bodies behind.

Our dreams dissolve

Like wisps of smoke;

The waters flow on.

Where are the joys of yesterday?

A plum-tree has shed its blossoms into the river.

(4) A SPRING DAY

In the south garden,

The ground is strewn

With piles of light catkins.

In sorrow I listen

To the sudden showers

Of early Spring.

与君便是鸳鸯侣，休向人间觅往还。

（二）更漏子

玉炉香，红蜡泪，
偏照画堂秋思。
眉翠薄，鬓云残，
夜长衾枕寒。
梧桐树，三更雨，
不道离情正苦。
一叶叶，一声声，
空阶滴到明。

（三）西江贻钓叟骞生

碧天如镜月如钩，泛滟苍茫送客愁。
衣泪潜生竹枝曲，春潮遥上木兰舟。
事随云去身难到，梦逐烟销水自流。
昨日欢娱竟何在，一枝梅谢楚江头。

（四）菩萨蛮

南园满地堆轻絮，愁闻一霎清明雨。

After the showers
Comes the evenglow;
The apricot-flowers fall
Incense-breathing to the ground.

Silently I smooth
My sleep-ridden face,
As I lie on my pillow
Behind the screens.

The twilight is closing in upon me;
I stand wearily leaning against the door.

Li Shang-yin (李商隐: 813–858) was not a hermit of the Green Chambers, but he had secret affairs with the nuns in the Taoist convents and with the maids-of-honor in the imperial harems. A considerable number of his poems deal with those adventures of love, and are couched in a language which is as obscure as it is beautiful. No poet has a greater mastery of the mysterious suggestions which lie concealed in words. This is how he writes:

From my room I gaze despairingly
Into the fathomless dusk.
A flight of jade stairs lies across the sky,
Severed from the hook of the moon.
The banana tree refuses to unfold its leaves;
The clove remains a closed bud for ever.
Each nurses a private sorrow in its bosom,
Though both breathe the same Spring air.

One does not know exactly what the flight of jade stairs is; and yet the lines convey inevitably the idea of an unbridgeable gulf between the lovers.

And who can ever forget such lines as:

The silkworm in the Spring goes on

Spinning gossamer threads until its death.

The wax-candle ceases not to weep

Its tears of blood until it burns itself to ashes.

*　　*　　*

The stars of yesternight!

The wind of yesternight!

West of the Painted Hall!

East of the Cinnamon Hall!

Our bodies possess no wings

Like those of the gorgeous Phoenixes.

But our hearts commune with each other

As those of the mystical Rhinoceros.

*　　*　　*

　　　　雨后却斜阳，杏花零落香。
　　　　无言匀睡脸，枕上屏山掩。
　　　　时节欲黄昏，无憀独倚门。

　　李商隐（813—858）不是一个青楼隐士，但是他同女道士和宫女的艳事倒有不少。他有许多诗讲的都是些儿女私情，诗中文字很是晦涩难懂，但也很美丽。诚然，没有别的诗人较他更富于玄妙神秘的幻象，这一首诗足以为证：

　　　　楼上黄昏欲望休，玉梯横绝月如钩。
　　　　芭蕉不展丁香结，同向春风各自愁。

我们不知道"横绝"月中的"玉梯"是怎样的一件东西，但是象征情人间不可跨越的深凹的意思是很明显的。

　　谁会忘记下面这几行？

　　　　春蚕到死丝方尽，蜡炬成灰泪始干。

*　　*　　*

　　　　昨夜星辰昨夜风，画楼西畔桂堂东。
　　　　身无彩凤双飞翼，心有灵犀一点通。

*　　*　　*

When heaven is desolate,

And the earth withers,

You will feel your heart rent apart.

But the pain is not half as intense

As when Spring mocks you

With all its rich splendors!

No one is so perfectly wintry, in sentiment as well as in style, as Li Shang-yin. The following are some of his representative poems:

天荒地变心虽折，
若比伤春意未多。

没有人在感情和笔调上有像李商隐那样"冬季"的，下面数首可以说是他的代表作：

(1) GETTING UP IN THE MORNING

A breezy, dewy, mild and clear morning.

Behind the curtains, a lonely man is getting up.

The orioles wail, but the flowers smile.

Which of them, I wonder, is the real Spring?

(2) SPRING

The Breeze of Spring is kind enough at heart:

But the things of Spring grow too exuberantly.

If Spring were a thoughtful lover,

He should have concentrated all his love upon a single flower.

My mind is different from the mind of Spring:

My heart is broken even before the coming of the flowering season!

（一）早起

风露澹清晨，
帘间独起人。
莺花啼又笑，
毕竟是谁春。

（二）春风

春风虽自好，
春物太昌昌。
若教春有意，
惟遣一枝芳。
我意殊春意，
先春已断肠。

(3) SORROW IN SPRING

Everyday the Spring is racing

With the rays of the sun.

The apricot flowers fill

The suburbs with their perfume.

Ah me! When will my heart

Be freed from the grip of sorrow,

So it can grow as long as the gossamer

And waft carelessly in the air without breaking?

（三）日日

日日春光斗日光，

山城斜路杏花香。

几时心绪浑无事，

得及游丝百尺长？

(4) WINTER

The sun rose on the east,

The sun has set in the west,

The lady Phoenix flies alone,

The female Dragon has become a widow.

...

Frozen walls and hoary-headed frosts

Join in weaving gloom and sending doom

To the flowers, whose tender roots are snapped asunder,

And whose fragrant souls have breathed their last!

...

The wax candles weep tears of blood

Lamenting the coming of the dawn.

（四）冬

天东日出天西下，

雌凤孤飞女龙寡。

……

冻壁霜华交隐起，

芳根中断香心死。

……

蜡烛啼红怨天曙。

(5) THE EVEN GLOW

Feeling fretful in the eventide,

I take a drive and mount the ancient plain.

How infinitely charming is the setting sun!

Only it is so near the yellow dusk.

（五）登乐游原

向晚意不适，

驱车登古原。

夕阳无限好，

只是近黄昏。

(6) FAR FROM HOME

Spring finds me far from home,

Far from home, and near the sunset.

（六）天涯

春日在天涯，

天涯日又斜。

If the wailing nightingale has tears,

Let her wet the topmost flower.

莺啼如有泪，

为湿最高花。

(7) SENT TO HOME

You ask when I shall come home.

There is no date yet.

Just now, here at Pa-shan,

Night rain is flooding the Autumn pools.

I look forward to the time

When we shall snuff the candle

Together by the western window.

And I shall tell you how I feel

This night at Pa-shan,

When the rain is flooding the Autumn pools.

（七）夜雨寄北

君问归期未有期，

巴山夜雨涨秋池。

何当共剪西窗烛，

却话巴山夜雨时。

(8) THE FALLEN FLOWERS

On the high pavilion,

Revels have ended and guests gone.

In the little garden,

Flowers are flying in disarray.

They cover up

All the meandering paths.

They form a long parade

To send off the glorious sunset.

My bowels have snapped asunder.

I have no heart to sweep away the scattered petals.

The more I strain my eyes,

The fewer flowers remain on the trees.

Their fragrant soul has given up

Its last breath with the Spring.

And what remains?

Only tears that bedew my raiment.

（八）落花

高阁客竟去，

小园花乱飞。

参差连曲陌，

迢递送斜晖。

肠断未忍扫，

眼穿仍欲归。

芳心向春尽，

所得是沾衣。

(9) THE LADY IN THE MOON

I sit behind the screens of marble
In front of a glimmering candlelight.
I have watched the Milky Way
Gradually going down,
And the morning stars sinking.

Ah, you Lady in the Moon!
How you must have repented
Your theft of the Elixir of Life,
For which you are condemned to live eternally,
With your heart bleeding from night to night
In the loneliness of the sea and the sky!

（九）嫦娥

云母屏风烛影深，
长河渐落晓星沉。
嫦娥应悔偷灵药，
碧海青天夜夜心。

(10) THE YO YANG TOWER

To disperse the pent-up sorrows of a lifetime,
I have mounted the Yo Yang Tower on the Tung T'ing
    Lake.
How I wish to ride on the endless waves to the bourne
    of Heaven!
Only the sinister dragons are too much bent upon the
    overturning of boats.

（十）岳阳楼

欲为平生一散愁，
洞庭湖上岳阳楼。
可怜万里堪乘兴，
枉是蛟龙解覆舟。

(11) TO THE WILLOWS IN AUTUMN

How you used to sway in the east wind,
Brushing gracefully the pretty dancers!
Now the Spring Garden is turned into
A scene of broken hearts!

Why have you lived to see
The days of pale Autumn,
To pine away in the fading sun,
Amidst the dirge of cicadas?

（十一）柳

曾逐东风拂舞筵，
乐游春苑断肠天。
如何肯到清秋日，
已带斜阳又带蝉。

(12) VISITING A MONK	(十二) 北青萝

The last beams of the sun

Have sunk behind the western hills.

I have come to the thatched hut

To call on the solitary monk.

Fallen leaves all around!

But the man is nowhere to be found.

Now the coiling path that has led me up here

Is enveloped in the chilly clouds.

All alone, I beat the stone-chime

To sound the knell of the day.

Attuned to the universal stillness,

I lean quietly upon a twig of rattan.

The world is contained in a little speck of dust.

There is no room for love and hate.

残阳西入崦，

茅屋访孤僧。

落叶人何在，

寒云路几层。

独敲初夜磬，

闲倚一枝藤。

世界微尘里，

吾宁爱与憎。

In connection with the last quoted poem, I wish to introduce a comparison of the seasons. Solitude is always an attractive theme for the poets, irrespective of ages and countries. But how one feels when in solitude is what makes the difference. Li Shang-yin could not have felt as the Spring poets did:

A NIGHT AT THE PEAK TEMPLE

I stop the night at the temple on the Peak.

Stretching out my hand I feel the pulse of the stars.

I dare not make any noise,

For fear of startling the folks in Heaven.

(Li Po)

AT A TEMPLE

In the clear morning I stroll into an old temple.

The tall trees are radiant with the first beams of the sun.

A coiling path leads me into a secluded spot.

The Dhyana Hall is hidden in the depth of flowers and trees.

The clear light of the mountains delights the nature of the birds.

The crystal face of the pond cleanses the heart of man.

All the discordant notes of the world are mute.

One only hears the serene music of the bell and the stone-chime.

(Chang Chien)

Nor could these Spring poets have sung as Tu Fu did:

A NIGHT AT THE LUNG-MENG TEMPLE

After guiding me in the excursions of the day,

The head monk invites me to spend a night at his temple.

The dark ravine oozes with the music of silence.

The moonlight casts the clear shadows of the trees.

　　讲到最后这首诗，我要介绍季候比较研究。不论年代，不论国别，孤独终是诗人爱好的题旨，分别就是在诗人对孤独的感觉上。李商隐决不会如春季诗人那般说：

题峰顶寺

夜宿峰顶寺，举手扪星辰。

不敢高声语，恐惊天上人。

（李白）

题破山寺后禅院

清晨入古寺，初日照高林。

曲径通幽处，禅房花木深。

山光悦鸟性，潭影空人心。

万籁此都寂，惟余钟磬音。

（常建）

春季诗人也不会如杜甫般唱：

游龙门奉先寺

已从招提游，更宿招提境。

阴壑生虚籁，月林散清影。

315

Between the cliffs hangs a scroll of throbbing stars.

Sleeping among the clouds, my clothes are drenched.

The morning bell has caught me on the point of waking,

Stirring me into a violent searching of the heart.

But this searching of the heart is a little too violent for an autumnal spirit like Po Chü-i:

AT THE HSIEN YU TEMPLE

A crane has come over from the sandy beach

And stands quietly on the steps.

The moon blooms like a flower

In the pond in front of the door.

There is something around here

That makes me feel at home.

After spending two nights,

I still feel like staying on.

I am glad to have chanced upon this secluded place,

With no companion to hasten my return.

Now that I have tasted the joy of solitude,

I shall never come here in a company.

天阙象纬逼，云卧衣裳冷。
欲觉闻晨钟，令人发深省。

这种深省，在秋季精灵像白居易看来，未免有些过分暴烈：

仙游寺独宿

沙鹤上阶立，潭月当户开。
此中留我宿，两夜不能回。
幸与静境遇，喜无归侣催。
从今独游后，不拟共人来。

XII.   LI YU: THE PRINCE OF WINTER

Winds wander, and dews drip earthward;

> Rain falls, suns rise and set,

Earth whirls, and all but to prosper

> A poor little violet.

—J. R. Lowell

Spring flowers and Autumn moon—how long is the pageant of seasons

> to last?

Who knows the countless events of the past?

—Prince Li Yu

Pile the pyre, light the fire—there is fuel enough and to spare;

...

Burn the old year—it is dead, and dead, and done.

—Sydney Dobell

If I am asked who is the greatest poet of China, I would say Tu Fu. But if I am asked what poet is dearest to my heart, I would say Prince Li Yu.

Prince Li Yu acted in his own person a tragedy that only Shakespeare could have written, and his lyrics are comparable to the soliloquies of Hamlet and Lear. Some of his best lyrics, at any rate, come so directly from the heart and are clothed in such perfect language that if Shakespeare were to write a tragedy of his life in Chinese, he would certainly have adopted them verbatim.

I have no heart to deal with his life in detail. It is too sad a story to tell. But his poetry is so bound up with his life that a few pivotal facts must be given here.

He was born in 937. In the following year his grandfather established the Southern T'ang, covering a territory of about a thousand square miles[1] on the south of the Yangtze River, and with Nanking as its capital. He assumed the title of an emperor. From the beginning it was a weak state, surrounded by more powerful neighbors. The star of the Sung

Dynasty was steadily rising, and the poor Southern T'ang was just like the morning star soon to be outshone by a greater light.

In 943, the grandfather died, and Li Yu's father, Li Chin, ascended the throne. During his reign, it was no longer possible to maintain the title of an emperor in his relations with other states, so he assumed the title of a

拾贰 冬之灵魂——李煜

> 大风漂泊，露水东流；
>> 雨落，日出日息，
> 大地旋转——一切都是为了培植
>> 一朵可怜的小紫兰。
>>>>> ——J. R. 洛厄尔

> 春花秋月何时了？往事知多少。 ——李煜

> 堆起柴堆，点火——燃料足够，用之不尽，
> ……
> 烧那旧年——它已死了，死了，完了。 ——悉尼·多贝尔

倘若有人问我谁是中国最伟大的诗人，我会说杜甫；但是，倘若有人问我谁是我最心爱的诗人，我要说后主李煜。

后主他本身即是一出只有莎士比亚才写得出的悲剧，他的抒情歌词也能同哈姆雷特或李尔的独语相比。他有几首好的词是直接从心灵中涌溢出来的，文字又美丽动人。我想倘若莎士比亚要拿他的生平写一出剧本的话，他一定会一字不改地采用它们。

我现在没有心肠记述他的生平，实在因为太凄惨了；但是他的作品同他的生平有极密切的关系，所以他生平最重要的几件事不得不在这里提起。

他生在 937 年，次年他的祖父便在扬子江南岸建立南唐，以南京为首都而称帝。南唐出世时便是一个弱国，周围都是强邻；宋朝之星渐渐上升，可怜的南唐只是像隐没在即的晨星。

943 年，李煜的祖父离世，父璟即位。那时候他已不能再以帝皇自居，只得改称"国主"。他不是一个次等诗人，曾写了下面二

king. He was a poet of no mean order, and has two exquisite little pieces to his credit:

AN EVENING IN SPRING

I have rolled up the pearl-screen.

But the Sorrow of Spring,

Like a bird inured to its cage,

Refuses to fly out of the window.

The flowers are falling in the wind,

Like guests taking leave

Of a world without a host.

My thoughts lengthen to eternity.

No fairy birds have brought to me

Any message from beyond the clouds.

My heart is like the clove

That has shriveled in the rain

Into a bloomless bud, in which dead Hope

Lies entombed in its very womb.

Turning my head backward,

I see green waves rolling and billowing

Through the dusk-shrouded land of Ch'u

Toward the azure sky.

A GIRL THINKING OF HER LOVE

The fragrance is faded from the lotus-flowers,

And the emerald leaves have withered.

The west wind is scattering sorrows among the green ripples.

Everything seems to be decaying with my years,—

I cannot bear the sight.

Interwoven with the silken rain,

My dreams are hovering round the remote Border of Cock-crow.

All alone I have been blowing the pipe of jade

Until my little garret freezes out and out with its icy notes.

With endless sorrows flowing in endless pearly tears,
I lean silently on my balcony.

In 961 when Li Yu was twenty-six, his father died, and he ascended the throne. By that time, the Southern T'ang was already a vassal state of Sung. The Founder of the Sung Dynasty summoned him several times to his capital, K'aifeng, Honan; but he persistently declined to go on plea of ill-health. Getting impatient, the Emperor sent his troops down to attack Nanking in 974. The city was surrounded for a whole year before it was surrendered. Li Yu was brought to the capital, and spent his last two years in captivity as the "Marquis of Recalcitrancy." In a letter to his former maids-of-honor, he said, "Here in exile, I wash my face with my tears day and night."

首精致动人的短歌：

摊破浣溪沙

（一）

手卷真珠上玉钩，依前春恨锁重楼。
风里落花谁是主，思悠悠。
青鸟不传云外信，丁香空结雨中愁。
回首绿波三楚暮，接天流。

（二）

菡萏香销翠叶残，西风愁起绿波间。
还与韶光共憔悴，不堪看。
细雨梦回鸡塞远，小楼吹彻玉笙寒。
多少泪珠何限恨，倚阑干。

961 年，李煜二十六岁的时候，李璟死亡，他便续位。那时候南唐已是宋朝的部属，宋太祖数次诏他入新都开封，他都托病拒绝；这惹起了太祖的脾气，于是他便兴兵进攻南京，那是在 974 年。南京经一年的围攻后，便投降了；李煜被俘，带到开封，此后二年便过着俘虏生活，人家叫他"违命侯"。在给他以前的宫女的一封信里，他说"此中日夕以泪洗面"。

In the night of the Double Seven, in 978, Li Yu celebrated his birthday with wine, women and song. The next day he was poisoned by the reigning Emperor.

Li Yu was one of the most affectionate men that have ever worn a crown. He was an affectionate son, an affectionate brother, an affectionate husband, an affectionate father, an affectionate friend, and an affectionate monarch. Even before his days of captivity, there were more tears than smiles in his life, for the little tragedies of life affected him more profoundly than they would a less poetic nature. For instance, there is a very touching poem in memory of his wife and his son:

> A sad memory clings to me eternally.
> A secret pain gnaws at my heart.
> The rain deepens the loneliness of Autumn,
> Sorrow aggravates my sickness.
> Standing to the wind, I gulp down my sobbing thoughts.
> Blear-eyed, I seem to see flowers in the air.
> O Lord of Emptiness! Hast thou forgotten me?
> Thy shiftless son is weary of wandering.

I am tempted to call him "the weeping king." He wanted always to remit death sentences, but his ministers remonstrated against his over-leniency, and he yielded to them weeping. He wept so much for his subjects that they could not help weeping for him when they heard of his tragic death.

His poetry may roughly be divided into two periods: before and after captivity. Naturally, the poems of the second period are more touching; but those of the first are nonetheless fine pieces of art, of which I want to give some specimens:

1. THE FISHERMAN'S SONGS

(1)

The foam of the waves simulates endless drifts of snow.
The peach-trees and pear-trees silently form a battalion of Spring.
A bottle of wine,

An angling line,

How many men share the happiness that's mine?

(2)

An oar of Spring wind playing about a leaf of a boat.

A tiny hook at the end of a silken cord.

An islet of flowers,

A jugful of wine,

Over the boundless waves liberty is mine.

978 年七月七日晚，李煜以醇酒、妇人及诗词庆祝他的生辰，第二日便被太宗毒死。

李煜是戴过皇冕中最多情的一个人。他是一个多情的儿子，多情的兄弟，多情的丈夫，多情的父亲，多情的朋友，多情的君王。就是在未被俘以前，他也是泪多于笑，生活中最微小的悲剧都给他普通人不能感觉的痛苦。看这一首思念妻儿的动人诗歌：

> 永念难消释，孤怀痛自嗟。
> 雨深秋寂莫，愁引病增加。
> 咽绝风前思，昏濛眼上花。
> 空王应念我，穷子正迷家。

我要叫他"泣王"。他时常要饶赦死犯，但是他的臣子却阻止他如此宽容，他也只得在泪中屈服。他为了他的臣民哭泣，所以当他的臣民听见了他的死讯以后，也不得不为他哭泣。

他的作品可以分作两个时期：前期是在他未被俘虏之前，后期是在他被俘虏之后。不容怀疑的，后期的作品是比前期的来得动人，但是前期的也可算是艺术上品，下面数首足以证明：

（一）渔父

（一）

浪花有意千里雪，桃花无言一队春。一壶酒，一竿身，快活如侬有几人。

（二）

一棹春风一叶舟，一纶茧缕一轻钩。花满渚，酒满瓯，万顷波中得自由。

2. TRYSTING SONGS

(1)

Her bronze pipe emits a crisp tune like that of cool bamboo.

She plays a new air with her ivory fingers moving gracefully.

She entices me furtively with her eyes,

Overwhelming me with their charming waves.

Clouds and showers in a secluded anteroom!

Whenever she comes, my heart sings like a melody.

But the feast is soon over, and the rest is silence.

My soul is lost in the cobwebs of spring dreams.

(2)

She has just finished her evening coiffure,

Sprinkling herself with a little sandal scent.

She sings a sweet tune,

Slightly revealing her clove-like tongue,

Which softly wedges her cherry mouth apart.

The gauze sleeves are enameled with ruby floods,

A deep cup is filled with the fragrant dregs of wine.

Leaning languorously on the embroidered pillow—Ah, what an image
    of tender grace!

Chewing a fragment of red wool to pulp,

She spits it out, smiling demurely at her sweetheart.

(3)

The flowers are scintillating in the dim moonlight.

A light fog suffuses the air.

'Tis an ideal night to go to my love!

In socks I walk tip-toe over the fragrant steps,

With a pair of embroidered shoes dangling from my hand.

I meet my love in a cozy corner south of the Painted Hall,

And throw myself trembling into his embrace.

"'Tis so hard for me to steal out:

Taste me to the full!"

3. A GIRL'S YEARNING

One range of mountains,

Two ranges of mountains.

The mountains are far, the sky high, the mists and waters cold.

My lingering thoughts have reddened the maple-leaves.

The chrysanthemums bloom,

The chrysanthemums wither.

The wild geese from the border fly high, but my love has not come
home.

The wind and the moon play idly on the screen.

（二）菩萨蛮

铜簧韵脆锵寒竹，新声慢奏移纤玉。眼色暗相钩，秋波横欲流。

雨云深绣户，来便谐衷素。宴罢又成空，魂迷春梦中。

一斛珠

晚妆初过，沈檀轻注些儿个。向人微露丁香颗。一曲清歌，暂引樱桃破。

罗袖裛残殷色可，杯深旋被香醪涴。绣床斜凭娇无那。烂嚼红茸，笑向檀郎唾。

菩萨蛮

花明月暗笼轻雾，今宵好向郎边去。刬袜步香阶，手提金缕鞋。

画堂南畔见，一向偎人颤。奴为出来难，教君恣意怜。

（三）长相思

一重山，两重山。山远天高烟水寒，相思枫叶丹。

菊花开，菊花残。塞雁高飞人未还，一帘风月闲。

4. THE REVELS ARE OVER

The cherries have fallen, and Spring has returned to Heaven.

The pair of light-powdered butterflies is frolicking in the air.

The nightingale is wailing the moon west of my little chamber.

The gauze curtain hangs gloomily from a jade peg,

Brooding in the mists of the twilight.

The guests have gone, leaving a little mansion in utter loneliness.

There remains only the dreary grass as a relic of happier days.

Wreaths of frankincense rise silently and linger around the stone Phoenix.

I find myself holding listlessly a silken girdle in my hand,

With my heart full of lingering regrets.

5. AGAIN

The flowing days of Autumn, they will not remain.

The steps are strewn with the scarlet leaves, the year is on the wane.

Ah, the Double Nine has come again.

And the arbors on the high plain

Are filled with the perfume of the dogwood again.

The breath of the purple chrysanthemum

Is wafting in the courtyard lane.

The evening smoke hovers ensnared in the silken rain.

In the cold air the wild geese faintly complain.

The same old sorrow and the same old pain!

6. THINKING OF MY LOVE

A tress of cloud!

A shuttle of jade!

A pale, pale robe of thin, thin gauze! [2]

A nameless grace playing about her knitted brows

Like a faint shade!

Autumn gales start,

Echoed by the rain.

Outside the window screen

A pair of plantain-trees grow wide apart,

The long, long night wears out a longing heart.

7. A QUIET NIGHT

A mansion secluded and quiet,—

Serenity dwells in the little courtyard.

Intermittent sounds of the cold anvil and pestle in the intermittent gales.

How they keep me awake during the long, long night,—

These solitary notes wafted on the moonlight into the screened-window!

If these and such as these were all he has done, he would still have a place in the history of Chinese literature as a *petit maître*. But it was in his days of exile that he produced the poems that have endeared him

（四）临江仙

樱桃落尽春归去，蝶翻金粉双飞。子规啼月小楼西，玉钩罗幕，惆怅暮烟垂。

别巷寂寥人散后，望残烟草低迷。炉香闲袅凤凰儿，空持罗带，回首恨依依。

（五）谢新恩

冉冉秋光留不住，满阶红叶暮。又是过重阳，台榭登临处，茱萸香坠。

紫菊气，飘庭户，晚烟笼细雨。雍雍新雁咽寒声，愁恨年年长相似。

（六）长相思

云一涡，玉一梭。澹澹衫儿薄薄罗，轻颦双黛螺。

秋风多，雨相和。帘外芭蕉三两窠，夜长人奈何。

（七）捣练子令

深院静，小庭空，断续寒砧断续风。

无奈夜长人不寐，数声和月到帘栊。

倘若这些便是他作品的全部，他已颇能自豪，在中国文学史上也能占一席之地。但是使他博取万人同情，争得冬之灵魂之衔者，

to the hearts of all his readers and made him the Prince of Winter. The following are some of his best known:

1. REMINISCENCE

A country with a history of forty years,

Possessing thousands of *li* of mountains and rivers,

With Phoenix Pavilion and Dragon Tower towering to the skies!

Dodders of jade with beautiful sprigs of precious gems,—that was all I
    saw.

How many times did I ever see the weapons of war?

One day I became a captive slave.

My graceful waist and delicate features have wasted away.

Ah, I can never forget that day when, after I had taken leave of my
    family temple,

The Academy of Music played a doleful song of farewell,

And I wiped my tears in front of the maids-of-honor.

2. TEARS, ENDLESS TEARS!

Tears, endless tears!

How they soak my sleeves and trickle on my chin!

Ah, let not your sorrow-laden heart drop with your tears!

Ah, blow not the Phoenix-pipe in tears!

Else your heart is sure to break or burst!

3. A DREAM

Ah, how sad!

Last night in my dream

I was again roaming in the Royal Park

Like in the old days—

Carriages were rolling like a stream

And horses prancing like dragons—

Moonlight flowers were quivering

In the warm caress of the Spring breeze!

4. UPON WAKING FROM A DREAM

Outside the window-screen the rain drizzles and drips.

The Spring is gasping away.

Under thin silken quilts I shiver in the cold tide of the morning watch.

In a dream, forgetting my homeless plight,

I feasted myself like a glutton upon the past joys again!

Ah, lean not upon the balcony all alone,

Lest you should see the endless rivers and mountains,

That make separation so easy and meeting so hard!

The stream flows on, the flowers have fallen, and the Spring is gone,

Leaving no trace in Heaven or on earth.

却是他的俘虏内的作品。下面数首是最脍炙人口的了：

（一）破阵子

四十年来家国，三千里地山河。凤阁龙楼连霄汉，玉树琼枝作烟萝，几曾识干戈？

一旦归为臣虏，沈腰潘鬓销磨。最是仓黄辞庙日，教坊犹奏别离歌，垂泪对宫娥。

（二）望江南

多少泪，沾袖复横颐。心事莫将和泪滴，凤笙休向月明吹。肠断更无疑。

（三）望江南

多少恨，昨夜梦魂中。还似旧时游上苑，车如流水马如龙。花月正春风。

（四）浪淘沙

帘外雨潺潺，春意阑珊，罗衾不耐五更寒。梦里不知身是客，一晌贪欢。

独自莫凭栏，无限江山，别时容易见时难。流水落花春去也，天上人间。

(NOSTALGIA

Upon the window beats the rain.

Spring is on the wane.

My silken quilt is too thin the pre-dawn chill to sustain.

In a dream, forgetting that I am a stranger in a strange land,

I slipped into the happy old days again.

Ah, lean not wistfully upon the window-pane!

Hills and rivers form an endless chain,

Which makes separation so real and yearning for home so vain.

The stream flows on, the flowers are falling, and the Spring is going,—

Between heaven and earth yawns the boundless inane!)

5. LIFE IS A DREAM

In life no one is wholly immune from sorrows and griefs.

But who ever felt as I do now?

In my dreams I return to my fatherland:

Upon waking a pair of tears drop from my eyes.

With whom can I go up the storyed mansion now?

I only remember how beautiful the fair days of Autumn used to be.

Past events have vanished without leaving a trace behind.

They are no more than a dream.

6. HOME THOUGHTS IN SPRING

My idle day-dreams carry me to the southern lands,

Where fragrant Spring is in full bloom.

In the boats pipes and strings make riotous music, and the face of the
river is green.

The catkins, mingled with the light dust, are flying pell-mell in the
whole city.

The sight-seers in the flowery gardens are busied to death.

7. HOME THOUGHTS IN AUTUMN

My idle day-dreams carry me far.

I see quiet, pellucid Autumn in the southern lands.

A thousand *li* of rivers and hills drenched in cool twilight.

In a thicket of rushes is moored a solitary boat.

The mellifluous notes of a flute come from a moon-lit tower.

8. HOMESICKNESS

Since we parted, Spring is half gone.

Every sight breaks my heart.

Below the steps the plum-blossoms fall in confusion with the flakes of
snow.

They are no sooner brushed away than they cover me over again.

The wild geese bring no news from home.

The roads are long, but my dreams are short.

Homesickness is like the grass in Spring:

The farther you travel, the thicker it grows.

（五）子夜歌

人生愁恨何能免，销魂独我情何限！故国梦重归，觉来双泪垂。

高楼谁与上？长记秋晴望。往事已成空，还如一梦中。

（六）望江梅

闲梦远，南国正芳春。船上管弦江面绿，满城飞絮混轻尘。愁杀看花人。

（七）望江梅

闲梦远，南国正清秋。千里江山寒色暮，芦花深处泊孤舟。笛在月明楼。

（八）清平乐

别来春半，触目柔肠断。砌下落梅如雪乱，拂了一身还满。

雁来音信无凭，路遥归梦难成。离恨恰如春草，更行更远还生。

9. PARTING SORROW

Speechless I am up here alone in the Western chamber.

The moon is like a sickle.

In utter loneliness the limpid Autumn is locked within a secluded
    mansion by the paulownia trees.

Scissors cannot cut,

Nor combs comb,—

That's parting-sorrow.

It has a taste of its own that's known to the heart alone.

10. 'TIS FATE

Vernal redness is faded from the flowers.

Ah, why so soon?

But who could prevent the cold showers in the morning and the cruel
    blasts in the evening?

How the tears, dyed in the rouge

Used to coax me to take more wine!

When will this happen again?

'Tis as inevitable for life to overflow in sorrows as for the waters to flow
    toward the east.

11. A SLEEPLESS NIGHT

Last night rains came in company with the gales.

The latticed curtain echoed the Voice of Autumn.

The candle flickered, the water-clock stopped, and many times I leaned
    upon the pillow,

And tossed in my bed and sat up restlessly.

The events of the world forever follow the flowing stream.

What is life but a floating dream?

In the Drunken Land alone are the roads even and smooth.

In no other lands can I walk without stumbling.

12. LONELINESS

What a pain 'tis to remember the joys of yesterday!

In my present plight, how they mock to prey!

The Spirit of Autumn haunts the courtyard, and mosses overgrow the
pathway.

A row of pearl-screens hangs idly and motionless like a painted wall.

Who comes to call throughout the day?

My golden sword is buried away.

My youthful dreams wither and decay.

This evening, the weather is cool, the sky clear, and the blooming moon
is in its full display.

Ah, fancy that at this very hour the jade towers and crystal domes are
casting their silent shadows

Upon the lonely waters of the Chinhuai!

（九）相见欢

无言独上西楼，月如钩。寂寞梧桐深院锁清秋。

剪不断，理还乱，是离愁。别是一般滋味在心头。

（十）相见欢

林花谢了春红，太匆匆。无奈朝来寒雨晚来风。

胭脂泪，相留醉，几时重。自是人生长恨水长东。

（十一）乌夜啼

昨夜风兼雨，帘帏飒飒秋声。烛残漏断频欹枕，起坐不
能平。

世事漫随流水，算来一梦浮生。醉乡路稳宜频到，此外不
堪行。

（十二）浪淘沙

往事只堪哀，对景难排。秋风庭院藓侵阶。一任珠帘闲不
卷，终日谁来？

金锁已沉埋，壮气蒿莱。晚凉天净月华开。想得玉楼瑶殿
影，空照秦淮。

13. HIS LAST POEM

Spring flowers and Autumn moon!

How long is the pageant of seasons to last?

Who can remember the endless events of the past?

My little chamber was astir again with the breath of the east wind last night.

Ah, how could I bear to think of my vanished country in the bright moonlight?

Carved balustrades and marble stairs must still be there:

Only faces cannot always be fair!

How much sadness, you ask, can be harbored in my breast!

Even as the swollen rivers in spring rolling eastward without a moment's rest!

The seasons of T'ang poetry have come to an end. A new year is beginning!

I can find no fitter conclusion for this long article than a poem by the springy poet, Chang Chiu-ling:

AN ALLEGORY

In Spring, how lush the leaves of the orchid!

In Autumn, how pure the flowers of the cinnamon!

All things are quickened by the same Breath of life:

But each has a blooming season of its own.

Who knows the hermits among the woods?

How they attune their moods to the changing winds!

The grass and trees grow from an inner urge,—

Not for the sake of being plucked by pretty hands!

（十三）虞美人

　　春花秋月何时了？往事知多少。小楼昨夜又东风，故国不堪回首月明中。

　　雕栏玉砌应犹在，只是朱颜改。问君能有几多愁？恰似一江春水向东流。

唐诗的季候终究到了尽头，一个新年又开始了！

结束这篇长文，张九龄这首诗是最好也不过的：

感遇

　　兰叶春葳蕤，桂华秋皎洁。

　　欣欣此生意，自尔为佳节。

　　谁知林栖者，闻风坐相悦。

　　草木有本心，何求美人折！

NOTES 注释

I. Introduction
壹 序幕

1 李白生于 701 年，杜甫生于 712 年，差 11 年。——编辑注

2 Dionysus、Prometheus、Epimetheus 俱系希腊神话中之人物，此文中皆用其形容词。Dionysus 又名 Bacchus，酒神也。Prometheus 以泥塑成人形，盗至尊无上 Zeus 之火以济泥人生命，后为 Zeus 所惩罚；Epimetheus 乃 Prometheus 之弟，曾劝其兄勿做触犯 Zeus 之事，因娶妻使整个人类受累。

II. The Spring
贰 春：李白的前驱

1 以下两段无相应英文。——编辑注

2 I am using the excellent version of Ayscough and Lowell with a few alterations which seem to be called for. The words italicized are mine.

我用的是艾思柯和洛威尔的版本，做了必要的改动。斜体是我自己的翻译。

3 从"他的精神的专一"至此无相应英文。——编辑注

4 前一句引文出自美国作家亨利·米勒《走入夜生活》（Henry Miller, "Into the Night Life," *The Cosmological Eye*）；后一句及下方引文摘自拜伦长诗《唐璜》（查良铮译）第六章第五十三节。——编辑注

III. The Prince of Spring: His Life
叁 春之骄子：李白

1 旧时一些外国殖民者对我国新疆地区的称呼。——编辑注

2 以下至本章结束无相应中文。——编辑注

IV. The Prince of Spring: His Poetry
肆 春之骄子：其诗

1 此句无相应英文。——编辑注

2 以下至段末无相应英文。——编辑注

3 At this point, I wish to mention that there are three great Taoists among the poets of T'ang: Li Po, Po Chü-i, and Li Shang-yin, representing respectively three types of Taoism. Li Po belongs to the type of Chuang-tzŭ, Po Chü-i to the type of Lao-tzŭ, and Li Shang-yin to the type of Pao P'u-tzŭ.

唐朝有三位道家诗人：李白、白居易和李商隐，代表三派道教。李白属于庄子的一派，白居易属于老子的一派，李商隐属于抱朴子的一派。

V.   Summer: Its Blazing Heat and Fire
伍 夏之烈焰

[1] This is a Chinese proverb. Compare what Marguerite said in Maupassant's *Rose*: "I need to be loved—I want to be loved, even if only by a dog." Indeed, Maupassant is some guy!

这是一个中国谚语。试比较莫泊桑的《玫瑰》中玛格丽特的话，"我需要被爱——我想要被爱，哪怕只是被一条狗爱着。"莫泊桑确实了不起！

[2] Literally means a king, but here it means a commander.

字面意是"国王"，这里指统帅。

VII.   An Interlude
柒 夏秋之插曲

[1] Meaning the Emperor is kind-hearted.

意指皇帝很慈悲。

VIII.   Autumn: Po Chü-i
捌 秋之灵魂——白居易

[1] 冥府河名，能令人忘记过去。

[2] 希腊神，宙斯之子。

X.   The Winter: The Anatomy of a Mood
拾 冬之心理分析

[1] From Euripides, "No More, O my Spirit," translated by H. D.

出自欧里庇得斯的《噢，我的精神不再》一诗，英文翻自希尔达·杜利特尔。

[2] See W. C. Lawton, *The Soul of the Anthology*, Yale University Press, 1923, p. 119.

出自劳顿的《选集的灵魂》（耶鲁大学出版社，1923 年），第 119 页。

[3] From Arthur Waley's *The Book of Songs*.

出自韦利译《诗经》。

[4] From T. S. Eliot's *The Waste Land*.

出自 T. S. 艾略特的《荒原》。

5 From Arthur Waley's *The Book of Songs*.

出自韦利译《诗经》。

6 From Edith Sitwell's "Solo for Ear-Trumpet."

出自伊迪丝·西特韦尔的《助听筒独奏》。

7 From one of the Anacreontics called "The Epicure."

出自阿那克里翁体诗《享乐主义者》。

8 *Ibid.* 同上诗。

9 From one of the Anacreontics called "Age."

出自阿那克里翁体诗《年纪》。

10 From Arthur Waley, *An Introduction to the Study of Chinese Painting*, Charles Scribner's Sons, 1923, p. 16.

出自韦利的《中国绘画研究入门》，斯克里布纳之子公司，1923 年，第 16 页。

11 From Gautier's "Posthumous Coquetry."

出自泰奥菲勒·戈蒂埃的《身后的妖艳》。

12 Arthur Symons calls Baudelaire "a hermit of the brothel": T'uan Ch'eng-shih（段成式）calls Wen T'ing-yuen "a hermit of the green chamber." They mean the same thing, but who are we that we can call any house "a brothel" or any girl "a prostitute"?

阿瑟·西蒙斯称波德莱尔为"妓院隐士"，段成式叫温庭筠"青楼隐士"。他们的意思都是一样的，但是我们有什么资格将任何一个房屋视为"妓院"，将任何一个女人视为"妓女"？

13 From Régnier's "Night."

出自亨利·德·雷尼埃的《夜》。

14 These words are adopted from Lafcadio Hearne's essay, "A Ghost."

此句出自小泉八云的《幽灵》。

15 These words are what Lytton Strachey said about Verlaine.

此句是利顿·斯特雷奇对魏尔兰诗歌的评价。

16 This sentence is a paraphrase of Goethe's "The Lay of the Captive Count."

此句是对歌德的《被俘虏的伯爵之歌》的改写。

17 From an anonymous German Song of Nativity "A Lovely Rose is Sprung," translated by Margarete Münsterberg.

出白一首德语圣诞曲《一朵可爱的玫瑰绽放了》，作者不详，玛格丽特·明斯特贝格英译。

18 In the Latin Poetry of the first century before Christ, I find Lucretius belongs to Spring, when "heavens laugh, and all the world shews joyous cheare"; Virgil belongs to Summer, when he invokes the Sicilian Muse to "begin a loftier strain," and so does Catulus with his Tufuish humor in the form of self-mockery; Horace belongs to Autumn with his mellow counsel of following "the golden mean"; and Ovid belongs to Winter, when, as he says, "They do not quaff a cup, they break a bit of wine."

在纪元前一世纪的拉丁诗内，我发现卢克莱修属于春季，那时候"天笑，全球都欢乐"；维吉尔属于夏季，那时候他令西西里缪斯"重唱一曲崇高的歌"，卡图路斯的杜甫式的自嘲幽默也将他列入夏季；贺拉斯属于秋季，他有成熟的智慧，采取中庸之道；奥维德属于冬季，他说："他们不一口而尽，他们只吃一点点酒。"

19 奥萝拉乃罗马神话中的司晨女神，门农乃其子。

20 There are many speculations about the occasion of this poem, but there could be no question as to its philosophy of the interrelatedness of life.

关于这首诗的创作有许多推测，但是它所包含的生命相互关联这一哲学思想是不容置疑的。

21 These two lines were brought to my attention by an old friend of mine, Mr. Ch'uan Su-sou (全甦叟), as expressive of the wintry mood. I am glad that a poet of the old school should have subscribed to my seasonal interpretation.

经友人全甦叟提醒，我想到这首诗能够充分表达冬天的情绪。我很高兴，一位旧派诗人能够赞同我对诗歌的季节性解读。

XII. Li Yu: The Prince of Winter

拾贰 冬之灵魂——李煜

1 此数据遍查未果，恐有误，译文中未补。南唐国土面积最大时约 76 万平方公里（951年）。——编辑注

2 This line I have taken from E. D. Edwards, *The Dragon Book*, William Hodge, 1938, p. 102.

此句摘自 E. D. 爱德华兹的《龙书》，威廉·霍奇出版社，1938 年，第 102 页。